I0640777

Sins & Secrets

TRUST IS EARNED......

NICHOLA HARVEY

Sins & Secrets, The Masquerade Trilogy

Copyright © 2023 NICHOLA HARVEY
All rights reserved.
ISBN: 978-1-7638328-0-0

DEDICATION

This book has been years in the making of some seriously late nights that included endless editing and story line changes. Procrastination and doubt usually followed, but here we are – finally!

To my rather large family, I sincerely thank you from the bottom of my heart for your tremendous support and encouragement. Without any of you none of this would have been possible. Especially my gorgeous daughter, who was often helpful when i needed her input, without her witty charm

And brains on my off days, I would never have finished. I love you all to the moon and back.

To my helpers along the way including fellow writers, Sonia Freitas (Maria Bernard) and Bryn Donovan, (your book was and still is my bible!) Without your help and advice this book would never have come to fruition.

Lastly, to my wonderful friends who've held the utmost faith in throughout this tedious process.

Love you xx

<u>TRIGGER WARNING</u>

Contains themes of sexual assault, suicide and domestic violence.

Recommended for Mature Audiences 18+

∞ **Denotes change of POV.**

<u>DISCLAIMER</u>:

Some places and names of business' depicted in this novel are purely fictional.

———————

1

Teddy

HAVING DRAGGED THE CURTAINS OPEN, I scrunched my nose up as I viewed what the day had to offer. Ugh. Dismal.

Dove grey clouds were slowly drifting across the sky, threatening to turn what would've been a warm, bright sunny day, grey and chilly. The weekend was fabulous too. I smiled coyly; in more ways than one. Oh well, the clouds would eventually clear, and we'd all be stripping off. Typical.

Melbourne was the only city I knew of that had four seasons in one day. It left me questioning whether moving to a warmer climate was the answer; North Queensland came to mind, as had the saltwater crocodiles. I shivered, ew, no thanks, I think I'd be safer sticking with Melbourne. Besides, considering the unpredictable changes in the weather, living anywhere else was inconceivable, it was home.

As I stepped under the shower, the steaming water immediately warmed my chilled bones through. A feeling I relished in as I reached for the shampoo sitting on the niche shelf, pouring the loads required for my thick mane into the palm of my hand, my eyes sliding closed as I worked my fingers over my scalp. Somehow, I felt that my day would be different – and for the better. Call it intuition, a sixth sense, whatever, I just knew.

Once I'd finished showering and drying off, I wandered through the walk-in-robe, scanning the numerous drawers and racks for something to wear. Warm was preferable, considering the dismal weather outside. Admittedly, I had far too many clothes; to the degree, my wardrobe resembled a small fashion boutique.

Designed to be every woman's dream, it wasn't exactly small either. Glass fronted drawers with sectioned open racks, plentiful for hanging all my stylish dresses, skirts, and blouses.

Lately though, my sister had been trying to poach one of the many pairs of heels I owned. We weren't even the same size.

My job as a graduate architect at Bricks and Mortar Architecture didn't require formal wear, thanks to my hunky boss, Spencer Hughes. He ran the business in a casual setting, making my life easier when it came down to choosing an outfit each day.

Having donned a black lacy bra, matching panties, and a pair of cheeky thigh-high stockings, I started scanning the racks for a dress. In the end, choosing a black, long sleeve fitted jersey dress. Lastly slipped over my feet was a pair of black knee-length boots, the soft leather giving the extra warmth I needed on such a ridiculously chilly day. I grabbed a denim jacket, and a grey wool scarf, wrapping it around my neck as I made my way back to the ensuite bathroom to blow-dry my hair.

The house was relatively quiet as I left my bedroom and headed for the kitchen, my other favourite room in the house.

With marble benchtops, stainless steel appliances, a porcelain farmhouse sink and off-white shaker cabinets, the kitchen was a chef's dream. As was the butler's pantry, where I prepared my usual breakfast; a cup of Earl grey tea and a bowl of oats drizzled with honey before the appearance of my roommates shattered that peace.

I spoke too soon and greeted them cheerfully, "Good morning, peeps."

Pouring hot water into a prepared coffee cup, Scarlett groaned indignantly. "And what pray tell, Teddy, is so damned cheerful about a cold and rainy Monday morning?" Too bright for some apparently.

Scarlett happened to be one of those three roommates, and coincidentally, my baby sister. She wasn't unlike any other twenty-two-year-old I knew; she wanted to live life to the fullest and party whilst she was able to. Regardless of the fact she was studying a Bachelor of Nursing at university with dreams to work in paediatrics, our domineering parents, Evan, and Therese, always fought over the choices she made – or did not. Consequently, their nagging drove her away, forcing her out of their house and in with me.

I sat at the table and dug my spoon into the bowl. "It's going to be a fantastic day. I can feel it in my bones."

Scarlett rolled her eyes mockingly. "Always the optimist, sis."

Unable to help myself, I raised a brow sardonically. "Well, someone has to be, Miss Misery Guts."

"Who's miserable now?" Dominique asked, sauntering into the kitchen. I giggled as her hands flapped sarcastically. "Oh, oh, I know Miss, don't tell me! Only one person I know behaves in such a manner; a certain little Miss Sunshine with a cantankerous personality?" she teased, averting her vibrantly blue eyes in Scarlett's direction.

Scarlett glared. "Ha-ha, hilarious little Miss Wise Arse."

I laughed, rising from the chair, and slotting my dishes in the top rack of the dishwasher. "Any case ladies, I'm off to work. See you all later!" I planted a quick kiss on my groaning sister's head. "Have a good day, little Miss Grumpy."

"Yeah, what ev," she grumbled through a mouthful of muesli.

As I ran to my car in the driveway, a Holden Captiva, the skies opened, making me wonder why I'd even bothered with makeup that morning. I jumped in, barely avoiding the sudden downpour.

My face now had the appearance of a panda, instead of the fresh look I'd initially done. With the rain coming down in buckets, the gutters quickly filled, overflowing onto the roads, making the simple task of driving to work hazardous. The trip to work was a nightmare. Dealing with impatient and angry drivers in the wet weather had me exhausted, already and it wasn't even nine yet.

Bricks and Mortar Architecture, a relatively small firm, sat on the fifth floor of 101 Collins; a postmodern building situated centrally in the fashionable business district of Collins Street. Little cafés and stylish, upmarket boutiques surrounded the building, making it perfect for unique lunchtime shopping or a simple catch up with friends.

Taking up an entire floor, the light and airy office space with its eclectic warehouse interior made it a joy to work. With views to the busy streets and laneways, the roomy glass cubicles were comfortable enough for two people to work in without cramping each other's style. Each space was set around the outside of a spacious communal area, great for collaborating or for simply relaxing.

I'd barely entered my cubicle and thrown my bags onto the desk when my boss, Spencer, called me into his office. I sighed. Fixing my makeup was my priority but duty called. Oh well, he'd have to deal with the smudged eyes.

Wandering over to his office, the heels of my boots clicked on the refurbished timber boards. I raised my hand and lightly tapped on the doorframe. "You asked to see me, Mr Hughes?"

Standing well over six-feet tall, with broad, muscular shoulders, and warm chocolate brown eyes, Spencer Hughes was every woman's dream and every man's worst nightmare. His presence alone was captivating.

Looking up from the folder on his desk, he brushed flopping chestnut brown hair off his forehead and greeted me with a smile most women would fall over; broad, and dashing, as was the person wearing it. "Please, come on in and take a seat." He gestured towards one of the replica Hans Wegner plank armchairs adjacent to his solid redgum desk, ideally situated in front of the widely arched windows behind him.

Peering over his desk, I quickly realised the folder in front of him was, in fact, my portfolio. Curious as to why he had it, and expecting the worst, I asked, "Is everything all right?"

"Yes, everything is more than all right, actually," Spencer assured me grinning. "Now, Teddy, I've been glancing over your latest work, and I must say, I'm impressed. You have talent, initiative and quite the instinct when it comes to the client's needs. By that, I mean, you listen, and follow the brief to a tea – even if you do disagree with them." He chuckled when I grimaced at him. "You're incredibly persuasive, by showing them what does and doesn't work without compromising on the client's style.

Furthermore, you're extremely thorough with your research. You ensure the whole development runs smoothly, and to me, as such, it shows you have passion. Which is necessary for this business, and you most certainly have it. You have become quite the asset to this firm," Spencer proudly shared, his steepled hands clasping in a relaxed manner in front of him.

My mouth gaped, astonished by Spencer's overly generous review. "I don't know what to say, Mr Hughes, other than I'm truly flattered."

He gave another beaming smile. "Spencer, please, you've been here long enough. We're casual here."

"I've only been here about two years," I corrected, blush flaming my cheeks. "But it does feel distinctly longer. I enjoy working here and have learnt such a lot in a brief time."

He nodded warmly. "Good. Now, last, but not least, you passed the Architectural Practice examinations with flying colours; I received confirmation Friday evening." Spencer continued his review, "So, I feel it's safe to say you are now a fully registered architect." He grinned rising from his tan leather office chair. "Congratulations, Teddy."

"Thank you, Spencer; I wouldn't have made it this far without you as my mentor." Beaming at him, I quickly pushed to my feet, his large hand enveloping mine as we shook over the top of the desk.

"No, no way. I assure you," he disagreed modestly, "it was all you. You've worked extremely hard and showed dedication; that's what got you here. I only guided you along the way." He gently ushered me towards the door. "Keep up the amazing work."

With an extra skip in my step, I bounced back to my desk and noticed my co-worker Emily Smith's dark eyes smiling up at me. "What? I'm just euphoric."

"You got the 'fully registered' speech I see." She grinned, jumping out of her chair to hug me tightly. It wasn't any secret that Spencer gave all newly qualified employees the same speech.

"Congratulations!"

"Thanks, Ems."

Only just promoted herself, Emily began at Bricks and Mortar shortly after I had. We clicked immediately, only in the professional sense. Apart from my roommates, I preferred it that way. After years of endless pain and heartache, it tended to leave you not only wary but also sceptical as to who I allowed in my life.

For the remainder of the day, my high spirits continued. Not even the deluge of rain outside could dampen my day.

I flicked a generic text to my roommates about my plans for a night out in the city, one filled with dinner and drinks for starters. Then after that, who knew? Our celebrations could lead us anywhere. The next question was, where? Melbourne was a city well known for never sleeping, even early on in the week. The options were endless.

Roll on five-thirty.

Once the elevator commenced its slow descent to the underground garage, I sagged against the reflective walls inside. My mood giddy and excited by the way my day had turned out. Now, I just wanted to head home, open a nice bottle of wine and wind down with a nice long hot bath before the girls' came stampeding through the door.

I'd come so far, not since... I shook my head. No, my past was just that. There wasn't any point giving it another thought, especially when we had a fantastic evening ahead of us.

The elevator jolted to a stop. An icy, blustery gale greeted me as soon as the stainless-steel doors glided open, taking my breath away. Holy hell! Where did that breeze come from? Antarctica? The day had started bleak and rainy, and now it was just downright miserable and chilly. Walking faster, I gripped the edges of my denim jacket, hugging it tightly around me. Perhaps I ought to reconsider our night out. Reaching my car, I chuckled; there wasn't a chance in hell of that happening.

About to dive into my handbag for the keys, the sound of an empty glass bottle rolled across the concrete subfloor. A reverberating noise that startled me enough to send my head swivelling as my anxious gaze darted around each darkened corner.

Blowing out a nervous laugh, I turned back to my car. "It's just your imagination, Teddy. Nothing more..." Then a familiar odour of burning tobacco wafted. A panic-stricken chill curled around my spine, and panic surged as slow, taunting footsteps echoed along with the whisper of my name. In desperation, I began raking for the keys in my oversized tote, profusely cursing, when I was unable to locate them fast enough. The footsteps sped up, as had the search for my keys. Relief washing through me as I found them buried under my purse at the bottom.

I rushed up onto my seat, swiftly locking the door behind me with one shaky hand while attempting to push the key into the ignition. Starting the car, I looked in the rear-view mirror as I jolted the gear stick into reverse. Regret swiftly followed. My eyes widening as a horrified gasp escaped me at the sight of the menacing smile staring directly at me.

I hightailed it out of there.

Running inside the safety of my house and slamming the door behind me, I dumped my bag onto the kitchen island and headed directly for the bar fridge in the butler's pantry. I had the bottle of Pinot Grigio open before I'd made it back through the opened doorway. On the sink, there was already an upturned glass from the night before; I must've known. Call me greedy, but I kept pouring, filling the glass until the wine licked the brim. I didn't take long to down it either, my watery gaze peering over the rim as I glanced at the clock on the stove. There was still ample time to take that bath.

Melodic tunes of Chopin streamed from my iPhone through the speaker perched on the double vanity while wisps of steam floated from jasmine-scented water, and lit candles burned, permeating the air with gardenias and frangipani easing my woes in a heartbeat. Adding a particular dark-haired suitor to the equation might have aided in that healing also — hmm...the possibilities.

A loud laugh rang through the hallway, killing my lustful musings. Scarlett's such a mood blocker. I flopped my head back against the edge of the charcoal stone tub and groaned; the time for relaxation was over.

Wrapped in a towel, I padded over the floors and out to the kitchen, greeting my three roommates cheerfully, "Hello there, my roomies."

Scarlett crossed her arms and huffed. "Well, what's this news you've been dying to share with each of us?"

Amused by my sister's lack of patience, my beaming grin grew wider. "Well, little Miss Grumbles, today, just as I predicted, was the best day ever! Spencer Hughes, my boss, informed me that I'm now a fully registered architect!"

"Oh my god, Teddy, that's fantastic news!" Poppy squealed, embracing me gently. "What you have worked so hard for all these years has finally paid off."

"Well done, sissy!" Scarlett simpered proudly, throwing her arms around my neck. Unlike Poppy, she nearly choked me in excitement. I squeezed her back. "Thanks, Scars."

Poppy's sunny gaze darted. "So, ladies, where are we taking this celebration?"

"What about the Rockpool Bar and Restaurant at Southbank?" Dominique suggested, smiling coyly. "It's also one of Ari's favourite places to dine..."

I deliberately ignored her jibe.

"The food is to die for, Teddy," a grinning Poppy agreed. "But you decide, it's about you tonight after all."

I replied with an exuberant laugh, "Okay, Rockpool it is. Girls', time to get all dolled-up!"

Having entered the restaurant in high spirits, a towering young waiter with slicked-back butter blond hair and a disarming smile greeted us. Recognition glimmered in brilliantly emerald-green eyes, his fixated stare making my heart skip anxiously. To my relief, he remained professional and instead queried, "A table for four?"

We all nodded in unison. He led us to a table with views of the open kitchen where delicious smells wafted, making our mouths water and our lips curve upwards in delight as the loud voice of the head chef barked orders across the chaotic space to his staff.

In Dominique's case, the food wasn't the only reason. Brazenly flirting, her hungry gaze remained firmly planted on the waiter's rounded behind and broad back until we reached the table.

"You're shameless," Scarlett murmured, sliding onto a seat with Dom flopping beside her.

Her slim shoulders shrugged in her usual carefree manner. "Quite possibly."

"My name is Leon, and I shall be your waiter for the evening." He gave a friendly smile, his deeply dimpled cheeks flashing at us.

"Might I suggest a drink to start?"

"Thank you, Leon," I murmured, taking a menu from his outstretched hand. "We'll have a carafe of Domaine de l'Arlot Clos des Forêts Saint Georges 1er Cru to start please," I rattled off in fluent French, surprising even myself. Taking French lessons had indeed paid off. I might learn Italian next.

"Excellent choice, ma'am."

"Don't panic girls; I'm paying," I mused to three very shocked grown women. "Close your mouths, you all look like codfish."

Poppy giggled as our dashing waiter walked away. "Ma'am?"

Wrinkling my nose at the old-fashioned notion, I leaned my back against the soft leather, checking out my surrounds for any unwelcome visitors. Since my encounter in the carpark, it had left me feeling quite paranoid, and rightfully so.

Leon returned a few minutes later, pouring the wine from a crystal decanter into four glasses, his blended scent of citrus and musk distracting me from my thoughts momentarily.

Sipping my wine, I coquettishly smiled, thanking him.

He winked and walked away.

Grasping my glass, I caught my sister's curious gaze eyeing me suspiciously. "What?"

"Whatcha looking at, sis?"

The corners of my mouth twitched. "Only the view." I wasn't lying, well, not exactly.

Scarlett's eyes rolled, something she did habitually. "Leave work at the office for a change; you're out celebrating!"

I shrugged and lifted the glass back to my lips, taking another generous sip. "Oh, you know me, I can't help myself." Which in truth, I couldn't. My gaze slid across the restaurant floor, earning yet another eye roll.

The five-star restaurant owned by world-renowned chef Neil Perry was bustling. Not that it surprised me; it was quite the place to eat. In addition to the menu, the interior was just as appealing. Dark timbers, stone, and steel dominated the space. Adding softness and colour were the deep russet leather chairs, bright red bench seats and delicately draping curtains in doorways. The dimly lit downlights tucked under a slatted timber ceiling, provided the textbook ambience for a flawless evening.

In my case, it had presented the ideal distraction, one that I undoubtedly needed.

"I'm positively stuffed," Scarlett moaned, pushing her empty plate away. "I'll have to work out twice as hard tomorrow." My brows shot up.

"Do you even know what exercise is, 'Miss I can eat whatever I want and not put on any weight'," I breathlessly mocked. With bright electric blue eyes and fair skin, Scarlett had always turned heads, earning herself quite the stream of lustful admirers over the years. I loved teasing my sister, and without fail, I'd always attract a bite.

She flicked her long glossy copper tresses over one petite shoulder. "I know I'm gorgeous."

Lifting the wine glass to my lips, I snorted. "Love yourself much, Scars?"

"Hmm, I do, a lot!"

2

UPON RETURNING TO THE HOUSE, everyone had immediately retreated to their beds, passing out the moment their heads hit the pillow. And unbeknownst to any of them, I took full advantage of their drunken state by quietly slipping out again only to reappear hours later, my body weary, but satisfactorily worn out.

Flopping heavily onto the soft mattress, I yawned and cuddled into one of the many, probably too many, soft pillows on my bed. My eyelids drooped heavily, and eventually, I gave in to the tiredness, only to have my sleep haunted by terrifying dreams.

A shadowy figure lurked in the dark, his rough whisper repeatedly calling out my name. My legs shifted restlessly beneath the blankets as I attempted to run away from him. It was pointless, lead-filled feet held me down. He closed in, roughly grabbing me from behind. I had to face him, and with fear engulfing me, I slowly twisted. Gleaming dark eyes menacingly stared back at me as his lips moved, whispering my name.

"Teddy..."

I jolted upwards, my anguished scream echoing around my darkened bedroom. My dream felt real. It was as if he was physically here, in my bedroom.

My dampened hands pressed against an equally sweaty face as I let out a despairing sigh. Chilling nightmares that had once disappeared thanks to a decently lived life had now returned. I frowned, wondering if the eerie encounter was to blame. That aside, I darted my blurry gaze towards the clock on the bedside table, and in exasperation, reached over, flicking off the alarm button, an hour before the scheduled time. I might as well be proactive. If only my legs would cooperate. Looking at the state of my twisted sheets, I forced them to move.

Throwing back the covers, I slid out of bed and staggered into the walk-in-robe in search of a pair of gym pants and my hot pink joggers. A run always alleviated the worries.

Each pounding step sprinted over the footpath was perfectly timed with each exhaling breath as The Frays, Love Don't Die blasted in my ears. They were my muse, and the overhead streetlamps were my guide, taking me from the dark and into the light.

I ran until I hit Gardner Reserve, a family orientated park a few blocks from my house and paused at a timber bench to stretch my burning limbs. I had always loved this park. With its oversized elms littering the billowing garden beds along a weaving crushed granite pathway, their full leafed branches created a canopy, keeping play equipment and picnic tables cool enough for use throughout the warm summer months. Currently, the trees were still bare, giving way to the dappled light of the rising sun peeking through, indicative of the beautiful day we had ahead of us. I flicked my wrist and checked my Fitbit noting it was time to start heading back. Surprisingly though, I felt energised, even after a terrible night's sleep and ran home barely exerting myself in the process. And as I walked through the house, the heavenly smell of coffee and toast wafted under my nose, hitting my empty stomach with a thud. Likewise, were the loud sounds that materialised from Scarlett's mouth. Surely not. It was far too early for that amount of noise from one person.

"Morning all." I waved, breathlessly striding past the island to the fridge. Reaching in to retrieve the bottle of pineapple juice, I closed the door and spun around. My quizzical gaze met gaping stares. "You may want to be careful leaving your mouths wide open like that or flies might think it's their new home," I stated, turning back to grab a tall glass from the overhead cupboard, and setting it down on the countertop in front of them.

Spreading a thin layer of vegemite over her buttered toast, Scarlett frowned. "Who on earth goes running this early in the morning?"

I shrugged unapologetically. "I do."

"You're either mad or stupid."

"Well maybe if you did a bit of exercise, you'd feel even better about yourself. Oh, but hang on, you don't need to, your heads fat enough already!" A piece of toast came skimming past my head and landed on the polished floorboards behind me at my feet.

Tutting, I placed my hands on my hips. "Oh, no, unless you follow the five-second rule, you can't eat that now, Scars."

My baby sister was also unimpressed by Dominique and Poppy's laughter and stomped her little foot loudly. "You can all go fuck yourselves!"

"Oh, come on, Scars, take a joke. Teddy was only stirring you because she knows how much you loathe exercise," Dominique joked, only for Scarlett to flip her off as she marched past her on the way to the stairs. "That's so childish," she murmured, carrying on with her breakfast.

Due to Scarlett's temper tantrum, it meant I ended up missing my usual breakfast, and had to stop by the café below Bricks and Mortar. Taking my vanilla latte and fruit salad upstairs into the confines of my cubicle, I sat behind my desk, enjoying them both while quietly reviewing a set of plans. I should think about coming to work early every day. It's so peaceful.

"Good morning, Teddy."

"Oh, Jesus, Spencer!" I jumped out of the chair, throwing the remnants of my fruit salad over my desk. "You scared the hell out of me!" I screeched as I frantically mopped up the juice with reams of tissues.

"I'm sorry, Teddy, I didn't mean to startle you." He clung to the edge of the glass and awkwardly rubbed at the back of his neck. "And here I thought I came in being quite noisy too."

"Well, you weren't!" I had just yelled at my boss. Cringing, I swiftly apologised, my voice a dull whisper, "I'm sorry."

Naturally poised, and ready to yell back at me, I expected quite the dressing down. However, to my surprise, Spencer's mouth snapped shut, forming a thin disapproving line. Chocolate brown eyes glared right before he stalked into his office, the door slamming behind him. I flinched.

What in the hell was wrong with me, and what did I just do? I sank back into my chair and flopped forward, banging my forehead on the desktop. Ground; please swallow me. Spencer looked so mad, not that I blamed him; he wasn't the one in the wrong, I was. I'd snapped for no apparent reason. Nor was it his fault I'd slept like crap, or my nightmares had returned.

I straightened in my chair and peered over at the closed door; I needed to either eat humble pie and apologise or quit. Then again, Spencer wouldn't accept my resignation over something so small. Humble pie it had to be.

Pushing off my chair, I fixed my appearance and bravely made my way to his office. I raised my hand and knocked on the closed door, tentatively waiting for a response.

His response came clipped and sharp. "Come in!"

"Spencer, may I speak with you...please?" Who was I kidding? I was a timid little mouse currently shaking in her designer heels.

"Take a seat please, Ms McGovern." If the taut nod and the formality of his tone as well as the furious tapping on the keyboard were anything to go by, I'd say he was highly irritated with me.

"Yes... Mr Hughes." I swallowed the lump of pride in my throat and slowly flopped into the chair in front of his desk. My eyes misted over. "I... I came in here to apologise for my outburst earlier. I honestly don't know what came over me." Ashamed, my chin tilted heavenward.

His hardened expression softening, Spencer sighed. "Look, I shouldn't have gotten angry with you; it was entirely my fault for sneaking up on you anyway." His brows creased in concern. "You okay?"

"Perhaps it's just tiredness as the girls, and I went out to celebrate my promotion, and as you can imagine, we got in pretty late." Relieved Spencer wasn't about to write a formal warning, or worse – fire me, I sagged against the backrest. "Again, I apologise."

"It's fine, we're all human, so in my book, it means we're entitled to have the occasional difficult day." Spencer smiled warmly, putting my mind at ease. The warmth in his chocolate, brown eyes reminded me of someone I knew, making me smile. "I'll be sure to make more noise the next time I arrive early though." He chuckled.

"Thank you. I won't hold you up anymore, Spencer, and I'll get back to work," I replied softly before strolling back to my desk.

However, my mind wasn't relaxed. Instead, I spent the remainder of the day in a daze, the ability to focus, gone. Regaining that focus and control before everything became overwhelming had to be my new goal, and I knew precisely where to start – the gym.

"Hey, I'm home!" hollered a cheerful Poppy upon sauntering into the kitchen where I busily prepped salad vegetables at the island bench with various piano compilations playing off my Spotify playlist in the background.

"Hi, Poppy, how was your day?"

Hanging her tote and satchel over the back of a barstool, her brow wrinkled. "You're home earlier than normal, Teddy. Is everything okay? You seem a little distracted?" she murmured, watching slivers of Lebanese cucumber slide from the cutting board into a clear glass bowl filled with spinach and rocket leaves.

"No, nothing's wrong." I gave a swift shake of the head and started dicing Roma tomatoes trying to ignore the disbelieving gaze staring at me.

"I call bullshit. Tell me what's really going on, or do I have to shake it out of you?" Poppy forewarned rounding the bench. Having carefully extracted the sharp knife out of my shaking hand, she set it down on the counter.

Taking one look into those coffee brown eyes, I dissolved. "Yesterday, as I left work, someone was watching me in the garage. I think it was..." I choked on my tears, unable to speak his name. I didn't have to.

"Are you sure? Maybe it was just a homeless person or somebody who looked like – him?" she inferred, compassionately rubbing my arm.

Poppy and I had met after her father's job transferred him from London to Melbourne, merely months before my life changed forever. She was the one and only person I had openly spoken to about my sordid ordeal. Mind you, when your best friend finds you crying your eyes out and trying to swill an entire bottle of scotch stolen from your father's liquor cabinet, it was bound to raise a few concerns. Her forthright manner always had a way of making you open up, even when you've tried to tell her, repeatedly, that you weren't in the mood to talk about it. Without her friendship, coming to terms with my past may never have happened. Her support hadn't ever wavered, sealing the bond we now shared, one so much stronger than sisterhood.

"No, I can't be certain, unless he has an evil twin. I'm sorry. Perhaps it was just my imagination, and it was just a homeless person?" Who was I trying to convince more, her or me? I smiled weakly. "That's why I went for a run early this morning, and to the gym this afternoon. I have to regain control over my life before my past takes ahold of me again."

"That's right, you do. Just keep focusing on the positive influences around you, and you'll be fine."

"Thank you for always being there for me."

"I'm always here if you need me, but next time – don't hide your issues from me, okay?" Poppy chided sternly, wagging a finger at me. Clear and direct; an approach she'd mastered and used in her skills as an English teacher at Beaumont Grammar, a prestigious school in Melbourne's northern district.

"Okay, but I won't say I promise to either," I responded, turning my guilty gaze away under the pretence I was grabbing the knife to finish my food prep. Some secrets just weren't meant to be shared; it was against the rules.

"Mmm, I'm starving. What's on the menu tonight?"

I chuckled in amusement as Dominique eyed the small feast spread over the long wooden dining table hungrily. "Spinach and ricotta tortellini deliciously coated in a mushroom sauce, with garlic bread and a simple salad, nothing too spectacular. I picked it up from the deli on the way home from the gym," I replied, setting a bottle of Pinot Grigio in the centre of the table as I slid into one of the empty seats either side of Poppy.

"Who cares where it came from, it's dinner, and it smells amazing. Let's eat," Poppy countered, shovelling a forkful of pasta into her mouth.

"So, girls', are we all set for Saturday night?" Dominique queried, through a mouthful of salad. "I'm so excited; mum throws the best parties. The food, the people, the booze, and let's not forget the hot guys in fabulous tuxes'!"

Scarlett picked up a serviette and playfully wiped down Dominique's chin. "For the drool," she uttered dryly. "You'll ruin your dinner with it."

Dominique giggled, swatting Scarlett's hand away. "You're an idiot."

"Have you got your dresses organised?" Poppy enquired, tearing at the garlicky baguette. The girls nodded in unison.

"I have too," I added, clutching the wine bottle, and filling everyone's glasses. "What time are we expected at your mother's soiree, Dom?"

"Seven, or eight, I can't remember exactly." Her nose scrunched. "It doesn't matter if we're a little late, mother would faint on the spot if we arrived on time anyway."

I giggled. Audrina Jaeger represented everything a mother was supposed to be: kind, loving, and most of all, fun. Unlike mine, they were opposites in every way. "Your mother knows us well."

"And you know… Ari shall be there," Dominique told me ever so casually, lifting the wine glass to her lips as she tried to hide her not so innocent smile.

"So?" I sighed, pushing to my feet. "What does Ari being there have to do with me?" I challenged, gathering dishes, and carting them to the sink. Inside I was delighted, but it was a sentiment I refused to share with my persistently intrusive roommates. As always though, their sixth sense to my take flight response whenever Ari's name came up was on overdrive.

"So?" Scarlett intoned, rolling her eyes and bouncing around me as I rinsed the plates under the hot water. "Is that all you've got to say about the man you've unequivocally lusted after your entire life? You two have it bad for one another," she uttered. "The moment you two are in the same room, the sexual tension blows the roof from its rafters."

I spun on my heel and shot her a deathly glare. "We do not!" The high octave in my voice was a sure sign she was right on the mark. Her smirking expression told me so. She was such a bitch. "We're just friends. We grew up together, so naturally, we're bound to have some feelings, you know, like a brother and sister," I argued nonchalantly, and again, not one of them bought it.

"That's crap, and you know it," Dominique interjected. "What you and Ari share, Teddy, is most definitely not like a brother and a sister. A brother-sister relationship is what we have – the whole love-hate thing. And I agree with Scarlett; Ari acts like a lost puppy whenever he sees you." Sticking a finger in her mouth, she gagged. "It's sickening."

Snap. There it was, and it had nothing to do with the crude gesture causing one of my brows to rise sharply. In my attempt to ignore the continually churning digs about Ari, I turned back to the sink and started stacking the dishwasher.

I loved Ari and had for years. But the problem was my past, it always stood smack bang in the middle of the road like a large crevice, preventing any chance of us ever coming together.

Scarlett bounded around the bench like that jacked-up rabbit I'd always thought her to be and grabbed me by the waist. "Come on, sissy; you know ya wanna!" Her eyebrows jiggled scaring me or scarring me. Whichever way, I was concerned. Moreover, she had me cornered. A shitty predicament to be in if you asked me.

"Yes, all right! You're a bunch of nags. I do like him! A lot!" Finally, and much to their impish delight, I caved. I was sure my cheeks burned the same colour as my hair; so much so, astronauts could detect me glowing from outer space. Mars to be precise. I'd just died of embarrassment twice in one day. "There, I said it. Are you happy now?"

"Of course, we are. Why wouldn't we be?" Dominique giggled, sidling up beside me. "Why don't you try on the weekend at mum's party? You may find my brother will be more than happy to reciprocate," she stated matter-of-factly. Cheeky bugger.

"Okay, okay," I conceded blushing. "This weekend I'll tell Ari – but only after a few glasses of champagne and all this nagging!" Loud satisfied screams deafened me.

I threw the dishcloth into the sink. "Right, who's finishing the cleaning up, because I most certainly am not?" Pointedly, I stared at my sister and Dominique. Surprisingly they took the hint.

Simpering, I clutched the wine bottle along with my glass and moseyed over to the family room, setting them both down on the coffee table before switching on my iPhone, the room automatically filling with the earthy voice of Etta James. I settled beside a slightly tipsy Poppy on the modular sofa to relax, if only Scarlett would quit complaining then I could.

A protesting whimper swiftly followed as Dominique flicked her on the thigh with the tea towel.

I smiled privately behind my glass at the familiar and arousing sound. In my dazed state, I began stroking the long stem of my glass, my thoughts tuning in elsewhere, somewhere more erotic. Something Poppy noticed as she bumped our shoulders together, knocking me out of my reverie.

"You're blushing. I imagine it has something to do with a particularly hot, handsome young man. And don't try to lie, I know that look!"

I sipped on my wine under the ruse of not hearing what she'd said.

"You were, weren't you?" Poppy pressed, grinning at me.

"You're as bad as the other two. Is this gang up on Teddy night?" I whined, my head falling back against the sofa.

Bobbing her head gleefully, she drunkenly giggled. "Yep…"

"You're all unreal." I laughed along with her; my thoughts were quickly sobering. "I just hope I don't lose my nerve and run away from him as I have in the past…"

"One should hope not!" Poppy determined in her soft English manner. "Perhaps, and this is merely a suggestion, take him somewhere quiet, away from prying eyes and ears?" As she not so covertly pointed in the direction of the kitchen, hiding my laughter became a tad challenging.

"Good thinking, ninety-nine, I may just do that." I polished off the glass and set it down in my lap. "I'll grab him by the belt and drag him upstairs to his old bedroom so that I can ravage him with all this 'sexual tension' we've allegedly harboured."

"No alleging anything!" she scoffed, prompting a dramatic eyeroll from me. "If I, were you, I would even go butt naked underneath just to save time," Poppy dryly endorsed.

"Poppy Fleming, I'm shocked!" I slapped a hand over my mouth as another bout of laughter bubbled to the surface. "And here I thought you were little Miss Prude."

"I'm a closet kink," she whispered, holding a finger up to her lips. "But shh, don't tell anyone."

She needn't preach to the choir; I was the Queen of secrets. "Your secret is safe with me. Anyway, I'm off to bed." My legs wobbled beneath me as I pushed off the sofa to stand. "Whoops."

"See, you're already weak at the knees just thinking about him." "No, the extreme exercise at the gym is to blame."

"You keep telling yourself that, but we all know the truth." Growling, I waved a dismissive hand. "Goodnight, lovely."

"Goodnight, Teddy Bear. Don't dream too much of him, though. You'll only frustrate yourself more, and then you'll be pulling out one of those many friends you own in the drawer...." Poppy snickered, gaining immense delight as she saw my cheeks flame. "Then all that tension..." Her hands circled the air above her. "Poof, gone!"

I picked up one of the overstuffed cushions and threw it at my hysterically laughing friend. "Goodnight, Popsicle!" Amused, I took off to my bedroom before she said anything more to embarrass me.

Throwing myself onto the bed, I flopped against the pillows and stared up at the ceiling, praying I wasn't making a massive mistake by finally giving in to my feelings.

3

WITH THE ARRIVAL OF THE WEEKEND after a long working week, the girls' and I cruised into Club Retro, a fashionable nightclub in the centre of Lonsdale Street. Its three levels and two bars crowded, and brimming with other young clubbers that were here for the same reason as us; to forget the pressures of their daily lives.

Hypnotically energetic music reverberated loudly around us, leaving our bodies humming and forcing us to shout. But then again, we weren't out at a noisy club to talk.

The moment we each collected our drinks, we manoeuvred our way onto the dance floor, struggling to find a space amongst the packed bodies. Revellers danced back-to-back, the thumping music their muse under the flickering strobe lights, blinding us as they lit up the darkened club.

Lethal cocktails became the fuel to an unlit match, reigniting the rescinding fire within. I let loose and danced like no one was watching. Except unbeknownst to me, or any of us, somebody already was.

∞

"**HMM, LOOKING GOOD THERE, TEDDY**. Just as good as the tight

Lycra pants you wear jogging." Licking my lips, I observed a luscious Teddy from the balcony above. The short, revealing outfit and the provocative moves made me want her more than ever before. "Such a pity you have company though."

∞

Teddy

THE WILD NIGHT OUT HAD cost me severely in the way of a vicious hangover and painful blisters on the soles of both feet. I needed food. "How about we do brunch?" I emphatically suggested to my equally suffering roommates. "I could quite easily go for one of those salmon bagels and a ridiculously strong coffee from the Pocket Café around the corner; it would be fantastic about now."

"Sounds like a plan." Poppy winced, easing onto a stool at the island bench and nursing her pounding head between her hands. "The fresh air might be nice too."

"Sunglasses are a must," Scarlett added in a hushed tone, her eyes squinting at the bright sun blazing in through the kitchen window above the apron-front farmhouse sink. "Why do we put ourselves through this?"

"And to think, we're punishing ourselves all over again tonight at my mothers," Dominique groggily murmured alongside her while downing a couple of painkillers with a glass of icy cold orange juice.

"Come on, let's go eat, and refuel ready to kill our livers again later." Sighing, I pushed away from the bench and hobbled back to my bedroom. Why did I suggest clubbing last night knowing we were partying again later? By the end of the weekend, an ice pack wouldn't cut it; I'd have to soak my entire body in the pool to recover.

The house grew into a hive of activity, and hidden somewhere under the piles of makeup and hair accessories was my dining table. According to Dom, it was everything we needed to beautify ourselves for her mother's party. She had also kindly offered to style our hair; more like threatened us if we went to anyone but her. She was a hairdresser after all.

With Jessica Mauboy's, Fallin' playing softly from the speaker, I sat back, soaking up every minute of the pampering while my liver soaked up yet more champagne. Curious about the party, I questioned Dom, "Not that your mother ever needs an excuse, but what's the reason behind this latest cocktail party?"

She snorted derisively. "No, you're right there, she doesn't. Tonight's about dad's law firm as he and Uncle Garrett have a new junior they want to introduce to everyone who matters, including Asher, Ari's lawyer. You remember him, don't you, Teddy?"

He was a hard man to forget; loud, brash, crass; a possible roadblock in my plans. With any luck, he'd find himself too distracted trying to worm his way into someone's skirt. One could only hope.

"Mum showed me a photo, and he's rather cute."

I frowned. "Asher's cute?"

"Ew, no, Asher's too old!" I laughed at her horrified expression as she twisted a narrow length of my hair around the straightener. "I was talking about the new associate."

"Sorry, Dom, anyway, carry on."

"What's the new guy's name?" Scarlett queried impatiently, "Dom, hello?"

Dominique blinked and stared blankly. "What?"

"A...name... please," she repeated slowly. "We want other details, too. You know, what he looks like, age, star sign, etc."

Rolling my eyes at my sister was a given. Unlike me, Scarlett was incredibly nosy, insisting on knowing everything, no matter how small the detail.

"Oh. Yeah, right. Damien Rivers and his eyes…. are the same colour as one, too." Dom dreamily describing him while she had long curls of my hair wrapped around the steaming straightener was not the ideal situation if I planned on seducing Ari later. A bald head might be a significant turn-off. I let out a sigh of relief as a hot curl flowed down my neck.

I chuckled. "What a yucky brown like the Yarra?"

"Nooo, they're a stunning blue, like the ocean on a bright day. His hair…it's the colour of caramel, like the ones I enjoy sucking on." Her lips twisted ruefully. "He has a chiselled jaw and face, and his body, from what I was able to tell by the cut of his suit, didn't seem too shabby either. His smile," she gushed, "made him, ah…dashing."

Scarlett's eyelids fluttered. "Dom's in love."

Switching from the straightener to hairpins, Dom let out a girlish giggle. "No, not love, just lust. Don't confuse the two. And if I'm right, Teddy might not be the only one getting lucky tonight."

I scoffed at the statement. "Let's not count our chickens before they hatch, shall we?" Inwardly though, I hoped it to be true. "Getting our heads back above the waistline, isn't this party a bit over the top for just one guy? Won't he feel a tad overwhelmed?"

"Hopefully not. Mum felt this party would be the perfect introduction for Damien. Me personally, a simple dinner party would have sufficed. My mother, as we all know, refuses to settle for anything less. Any excuse for kicking up her heels really," Dominique stated, grasping the small hand mirror beside me and waving it around the back of my head. "There, all done, Miss Teddy, do you approve?"

As always, she had outdone herself.

Apart from the few loose strands falling gently around my face, she had swept my hair to one side, leaving masses of curls pinned neatly just above my nape. My neck left exposed, ready for Ari's sweet lips, his hands, and…oh boy, I had better stop right there. Just envisaging his sexy arse body had the warmth igniting between my thighs.

"Earth to Teddy," Dom murmured, waving a hand in front of my face. "Just now, that flush in your face was rather disconcerting."

I pushed from the chair and looked anywhere except at the three sets of eyes laughing at me as the flush rose over my neck and face. "It's lovely, Dom, thank you."

"Thank you. Ari should hopefully love it just as much." Dominique's charismatic smile flashed, tapping the top of the chair with the hairbrush. "Now, who's next?"

Realising that was my cue to move, I sidestepped to another chair.

"Wear your eye makeup heavier tonight, Teddy," Scarlett conveyed, occupying the seat I'd just vacated. "Make them look...seductive."

I shot her a quizzical look as I slowly dabbed the foundation sponge over my nose and cheeks. "I don't want to look like a high-class hooker either."

"You don't want to look like a nun either. Otherwise, you might not get none!"

My eyes rolled. "Good to see you paid attention in English, sis." The torture didn't end there as she passed the gold-encased lipstick pulled from her makeup case over the table to me. Blue eyes mischievously glimmered as she watched me slip off the lid and inspect the red stick inside.

"Ari has a real fetish for clowns, or so I've heard."

Dominique swiftly reacted and tapped the top of Scarlett's head with the back of the brush. She wasn't gentle about it either; Dom had the Jaeger temper that's for sure.

"Ow, what was that for?" Scarlett whined, rubbing the crown of her head. "That's probably going to bruise."

I sniggered behind the safety of my hand.

"All that shall bruise is your ego," Dom growled, waving the pointy end of the pintail comb at her. "Your sister's nervous enough as it is. Keep it up, and you'll be the one looking like a circus freak instead. Good luck getting a man then!"

Scarlett shrank down in her seat. "Okay, I'll stop. I'm sorry, Teddy."

I narrowed my eyes. "I'm sure you are. And while I do appreciate the advice, even if in part it was you being nothing more than a nasty cow, I only want to appear alluring, not desperate."

Scarlett nodded in defeat. "Fair enough, but seriously the red lipstick would look amazing with your dress and nails."

"I'll wear it then," I murmured, setting the lipstick beside me.

For the next twenty minutes, I applied my makeup in peace, without any further ribbing from my obnoxious sister. Once finished, I sat back and admired my handiwork in the mirror. "Well?" I asked, pushing the mirror aside.

"Stunning," remarked Poppy.

"You go, girl. If that doesn't blow Ari away, well, he's more of an idiot than I thought," Dominique assured.

Pushing off my chair, I placed a hand on my dancing stomach and blew out a shaky breath. "What if tonight's proposition goes wrong? Or Ari laughs at me? Or worse, he rejects me for making him wait this long?"

"You'll be okay," Dominique whispered, placing a reassuring hand on my shoulder. "I just happened to overhear along the grapevine, my brother's just as nervous. He's worried you'll reject him."

Whenever gossip was involved, Dom never just happened to overhear anything; she was usually right in the thick of it.

"Oh, that makes me feel better. I think." Unconvinced, I grimaced. "Regardless of what happens, I am now going to go and finish getting myself ready, so that I am hot enough for Ari not to turn me down!" A girl could dream, couldn't she?

I padded back to the bedroom and dropped my dressing gown to apply moisturiser to every inch of my body, leaving my skin soft and supple to the touch. Then I sprayed my favourite perfume, Marc Jacobs, Daisy, dotting the delicately alluring scent around the pulse points of my throat, and wrists.

My meticulously planned outfit for the night ahead lay on the bed; black lacy Victoria Secret panties, their delicate lace see-through, giving the slightest of hints to the treasures lying beneath a simple backless one-shouldered bodycon dress in black. No bra required. Extremely short, the hem barely stopped mid-thigh. I had to say, as I admired myself in the full-length mirror, the fitted dress was definitely worth the expense.

I moved toward my antique dresser and perched on the chair, slipping a pair of four-inch black strappy diamanté heels over my feet. Cute. I knew the perfect piece of jewellery to complement them too — my square-cut eighteen-carat white gold diamond earrings, a twenty-first birthday present from my grandfather, Barrett McGovern. I pushed the studs into my lobes and took one last look in the mirror before exiting the room to join the others in the kitchen for yet more celebratory glasses of champagne.

"Looking spectacular ladies." I smiled, handing them each a flute. "Now a toast: here's to a successful evening and to hopefully getting laid."

In our typical manner, we were fashionably an hour late, eventually arriving at the Jaeger's residence, a sprawling French inspired mansion residing in the leafy upper-class suburb of Toorak. The town car curved smoothly around the crescent-shaped driveway with our driver halting beside a brightly lit water fountain, it's centrepiece a mother nursing her child. A sure sign Audrina loved her children, I thought.

Dominique clumsily stepped out first. "Oh, whoops! I had better not fall into that." She laughed loudly, adjusting her fitted cranberry red midi dress.

"I'm so buzzed," a slurring Poppy announced, sliding across the black leather seat. "That bottle of champagne Audrina had waiting in the car has put me over the edge." Elegantly swinging her legs and climbing from the car without falling at least, she stood to straighten her short V-neck chiffon daffodil cocktail dress. With her warm, honey blonde hair slicked back and natural makeup highlighting coffee brown eyes, she looked stunning.

"I know what you mean." God, I was equally drunk. I giggled like one too. Falling out behind her, I made a point of avoiding the fountain myself. Hours spent getting dressed up would've been a pointless exercise otherwise. Teetering on high heels while drunk was not a great mix either, making the amble up the vintage redbrick paved footpath to the front door quite the tricky task.

Dominique's attractive parent's, Jaxson and Audrina stood in the covered breezeway, greeting each guest as they arrived, directing them in through the house and out to the open marquee in the expansive backyard. Ruby red lips mischievously quirked as Audrina embraced each of us.

"Oh, my goodness, girls', you're sloshed already," she murmured in her ever-present English lilt.

A classic beauty with alabaster skin and flowing locks of glossy jet-black hair, Audrina had always reminded me of Snow White. Well, that's who I'd compared her to as I grew up.

Nevertheless, it was a term of endearment she grew to love.

As a small child, whenever our families came together, I'd stand by the doors, eagerly awaiting to see if any forest animals followed her inside. It was a dream that never once took place, quite disheartening really, particularly when you're only three years old.

"That, Snow White, would imply we drank copious amounts of champagne," I asserted giggling, returning her embrace. "Which I might add...you just happened to supply."

She laughed. "In my defence, I only provided one bottle." Her deep chocolate gaze playfully narrowed, scanning each of us. "But by the looks of you four already, you drank a bottle before you left home."

"A whole bottle doesn't go far between four, does it, Daddy?" Dominique insisted, hugging her beloved father.

"Aye, it doesn't. But then your mother wouldn't know because she doesn't like sharing, even with me," Jaxson dryly agreed, earning a deathly glare from his wife. "You all look positively stunning."

Glowing sapphire blue eyes twinkled brightly. "You'll be spending the night trying to run away from those handsome suitors we have here. How in those shoes, I haven't the slightest?" he questioned, bending at the waist to kiss each of our cheeks. "Perhaps I might suggest giving you each a cricket bat to swat them away?"

"No bats needed, Dad. Now promise the girls' and me here, you won't go chasing them off?" she haughtily demanded, grabbing the lapels of his black dinner jacket roughly.

"Now, Dom, the lack of faith in your father's disheartening. Why on earth would I need to chase any suitor off?" His mouth twitched in wry amusement. Considering the length of time, the Jaeger's had lived in Australia, his Northern Irish lilt hadn't lessened much either.

"I'll just send Ari after them if they dare dishonour any one of you." Jaxson was Audrina's Prince Charming. Dressed in his black dinner suit with his neatly combed raven hair substantially greying, he was still quite the head-turner, even at sixty.

"All righty then, you know it's time to go and join the party when the 'rents are embarrassing you already," Dominque grumbled, turning to Scarlett. "Are you coming?"

"Yes! I need to find me a man!" Linking her arm through Dominique's, they promptly made their way towards the open French doors at the back of the house.

I just shook my head and followed. I was too busy perusing for somebody much older and much more handsome.

Dominique stood at the top of the brick-paved steps, her gaze keenly scanning the yard for Damien until she spotted him. "Ooh, there he is." She excitedly pointed him out amongst the multitude of sleek suits and the rainbow of cocktail dresses.

I raised a dubious brow. How? They all looked the same.

Impressed, Scarlett gushed, "Wow, you were right; he's adorable." If jocks were their thing, who was I to judge?

"Who's cute? I hope you were talking about me?"

The four of us pivoted on the spikes of our heels simultaneously to find Bryson Jaeger's eyes sparkling like freshly polished sapphires, ready to inflict mischief on an unsuspecting victim; mainly his youngest sister. Having inherited his father's build; broad shoulders, long legs, and a dashing smile to match, the dark, slim-fit suit he'd donned for the evening, only accentuated every inch of his good looks.

"Bryson!" she squealed, hugging him tightly.

"Yeah, happy to see you too, sis..." He grinned, pulling away. "Ladies, how are you all tonight? You're all looking ravishing as always," he stated before motioning to the petite blonde standing next to him, her large crystal blue eyes glittering under the fairy lights strung above us. "You remember my long-time girlfriend, Olivia Gilbert?"

"Of course, we do!" Dom scoffed hugging her just as tightly.

Bryson's eyes rolled. "We know you do; I was talking about the others ya daft bugger!"

Not wanting to be rude, I ushered forward and hugged her. "It's good to see you again, Olivia."

"Same," she sweetly replied. "Enjoy the party."

Dominique squeezed her brother's arm affectionately. "Lovely to see you, bro, but we are on a mission tonight. But first we need to swing past the bar to grab another glass of bubbly, and then, we're partying hard."

Bryson's eyes twinkled, his soft expression glowing in amusement. "You look like you've had an early start as it is." Long fingers strummed his chin. "Let me guess: mother threw a bottle of champagne in the town car for you?"

"Perhaps..." She giggled, walking off towards the bar at the edge of the dance floor to grab a fresh glass of champagne before veering away in search of her jock. I set off in the opposite direction in search of Ari.

As usual, Audrina had spared no expense, setting the backyard up beautifully. The marquee with widely opened draping curtains housed several well-laid tables, each decorated with small glass vases filled with fragrant flowers. While tea light candles inside filigree metal hurricane lamps glowed, their intricate patterns adding a soft romantic shine over the fabric walls. In the corner of the makeshift timber dancefloor, a band gently played, their female singer crooning Billie Holiday renditions beautifully.

Confidently strolling across the floor, my head repeatedly swivelled in the hope I'd run into Ari. Instead, I witnessed Scarlett fawning over Dom's older cousin Gabriel on the edge of the garden. Not that I blamed her; he was rather handsome in a rugged kinda way, I suppose. Then my wandering gaze spotted Asher's golden blonde hair as his towering frame slinked through the crowd, his sights squarely set on the gorgeous brunette beside Caleb, another cousin, whom I assumed to be his date.

Oh, dear, I wouldn't if I were you Asher; you're bound to have your arse kicked.

The Jaeger men's volatile temper was infamous amongst their social circle and the business world, Ari's specifically. He had earned quite the reputation when it came to losing his, especially when it came to the media. That was a love-hate relationship, and he hadn't ever shied away from telling them so either.

Speaking of which, if Asher was there, then where in the hell was Ari. Practically joined at the hip, surely it meant he wasn't too far behind him.

I leaned on the bar and ordered a glass of champagne while still busily spying on Asher in the hope he'd dismally fall flat on his face. As the bartender passed me my drink, I stepped back, inadvertently stumbling backwards against a solid wall of muscle.

Thankfully, a pair of smooth masculine hands caught me beneath the arms before I completely fell and embarrassed myself even further. Using the firm biceps to my advantage, I slowly raised back to my feet and straightened with my champagne glass miraculously intact. Whoever he was, he smelled sinfully inebriating.

"I'm so sorry, I didn't see you there," I muttered, carefully twirling around to meet my rescuer. My face flamed as deliciously dark chocolate eyes glinted at me. "Oh, Ari...um, how...hi, oh God!" The proximity of his closeness and the muskiness of his cologne had left me weak at the knees and foolishly incoherent, making it impossible to form words that were worthy of any response.

His long fingers grazed my arm, setting my body on fire. "No, I'm not God, but if you see me that way then... I say thank you," he cockily murmured, tilting his head, and greedily raking his heated gaze over my body. "You, Teddy, look beautiful, as always."

That voice. Swoon. I gulped nervously. "Ari.... there's something I have to tell you."

"As do I," he whispered, gliding a hand over my bare shoulder. My eyes slid closed as I shivered in delight.

Reality suddenly dawned and confessing my feelings wasn't going to come easily. My eyes flicked open, and desolate, I pushed off Ari's chest, staring regretfully. "I'm sorry, but I can't do this. Excuse me." Brushing past him, I stormed off into the house, leaving him behind, well and truly confused.

As fast as my legs would carry me, I ran up the stairs and sought refuge in Dominique's old room. I closed the door behind me and sagged against it, verbally castigating myself. "I'm such an idiot." But out of nowhere, hysterical laughter erupted. It was either the numerous glasses of champagne I'd speedily downed, or it was Dominique's eclectically styled room.

It was whimsical, a crazy, mishmash of colours, nothing matched, yet somehow it worked. My favourite feature, of course, was the giant wall of framed photos, each of them filled with the many memories us girls' had shared over the years.

I bounced off the door and strolled across the room, my heels sinking into the plush, hot pink carpet — so many memories, with each one as memorable as the last. Our Gold Coast holiday especially. Now that trip was wild; I recalled that much. We had squeezed in as much as possible into one short week, including the fun parks. Between the four of us, I was highly confident we had drunk each bar and nightclub we visited along the strip dry. The hangovers were horrendous to boot if that was any indication.

I heard the handle on the door turn, compelling me to swiftly pivot and my breath to hitch. The butterflies had returned.

Ari smirked, his chin jerking towards the photos. "I bet my bottom dollar not one of you shall ever forget that week. Well, what you probably remember of it anyway," he murmured, leaning his broad frame in the open doorway.

"My liver and kidneys certainly didn't thank me for the abuse I dished out, that's for sure."

His heated and darkened gaze appeared to be undressing me, making me feel hot and wet with an unabashed need to rip my clothes off.

Likewise, my hooded gaze drifted correspondingly.

From the unruly, spiked jet-black hair on the top of his head to the long, taut legs crossed at the ankles, dressed in an expensive black suit and a white shirt, sans the tie, with the top button undone, he was quite the mouth-watering sight. Along with that designer stubble growing along a defined, masculine jawline – the pleasure alone would be worth the facial rash.

Conversely, my shyness held me back. Otherwise, leaving my inhibitions behind and scattering them over the floor along with my clothes wouldn't have been an issue.

Peeking coyly from beneath my lashes, I asked, "Are you in here to make more fun of me, Ari?"

In slow measured steps, he strode leisurely towards me, a ghost of a smile crossing his sinful mouth. "No, I'm not. And I wasn't making fun of you earlier; I was merely making a joke, a bad one at that I'd say."

"Clearly," I uttered, slowly stepping backwards until my back connected with the wall behind me.

Ari closed the gap between us as his sultry gaze stared darkly. His intent evident as his palms flattened against the wall, caging me in with his muscly physique.

"You know how much I like you, Teddy? I always have," he spoke softly, his raspy accent striking every nerve throughout my trembling body. The fire within reignited as his soft lips repeatedly brushed in tender kisses over my parted mouth.

My tongue darted out, tasting his bottom lip. "Yes, as do I."

Ari inhaled sharply, his fingers lightly gliding along my jawline and down my throat. The stirring feeling headed south, curling around my spine and into my groin. A triumphant smile danced on his lips as his hands travelled over the curves hiding beneath the figure-hugging dress. I felt his warm breath against my skin as a low, raspy growl rumbled. "You are...divine."

His fingertips brushed along my thigh, and slid under the short hem of the dress, slowly finding their way inside my panties. Another low growl escaped. Somewhat an erotic sound, I thought as his fingers worked their magic over my aching nub, rubbing and applying pressure until my body stiffened and shook in response.

Overwhelmed by my climax, I gripped the lapels of his jacket tightly, moaning, "Ari..."

"I'd say you feel the same way," he whispered hoarsely, stroking along the bare silken folds of my cleft, my climax soaking his probing fingers.

I was about to respond when a ruckus in the doorway interrupted us, not that Ari allowed the noise to divert his attention.

"Oh, here you BOTH are!" Dominique exclaimed loudly, stumbling through the doorway.

"Get out, Dom." Regardless of her intrusion, he discreetly kept up the tantalising strokes.

My jaw gaped at the relaxed demeanour. How was Ari so damned calm? I certainly wasn't! Oh, sweet Jesus, this was pure torture. Worse when I felt my legs stiffening from the strain.

His encouragement purred in my ear, "Just let go." My brow furrowed; was he mad? Oh, fuck it.

I leaned into his shoulder, muffling my cries as another intense orgasm ripped through me.

"Will you two go ahead and just do it already? You know you want to. Put yourselves, and us, out of our misery for goodness sake!"

An irritated growl rumbled low in Ari's throat, making me giggle. "I'm trying, but you won't take the hint and leave."

"It's my room, so how about you leave! Go to your old room if ya wanna fuck each other senseless!"

Ari peered down at me and smiled warmly before peering over his shoulder at his sister and growling at her. "Are you quite finished my darling sister? You're not only embarrassing Teddy but also yourself. Now, go, and have some food, and water, whilst you're at it!" he scolded in a fatherly fashion. "I believe you've had enough alcohol for one night."

She stubbornly folded her arms over her chest. "Don't tell me what to do, brother!"

"Are you coming, Teddy?" Blowing out a disgruntled sigh, he straightened and held out a hand, his face glowing with immense pleasure when I gladly accepted it. Anything if it meant we could be alone elsewhere, and away from prying eyes.

Dominique giggled uncontrollably. "I'm sure she wants to."

Fed up and flustered, his hand dropped from mine. "Out!" he barked, pushing his sister towards the open doorway.

"All right, I'm going! And don't touch me!" she growled fiercely poking his hands away. "Who knows where those hands have been!"

"Go! Now!"

"And stay off my bed!" In a drunken huff, Dominique noisily stumbled and took off. Quietly and inwardly, I prayed she'd made it to the bottom of the winding staircase safely.

"Right, now my annoying little sister has left the both of us utterly embarrassed, shall we proceed to somewhere a little less noisy?" Ari queried, holding out his hand once more. "Perhaps my bedroom might be more suitable as opposed to this pink nightmare?"

Stupidly, I refused his gesture and instead, I just stared, clasping my hands close to my chest. "I can't."

He expressed his dismay, "Why not? Have I done something wrong, Teddy?"

Facing the puzzled gaze on his face pained me beyond repair. "It's...I feel the same way, and was hoping..." Blinking pooling tears away, I sighed despondently. "I was hoping tonight would finally bring us together."

Ari tugged at my chin. "Look at me, please?" he whispered, cupping my face. As he wiped my falling tears away with the soft pads of his thumbs, his intense gaze softened. "Believe it or not, I had the same notion." Suddenly he launched himself at me, and firmly grasped my nape as his mouth hungrily claimed mine.

My fingers twisted through his thick hair, as the seduction and desperation left me lost in the electrifying kiss.

I moaned and arched into the hard slab that was his body, absorbing the feel of his hands as they began roaming. One slid down my back, pinning us together. His noticeably impressive bulge strained against the soft curve of my stomach, an indication if I ever felt one of the apparent effect I had on him.

Then unbidden thoughts raced through my mind, tragically reminding me why we never came together to begin with, and why we were never meant to be. Panting harshly, I pushed away from Ari, my hand flattening against his firm chest as he endeavoured to lose the separation between us. "No, I can't."

Heavily panting, Ari's brows knitted together. "Why not?" Again, he attempted to reach out to me. I shook my head heatedly. His disappointed gaze eyeing me with longing as his arm dropped back to his side.

Never again, could he look at me the same way if I explained the truth behind my reasoning. It just wasn't possible.

"It's...I just can't. Excuse me, Ari." Like the coward I was, I ran from the bedroom, leaving him behind, lost, and perplexed. Again.

4

Ari

A FRISSON OF ANNOYANCE FLARED as I speculated Teddy's reticence. As it stood, our little tryst had earned me a rock-hard erection, one I desperately needed to rid myself of, and quickly before my balls turned a lovely shade of blue. Whilst I imagined ice cubes easing my woes, I weaved my way through the crowded dancefloor towards the bar, I made the gut-wrenching decision to maintain distance from Teddy for the remainder of the evening. Visiting with her at her North Melbourne home appeared to be the preferred choice. Privacy would be a given at least.

"Bourbon, straight, and no bloody ice!" My curt demand quickly met, I threw the dark liquor back, its burn felt on the way down. It wasn't enough. I slammed the small crystal tumbler onto the bar indicating for another.

"Another, Mr Jaeger?"

Irritated the bartender couldn't take the hint, my brows shot up. "Does a bear shit in the woods?" Only then did the young, inexperienced red-faced bartender understand. He swiftly poured and slid the drink back to me.

My gaze inadvertently slid across the yard as I casually leaned my forearm on the bar. I frowned; considering our steamy encounter earlier, Teddy was rather lively. It had to be nothing more than an act, surely. My silent question furtively answered as her daring gaze glanced over at me, and creamy cheeks turned a deep crimson.

A perceptive smile flittered across my lips.

Knowing Teddy was as equally affected by my presence as I was hers, offered a fragment of hope. Even if it was small, tomorrow was bound to be an improvement on tonight's epic failure.

Then I was given a glimpse of the reason behind Teddy's animated persona: Eve, my mother's younger sister. She peered past Teddy's slender shoulder and waved. I raised my glass, acknowledging her. She added a wink for good measure. Cheeky bugger.

Eve Whittemore, what could I say, I adored her. She was more of a second mother than an aunt. Whenever I required an indifferent or objective opinion, she always delivered. Another expertise of hers I admired and applauded was her ability to speak her mind. Then, her diplomacy skills or lack thereof, weren't all she endowed.

Having earned quite the reputation as a seductress and a maneater, she was highly skilful at luring anyone to her bed. She proudly owned it too. Over the years, I'd observed her orchestrate many a dalliance with a simple glance or a feather-light touch. The moment their entranced gaze stared into fathomless chocolate brown eyes; they were instantly lost. Unwittingly, men, and women alike found themselves worn down, giving in to whatever she desired. As beautiful as my mother, it wasn't surprising, but that's where the similarities ended.

Eve oozed sexual dominance, surpassing any of the women I'd briefly dated over the years. Come to think of it; they had nothing on her. So self-assured, every member of the family had often wondered how her bumbling husband Nicholas had snagged her; he was quite the marshmallow compared to his seductress wife.

I turned back to the bar, ordering yet another drink.

"I'll have one of those too, please." Speak of the devil.

I grinned at the person behind the posh voice sliding up beside me.

"Eve, my old darling aunt, how are you this fine evening?"

She snorted and bumped shoulders with me. "I'm well preserved, not old."

"There's a difference? I had no idea."

Laughing, Eve opened a silver cigarette case and slid one between her plump lips. I tugged a Zippo lighter out of my pocket and lit it for her. Her mischievous eyes glittered as she dragged pleasurably and blew a stream of smoke into the fresh night air. "I'm also a little spice and no sugar."

I snorted derisively. "Tell me something I didn't know."

"Having spice in one's life never hurt anyone, Ari." She sipped on her bourbon. "You know what they say?"

"I'm sure you shall take immense pleasure in enlightening me, my darling, Eve," I riposted, smiling warmly.

"All work and no fun can make you a dull and lonely boy."

I smirked. "And your point is?"

With her white long-sleeved dress fitting her willowy body like a glove, Eve was dressed to kill. She twisted and leaned against the bar, exposing the backless cut-out along with her shapely back. Just as leisurely, she spun back, conspicuously dropping her twinkling gaze to the crotch of my black dress pants. "Go and sort out that pole inside your pants before you poke everyone's eyes out, will you?"

Raising a brow at my loquacious aunt, I lifted the drink to my lips, taking another tentative sip. "Isn't going blind a prerequisite of growing old also? I guess I thought wrong."

Her mouth quirked as she picked at the nibble tray on the bar, deftly shelling the pistachios before popping them one at a time into her mouth and slowly chewing. "You do realise you and Teddy have it awfully bad for one another."

"Getting slow is another prerequisite too, you know." My smart mouth earned me a firm punch to the bicep. "Ow!"

She laughed heartily. "Pussy."

I set my glass on the bar and slumped in defeat. With any other woman, I exuded confidence, yet when it came to a gorgeous young woman I'd known my entire life, I fumbled like a pre-pubescent teen.

Eve knew it too, and wasn't about to let me live it down. "Yeah, I've been watching the two of you all night. It's better than any movie I've ever watched. Any hotter -" She smiled devilishly, fanning her face. "- we'd all be on fire."

"Well, it hasn't exactly gone to plan tonight for either of us, Eve. Believe you me; we both tried but..." I trailed off upon noticing my doe-eyed cousin, Gabriel fawning over her. My chin jerked in their direction. "Although, I noticed just now, your son appears rather enamoured. I might have some fierce competition."

Her lips twisted wryly, viewing them quickly. "She's a beautiful woman, no? What's not to love," she stated, stubbing out her half-smoked cigarette in the ashtray on the bar. "Besides, Gabriel doesn't like Teddy the way you do, and with the way he's been acting of late, I'd say there's someone in the picture – and it's not a woman. Trust me, I know."

"Mothers intuition?"

"If that's what you call it," she countered, making me laugh.

Everyone in the family and our social circles knew it was no secret about Gabriel's sexuality and his preference for either sex. The apple hadn't fallen too far from the tree in that regard, and as I scanned the marquee, one could only speculate amongst the guests, who he'd shared his bed with.

Regardless of his upper-class upbringing, dressed in a black tuxedo, he looked uncomfortable and oddly out of place. The dirty blonde dreadlocks certainly didn't serve him any favours either. Nevertheless, with a charisma identical to his mother's and kind, chestnut brown eyes, most overlooked his unkempt appearance.

"So, go grab her. Put both yourselves and us -" Eve's slender hand regally circled the marquee, "out of our misery."

"As much as I would love to, I'm more of a gentleman than you are," I murmured winking.

"That's debatable," she quipped.

My beaming smile faded as I stared longingly at Teddy from afar. "No, I'll visit with Teddy tomorrow, when we're both sober."

"Be sure to let me know if you're successful or fall flat on your face!" she gleefully shouted over one slender shoulder, walking off.

"I've deleted your number!" I retorted, laughing when she flipped me the bird. All class that woman.

Having met my father's shiniest new toy, and failed dismally with Teddy, I just wanted to head home where I could wallow in self-pity with dignity. I tossed back the rest of my drink and lamented as I peered over at Teddy one more time. Tomorrow.

I eventually tracked down my parents inside the house, playing doubles at the twelve-foot billiards table in the rumpus room with my Uncle Garrett and his wife, Michaela. His usual cigar clenched between his lips, dad stretched over the green baize and took his shot. A loud exclamation escaped his tightened lips as he missed the pocket.

I patted his back and shook his hand, chuckling. "Bad luck, old chap." I glanced across the table. "Uncle G's kicking your arse. Still, I see?"

"The table mustn't be level."

I grinned as Garrett poked back. "No, brother, it's just your aim that's crooked." Then the usual slinging started.

"I'm leaving before you two involve me in your little games." Kissing Michaela on the cheek, I wished her good luck.

Her nose scrunched playfully. "It's gonna be a long night I feel."

Mother's customary goodbye took longer thanks to her inquisition.

"Lovely party, but I have a busy day ahead of me tomorrow." Hopefully between Teddy's legs.

"A new acquisition?" she teased, lovingly rubbing my arm. She knew me well.

I smiled affectionately. "Something like that."

"I trust you had an enjoyable evening?"

"Of course, I always do at your soirees."

"Be sure to join us for dinner one night this week, darling, hopefully with a date?" A glimmer of optimism twinkled in my mother's glassy eyes.

"Yes, Mother. Keep your fingers crossed on that one."

Down in the mouth and with my hands in my pockets, I strolled out the front door to my Imperial blue M6 Gran Coupe BMW already parked and waiting for me in the curved driveway. One of the two surly attendants my parents had hired for the evening held the door open for me. I thanked him and slid onto the supple leather of the black sports seat, turning the key. The V8's throaty engine sprang to life, a sound that would never grow old, raising a smile. Something had to. Intentionally revving the accelerator, I sped out of the driveway, the tyres spinning in my haste to go home. The black skid marks left behind I guaranteed shan't be received well. Nor will mother's earbashing over her ruined driveway.

Apart from the few cars I passed, the drive home was quiet. The lit streets were practically empty, leaving me alone on the road and alone with my thoughts, mostly about Teddy, and that hot, wet, heated kiss. The night I presumed was a teaser, a prelude for the future.

I pulled into the garage of my seaside Beaumaris home just after eleven and wandered inside, heading straight upstairs and into my ensuite bathroom where I dove under a shower. The warm water cascaded over me, barely easing the tension in my tightened sac.

Gripping my cock, I leaned my back against the shower wall and began softly stroking as evocative images of Teddy's sensuously naked body appeared. Her narrow hips squirming as my tongue fluttered over the sensitive bud between endlessly long legs as I drew out her orgasm. Suggestive imagery that only made my cock harder. I began fisting savagely, my release coming hard and fast as it spurted in long streams, over my hand and onto my belly. I moaned, sagging against the charcoal tiled wall. The relief couldn't have come fast enough.

Reaching for the body wash from the inset shelf, I poured the scented liquid over my loofah and began scrubbing. My mind stuck on Teddy, I inwardly questioned the lack of explanation behind her pulling away from me. Something had stopped her. The distress in her voice and the agony in her eyes told me that the same girl I'd loved since we were children was no longer there.

Was I simply chasing a fantasy?

The Jaeger's and the McGovern's, two families introduced by chance just after we'd left the freezing shores of England for the warmer climate of Australia. I was a mere four-year-old more fascinated by the tiny infant girl with strawberry curls in the pram, rather than the fancy parties that our parents frequently threw. My mother claimed Teddy had me love struck from that moment on; she was spot on, she had.

As we grew, so did the fascination. Whether it was building sandcastles in the sandpit, or swinging on the swings in each other's backyards, we were inseparable. Or as my mother would say, not even surgery could've severed us.

Over the years, the dynamic changed. More so as we hit our pubescent years.

Teddy had blossomed right before my eyes, transforming from an awkward teenager into a ravishing beauty. And as an adolescent boy, I became a walking hard-on whenever she was around.

Conversely, the turning point for us was Teddy's lavish twenty-first birthday party. The minute I laid eyes on the stunning beauty politely greeting her guests, my entire world shifted. She was striking, and from then on, the allure I felt towards her grew.

As Teddy slipped a slender hand inside mine, her soft creamy skin deepened, much like the roses in my mother's garden by the illustrious touch. Glossy pink, plush lips shamelessly parted as her tongue glided smoothly along a full bottom lip. An erotic sight that headed south, hitting my nether regions with quite the pleasurable thud.

That pleasure swiftly turned painful as soon as Teddy's overbearing mother Therese waltzed over and rudely stepped between us. She openly proceeded to scold her daughter, sternly warning her that our interaction was lewd and unacceptable. Displaying such actions in front of their guests was utterly distasteful apparently, forcing us to part ways.

The entire night I had stared wistfully, hoping for a glance, or a mere suggestion, anything, just to put me out of my misery. I had expected to kiss Teddy's full, pink lips, if merely for a taste. Sift my fingers through the thick wavy copper locks flowing down her elegantly curving spine. A naked back I was lucky enough to catch a glimpse of as her hair swayed or as she tucked it over a shoulder, curling the ends over her delectable breasts.

It drove me wild the entire night knowing I couldn't touch her.

Now I had another erection. Just fabulous.

Gruffly flicking the tap, I shut the water down and stepped out, grasping one of the towels off the heated rail beside me. I barely dried myself as I sauntered into the bedroom, tapping the lights off on my way past. I fell into bed, hoping the next day would lead to a promising future with the one woman who had forever haunted my dreams.

5

Teddy

THE ATROCIOUS ACHE IN MY head matched my guilt. I'd call that karma; one for drinking too much, and two, for rejecting the man I loved. Again. And why I asked myself? Because I was an idiot, that's why.

Downing a few more glasses of champagne, I had floundered around the yard looking for Ari only to be left dismayed as a slurring Audrina informed me that her beloved son had departed much earlier. Not without painfully adding, despondently, too.

Now, as I threw myself into a shower and leaned my back against the cold herringbone marble tiles on the wall, the karma continued in the way of torturous thoughts.

Light droplets of tepid water glided, reminding me of Ari's grazing fingers over my bare skin. Our lips as they brushed, his so soft and so tender. That darkened gaze had seen me like no other, searing so deep, it burned within the depths of my darkened soul.

Then there was his body. A firm muscular body with a prominent bulge that kept pressing against my thigh, an image so delicious, it filled me with a desperate want, and need, for an orgasm.

I imagined Ari's long fingers slithering between my silken folds, caressing the soft flesh. I palmed both breasts, rolling my stiffened peaks between my fingers....

A loud bang on the bathroom door abruptly ripped me from my sensual daydream.

"Theodora! Are you drowning in there?" Bloody sisters, they're such a pain in the arse!

Frustrated, I yelled, "Yes, I am! And don't call me that!" If there was one thing I despised in this life, it was the use of my full name. "I'm trying to drown away last night's embarrassing behaviours."

"Well quit feeling sorry for yourself and join us outside for brekky. Make sure you put on a bikini, too; we're swimming our hangovers away in the pool. It's a beautiful day outside!" she singsonged.

"Okay, I'm coming!" I winced. Shouting did not help when one's head was pounding. Now, I was starting to sound just like Ari, so damned English.

To appease my nagging sister, I hurried in and out of the bathroom, slipping on my favourite blue halter neck bikini and covering myself with a white knitted cover-up. I might have lost my dignity at Audrina's party, but I wasn't about to lose it at the table. Having slid my feet into a pair of Havaianas, I ran a brush through my hair, leaving it to hang loose in soft waves around my shoulders before hastily walking through the house.

I had barely reached the French doors off the family room when Scarlett piped up, "About time, you joined the living."

I swore my sister lived to torment me, a ritual that started the second she woke each day. Although, Scarlett was right to nag me, the day was beautiful.

For this early in the spring, temperatures were unseasonably warmer. But if it meant wearing less than the thick coats required for Melbourne's bitterly cold winters, I couldn't imagine any one of us complaining. That glare though, damn it was blinding. I slipped my sunglasses over my eyes before joining the girls' on the alfresco patio where Adele's soulful voice faintly serenaded us in the background. I winced. It was far too early, even for music.

"I feel far from alive, let me tell you!" I moaned, plonking down into one of the softly padded chairs surrounding the eight-seater timber table and tucking a leg beneath me.

Scarlett's eyes rolled as her attention diverted back to Dominique. I shook my head in disgust. I despised gossip, something the pair of them conversed in far too often.

Leaning forward, I grabbed one of the fresh blueberry Danishes from the platter in the centre of the table and zoned out, preferring to fantasise about a future with Ari instead. That's all it would ever amount to anyway. Fate had kept us apart for a reason. With my present lifestyle as well as an unsavoury past, to include Ari in that equation would be disastrous. A toxic mix.

Where he longed for white picket fences, I yearned for something else entirely. I blamed my upbringing.

My childhood wasn't the dream most children wished for thanks to the complicated relationship with our parents, our mother more than our father for the most part. That altered too, when everything in my world horrifically changed.

Our grandparents, on the contrary, were an entirely different story. They adored their grandchildren and often expressed their affections, more so when something was worth celebrating. Hence the double-fronted early Victorian cottage, an overly generous graduation gift from both sets. Most presumed it was because I'd graduated University, with honours. Alas, no, it was only high school. Admittedly, I had received the DUX award, giving them another reason to be incredibly proud.

Nonetheless, I'd always thought small gifts were a given, such as a necklace, or even a fancy pen; I assumed wrong — big time. So, not only was I presented with the house, but my grandparents ensured they spared no expense renovating it, front to back, to my style, of course.

So besides not experiencing life living at RMIT alongside other students, the time spent on campus, I enjoyed anyway.

Studying Architecture and Design, as well as Interior Design, I had surpassed all expectations, surprising even myself. The high recommendations from each of my professors and the Dean, were the icing on the cake, and thus, landing the job at Bricks and Mortar.

Then, there was Ari. I loved him, always had. My sixteenth birthday was the day I had planned on asking Ari to wait for me until I turned eighteen. It was a day that never came, nor was it celebrated. Instead, I locked my feelings away, building impenetrable walls around me, making it impossible for anyone to breach beyond them.

After ten long years, I finally possessed the courage to take a precarious leap of faith – and like the coward, I was, and still am, I stumbled. I ran away, leaving the one man I'd yearned for confused. Desolate. A decision that left me wracked with feelings of guilt and regret — the thought of not repairing that damage soured an already dampened mood. I'd call him later.

"Teddy, wake up!"

My head jerked towards a curiously frowning Poppy. "What?"

"What, or should I say whom, were you daydreaming about?"

"Nothing in particular," I replied shrugging dismissively.

Poppy smirked as I reached over the table, grabbing another Danish. Lucky, I loved her.

When an attractive male visitor stepped outside, his hand awkwardly rubbing the back of his freshly washed hair, my hand paused mid-air as my jaw dropped in shock. Oh, it was the jock. What's worse, he'd stayed here with Dominique. Oh. Oh, her domineering brother would not be pleased one little bit.

A shy smile formed blinding us with glaringly white teeth. "Um, hi."

He clumsily took the seat beside a beaming Dominique at the table, his gaze nervously darting between our gaping mouths and us.

"Whoops! Sorry girls', did I fail to mention I had company? Girls', this is Damien. Damien, girls'," she announced, casually flipping her hand around the table at each of us. A bit late for introductions, I thought. "Close your mouths, you all look like codfish."

The front doorbell began ringing incessantly. I ignored it in the hope someone else would think to answer the door. Not gonna happen by the looks of it.

I tried yelling out. "Can one of you get that, please? I'm kinda busy here!" Not one reply, typical. I sighed and ducked my head, glancing outside. The probability of anyone amongst that rowdy lot hearing anything over that blaring music was nil anyway.

I had barely tipped the last of the ice cubes into the jug of homemade iced tea when the bell shrilled once more.

"All right, I'm coming!" Yelling, I barely had enough time to shove the jug into the fridge before it rang again. "I hear you, as can the neighbours down the street!" I marched towards the front door, my footsteps thudding on the floorboards beneath my feet. I reefed it open, huffing, "Impatient mu...ch." Oh, it was Ari. On the porch. My porch. Like a deer caught in headlights, I stilled, my voice gone. It had probably disappeared out the door and taken off up the footpath along with my manners.

His mouth twitched at the state of my obvious fluster. "Hi there."

My brows creased at the black sports bag slung over his right shoulder. Had he planned to move in already? Perhaps he was using it as a ploy, so I'd give in to him. Don't be paranoid, Teddy.

I cleared my throat and found my voice. "Ari, what...what are you doing here?"

Pushing his tinted sunglasses off, he slid them through his unruly hair to the top of his head, allowing his darkly hooded eyes to roam unashamedly.

My body naturally responded as my nipples hardened beneath the scorching gaze. If we kept this up, we'd never move past the porch. Wouldn't that give the neighbours something to talk about over their afternoon tea? The thought made me smile.

I intentionally cleared my throat, raising his ogling gaze off my chest. "Ari, why are you here?"

"I um...came to see you." He was just as nervous as I was, that much was obvious. "To chat about us and what happened.... or didn't last night." Of course he was, you idiot.

My face flamed; this dancing around each other had to stop. "Well, you had better come in then." Smiling softly, I opened the door wider and stepped back, waving my hand at him. "After you then."

A charming, crooked smile formed. "Thank you."

"We can go to my bedroom; at least we won't be interrupted in there."

His eyebrows shot up in question as he stepped over the threshold into the foyer. "Does it have a lock on the door?"

I gently closed the front door behind us, eliciting a small laugh. "Actually, yes, it does. So, there's no chance of your sister barging in on us this time."

"Well, after you." He politely gestured, following me into the bedroom.

I stood back, watching his soft gaze quietly soaking in every detail as he set his back down on the floor nearest to the bed. Stylishly decorated in various shades of blues and whites, my room had remained soft, yet feminine. It was my sanctuary.

"Why do women love pillows?" he muttered, shaking his head at the piles neatly stacked against the diamond-tufted headboard.
I giggled. I loved my pillows. If he didn't, then too bad.

He drew his gaze upwards to the room's centrepiece, an antique crystal chandelier hanging from the centre of a replicated decorative ceiling rose. From the architrave to the wide skirting skimming darkly stained Baltic timber floors, and where possible, almost every feature in the bedroom was entirely original, painstakingly, and lovingly restored, including the fireplace facing adjacent to my king-sized bed.

Ari's eyes lit up like the bright lights on a Christmas tree. "There's something to be said about a warm fire on a crisp, winter's night, wouldn't you say?" His wandering gaze openly ravished me. I swallowed tightly.

"Um...yes, I suppose there is." I had to shut his advances down, quickly, before he advanced any further.

"Sit, please." I indicated to one of the two striped wingback chairs beside the bay window. He promptly sat. "I want to start by apologising for taking off without explanation last night," I began, perching on the edge of the bed and crossing my legs, "I have secrets, and, well...they're quite dark."

"We all have secrets we don't like to share." Convincing him to back away was going to be harder than I initially thought.

I shook my head vehemently. "I can't imagine you having anything deep or dark for that matter. If I do choose to divulge, you may change your mind about me – and about us."

"Don't worry; there may be certain aspects you might not like about me. Isn't that what relationships are all about?"

"I suppose so." I closed my eyes and sighed. Dammit. Opening them again, I peered up at him. "To honestly answer your question from last night – yes, I do like you...and have for some time now. But..." Before I had the chance to finish explaining, Ari's lips were on mine.

A hand rested on my shoulder, pushing me back onto the mattress. His kiss was seductive and skilful, and the more he kissed me, the more I grew lost in the moment. More so as his hands roamed every inch of me, caressing my shoulders, my breasts, my midriff, along my thighs, and back up again.

Despite myself, I weakened, giving in to a lifelong yearning. Passion and desire soared, burning through my core with each passing minute.

My body had betrayed me.

Breathless, Ari's heated kisses slowed. He pulled back, looking down at me with a tender gaze. "You have no idea how long I've waited to hear those words from you, and about last night, let's not talk about regrets. Let's live in the now, as if these wasted years never occurred."

Embracing his touch, I leaned into the hand cupping my cheek and slid my fingers through his hair, massaging his scalp with the tips as I tugged him closer reconnecting our mouths in a hard, deepened kiss.

Agile fingers tore at my bikini top. "So, beautiful," he murmured, curving his palm around my breast, and rolling a pebbled nipple between his fingertips. His head dipped, clamping onto the other breast, his lips suckling gently to elongate the nipple. Delightful shivers coursed through my body, making me crave so much more.

As if he read my mind, Ari stealthily untied my bottoms and probed the delicate flesh between my thighs. I moaned, gasping as one long digit slide inside of me.

"Shouldn't...we take...this slower?" I whimpered as he began palming my clit.

"What?" His head jolted upwards, his confused gaze staring incredulously. "You ask me that now? When we're practically naked?"

I cocked my head. "You aren't."

"Fair point," he murmured, glancing down at his clothes before swiftly pushing off me and standing at my feet.

I avidly observed as he tugged his T-shirt over his head and threw it to the floor. His chino shorts and boxer briefs instantly followed, my teeth sinking into my bottom lip as his ravishing cock sprang free. Damn. That's impressive.

Ari inched closer to the bed and spread my legs wide, crawling between them. His rigid length bobbing against my aching cleft as he grasped my head and flipped us over.

I sat back and straddled his thighs, rhythmically skating my fingers along his silky shaft. "What about contraception?"

"You ask me that now? When we're about to have sex?"

I huffed in exasperation. "I'm on the pill and have been for a long time."

"Touché."

My eyes narrowed as my stroking paused. "You did that on purpose."

He grinned wolfishly and reared up, his hands sweeping restlessly up and down my back. "I did."

"Arse. Now fuck me."

He chuckled. "Your wish is my command." Likewise, his touch and the zeal in his kisses reflected my desperation. It seemed he also wanted to enjoy the moment and was taking his sweet arse time.

As he skimmed his lips along my jawline and down my neck, my frustration grew. "Ari, please, delayed gratification isn't my style!"

His chest rumbled with laughter. "I noticed."

Loud groans echoed as he suddenly lifted me, impaling me over his hardened length, stretching and filling me.

Ari felt just as I imagined he would, unbelievably amazing. He grunted loudly as my inner muscles contracted around his shaft, squeezing tightly, more so as I attempted to undulate my hips.

"Don't move, just feel," he murmured quietly, clinching me at the waist.

"Ari..." I mewled in protest.

"I know." He flipped us back over, his heated gaze maintaining eye contact as his bulky weight hovered above me. And as he pushed off his elbows, pleasurable moans escaped harmoniously.

The gratification was indescribable. My fingers lightly skimmed up and over Ari's body matching the slow drawn-out rhythm. The sinuous feel of the veins bulging in powerful forearms as he thrust forward, past his flexing biceps and over strong shoulders to trail along the soft curve of his spine. I paused at his perfectly rounded rear and splayed my hands, relishing in the feel of the muscles contracting beneath each cheek with each slickened movement.

Somewhere in my clouded mind, it felt like he wasn't close enough and began rocking my hips, my legs lifting to suck him in deeper.

Ari grunted and sped up, sweat beading the broad width of his back while each hard lunge stroked my inner wall, bringing me closer to the precipice.

My back bowed off the mattress, a garbled cry escaping from my gaping mouth as an intense climax suddenly rippled. Regardless of the slowing thrusts, the continual caress of Ari's cock inside me triggered shuddering aftershocks. Suddenly, his thrusts hardened before he stilled, his neck corded from the strain as he spilled his warm seed inside of me. Collapsing breathlessly into the valley between my breasts, he nuzzled my flushed skin with his nose. "Wow, that was...unexpected."

Raking my fingers through his dampened hair, I peered down at him. "Why was it?"

Ari leaned up on his elbows, his provocative gaze staring as he pushed a dampened strand of hair off my face. "I came here to talk, and somehow we ended up here."

"Are you complaining?"

His sculpted mouth curved wickedly. "No, not in the slightest. We needed to deal with years of pent-up feelings, therefore explaining my inability to last longer."

An inappropriate giggle erupted, and Ari cocked his head eyeing me quizzically. "What's so funny?"

"You pretty much confirmed what the girls' had said all along."

"Enlighten me, please."

"Somewhere in their warped minds, they all decided whenever we're around each other, this supposed sexual tension between us is capable of blowing a roof off its rafters."

Ari let out a small laugh. "Really? According to Eve, if we were any hotter, everyone would be on fire."

I chuckled. "Well, now we can happily inform everyone there's no need to go calling the fire brigade, or a builder."

"About bloody time, too." He chuckled rolling off me and onto his back, his forearm coming to rest across his eyes. "We really ought to leave this room before someone comes looking for us." Running a hand over his damp face, Ari blew out a disgruntled sigh. "Namely my sister."

Considering us sleeping together hadn't been part of my plan, I sadly agreed, "And mine. It seems our sisters' have an uncanny knack for bad timing. I'm amazed they aren't banging the door down right now." Rolling into his side, I drew circles through the smattering of dark hair across his chest.

"Give it time," he groaned, stretching out his limbs along the length of the bed.

I furtively peered up at him. "Maybe we should make the most of the time alone? Persuading you to stay in bed for the rest of the day shouldn't be too hard, should it?"

"Generally, no..." he remarked candidly, darting a dark gaze down at me before sitting up and swinging his feet to the floor. "But we need to make an appearance before they do." He twisted at the waist and skated a hand along the top of my thigh. "Come on."

"Gimme a minute."

As Ari moved about the room, my intrepid gaze followed. Well defined muscles in his arms and back rippled, flexing beneath flawless skin with each fluid motion. He bent down to scoop up his discarded clothes off the floor, and my head tilted, highly appreciating the lovely sight of his rounded rear.

Slipping his shorts over his feet, he tugged them the rest of the way up wearing a knowing smile. "What's the matter? Is my hair a mess?"

"You have seriously bad bed hair," I teased, my amused gaze watching him as he approached the mirror and adjusted the thick strands, so they were just so. And here I thought I was terrible. "Better?" he asked, swinging back to me.

"Much. Now come here." I crawled to the foot of the bed and rose to my knees in full view of Ari's searing gaze. Although slickened with his seed between my thighs, I couldn't help but want him again. "Make love to me again."

A long finger stroked my cheek as curious eyes studied me. "Demanding little thing, aren't you?"

"Always," I whispered, grabbing the edge of his shorts to haul him back to the bed. That time, my mouth and tongue commanding him.

6

Ari

FRESHLY SHOWERED, AND SATISFIED, Teddy and I eventually decided we needed to move past the bedroom and join everyone outside before someone came breaking the door down. Thankfully, no one hadn't.

My steps slowly faltered in the doorway as I saw the reason why. My sister was otherwise preoccupied – with bloody Damien, my father's new junior associate of all people. Won't our father be pleased once he's discovered their little dalliance?

The sudden stop caused Teddy to run directly into my back. Noticing my deathly glare, she circled me to my front, her chin jerking towards the unsightly view. "Leave it," she firmly whispered, hastily turning her irate gaze back on me.

"Yeah right, like that's going to happen," I scoffed, stepping onto the patio to the sound of jeering wolf whistles and loud clapping, distracting us away from our little disagreement.

I slung an arm around Teddy's shoulders, chuckling as she buried her crimson face in my shoulder. "Okay, settle down you bunch of degenerates. We're aware you're all as equally delighted as I am, but please, my poor girl's blushing like a tomato." The poking comment earned me a smack to the chest. Feisty. I had better watch myself.

Snaking my other arm around her shoulders, I pulled her closer and pressed my lips to her temple as my narrowed gaze furtively observed the cosy couple over the top of her head. My jaw ticked tightly as the pet project whispered sickly-sweet nothings in her ear, leaving Dominique in a fit of riotous giggles.

"I'd need more wine for that," she murmured, biting down on her lip, and looking at him like …. Ugh, I now had a ghastly image seared into my brain. I needed a drink, something stiff preferably. Oh Christ, another gruesome image worse than the last one just gave me third-degree burns.

"I'll be right back," I heard her offer as she jumped off his lap, not before performing a lap dance much to the drooling idiots delight. My watchful gaze followed her as she sauntered into the kitchen, an opportunity that was well worth seizing.

"I'll be back shortly." Cupping Teddy's cheek with my palm, I gently pressed my mouth to hers. Ever so slightly, I pulled back. With a well-shaped eyebrow raised questioningly at me, I simpered, "Something requires my attention."

The shake of the head said it all; I was in the shit. Already.

Dominique's happiness was apparent as she strolled back inside the house. She hummed, retrieving another two bottles of Pinot Grigio from the bar fridge in the butler's pantry, twisting their lids off at the island bench.

"What do you want, Ari?"

Crossing my arms over my chest, I snorted; our mother certainly hadn't raised a fool. "Is dad aware his new protégée came home with you last night?" I enquired, glowering at her over the marble counter.

"No, he doesn't," Dominique haughtily informed. "And you aren't to go dibber dobbing either. Daddy doesn't need to know," she boldly added.

I scoffed. Attitude plus that one. Whatever happened to my sweet, innocent baby sister?

I scowled. "What were you thinking, Dom? Bringing him home to screw his brains out hasn't been one of your brightest ideas, has it?"

"I wasn't…thinking – and anyway, I like Damien!" Defiant, she shrugged. "Regardless, daddy shouldn't stop his staff from having a relationship with anyone, even if it is me."

Frustrated with the blasé attitude, I scrubbed at my forehead. "Stupidly, I find myself agreeing with you, but please, try to be pragmatic here; what if there's a lover's spat? Or, God forbid, this 'relationship' doesn't work?" One held out hope. I rounded the bench and inched closer. "The conflict would displease both our father and Uncle Garrett immensely, and you being his daughter is no exception; another reason as to why you shouldn't pursue this so-called relationship. I'm just simply throwing caution to the wind, little sister."

She held up a hand in front of my face. "Well, big brother, I'm not sure if you've noticed, but I'm no longer a child! I'm now an adult and have been for the last four years! So, you and that wind you blew in on can fucking butt out!" Seizing both bottles by their necks, she angrily spun away and stormed off outside.

I stiffly twisted at the waist and trailed after her, my head shaking in disgust as she perched on the pet project's knee and kissed him passionately.

"Stubborn. Like mother, like daughter." Exasperated, I ran my hands through my hair before reaching into the stainless-steel fridge behind me, grabbing a stubby of Carlton Dry. I twisted the top and threw the lid in anger. Icy cold beer was just the ticket.

Laying my forearms along the marble island, I continued sipping, observing Damien closely from afar. Watching as he pushed his sunglasses down his nose and followed Teddy with a wide-eyed gaze the moment she left her chair and walked towards the pool with my sister, whom he was presumably dating. My jaw tightened; right, time for that little chat with the pet project.

"So, Damien, is it? Ari Jaeger, Dominique's big brother." He eyed me suspiciously before cautiously shaking my hand. I almost burst out laughing. A punctured balloon had a sight more grip.

"I have a question for you, Damien." Self-assured, I took the seat beside him, and casually leaned back in the cane chair, resting an ankle on my knee. "What are your intentions with my sister? Are you only fucking her? Or do you intend to string her along under the pretence you want a relationship all the while lusting after my girlfriend?"

"That's three questions, and I don't believe it's any of your business, Ari," Damien retorted smugly, covering his eyes with his sunglasses. Wimp. "Dominique's a grown woman who can make her own decisions."

I glowered. "I didn't realise you could count, you impertinent little shit. Did you happen to include jackarse on your résumé when you applied to my father's firm?"

"Presume whatever you want, I don't have to answer to you and quite frankly, nor does your sister," he argued, rising from the chair and standing over me — attempted to anyway.

I looked up and laughed in his face. "You're right; you don't. But you forget one minor detail..."

He crossed his arms and smirked. "I'm sure you'll enlighten me."

"You answer to our father and uncle. Neither of them would be pleased to learn you'd screwed my sister over after you'd screwed her. Your new job at my father's firm might be very short-lived, especially if I have anything to say about it." I smirked triumphantly observing as the realisation dawned on the pet projects smug face. "Not so cocky now, are we?"

His puffed-out chest deflated. As I said, limp. "Look, we only just met, and we haven't exactly talked about having a relationship. I assumed it was only going to be a one-night thing."

My expression hardened. Rushing to my feet, I closed the gap between us, placing Damien's terrified face only millimetres from mine. "You either have good intentions, or you don't? Simple."

"I need to find out what Dominique wants first," he nervously spluttered, tugging the short sleeves of a plaid shirt over his arms. "She might not want a relationship, and truthfully, neither do I. As you obviously stated, I have only just started at the firm...and besides, she was the one who threw herself at me!"

Outraged by the suggestive insults directed at my sister, I swung a fist, the impact sending him toppling backwards. Like the bag of shit he was, he dropped, hitting the timber decking with a resounding thud. "Now get out, before I throw you out!"

Touching his swelling nose, he winced. Then he proceeded to wag one of his bony fingers up at me. "Don't even think about touching me again!" he uttered through clenched and bloodied teeth.

I snorted. "Or what, you'll sue me? Go your hardest." Glowering, I squatted; the pet project clearly required one of my stern warnings. I kept my voice intimidatingly low. "Are you incapable of saying no? You're a grown arse man who has choices, and if I ever catch you sniffing around my sister again, you'll be extremely sorry."

Having heard the commotion, Dominique hurried from the pool and gaped, boorishly sharing her mortification. "How dare you do this to Damien, Ari!" She squatted, giving him a towel for his profusely bleeding nose. "Stop trying to run my life! You're as bad as mum and dad! Actually, no rephrase that – you are worse than they are. And whom I see is my business, not yours!"

"Having a devil may care attitude won't help anyone, Dom. Especially you, taking up with the impertinent one."

My defiant sister shot me a deathly glare helping Damien up off the ground. "I'm not interested in your opinions, Ari!"

"Of course, you aren't," I mocked, unconcerned until I spun around spotting both Teddy and Poppy frozen to the spot. Their eyes wide after having witnessed the volatile argument unfold in front of them.

Poppy cleared her throat, excusing herself, "Um, I'm leaving you both to it. Good luck," she whispered sympathetically to Teddy before disappearing inside.

"Thanks, I'm going to need it," she uttered, grabbing the knitted cover-up from the back of the chair and slipping it over her head. Rigid arms folded over her chest, covering her soaked breasts from my wandering gaze. "Do I dare ask what that was about?"

"Damien made my sister sound easy," I grumbled sheepishly.

She scowled. "So, your way of dealing with Damien was to punch him?"

"He deserved it."

Her scowl deepened. "Nobody deserves getting punched in the nose, Ari." Teddy exhaled roughly. "In case you failed to notice recently, Dom's an adult now. Meaning she's quite capable, and old enough, to make her own decisions. She needs to learn to make mistakes and to grow as a person without you. You can't go controlling every aspect of her life, Ari; that caveman behaviour," she purred, waving a hand in the air, "only pushes her away."

A ghost of a smile twitched at my lips. Yep, Teddy had my number. "...Caveman behaviour?"

She bit down on her bottom lip as a feeble attempt to curtail her laughter. "Out of that entire conversation, that's all you heard?"

"I'm a caveman, am I?" Tickled, I shook my head and chuckled. "Wow, never have I ever been called that before."

Hazel eyes alight with amusement, begged me to challenge her as I rubbed my chin. Well, challenge accepted.

I swiftly disposed of gentleman Ari and ran at her, throwing her over my shoulder as I made a beeline for the pool. A crudely loud Teddy objected, slapping my back as I jumped in, sinking her screams below the water's surface.

In a spluttering rush, Teddy resurfaced, angrily shoving her gloriously sodden copper tresses off her face. Her eyes narrowed as I rose calmly beside her. "That was mean! Nor was it funny!"

"You needed cooling off." I shot her a mock glare and yanked at her arms, violently crashing our mouths together. She melded against me, pushing her soaked breasts against my chest.

Between soft, chaste kisses, Teddy mischievously glanced up. "Nice distraction there, Mr Jaeger." Sharp fingernails scraped over my soaked abs. "Hmm, what do we have here?" Untying the string to my shorts, her hand slowly shovelled its way inside, springing my flaccid cock back to life with each teasing stroke of her fingers. In turn, she smirked proudly.

I inhaled sharply, surrendering to the audacious touch. My arm snaked around Teddy's narrow waist. "That was impudent. Now, what am I to do with this?"

"I don't know. But I'm sure Mrs Palmer and her five daughters' would happily oblige you," she simpered, curling her arms and legs around me. Bloody monkey.

Haughty laughter escaped me. "That would be your Mrs Palmer and her five daughters', not mine," I murmured, bending my head to capture her mouth. My tongue leisurely dipped inside, licking, and tasting as we moved towards the pools edge. I slid my splayed hands inside her bikini bottoms and tantalisingly caressed both cheeks.

Teddy's mouth curved wickedly against mine. "I'll see what I can arrange..." She gasped as the pad of my finger grazed the puckered rosebud between her buttocks. "Let's take this inside." She climbed off me and hauled her lithe figure over the coping where she remained towering over me at the water's edge. I intrepidly observed the removal of the drenched cover-up and the dropping of it to the ground from an outstretched hand before reaching around to undo the straps of her bikini top. It too, was tossed away.

My tongue swept across my lips as her nipples puckered against the light afternoon breeze. Perfect little mounds.

Teddy's crooked fingers grasped the side ties of the bottoms and tugged, allowing them to promptly peel off her wet behind and drop at her feet. Her naked body was now indecently and unashamedly on show, making my cock harder than the stone wall behind me. I'd come harder than the waterfall rushing from the stainless-steel spouts too if I wasn't inside her soon.

An impassive Teddy clutched one of the large beach towels slung over the back of a lounge chair. "Surely you realised I wasn't going inside all wet now, did you?" she purred, wrapping it around her slender frame. The little minx strutted towards the house only to pause in the doorway.

What was she up to now? Curious, I took a few tentative steps, bringing my hands to rest on the coping. My heated gaze piqued as she glanced over her shoulder and cheekily winked, before venturing inside – without the bloody towel!

I had to stop my jaw from hitting the bottom of the pool. Clambering from the water, I pushed my wet shorts down my legs in double time. "Right, if this is how the cheeky wench wants to play, then so be it."

Determination had me taking Teddy against the wall the instant I reached the shower. Splayed fingers wrapped around her throat from behind, brushing the edge of her jaw with the tips.

She moaned. "About time you joined me. I was beginning to think you weren't coming."

"Oh, I have every intention of coming...inside of your tight little pussy," I taunted, softly grinding my painfully hard cock between the crease of her delectable behind. "You want me, you got me. Now, it's my turn to tease you."

"You. Are. One voracious woman." I buried my head in the crook of her neck, my heaving chest rising and falling as I attempted to catch my breath.

Teddy unwrapped her long legs from around me and leaned her delectable body against my rasping chest. "With you I am," she pleasurably hummed, running her hands over my biceps and up my shoulders. "You are so...sexy and charismatic."

"You know how to stroke my ego – in more ways than one." That sounded smug, I know, but she did more than that. Much more. And I wanted more, my mouth finding hers once again.

7

Teddy

ARI HAD SPENT THE LAST few minutes meticulously ensuring every section of his well-defined body was dry. I was far too busy leaning in the doorway of my wardrobe, admiring him instead of dressing. I had gotten as far as my lilac silk dressing gown, which was a start, I suppose. Then my unabashed gaze zeroed in on the delightful package swinging between his taut thighs, stirring a familiar ache between my own. Oh, so worth it.

Throwing the towel over one broad shoulder, he glanced up and smiled perceptively. "Enjoying the show, are we?"

My mouth curved. "Vastly."

A jet-black brow raised intuitively. "Are you torturing yourself?"

"Maybe..." I sidled up to the bed as he sprayed deodorant under his arms, followed by his cologne around the base of his neck, soaking my bedding with the inebriating fragrance.

Ari made a point of swiftly throwing on a pair of boxer briefs as he looked askance and tutted, "Stop it."

I smiled eloquently in return. "I have to say, you brought quite the collection of clothes with you," I noted, jerking my chin at the countless choices laid out across the bed. His clothes were expensive, but his taste, impeccable. "...Unless you had plans of secretly moving in with me already?"

Ari briefly glanced up and scowled. "You ought to talk. It has me baffled how the weight of those oversized suitcases you call handbags don't send you stumbling all over the footpath." I got the feeling he was deflecting.

"It's arduous being a woman. Preparation is the key you know, 'cause the moment you drop the ball...anything could happen," I taunted. "Knocking out a potential mugger is another advantage."

He snorted irreverently. "Or bloody well kill them with it."

I giggled. "Wouldn't that make for an amusing front page; death by handbag." My stomach suddenly rumbled, loud enough for Ari to hear. I blushed. "Sounds like I've worked up quite the appetite."

His mouth quirked as dark eyes twinkled at me. "Well, what do you want for dinner?"

"Not sure. You decide."

"Well, what about we go out then? It's a lovely evening," he suggested shrugging on yet another shirt. "Perhaps ask the girls' what they're doing for dinner..." Hesitant, he paused.

"But?"

"My earlier misdeed left Dominique rather upset with me." A frown marred his handsome face. "She hates me, and honestly, I can't blame her. She's rather adept at knife throwing too, you know?" A peculiar comment that had my brows furrowing.

I slipped my arms around his waist and reassured him, "Dying would be such an imposition..." I mock sighed, raising a chuckle. "So, how about, rather than risk your sister's wrath, I go speak with her?"

Ari smiled weakly. "Okay."

"If I don't return – run like hell," I joked, slipping from his embrace and swanning across the floorboards. His bright smile abruptly faded. "Lighten up; I was only joking."

I left the room and made my way towards the stairs, pausing at the bottom; I must be a glutton for punishment.

Knocking softly, I tentatively pushed the door ajar to Dominique's room and poked my head around the corner. "Is it safe for me to enter?" My presence was met with a heavy sigh.

"If you must…"

Upon entering the room, I noticed my sister was presently hiding with Dom, saving me a trip to her bedroom. The pitiful sight of two grown women sulking like children had my eyes inevitably rolling. Except neither Dom nor Scarlett were children, nor was anyone punishing them. Mind you, with the way they were behaving, a good spanking wouldn't hurt either of them.

I perched at the foot of the bed, crossing my arms and legs, my pensive gaze eyeing both women. Neither had bothered to look up from their iPads either. How bloody rude.

"I see you and my brother have been rather busy!" Dominique snapped frostily.

Taken aback by the frosty reception, my mouth tightened. "Not that it's any of your business, but yes, we have." She glowered at me. Lucky Ari hadn't come upstairs then. "Anyway, I'm not here to discuss my private life; I came to see if you would like to join us for dinner?"

"Us, as in you and Ari? No thanks," she uttered irritably. "Besides, the thought of hanging around my interfering brother causes one to lose one's appetite."

Disheartened by her attitude, I sighed. "Are you sure you can't forgive Ari? He was only looking out for you, not that I agree with how he handled it." Which was the truth, but I reasoned anyway, "I know he feels terrible about the entire episode."

Dom shrugged her shoulders indifferently. "Good, he should."

Not wanting to cause any further angst, I relented and pushed to my feet. "Fair enough… I guess I'll see you both later then."

Aggravated, I breezed from the bedroom and made my way down the hall into Poppy's only to receive the same response, without the tantrum or the anger.

"I have a ton of marking that requires completion by tomorrow morning, sorry, Ted. Go out, have an enjoyable time. I'd only be a third wheel, a position no one wants to be in, not with you pair anyway." She winked.

I laughed. "True. Don't wait up."

"Wasn't planning on it!"

Ari sliding an entirely new pair of jeans up his legs and over his boxer briefs as I re-entered the bedroom had my irritation sweeping away in an instant. The tapered cut of the faded denim hugged his rounded rear perfectly. The next item lifted from the bed was a white long-sleeved T-shirt, which he studiously pulled over his head, avoiding his artfully styled hair. The tight T-shirt fitted just like a second skin, showcasing every inch of a well-defined body underneath — what a mouth-watering sight.

"Weren't you dressed before?" I asked, snapping out of my lust filled reverie.

"And weren't you supposed to be getting dressed?" he countered dryly.

He let out a small laugh when I smiled coquettishly and shrugged at him, setting my hands on my hips. My gaze cut back to the clothes spread over my bed. "I've concluded you're a fashionista."

"And how, dare I ask, did you arrive at such a conclusion?" Taking a seat in one of the wingbacked chairs, Ari tugged a pair of russet brown leather boots over his feet and tied the laces. Deep brown eyes surrounded by jet-black lashes glinted up at me.

I bent at the waist and picked up his expensively Swiss-made watch, admiring the textured dial and intricately engraved pattern on the face. "Well, for starters, you've seriously put a lot of thought into what you packed and not only that, you've changed at least three times in the last half an hour. I must say, it's nice to see a man who follows the latest styles and has great dress sense."

Ari shook his head and rose from the chair, his long strides swiftly closing the gap between us. My body tingled breathing in his masculine scent. "Are you getting dressed?" he queried once again. "That is unless you're planning on going out for dinner in nothing more than your dressing gown? What a delicious thought." Deft fingers loosened the sash and parted the soft silk, each nipple stiffening under his scorching gaze.

The moment he cupped each breast and rolled their peaks, I was putty in his hands. "Feasting on me now sounds like a much better offer." Heat radiated between my thighs. "Don't you agree?"

Catching one of my lobes between his teeth and nibbling, he breathed huskily, "Much."

Everything inside me clenched.

"But we can wait until after dinner."

I let out a disgruntled growl, "Why not now?"

He lifted his head, raising a perfectly arched brow. "Don't sound so disappointed. Eating actual food is a necessity, you know. Besides, we have the entire night ahead of us."

"Only all night?"

"You might tire of me eventually."

Snaking my arms around his neck, I captured his mouth, kissing him deliberately and seductively. "I would never tire of you..."

".... I hope not."

I slid the gown down my shoulders, pooling lilac silk around my feet. "Never ever," I murmured, sauntering my naked body away from him and into the wardrobe. With his darkened gaze planted firmly on my bare behind, I remained hopeful that spanking was a big part of that plan.

Grabbing my clutch off the dresser, I informed a patiently waiting Ari I was ready. "Don't dither; let's go."

His luscious mouth twitched in amusement. "Yes, ma'am." Trailing after me out the door, he gestured to the sleek Imperial blue BMW sitting at the kerb.

"Nice car."

A boyish grin formed pressing the button on the keys in his hand. "Indeed, it is." He leaned down to grasp the chrome handle, opening the door for me. What a gentleman. "Your ride, ma'am."

"Why, thank you, kind sir. I'll be sure to give you your tip later," I purred, sliding onto the soft seat, the smell of leather and citrus permeating my senses.

"I don't doubt it." He chuckled, closing the door. Long legs quickly strode around the bonnet to slide in beside me, inside me was preferable. His mouth curved leisurely into a breathtaking smile. "Well, where to?"

Uncertain, I shrugged. "I don't know, you decide. Any brain cells I had left, you sucked from my body."

Smirking, his hands flexed over his thighs. Hmm, interesting. "I have a craving for Italian, and coincidentally, I know a lovely place on Lygon Street."

"Sounds good," I replied, snuggling into the seat.

"Okay, Italian it is then," Ari responded, reaching across to kiss me tenderly before starting up the car and roaring away from the kerb. That would never get old.

If anyone ever asked me about my favourite pastimes, one would be dining on Lygon Street in Carlton. The long length of street was buzzing, similarly to most nights no matter what the season, with summer naturally being the busiest. Couples and families casually strolled a busy walkway that was awash with an array of cultured restaurants, cafés, and sports bars. Whilst their staff hovered about the open doors ready to refill glasses for their jovial patrons already seated at the rows of tables edging the widened footpath.

So busy was the night, Ari had trouble finding a car park close by, forcing him to park around the corner in Argyle Street. "Here we are. Wait there, I'll get your door," he firmly stated, switching off the car and stretching for the jacket laying across the backseat. I knew there was a reason I wanted and loved that man — pure gentleman.

I obediently waited as he climbed from the low vehicle and hastily walked his gorgeous body around the bonnet to open my door. His hand extended ready for me. "Thank you, kind sir."

Closing the door, Ari roughly tugged me to him, landing a heated kiss on my lips. "Behave." He growled, liberally brushing his lips against mine. "Or I'll take you here on the footpath, and I don't care who sees." His domineering reaction had me wondering whether he understood the reference or not.

God, he smelled intoxicating. I would've happily lost my inhibitions in front of everyone, except without the ramifications. "Hmm, an enticing proposition, however, there are a few issues with venturing down that road."

His head cocked. "Such as?"

"Well, for starters, we'd be arrested for lewd behaviour and indecent exposure," I cautiously qualified, skimming my hands over the curve of his well-defined back. "Then we'd have to face the wrath of our families for getting arrested, and for embarrassing them. Not so enticing now, is it?"

Ari scrunched up his nose. "No, most definitely not. The thought of facing my mother sounds awfully frightening." He was right; trifling with an angry Audrina was not ideal on any given day.

I offered up a sensible substitute instead, "Dinner then?"

He pushed a soft, chaste kiss to my lips. "I knew there was a reason I was dating you."

"Yeah, I'm the sensible one."

Feigning offence, he grabbed my hand, the two of us laughing as we sauntered down the footpath. Enticing smells wafted out the restaurant doors, making our mouths water. We were both starving, which wasn't surprising considering our rather carnal afternoon.

Vendors shouted from their doorways, hoping to lure prospective customers with their competitive prices and decadent menus. We strolled straight past them until we reached Buona Compagnia, a quaint Italian restaurant that made you feel as if you were in Venice, only without the canals.

"Here we are. Buona Compagnia not only cook genuine Italian woodfired pizzas; they also have the best wines," Ari murmured, rubbing a hand over his growling belly.

My eyebrows shot up. "Why am I not surprised?" A dark brow raised above an even cheekier smile. I tutted as he dragged me through the open door.

Immediately, a waiter dressed as a gondolier kindly greeted us. He directed us to a table situated beneath an open bi-fold window with views of the busy street where he duly informed us his name was Antonio, and he was to be our waiter for the evening.

"Your menu," he said, placing two black folders on the table directly in front of us. "Would you like a drink to start, signor, and signora?"

Responding in fluent Italian, Ari requested his preferences while slinging his leather jacket across the back of a chair. He slid into the opposite seat.

Antonio beamed, clearly pleased with Ari's reciprocation in his native tongue. I wasn't even aware Ari could even speak Italian but was impressed, nonetheless.

They switched back to English.

"Of course, do you want to order your main as well, signor?"

"No, thank you. We'll order those after our entrées."

"Eccellente. I shall be back shortly with your wine," Antonio replied before turning and heading towards the bar.

Ari's dominant side hadn't shocked me either. In fact, it did the opposite and turned me on, immensely. "You command, and people seem happy to jump."

Filling our water glasses, he unapologetically answered, "I know what I want. Procrastination is a pet peeve of mine, and besides, eating whilst drinking was a foregone conclusion, I thought."

"Fair enough, I can't argue there," I conceded, resting my folded arms across the table. I gazed curiously. "So, tell me about your business; what does an enigmatic CEO do with his day besides ensuring his hair remains perfectly intact all the while barking orders at his minions?" The corners of Ari's mouth quirked in amusement.

"Jaeger Property Development oversees a multitude of items, ranging anywhere from rebuilds to new builds, commercial and residential. I also own several properties, as well as shares in businesses around Victoria and New South Wales. The business has increased quite profitably, so much so, our Sydney branch has recently expanded. The staff there are amidst packing as we speak and are moving mid next month into brand new offices right in the heart of the CBD. With one of the best men I know to run the place...."

As I listened intently to him, the soulful voice of Ella Fitzgerald crooning in the background slowly drifted away. All I heard was Ari's lilted voice and the evident passion for his job. My eyes wandered, soaking every aspect of him in, in the same manner he had during our shower.

From his artfully tousled, and wayward short, thick, jet-black hair to the colour of his almond-shaped eyes. Pure dark chocolate that turned ebony when they darkened. A straight nose, sitting perfectly above his beautifully sculptured mouth, and last but not least, his raspy British accent, a voice that was capable of seducing me, without even the slightest of touches.

Antonio eventually returned to the table with our bottle of Shiraz and entrées, snapping me out of my reverie. As I looked up, I caught Ari staring with an inquisitively raised brow.

"Are you okay? All that dreary talk of business must have bored you, surely?" He cut the Bruschetta in half and lifted it to his mouth, taking a bite. I copied.

Balsamic vinegar combined with ripened Roma tomatoes and fresh basil tingled my taste buds, delicious. Swallowing, I gave a slight shake of the head. "No, you weren't boring me. It was quite the opposite actually; I was simply admiring the view. Again." Bringing the glass of wine to my lips, I smiled coyly.

Closely observing as I slowly sipped, Ari inhaled sharply. "You're quite the naughty girl. Who knew?"

"I've never felt this way with anyone before you," I admitted, lowering my eyes. I hadn't bothered looking either.

In a smooth caress, Ari slid a hand over mine. Like two magnets drawn to one another, our eyes locked. "I feel the same way about you, Teddy. I always knew feeling this way was possible, but I was beginning to lose hope." His throat bobbed tightly. "I had reached the stage where I was ready to give up and as pathetic as it may sound, I wasn't prepared to even settle for less. Loving someone else when I have loved you my entire life was inconceivable." His admission blew me away.

Curiosity got the better of me. "But when did you realise that you were actually in love with me?"

"I had just celebrated my twentieth birthday, and you had barely turned sixteen. Legally though, I couldn't do anything about it. Therefore, I waited. Patiently, until you finished high school; then you went off to university."

"But I was still here, in Melbourne," I sadly disagreed, even if it was only in body.

"I know, and honestly, I thought some other suitor would have come along sweeping you off your feet whilst you were there. As it stood, we scarcely crossed paths. I was busily trying to establish my business, and just when the timing was right, it seemed as if you'd locked yourself away from the world."

I had. If only Ari knew why. Courage lacked for me to tell him why.

"The next time I saw you, it was at your twenty-first birthday party. Taking my eyes off you was difficult." Sexual tension crackled around us and rose with each candid confession. "You were so beautiful, and still are, and that dress, wow."

"I still have 'the' dress. I've never wanted to get rid of it, mainly because my father bought it for me. Mother told me it was terribly indecent and far too short." Another night wasted. If only my path had led me directly to you, and not in another direction.

"And in those heels.... It was awfully tempting to drag you into the toilets then and there." He blushed. Hmm, the possibilities, I'd be sure to wear them again.

"Ari Jaeger! Are you blushing?"

"Yes, but don't tell anyone, will you? I do have a bad boy image to uphold after all."

"So, the mysterious CEO does have a human side," I teased, perching an elbow on the table, and resting my chin in the palm of my hand. "So, why didn't you?"

Ari's perplexed gaze stared. "Do what exactly?" Really? He had to ask why?

"You know, drag me into the toilets and have your wicked way with me?"

"Quite the unhygienic place for a sex romp, don't you think?" His nose crinkled in disgust. Then he softened. "See, I can be a gentleman, and on the odd occasion, a caveman, so I was recently told."

I laughed softly. "Unhygienic or not, I wished you had. It might've stopped mum from trying to set me up with her friend's jerk of a son Carter Jenkins at least. What a sleazeball." Nothing's changed.

"He kept groping your arse; I remember that much. Bryson and I were both ready to teach him some manners. As it turned out, you weren't in need of our assistance; you handled him rather appropriately if I recall." Ari grimaced at the memory.

"Ah, how could I possibly forget? Or the fact he squealed like a pig after my shoe connected with his foot." My mouth twisted ruefully. "Carter deserved every bit of what I dished out. Although, my mother failed to understand my reasoning and scolded me like an errant child for my undignified behaviour for weeks on end after that." God forbid I ever embarrassed her in front of her high society friends. "Then she insisted I apologise to that weasel and his snobby mother, Miriam, which I refused, of course. He ought to have thanked his lucky stars the spike of my heel hadn't connected with his balls instead."

Ari winced. "Yes, those stiletto spikes certainly had a bit of a kick to them. Pun intended." He chuckled. "And from what I've heard, Carter still has quite the limp." A piece of information I was quite familiar with, unfortunately.

"It was just my reflexes. A girl has to protect herself," I muttered, staring wistfully at the flickering candle in the middle of the table.

Ari gently wiped away a stray tear I hadn't realised had fallen with the soft pad of his thumb. I met his unwavering gaze, and for a fleeting moment, a past I wished, in reality, wasn't there, vanished.

Seated across the table from me was a man I'd desired my entire life. He knew nothing of my history, past or present. Frankly, I wasn't interested in sharing either. Circumventing might be another issue.

The sound of a throat cleared, interrupting our intimate moment. "Are you ready to order your mains, signor?"

Ari glanced up at Antonio and brusquely ordered veal scallopini before returning his heated gaze to me. Our yearning for one another openly radiated, sending our crimson waiter scurrying away without our half-finished entrées — poor fellow.

So enthralled, I failed to notice Ari picking up the wine bottle or topping up both glasses. I took mine from his outstretched hand as he passed it to me over the table.

"Are you trying to get me drunk?"

Glinting chocolate orbs dipped to my fingers as they glided over the narrow stem. "No, just pliable." I squirmed in my seat.

"I'm already quite flexible, without the alcohol. But it's a little detail you're already aware of."

The corners of his delicious mouth eloquently rose. "That I am."

I smiled knowingly before broaching another minor element we had yet to discuss. "Do you care to explain the fully packed bag of clothes you brought to my place today?" Clutching and balancing the stem between my fingers, I swirled the wine around inside before taking a tentative sip. "Rather presumptuous, wouldn't you say?"

"Nothing wrong with feeling hopeful," Ari professed. "And well, it certainly paid off."

"Ah, so does that mean you're staying at my house tonight?" I silently prayed the answer was a yes, spending another minute apart from him was unthinkable.

"I can," he softly responded.

A victorious smile flittered across my lips.

Ari reached across the table and took my hand, pleasantly stroking the knuckles with his thumb. "I take it you're pleased with my response?"

Slowly nodding, I shivered deliciously at his touch. "Yes, sir, I am."

He frowned and was about to respond when our waiter Antonio interrupted once again.

"Signor, signora, your Vitello Scallopini," he announced, setting the steaming meals in front of us.

"Thank you, this looks delicious," Ari informed the ever-patient waiter.

"You're welcome, signor. Will there be anything else?"

"No, thank you, that shall be all," he sternly replied.

"Enjoy." Realising he was no longer needed, Antonio took haste, ensuring he took the entrées with him.

Ari dug his fork into the thin tender steaks smothered by a creamy mushroom sauce. "I'm going to enjoy my meal, and then enjoy having my dessert later at home." The sensual tone of his voice was full of promise and longing.

My body quivered in shameless anticipation. Everything about the divine man sitting across from me, I craved, my thirst unquenchable. All I wanted to do was reach over and maul him; patrons and the consequences be damned.

We finished our meal in relative silence, speaking only through our body language, with a touch here, and a touch there, sending heat coursing through my veins. As soon as we swallowed the last bite, and drank the last drop of wine, Ari was calling the waiter over for the bill. He barely glossed over the receipt. With his darkened gaze resting solely on me, he promptly tugged a wad of cash out of his leather wallet and placed it inside the black folder, leaving a ludicrously large tip for the suffering waiter.

"Thank you, signor, and please, come again."

"Oh, I plan on it."

Grasping each other's hands, we rushed out the door and back to the car, both as eager as the other to get home.

8

UPON INSPECTION OF THE crumpled state of the bed, the result of passionate and the occasional ravenous lovemaking, my mouth curved. Usually, crisp Egyptian cotton sheets were twisted and hung off the mattress. Cushions and pillows were scattered, landing wherever we'd thrown them in our haze of hunger.

Ari's decadent lovemaking had taken me to entirely new heights. Whether it was his fingers, his mouth, or his tongue, he had worshipped every inch of my body, making my body sing from the pleasure alone, leaving me deliciously sore. Everywhere.

"I hope I'm the reason you are smiling like that?" Ari presumed, strolling from the bathroom. He leaned over me, brushing his soft lips over my cheek. His freshly showered scent an intoxicating blend of orange, grapefruit, and mint with a subtle hint of roses drifting over me, leaving me high, high on him.

My head rolled over the pillow, meeting Ari's tender gaze. His hot breath tickled my skin as his arm slowly slithered around my waist, raising me off the bed. His ripped stomach flexing as he drew me closer. So close, not even a whisper of air could've passed between us. Pressed against my midriff was his growing cock; I ground my hips, indicating my desire for more.

A loud, harsh smack connected with my behind; I moaned in ecstasy. A low growl rumbled. "Did you enjoy that?"

"Perhaps you could do it again sometime?" I articulated, tugging at his bottom lip with my teeth.

"Really?" Ari flinched as I bit down. "You would let me spank your delectable arse again?"

"I've dropped enough hints, haven't I?"

"I suppose you have," he murmured as the tip of my tongue swept between the parted seam of his mouth. His scorching expression searched my face as his long fingers skated along my jaw and throat in a light caress. "Is there anything else you desire?"

Where did I start? "A little bondage, maybe a few toys; I have a few already if you must know," I unashamedly divulged.

Astonished, he tilted my chin, grazing his lips over mine. "You are full of wonder. I look forward to our experimentation then..."

"I'll be right back, sir," I whispered, stealing a quick kiss off a frowning Ari before disappearing into the bathroom.

"Nice tent you have there," I casually remarked, tugging my thick tresses from a hair tie as I stepped back into the bedroom.

"Well, I wonder why that would be," he uttered, rising off the pillows and dragging the sheet away, leaving his rock-hard member exposed to my hungry gaze. He held out a hand for me. "Come."

Sliding my hand into his, I gracefully crawled up onto the bed, and settled between the widespread of his taut thighs. My lustful gaze leisurely slid over his well-sculpted body until it halted at the impressive length encased by his gently fisting hand.

Dark chocolate orbs darkened, becoming pools of ebony as his sculpted mouth slackened, eliciting soft pants. A familiar warmth spread, filling my aching core with each measured, titillating stroke.

Precum seeped, dripping over the broad crest. Oh, yes, please. I had been dying to have a taste. Sweeping my hair to one side, I leaned forward and suckled gently, swirling the tip of my tongue over the swollen head. Delighted by his decadent flavour, I hummed and took him deeper, brushing my lips against Ari's fingers, tightly resting at the base of his rigid column.

His other hand sifted through my tresses, holding me firmly in place as his long fingers gripped them by the roots. The painful pleasure making me moan as he tugged out of ecstasy.

Dragging my bared teeth up the velvety shaft and back down again, I reciprocated the pain, extracting an appreciative hiss from Ari. Our pleasure quickly converged into a game of tit for tat.

Hard and repeatedly, he thrust his hips, plunging his cock deeper. "Jesus, Teddy!" he uttered, obviously astounded by my gag reflex or lack thereof.

I hummed again, working his cock with one hand while skating the other along the inside of his thigh, cupping his tightened scrotum in my palm. A move that provoked a guttural moan, as did the circling pads of my fingers over his perineum. I pressed harder.

He muttered incoherently, "For the love of God, Teddy, don't stop." Oh, I hadn't planned on stopping, not until I'd pumped you dry.

Taut, muscular legs quivered, and veins pulsated over his length as his cock swelled. Warm salty fluid swiftly followed, gushing copiously down my throat.

"Ah, fuck!" My mouth continued to pump him as I swallowed every last drop. Ari's gratified moans filled the room, my reward for a job well done. He sagged further into the pillows, gazing sleepily at me as I licked his shaft clean with a small, satisfied smile resting upon his face. "That was...wow."

Beaming up at him, I crawled up along the length of his body and stretched out, laying between his thighs. "It was something, wasn't it?"

Ari chuckled, one hand softly stroking my head and the other strumming over the length of my spine. "You blew my mind. Literally."

My mouth curved decadently. "I'd be more than happy to do it again, you know. It was rather tantalising, not to mention delicious."

Studying me intently, a hand cupped the back of my head. "You're insatiable, aren't you?"

"I am, but I can't help it." Well, that was the truth.

"Aren't you sore after all this sex, I know I am." No.

"A little, but nothing bath salts won't fix." Ari wasn't sure what to make of my nonchalant attitude. In fact, he looked perturbed by it.

"I seriously have nothing left. You have worn me out."

"Pity," I blatantly admitted, and then thought it best to mollify Ari when his face dropped, ".... We can wait."

∞

Ari

ASTOUNDED BY TEDDY'S UNWAVERING APPETITE, I sank back against the pillows, watching her as she climbed over me and curled into my side. Something was amiss here, but what it was, I had no idea. It was a conversation for another day, perhaps. For now, I was far too tired, as was Teddy. She had invariably drifted off and had begun talking in her sleep.

"Hmm, love you."

I turned my head and lovingly gazed down at her. "Goodnight, my lovely," I whispered gently pressing my lips to her head.

An alarm beeped madly on Teddy's bedside table, waking me with a start. My bleary eyes peeled open in time to observe an arm flinging out from beneath the sheet. A slender hand violently hit the button, silencing the deafening noise.

"What did that poor clock ever do to you?"

Swivelling her head over the pillow, Teddy smiled, her hazel eyes shining brightly, and mischievously as she stared at me. I too, had her number.

"Hello, gorgeous."

Her cute nose wrinkled. "Good morning to you too, handsome." Lifting the bed sheet, she peaked underneath, and then back at me, biting down on her bottom lip. "Such a shame to waste this...," she simpered, floating both hands over my torso. I silently thanked the heavens above they were warm before she shamelessly began exploring my nether regions.

I grunted at the feel of her long fingers cupping my balls and the tip of her tongue tickling the swollen head of my cock. "We.... can't leave...your day unsatisfied now, can we?"

"Hmm, yum," she purred, licking away the precum seeping over the swollen crest.

I pre-empted her next move and subsequently flipped us over, pinning her wriggling body beneath me. Pushing her legs wide with my knees, she moaned, her back arching off the mattress as I rapidly sank inside her warm, glistening sex. "No, my turn. You had your wicked way with me last night."

"No fair." Succulent lips pouted and panted with want. We locked eyes, and her pupils dilated. Her guileless gaze darkened to a deep sea-green completely possessing me, so I completely possessed her, mind, body, and soul.

"We need to get out of the shower. Otherwise, we won't ever get out, and we'll both be late for work," Teddy informed me, reaching for the tap. I swatted her hand away and took her into my arms.

"So, be late," I murmured, peppering kisses along her clavicle, and biting down on her shoulder.

"All right for some, but I can't imagine Spencer being impressed by my tardiness," she retorted tartly, wriggling against me.

"You can just blame me," I countered, skimming my lips up the side of her throat.

She moaned. "No, I can't...as much as I want to."

"Well, what's the problem then?" I joked. That was my first mistake; the second was my attempt to grab Teddy as she took a step back.

Terror flashed across her face. "I said NO!" Leaping from the shower, she ran away from me and out of the bathroom, sans the towel.

Puzzled as to what scared her off, I stared after her. That went without saying, ascertaining any answers wouldn't happen if I stayed in here. I shut the water down and stepped onto the mat, reefing two towels off the heated rail on my way past as I wandered out of the bathroom.

I didn't have to look far. I found a shivering Teddy huddled on the floor in the corner of her expansive wardrobe. My first instinct was to wrap the warm towel around her; it was fruitless. She shook her head heatedly and proceeded to shuffle farther away from me. "Teddy, please, you're freezing."

"No!"

Dejected, my knees dropped to the hard timber floors. "It was never my intention to frighten you."

"I know," Teddy whispered, so quiet it was barely audible.

Concerned, my brow furrowed. "If I did, I apologise. I couldn't…would not. Not in that way; it would be abhorrent," I added, running a hand through my wet hair. "Teddy, please say something, I'm starting to freak out here." I was too afraid to touch the woman I loved all because she was frightened. Of what though?

"I know you wouldn't – not like he did," she sniffled, fighting a losing war with her tears. "I'll explain to you one day, but…not right now…I…I just can't."

Who was he? Moreover, what did he do? Although my gut told me otherwise, I wasn't about to speculate either. I stiffly nodded, agreeing with her. What else could I have said? "Okay, I'll wait for you." Like always.

"You'll hate me," Teddy quietly told me. That was a load of bollocks right there.

"No, Teddy, I could never; I love you," I declared reaching out, only to have her cower away from me, taking me aback. "Trust me, please."

"I do. I'm sorry."

"Don't apologise. Can we cover you up at least?" I sensed her trepidation and prodded gently, "Please? You're shaking." Precariously, she moved into my lap, permitting me to cover her with the now cold towel. Relief flowed through me.

Resting my cheek against the crown of her sopping hair, I tightened my embrace, wondering what on earth had happened to the rambunctious girl I remembered growing up with all those years ago.

∞

Teddy

TUGGING MY DARK BLUE DENIM DRESS OVER MY HEAD, I mulled over my request, making Ari leave me be while I dressed. Even though he'd seen me naked many times already, I just felt dirty and unattractive, and facing him right now was inconceivable. How could I, after that little freak out in the shower? He might not want to confront me either; the thought depressed me.

I slumped into the upholstered chair in the corner of my wardrobe and perched my elbows on my knees, covering my blotched face with my shaking hands. It had taken me ten years — ten bloody years to face my fears, and just when I finally had the man of my dreams, I freak out, scaring him half to death.

Why did everything have to be so damned complicated? Swiping away my tears with the backs of my hands, I snatched up my tan peep-toes off the floor and tiptoed over the floorboards. The adjoined door soundlessly slid open and disappeared inside the wall cavity as I looked over at Ari, his beautiful frame standing by the bay window as he dressed. He was clearly struggling too, making my heart painfully wrench more than it already was.

Oh, Ari, I am so, so sorry for the way I've made you feel. As I warred with my thoughts, my brows furrowed; I realised losing him was no longer an option, but then neither was destroying him. Now, as I watched Ari staring off into the oblivion, I saw my past already was – I had to let him go.

9

Ari

AFTER THE BIZARRE TURN OF events in the shower, forgetting my morning might be a considerable challenge. In all my life, I hadn't ever dealt with this type of situation before; no wonder my head was in a spin.

The terror and the fear were both so real. So were the tell-tale signs of a headache, forming a strangling band around my head. It too, added to the agitation already surging, making my preparation for work seem like an effort.

I heard the soft shuffling of feet padding across the timber floors and looked up. Teddy stood statue-still, watching me. Her pained expression mirrored mine. She also showed signs of nervousness, the fidgeting with the glossy curls at the ends of her waist-length mane was an inherent habit I knew well. "Hi there."

She timidly approached the bed. "Do you mind if I come and sit with you?"

I shrugged and gestured to the empty spot beside me. "It's your house."

She sat down, leaving quite the gap between us.

I stiffened and shuffled, turning towards her. "Are you all right?" I knew the question was absurd the second it left my lips but felt the need to ask it anyway. Her demeanour told me she was far from all right as did the glassy eyes staring back at me. Droplets of tears balanced precariously on long, auburn eyelashes. Even vulnerable, she was still so beautiful.

Her tearful gaze swiftly dropped to the floor. "No, and I don't know if I'll ever be."

"Why would you say that?" Perplexed by such a negative statement, I frowned and shuffled closer. I grasped her hand, brushing my thumb over the knuckles. "You're perfect."

Teddy glanced hopelessly up at me from beneath her wet lashes. "Please don't put me on some goddamned pedestal, Ari!"

Taken aback by the sudden vitriol, I dropped her hand and gaped. "Where's this coming from?"

She held up a hand. "Don't! Just let me speak!" I reluctantly nodded. "I'm far from perfect. Compared to your life, mine hasn't ever been a fairy-tale, and once you eventually learn my secret...you won't want me, and your family definitely won't want me with you either," she refuted, her voice strangled. "I do love you, and have for a long time, but now, I'm not so sure if my problems should become yours. They'll only bring you down, and I'd forever hate myself if I inflicted that upon you."

I couldn't believe what I was hearing; Teddy was breaking up with me. We'd barely begun. No, no, no! "I told you it doesn't matter to me whatever...it is." I waved my hand around and irrespective of how pathetic I sounded, I begged, "Please ... don't do this, I beg of you. We've waited far too long."

Her sad expression told me otherwise. "I know we have, but this needs to be my decision. What happened in the shower was an epiphany, a wake-up call to something that could never be anything more than a fantasy. None of my craziness would be fair to you."

I swiftly pushed to my feet, directing my irritated gaze towards the opposite side of the street. Folding both arms over my chest, I swallowed tightly before daring to ask the question dangling on my lips, "Is this secret the sole reason you've been holding back all this time?" I twisted at the waist, darting my teary gaze in her direction.

Her bottom lip trembled. "Yes, yes, it is." Finally, an answer to one of life's little mysteries!

Peering back out at the busying street, I observed the neighbour over the road blissfully kissing his wife and leaving for work, whilst I was amid an argument wishing I was doing precisely the same. I scrubbed at my jaw; were their lives truly peaceful or was it secretly just as complicated? I wanted that life with Teddy by my side. Although right now, that blissful life was disintegrating right before my eyes.

"Whatever this secret is...I won't allow it to hold us back, ever! I meant every word. I'll be here for you, always," I implored, tilting her face to meet my unyielding gaze. "Please let me in and don't push me away. I'll never stop fighting for us. I love you..."

Desperate to show Teddy just how much, I lunged, pushing her back on the bed, fervently taking her mouth. Breathless, I leaned my forehead against hers and closed my eyes, my throat thickening as I expressed my love for her. "Love is the antithesis of selfishness. Is that proof enough?"

"Is love enough though?"

"Yes, it's more than enough," I stressed. "Just promise me you won't give up on us this easily."

Teddy rose off the mattress and sat on the edge of the bed. Deep in thought, she pensively chewed on her bottom lip. "Are you prepared for whatever happens, Ari?" she finally asked.

I nodded eagerly and shuffled up beside her. "I am."

She blew out an exasperated sigh. "To be honest, I'm a mess, both mentally and emotionally. My baggage is heavy, as is my secret. I have severe trust issues, and I'm frightened...frightened of my feelings for you." A renewed sense of hope rushed through me, one that made me believe there was a chance for us.

"We'll work on everything, together, I promise."

Tilting her head, she eyed me speculatively. "For some unknown reason, I believe you, and I know you would never have any rhyme or reason to hurt me."

"No, I would never, I couldn't." Crushing her to my chest, I let out a shuddering breath. "I love you, Teddy, that won't ever change."

"I hope not." I peered down as Teddy feebly spoke. But the unspoken fear, and the worry that I might, I most definitely heard. What had happened in the past to make her so scared of our relationship?

∞

Teddy

"**MORNING, TEDDY,**" Dominique greeted, smiling brightly as I rounded the corner into the kitchen. The beaming smile quickly faded as Ari came into view, and instead received her brother by way of a flipped finger on her way past to the downstairs bathroom.

"And good morning to you, Dominique. So childish," he uttered, shaking his head. "How are the rest of you ladies on this glorious Monday morning?" He perched on a stool at the island bench while I set about making coffee for him and a green tea for me. Considering our rather emotional morning, I'd prefer something stronger, sans the glass. Although, I had a feeling Spencer wouldn't appreciate it if I showed up to work drunk.

Pushing my woeful thoughts away, I turned my attention to something meaningful, like Ari and Poppy's in-depth discussion about education.

"I have a full day ahead preparing my senior students for upcoming exams, and I'm not looking forward to it," Poppy articulated. "Kids get stressed, teachers get stressed; no wonder we look forward to a glass of wine, or the entire bottle once we make it home at the end of each day!" she added with a giggle.

"I can well imagine. Trying to deal with kids these days must be a nightmare," Ari remarked, blowing on the steaming coffee I'd just handed him before taking a tentative sip. "They lack self-discipline and have this belief that the world owes them a living. On top of that, they want their arses wiped for them. Children today are simply revolting."

Poppy nodded in agreement. "Unfortunately, there's not a lot of difference between publicly or privately educated students either. Although saying that, a child's socio-economic background can impact on their education."

"I hear you, Poppy, but if a child wants to learn as a means to escape that cycle, they'll do whatever it takes to see that they do."

My gaze darted back and forth as if I was watching a tennis match.

"Yes, but still, there's no excuse for something called old-fashioned manners," she noted, her eyes cutting back to the notes open on the computer screen in front of her. "I don't ever recall behaving that badly growing up – then my parents may beg to differ." Her nose scrunched, making me laugh.

"You were the perfect child, Poppy, and honestly, I don't ever remember you giving your parents any grief," I interjected. "They probably wondered why their daughter was hanging out with someone like me."

Poppy peered over the top of her computer screen and smiled warmly. "My parents adore you and think the sun shines out of your arse. They're always saying what a sweet girl you are."

"Oh, my God? Teddy perfect, please! Maybe I should tell your parents otherwise!" Scarlett chortled loudly, provoking an eyeroll from me.

"Your sister is perfectly marvellous," Ari stated, blissfully smiling at me from across the island. Swoon.

Scarlett feigned coughing. "Well, aren't you pussy whipped!"

My head swiftly whipped in her direction. "Scarlett! Take that back and apologise, now!"

"Well, that's the truth. Ari only said it because he's screwing you," she goaded.

Vexed by her sudden hatred and attitude towards Ari, I gaped. "That's my boyfriend you're referring to, so I suggest you stop and apologise like I told you to!"

Unfazed by my anger, she just shrugged her shoulders and smirked. "I'm sorry, okay!"

I immediately knew that my sister's apology was bogus. She had pushed me too far this time. "Say it like you mean it, Scarlett, NOW!" Even my yelling was to no avail; she stubbornly ignored me and stormed off, thumping the entire way up the stairs and to her bedroom. The door slammed with a bang along with my last nerve. "Dammit, Scarlett!"

About to hotfoot it upstairs, Ari rapidly slid off the stool and sidestepped, halting me in my tracks.

I glowered. "Move!"

"No. Let her go," he firmly ordered.

I folded my arms over my chest and huffed. "Why? She was blatantly rude to you!"

"She's only lashing out because she's shitty at me."

"But why? I don't understand. You didn't do anything wrong, to her anyway."

"Scarlett perhaps feels the need to defend Dominique after my less than civilised behaviour yesterday," he explained, tucking a loose tendril of my hair behind my ear.

"They're young and immature, and one day with any luck, they'll realise, and regret, how badly they've behaved. Which won't be until they've had children of their own more than likely."

Our sisters and children? What a ridiculous notion. "I'd call that karma."

Ari's mouth twitched in amusement. "You heartless beast."

Impishly shrugging, I kissed him softly on the lips. "I know I am," I murmured against his delectable mouth. About to devour Ari further, a barstool scraped across the timber floors judiciously reminding me we weren't alone. Clearing my throat, I profusely apologised, "Oh shit, Poppy, I'm so sorry...."

She waved a dismissive hand. "Forget it. Your sister, and yours," she pointedly looked at Ari, "are simply chucking a temper tantrum. They'll get over it, eventually, and then all shall be forgiven."

My brow raised sharply. "It seems I'm not the only optimist lately." I wasn't earlier; in fact, I sounded downright contradictory.

Slipping her laptop into her satchel, she gave me a crooked smile. "Quite possibly. Anyway, I am off to work." She slung the strap over her shoulder. "I'll catch you two lovebirds tonight."

Waiting until I heard the door close, I slumped back onto a barstool and raked my fingers through my hair. "I feel terrible. Poor Poppy, she shouldn't have to listen to our family spats."

Ari pushed my legs apart with his knee and leaned into me, cupping my cheeks with his hands. The tips of his fingers grazed my skin as I gazed, mesmerised by his darkening orbs. Scarlett who? Then he brought me crashing back to earth where I landed with a thud. Where were we? Oh, right, our annoying little sisters.

"That's one of the many perks of Poppy's job; dealing with multiple personality disorders is all part and parcel of it."

I snorted at his analogy. "True."

Darting his gaze from me to the clock on the oven, he sighed despondently. "I really must get going as I have a few meetings to attend this morning. I'll call you later, okay?"

No, don't go. I sighed heavily. "Fine." The weight of the morning had come at me like a ton of bricks; all that was left was my wounded pride.

Ari bent his head and passionately captured my mouth. I twisted my fingers through his thick hair, clinging tightly to the roots. I didn't want to let go. Couldn't we just stay home, in bed? Don't stop. But to my disappointment, he did and gently pulled back. His stubbled jawline nuzzled my cheek.

"I must go, even though I don't want to either."

Grappling his lapels, I slid off the stool. "I know. I love you."

"And I love you," he murmured against the edge of my mouth, giving me one last lingering kiss before we eventually parted, our outstretched hands and fingers grazing as he walked away.

The door opened and then closed, leaving me alone with my thoughts, and my bratty sister. How remiss of me to forget? I reluctantly pivoted and gazed at the stairs. Exhaling a sharpened breath, I ran up the stairs to her bedroom.

I pushed the door open and looked across the room to the white antique desk beside the open window. Scarlett refused to slow down the fast-paced strokes long enough to acknowledge my presence. Bugger it; she could like it or lump it. I was over the attitude.

I crossed my arms over my chest and stayed in the doorway, propping my shoulder against the doorjamb. "Haven't you got uni today?"

"Your stuck-up boyfriend hasn't taught you it's impolite to enter someone's private space without knocking first obviously!" Snarky Scarlett, lovely.

I pinched the bridge of my nose and counted to ten. "You're treading on some seriously thin ice, sis!"

She glared darkly. "Whatever...just get out of my room."

"Not for much longer if you keep this up!"

She snorted derisively.

Exasperated, I threw my hands in the air. "This conversation is far from over!" Why was I shouting? She wasn't my child, and I was most definitely not her parent. Maybe I should call dad, and he could deal with her? Perhaps I should threaten to kick her out. More to the point, why was I arguing with myself?

Growling, I slammed her door. I stalked back downstairs and snatched up my bags off the hallway floor. The front door wasn't immune either; it too, wore the wrath of my temper.

Seriously, what a clusterfuck of a morning! The back of my head hit the headrest in my car with a thud. I connected my iPhone to the Bluetooth and opened up a playlist. Ah, much better. Nothing beats

Van Morrison's creamy voice to calm my nerves on the way to work, but then so did Ari. Everything about Ari Jaeger calmed my nerves.

Having flopped down at the desk, I checked the diary on my computer and groaned. My drama-filled morning, it seemed, was spilling into the afternoon thanks to our super awkward client, Mrs Elise Travers. The appointment had completely slipped my mind. Could my day have gotten any worse?

Clicking on the folder for the Travers, I pulled up their plans and glanced over them. As far as I could see, the plans were complete; all that we needed was the Travers' signatures to get the ball rolling on construction. It still puzzled me as to why Mrs Travers needed such a large house when it was just herself, her husband Patrick, and let's not forget the two rats she called dogs.

To survive the rest of the day, I'd need coffee by the bucket load. "Do you want coffee, Ems?" I asked, rolling my chair backwards and pushing to my feet.

With a shake of the head, she gestured to the mug beside her, all the while keeping her eyes fixated on the screen in front of her. "No thanks, all good here."

As I made my way towards the staff kitchen located at the front corner of the building, a powerful expletive echoed, halting me outside Spencer's office. I took a step back and peered in. By the looks of the massacre taking place, it was just in the nick of time too. Why do men always grab their hair when they're frustrated?

Coffee, he needed coffee. Chocolate biscuits wouldn't go astray either. Or if that didn't work, perhaps I could offer to shave his head instead?

Knocking tentatively on Spencer's door, I entered, instantly greeted by his trademark smile beaming up at me.

"You must have ESP," he acknowledged, eyeing the tray in my arms. I think a line of drool just dribbled down his chin.

"No, not ESP," I retorted, setting it down beside him on the desktop. "I saw and heard you, luckily, so I figured coffee and Tim Tams were the ideal solution for your frustration."

A deep chestnut brow raised inquisitively. "What was the alternative?"

"...Shaving your head," I slowly replied, a giggle erupting when a horrified expression crossed his face. "Just kidding!"

He held a hand to his broad chest and breathed a sigh of relief. "Thank god for that."

I smiled at him. "I was grabbing a coffee for myself in preparation for the afternoon's onslaught with Mrs Travers anyway."

Spencer grinned dipping his biscuit into the coffee before taking a chunk off the corner, leaving his lips coated in melted chocolate. "Yeah, good luck with that one. Without a doubt, you'll have her eating out of your hand by the time she leaves."

"I hope so, or it'll be my knuckles she'll be chewing on if she keeps being rude to me," I murmured dryly, clutching my cup.

He threw his head back and laughed loudly. "Let's hope it never comes to that. Thanks for the cuppa and the bikkies too. Perhaps now, I can finally stop cursing at my design."

"Moreover, pulling at your hair. Glad I could be of assistance. I'll leave you to it then."

Striding back to my desk, I set my coffee down and sat back in my chair. "Right, now let's make sure I have everything in these plans of my own."

"You know talking to yourself is the first sign of madness, Theodora." Oh, my day had just deteriorated even further. Fabulous. I groaned inwardly at the person behind the voice.

I plastered a smile on my lips, one that was more of a grimace really and spun the chair around to face the permanent thorn in my side. "Mother, what a pleasant surprise; what do I owe to this – unscheduled visit?"

In a form-fitting baby blue dress with her copper tresses pinned back in an elegant chignon, my mother was as always, impeccably dressed.

Her dour laugh rang in my ears. "I hadn't heard from you or seen you in a while..." There was a reason for that. Her green eyes stared, cold, and emotionless much like the person talking, "...And as I was in town, I thought I'd see if you were available for lunch?"

My brows furrowed, meeting her soulless gaze. That's odd. She never took me out for lunch. "Mum, I'm sorry, but I can't. You've caught me on quite a busy day as I have a client coming in at one and need to prepare before they do."

Her glare darkened, which I expected. Mother wasn't a fan of the word no, from anyone besides herself of course.

"Perhaps I should just make an appointment then, like everyone else!" she barked, bringing the onslaught of verbal guilt with her.

Again, expected.

"What kind of daughter are you if you won't even make yourself available for your mother? I'm certain if it were your grandmother's, you would make the time."

"At least they would be more understanding!" I snapped back, feeling proud as mother flinched at my unexpected outburst. "This is my job, Mother, and if it were any other day, I would have said yes," I firmly and diplomatically argued, which was not my style at all. Inhaling and exhaling sharply, I instead, calmly offered a compromise, "I'm sorry, Mum, but this is a critical client." More to the point, they were damned frustrating. "What about dinner? I would love to catch up with dad, and the rest of the family, only if they're available, of course."

Mother scoffed. "I suppose it must do. Does tomorrow night fit into your busy schedule?" Ignoring my mother's facetiousness, I smiled tightly. It was a tone we'd all grown accustomed to over the years.

"Yes, Mother, tomorrow night is much more suitable. I'll let Scarlett know, and we'll both be there around seven."

"No, I expect you both *by* seven, and not a minute later."

I couldn't help but roll my eyes with the dramatics. With an air kiss goodbye, mother paraded out the office, leaving me in a choking cloud of her sickening perfume.

As she waited for the lift, I observed my mother from afar. How was it possible to love and despise someone at the same time? With her, it was more the latter sadly.

She always had a way of making me feel guilty, no matter what I did, or didn't do, and for the sake of my sanity, I kept my distance. She had dealt me enough grief over the years, enough to last me a lifetime.

As soon as I saw her step inside the elevator, I apologised to Emily for the disruption and thudded back into my chair, hoping there weren't any more.

The Travers project was a large one, even with Emily and I collaborating, it still wasn't any easier thanks to the client's everchanging mind. Mostly, it felt as though we were back at school, cramming for an exam we knew we were both doomed to fail.

The morning had flown by with lunchtime rolling around quickly. Famished, I made a snap decision.

"Do you feel like walking to stretch our legs, Emily? I am in desperate need of a good sandwich before tackling Mrs Travers. So, what do you say, De'lish on Collins?" I suggested, picking up my bag and slinging the tan leather strap over my shoulder.

"I couldn't agree more."

As we entered the busy café, it was already buzzing with other lunchtime goers all wanting the same, one of the delicious choices on their extensive menu.

"I'll meet you at one of the tables at the back, Ems." I paid for my order, and grabbed the plate, manoeuvring around other tables to find an empty seat amongst the maddening crowd.

"Mmm, this is delicious," I moaned taking a bite out of my roast chicken, avocado, and salad sandwich as Emily finally joined me.

She grinned. "If your food can make you sound like you're having an orgasm, maybe I should have bought that instead of this schnitzel focaccia."

I winked. "I don't need food to give me an orgasm."

Emily sank her teeth into her focaccia. "Mmm, nah, not doing it for me. Let me try yours."

Laughter bubbled as I slid the plate across the table.

"What? I've got to get mine from somewhere, and unlike you, I don't have an Ari Jaeger to give me mine...." Damn straight.

"Or you need a bigger vibrator." Something I had aplenty. "And loads more batteries."

"So, how's the sex with Ari?"

I choked on my orange juice, spitting it down my chin. My hand struck out, reefing reams of serviettes from their holder to wipe up the mess.

Emily Smith, I quickly realised wasn't in the least bit shy. Which happened to be the first day we met. Asked if I preferred aggressive sex over passive sex among other intrusive questions was a conversation I'd never forgotten.

"It's great, more than great if I'm to be honest. Ari's everything a girl could want in a man; for starters, he's as handsome as hell and sweet as pie. Did I mention earlier that he was amazing in the sack too? I'm surprised I even managed to walk today!" I knew I was bragging but didn't care and proceeded to tell her about the Jaeger party and our behaviour at Buona Compagnia.

Emily listened enviously. "Wow, you're a lucky girl. I have yet to meet a man who can do that to me. But that poor waiter, he's probably hoping you two never come back!" she commiserated, giggling.

"That's why Ari left him a big tip!" I simpered, glancing down at my watch. "Ugh, it's that time already. We had better get back to work before her ladyship accuses us of making her wait."

As opposed to us, Elise kept us waiting; deliberately, I'm sure.

Ten minutes late and without the decency of an apology, she swanned into the conference room and flopped into a chair, sneering rudely as cold grey eyes pinned me across the table.

"Perhaps if you ladies got it right the first time, then I wouldn't have to waste my days coming back!"

Taken aback by the condescending tone, I gave her a tight smile. "Let's get started then, shall we?"

Spencer entered the room amidst our packing up. He paused in the doorway and sniffed the air. Coughing, he asked, "Blimey, what is that god-awful smell? It smells like somebody farted in here."

I laughed. Although highly educated, Spencer's pure Aussie mannerisms never lingered too far from the surface. "That putrid stench you speak of would be our client's god-awful perfume." I never thought I'd smell another worse than my mothers. Elise Travers had shot that out the back door along with her manners.

Spencer's chestnut brows shot up. "Well, her husband mustn't have any working senses then, or he just has bad taste. On a more serious note, how'd today go with her ladyship? Any more requested changes?"

"Surprisingly, she was happy with the result," I happily informed him rolling up the house plans and shoving them back inside their plastic tube.

"She was happy? I never thought I would live long enough to see the day." In obvious shock, Spencer's chocolate gaze widened. "Wow, Teddy, you could've at least warned me to sit down first."

"I was closely watching to see if any cracks appeared on her face when she smiled," Emily uttered dryly, making Spencer laugh.

"They'll be well hidden under the mountains of makeup she wears."

"Yeah, the makeup she applied with a front-end loader," I added, giggling. "But she happened to mention in passing that Mr Travers was growing impatient with the process and requested that we finalised – today. She acted a little sheepish about it too."

"You two are baaad," Spencer scolded, chuckling. "Well, that is good news then. I'm positive you two are more than capable of organising the remaining papers, yes?" We both nodded in unison. "Great. The sooner they're signed, the sooner the contractors can begin." Spencer smiled. "Splendid work, ladies. Take a break; you look like you need one."

Emily and I didn't need telling twice and ventured off to Le Petite Gateau, a French patisserie in Little Collins Street. The irresistible cakes and tarts in the glass display cases looked delicious, making it hard to choose.

"I might settle for a slice of the Brownie passionfruit gateau and a latte. What about you, Ems?"

Emily shrugged, pulling out her phone and sending a text. "I'm still unsure what I want, but you go ahead and order yours."

"Okay," I ordered mine and settled into a seat. The waitress trailed by with my order shortly after. My fork dug straight into the soft slice. I moaned the second the sweet, moist chocolate hit my mouth. "Oh wow, this is divine."

"Mmm, this chocolate cake is an orgasm on its own. I'd offer you some, but you've had plenty this weekend!" Emily winked, popping a chunk into her mouth.

I laughed and shook the fork at her. "I need to find you a nice man; orgasm by food is just not acceptable."

10

MOST DAYS, I handled my anxiety by pushing it back and using breathing exercises the last therapist gave me. Not even they were working. I needed a different kind of activity, something that would alleviate some, if not all. The possibility was currently zero. I settled for the gym.

I yanked the glass door open, and the smell of sweat-laced bodies hit me like a pair of stinky shoes, as had the loud music reverberating throughout the brick walls.

The Gym, a distinct and straightforward name, was a hundred-year-old warehouse conversion, and proudly, one of my first projects. The outstanding pitch I gave the owner was what sold him, hence commissioning me for the job. Taking most of my suggestions on board, he even went as far as insulating and adding reverse cycle air conditioning, sustaining a pleasant temperature throughout the seasons.

Original signage remained on the faded red brick walls, and matte black steel beams ran across the towering ceilings, maintaining that old industrial vibe. Included was a women's only section, housed on the mezzanine level. A space that gave women such as myself the confidence to exercise without fear, with uninterrupted views of the floor below. Attached, was a room available for spin classes and the likes, which I used on the rare occasion I required a rigorous workout, or for merely increasing my stamina.

I passed by the front counter, swiping my membership card, my suspicious gaze scanning the vastly open space. I knew my behaviour was nothing more than my irrational fears looking for someone who wasn't there. I snorted. My shrink would've diagnosed me with paranoia and given me medication. A tactic tried and failed once before.

Once I'd changed out of my work attire, I threw my bags into a vacant locker and made my way back to the main floor in search of a treadmill. I found one; smack bang between two middle-aged men. Both thumping heavily, they failed to notice my apprehension. I should've followed my instincts and just gone upstairs.

If I wanted a workout, I just had to face my fears. It wasn't as easy as it sounded though. Suck it up, Teddy and move your arse up onto the treadmill, they won't do anything. I jumped onto the treadmill and started pressing buttons without setting a time limit. I needed to run hard. And run hard, I did. I ran until the muscles in my legs protested from the burn, and the sweat dripped from my pores.

Next on my agenda was a punching bag.

I threw as much into it as I had the treadmill, each jab firing hard and sturdy. The pretence that it was *his* face made my workout all the more satisfying. Spurred on, I hit a circuit of weights.

With my last set of dumbbell lifts near completion, a hulking bodybuilder approached. His beady eyes ogled me as if I was a piece of meat he hoped to devour. I wasn't about to give him the opportunity.

"Hey, beautiful, do you need a hand with your workout?" I glanced up at him, my nose screwing up at the awful sight.

Sculptured, muscular and toned, Ari was attractive, whereas this guy was revolting; overextended muscles, veins popping in both arms and legs, great for giving blood no doubt.

He was several inches shorter too, leaving his line of sight aimed directly at my breasts when I sat up. He ogled the fuchsia crop top openly leaving me alarmed, and with a desperate need to cover up.

As politely as possible, I declined, "No, thank you, I'm finished and now going home."

The problem with bodybuilders, they were far too narcissistic for my liking. So much so, his pea-sized brain failed to register my disgust, or the effect his proximity was having on me. Anxious, my breathing increased as my sweaty palms rubbed along the tops of my thighs. Whilst the pungent stench of cheap aftershave and sweat caused overwhelming nausea to rise.

His persistence knew no bounds and blatantly refused to give up. "Well, maybe we can get outta here? My place isn't too far from here; in fact, it's just up the road. Whattaya say?" He leered brushing short, stubbly fingers along the length of my bicep.

I gagged. Seriously, had muscles ever heard of a toothbrush and soap, because this guy reeked!

A cold shiver ran down my spine, swiftly turning fear into anger. I shoved the sweaty and unwanted hand away. "You have some nerve! Why would I ever go home with a slimeball like you when I have a boyfriend, whom I am now going home to. So, move the hell outta my way!"

The grip on my arm tightened. "The boyfriend doesn't need to know." My stomach churned.

"Do you know what I hate most?" Pushing to my feet, I pointedly stabbed my fingernail at his chest. "…. are pigs like you who believe it's their God-given right to take whatever they want!"

He smirked. "Maybe you should've covered up and not paraded around in that skimpy outfit looking like a slut."

My eyes widened. Oh, muscles didn't just go there.

"Truth hurts, doesn't it, sweetheart?"

I glared. "Do you want to know what else hurts?"

Muscles smirked again. "Besides your ego getting bruised, what?"

"This!" I growled, delivering a sharp kick to his groin. I watched on in delight as he crumbled to the floor. "Now whose ego's bruised – sweetheart?"

Squealing like a pig, he clutched his crotch, "You fucking bitch! You'll pay for this!"

Staff rushed over, showing no sympathy whatsoever and promptly sent him packing, revoking his membership on the spot. I paid no mind to their apologies or the crowd mindlessly gawking or that I'd left muscles on the ground curled up and choking on his nuts either. I rapidly took off running towards the locker room.

Hot tears stung, and my vision blurred. The fear of another man's unwelcome touch had my skin crawling and my body shaking. All I wanted to do was go home, my one safe place, and shower to scrub away the filth.

So desperate to be rid of my infected clothes, I began stripping, leaving a trail along the hallway and over my bedroom floor. Numbness had overtaken any thoughts of self-preservation. Even as I scrubbed at my skin under the searing water until it turned red raw. I still felt his touch, and no amount of scrubbing would ever wash it away. Feelings of every nuance had set in, triggering streams of never-ending tears. Exhaustion flowed from there, leaving me sagging against the tiles.

My entire day had been one colossal fuck-up after another. Another day like that... I'd lose it entirely.

Shutting the water down, I grasped a bath sheet off the heated rail, wrapping it around my weary body. Combined with the hot shower, I ought to be warmer. But the shaking refused to subside, and my head was hazy, making it impossible to think. I just stood in the open doorway between my bedroom and the bathroom.

What was I about to do? Nothing registered, not even the soft knocking on the bedroom door.

"It's only me, Teddy." Poppy quietly opened the door and peered her head around. A strange frown appeared on her face.

"Are you okay? You came rushing in and seemed to be in the bathroom for a lengthy amount of time. Which is not like you at all," she stressed. Darting into the bathroom, she quickly returned with another towel and climbed onto the centre of my bed, her hand patting the quilted blanket softly.

"Come and sit." Bossy Poppy had come to visit. Dutifully, I perched on the edge while she knelt behind me, tenderly drying my dripping hair. "What has made you this upset?"

Dried up tears flowed freely once more, and amidst my sobbing, I tried my best to explain. "That man triggered all those feelings and all of those wretched emotions I'd harboured for the last ten years. Why do men think they can take whatever they want? Why do they feel the need to invade your space, even when you tell them no? Do they do it to intimidate you, hoping to frighten you into submission?" I viciously stabbed at my bare leg with the tip of my finger, leaving an indent from my manicured nails. "Even then, some don't get it – and they take it anyway!"

Over the years I had attended numerous counsellors, each offering the same advice; *'Move on with your life. Find a hobby.'* They also prescribed anti-depressants and sleeping tablets.

My mother helped too, by shoving them down my throat. So sick of their so-called solutions, I signed up for the gym. Exercise seemed to deal with my anxiety better than any doctor had, much like my secret lifestyle had.

My job at Bricks and Mortar along with my love of architecture were the one sure thing's in my life that hadn't let me down, an achievement that my past or my parents hadn't sunk their claws into and corrupted. Playing the piano also calmed me, as did listening to the great classics. Self-defence classes had taught me strategies for keeping unwanted people away, which had proven effective earlier, but it wasn't enough. Nothing could ever take away the anger bubbling away inside of me. I was a ticking time bomb, and it was only a matter of time before I exploded.

Poppy listened as she always had, letting me vent. She usually kept her opinions to herself, until it came to Ari that was. Rightfully so, given the length of time, I'd been in love with him.

"How am I ever going to continue a relationship with Ari? I'm damaged goods. This secret could ruin his family if he ever knew. Maybe we aren't meant to be?"

Poppy inhaled sharply. A tell-tale sign that her opinion was coming whether I wanted to hear it or not. "At the cost of ruining our friendship, there may be a point and time where you may have to tell Ari about your past," she reasoned. "Ari loves you irrevocably and would stand by you no matter what."

I leapt off the bed and stared at my best friend in disbelief. "How can you be so naïve? Ari will be repulsed! Not just by the thought of me, but he'll never look at me the same way again once he discovers the truth about me. His family have a lot of pull in this city, a reach that would leave me little choice but to move as far away as possible. The scandal it would create would bring down both our families."

Poppy's eyes rolled dramatically. "That's crap, and you know it. Your mother, as usual, has filled your head with her lies, and surely, even you, a well-educated woman must realise this! Teddy, please listen to me! I love you like a sister and have no rhyme or reason to lie to you." She threw the towel down and clambered off the bed.

Grabbing me by the shoulders, her coffee brown eyes blazed, scaring the hell out of me. "Ari loves you, and any damn fool can see it. He worships the ground you walk on. I'd even go as far to say he'd take a bullet for you," she pleaded. "Have you tried speaking to Ari about your past at all?"

I couldn't lie to my best friend, even if I tried. "He has a small inkling something happened, and that's only because of my freak out during our shower this morning. But I couldn't bring myself to go into any details," I explained, my voice small and childlike.

"I take it because Ari was still here and all over you this morning, he was very supportive... telling you it didn't matter to him?"

Sadness tore at my chest. "Yes, I suppose he was, but I'm still worried about Ari's reaction to the rest." Overwrought, I fell to my knees, my fingers clawing at my throat as I struggled for that breath of precious air. Oh, shit. "Pop...py."

Poppy immediately knelt beside me. "Try and steady your breathing, slowly, in through your nose and out through your mouth," she coaxed, pushing my head between my knees. "That's it, Teddy, slow breaths."

With each gentle rub of my back, the erratic breathing steadied. As I lifted my head, my throat clenched. "I'm sorry."

She held me close, her hand tenderly caressing my back. "Don't apologise; just do me a favour and stop allowing your past to control your life. At the very least, go back to your counsellor before your past takes a firm hold, and you start making rash decisions, decisions you'll come to regret later," Poppy lovingly implored. "If you want a future with Ari, then let him in. Talk to him. Your past will always remain present and stand in your way otherwise."

My dampened head came to rest on her shoulder. She had aimed the truth straight at my heart. Telling Ari was a decision I needed to make, and soon.

Yawning loudly, Scarlett stretched and caught me off guard as her arms snaked around my shoulders in a loving hug. Our morning argument appeared forgotten, which it wasn't. Mentally depleted by my earlier panic attack I was in no mood to rehash, nor did I have the energy to.

"Goodnight, ladies, I'm off to bed."

"Don't forget about dinner tomorrow night, Scarlett," I reminded her as she straightened.

She groaned. "Dinner with the 'rents; what could possibly go wrong?" The sarcasm dripped from her voice.

I chuckled and pushed off the sofa. "I might do the same; I'm exhausted. Night girls'," I mumbled, shuffling in the opposite direction.

On the way to the bathroom, I picked my iPhone up off the bedside table, hoping there was either a missed call or messages from Ari: there was neither. Upset, I set it down on the marble counter beside the sink and stared, willing it to go off as I brushed my teeth and rinsed my mouth. Oh, this was nuts, even for you, Teddy.

Mentally, I wished for Ari to call, and continued staring at my screen, even as I absently switched off the bathroom lights on the way past and crawled into bed. I flopped against the pillows. "Bugger it, what have I got to lose," I said aloud to no one really. Perhaps I was crazy after all. I punched out a quick message.

'Hope everything's ok? Haven't heard from you all day.
Goodnight. I Love you xxx.'

And like an overeager schoolgirl waiting to hear from her high school crush, I impatiently waited for a reply. Ari was probably busy, or he'd finally come to his senses. Having to witness a freak out like mine, I'd run too.

Eventually, my eyes drooped, succumbing to the tiredness coursing through my body. The phone still clutched inside my hand and close to my heart.

∞

Ari

MUCH LATER THAN INTENDED, I pulled up at the kerb outside Teddy's and glanced towards the house, smiling at the simple but thoughtful gesture of the glowing light on the front porch. As did the fact I was about to make my way inside to see my girl.

Thanks to certain people, my day was filled with useless meetings, leaving me without one spare minute to check in on her. I felt like absolute shit for failing to do so. Teddy apparently shared the same sentiment due to the rather passive-aggressive text I received earlier, astounding me.

Having gathered my briefcase and jacket from the passenger seat, I climbed from the car and closed the door. The darkened street was eerily quiet. So quiet, I was confident I heard the neighbours breathing. Surprising me the most were the willy wagtail birds nesting inside the blossoming crepe myrtle outside Teddy's window, they were also silent, noisy little blighters otherwise.

Unlocking the door tastefully painted in duck egg blue with the key given to me that morning, I stepped into an unusual silence and darkness. And with only the muted light from the dimmed lamp on the inherited antique hallstand from Vivienne to guide me, I was careful not to make any noise. Expressly as I soundlessly tiptoed into the bedroom. But as I caught sight of the amusing vision sprawled across the bed, I struggled to contain my bubbling laughter. Teddy had seemingly waited for me to call, which in turn, reiterated my failure to contact her. My smile rapidly disappeared. Clearly, somewhere in the back of her mind, she probably thought I had run for the hills after her breakdown.

Why would I?

I, Ari Colton Jaeger, loved Teddy Vivienne McGovern irrevocably.

∞

Teddy

A SURGING PANIC BEGAN TO rise through my chest at the realisation that something or someone had me pinned to the bed. I couldn't move, even if I wanted to. I forced my eyes open and slid my anxious gaze along the length of my body, relaxing instantly as I viewed Ari's veiny forearm casually draping over my waist. His nestled fingertips brushed my midriff, producing pleasant shivers that curled around my spine. Excitement and warmth suddenly filled my chest; he hadn't run for the hills after all!

I rolled over and tucked a hand under my cheek, my lips curving into a coy smile as I stared at the welcomed sight beside me.

"Didn't your mother ever teach you it's rude to stare?" Ari unexpectedly asked with his eyes still closed. God, he's gorgeous and smelled heavenly to boot.

"I have a good reason to stare," I crowed, grazing my fingertips over the stubble running along his strong jawline. "I have an incredibly hot man in my bed."

He looked adorable, peeling his sleepy eyes open. "I wonder how your boyfriend might feel about that."

The gym junkie's words prickled my skin. Pushing him out of my mind, I rolled Ari onto his back and excitedly straddled his lap.

"Ah! You're rough," he protested as I thumped down. He gazed sleepily up at me.

Leaning forward to nibble on his right earlobe, I whispered, "He doesn't need to know." Repeating that idiotic man's words made me inwardly cringe; why couldn't I have thought of something better?

"You're so naughty, and I like it." Scorching darkened orbs melted my insides; oh, you have no idea just how naughty I could be.

Cradling my head in one hand, and slanting his lips over mine, he slid the other down the gentle curve of my spine and into my underwear. Cupping my behind, he groaned salaciously at the heat transpiring between my thighs.

Moaning, I writhed against the probing fingers. "Fuck me, Ari, fuck me hard and spank me. I need to feel you everywhere." I wanted him desperately. I wanted him to make me forget. Grinding my pelvis against his hardened cock, I began to strip, my kiss turning ardent and frantic.

Sensing my desperation, Ari abruptly withdrew and stared up at me with a furrowed brow. "Not that I'm complaining, but why are you kissing me like there's no tomorrow? Has something else happened between this morning and tonight that I'm not aware of?"

Calmly, I hauled my baby pink singlet over my head. "No, nothing happened. What I missed, is you," I murmured dismissively, peppering kisses around his neck. "And I want you to fuck me hard, what's wrong with that?"

"Nothing, but you seem...I don't know...off. Like something's bothering you?" Ari was cautious with his words, and I refused to budge. "Is it because of this morning?" he persisted. Didn't mean I was caving.

The constant questions undoubtedly evaporated my good mood. Irritated, I lifted my lips away from his neck and sat back on his thighs glaring at him. I climbed off his lap and thumped down on the pillows, my back facing away from him. *There's nothing wrong with me, Ari.*

"Are you sure, Teddy?"

The gritted teeth ought to have indicated he'd hit a nerve: how obtuse of him. Exasperated by the constant questions, my eyes rolled. "Yes! I just missed and wanted you is all!"

"Okay, if that's all it was, then I apologise," he conceded, tenderly grazing his knuckles over my shoulder blades. He felt me stiffen and lifted his hand.

Tears shamefully prickled. I hated that I felt afraid, and I hated that we were arguing.

"I missed you today as well, and I apologise for failing to call you." Ari remained troubled by my attitude, even as he lay down beside me. I sensed it in his voice. "Today was just one big headache after another."

I rolled over needing that closeness and snuggled into his chest, slinging an arm over his waist. "Why, what happened?" I asked, peering up at him. Ari's brows rose, in disbelief I imagined. The poor man probably suffered from severe whiplash because of my mercurial moods.

"I had a handful of contractors that seem to have forgotten their place. Firstly, they ignored the initial warning given to them, and as a result, I refused to give them a second chance. Therefore, I sacked these wankers and their oversized egos." A low disgruntled growl rumbled inside his throat. "As it stands, the build's already behind schedule, and it's going to take a miracle for us to meet the original deadline. The prospect of having to hire more contractors doesn't thrill me one bit either, as it means longer delays whilst getting them up to speed," he explained, trailing his fingers along my spine.

"I'm sure you'll have them sorted out somehow. You're tough like that."

He snorted, tipping us back to the mattress. "I'm glad someone has faith in me." The gruff expression was replaced by a much softer tone as the atmosphere around us shifted. "I love you, Teddy McGovern, and no matter what's thrown our way..." I leaned into the palm caressing my cheek. "I'll always be there for you." Chocolate orbs gazed deeply, past my darkened and damaged soul. It was as if he held out hope, that he would be the one to offer me the absolution I so desperately sought.

Poppy's stern words began to rattle around inside my head. Perhaps she was right. Could I drop the mask I wear and expose a past I desperately wanted to stay buried, along with my secrets? What were the chances of our relationship surviving if I took that risk? Could it weather the storm that followed? Exposing the mountainous waves of lies surrounding my life could mean a disastrous end, for all of us.

I sighed heavily as doubt plagued my thoughts and questions.

"What's going through your mind, beautiful girl?" Ari's concerned gaze intently searched my face. "You appeared to be miles away." I was.

"No, I was only thinking about us and how lucky I am to have you in my life. You give me a reason to smile every day." Liar.

"I feel the same way. Even my staff noticed the extra bounce in my step when I entered the office today. If only they knew why," Ari murmured, smiling as his nose skimmed along mine.

"Are you ashamed of me?" I joked, feigning offence.

"No, I could never be ashamed of you," he wisely replied, his voice a silky rasp. "I want to share my joy with everyone, but for now, I want you all to myself. Besides Asher, my colleagues ribbed me the entire day by implying you're nothing more than an imaginary friend I made up."

I tempted fate and ran a hand down his back, squeezing his luscious behind. "Does this feel real?"

"I know what else is real." He drew me closer, and lowered his head, sealing his sculpted mouth over mine. Ari was ardent, pouring every emotion into the kiss. Likewise, his touch as he ran a hand over the curve of my spine, and along the curve of my buttocks. Over the next couple of hours, we spent every waking minute cherishing every inch of one another's bodies, showing what we meant to each other.

The sun streamed through the open windows, disturbing me. I awoke to find Ari entwined around my overheated body, his hips flexing, pressing an impressive morning erection into my lower back.

I squirmed against the warmth of his body. "Do you want some help with a 'little' problem this morning, Ari?"

"I'll have you know it's not a problem, and it's far from little," he admonished cupping one of my breasts and tweaking the nipple, inducing quite the pleasurable gasp. "I have an early breakfast meeting with a union representative over yesterday's fiasco that I need to attend, otherwise tending to you would be my main priority." Groaning aloud, he rolled off the bed, smacking my bare bottom in the process. "Come on, sleepyhead; we need to move."

"Do I have to?" I moaned, pulling the sheet back over my head.

"Come on, lazybones." Ari pried the sheet from my tight grip and scooped me off the bed and into his arms. My protesting ignored, he carried me right on into the shower and flicked the tap. A cold spray shot from the shower head.

"Ah, that's freezing!"

Ari chuckled and held on tight, not letting me go. Ever.

I waltzed into the kitchen with my spirits higher than ever. Great sex and reassurance would do that to a person I suppose.

Bent over sorting through the pantry shelves for my breakfast oats, an eager pair of hands rubbed my backside over the top of my indigo blue skinny jeans, stirring a need we both craved. I sighed and straightened, pressing my back against Ari's firm chest. "Are you right there, Mr Jaeger?"

"Hmm – mmm, your arse looks amazing in these jeans, so tight, and so firm," Ari murmured, caressing my rear as his mouth skirted over my exposed nape.

"Don't you have a meeting to go to?"

He growled at the frustration of having to let me go. "I do, so I had better take off."

"I offered to help you with your 'little' problem, but just remember – it was you who turned me down." I raised a brow when he adjusted the bulge straining inside his charcoal grey suit pants.

"I now regret not taking up the offer. My balls shall be the size of tennis balls by the end of the day," he grumbled, folding me into his warm embrace and nuzzling my hair, which was up in a stylish updo for a change.

"I suggest you stay behind your desk today and if you're lucky I might, and only might come and pay you a little visit so I can have my lunch." I slid my fingers beneath his jacket tails, skimming my hands up and down the length of his broad back.

"You are so bad; admittedly, I do love it." Hips flexed as he captured my mouth in a kiss that had all ten toes tightly curling in the ends of my nude heels. "I'll catch you later, me and my blue balls."

"Wait! Ari hold on, please?" Scarlett shouted, breathlessly running into the kitchen, her words flowing out in a rush. "I wanted to apologise for my childish behaviour yesterday. It was truly uncalled for and this issue between you and Dom...well, it has nothing to do with me, so I should never have acted so horrible to you, or Teddy."

"All right, apology accepted. Now, I believe, there's a slice of chocolate tart with my name on it as part of this apology?" Ari murmured in wonder.

Scarlett fetched the container from inside the fridge she expressly put away and handed it to him. "There's even Chantilly cream to go with it." She profusely blushed when he bent at the waist, kissing her on the cheek: my man, the charmer.

"At least this shall satisfy me, if only slightly." He winked, turning my face crimson. "And, Scarlett, thank you."

"You're welcome. I need to get going to uni, see you tonight, sissy."

We watched with wry amusement as Scarlett happily skipped out the door.

"Well, that was unexpected," Ari acknowledged, turning back to me. "I really must go. Love you." Giving me a chaste kiss, he disappeared out the door just as quickly.

11

Ari

LONG, ARDUOUS MEETINGS occupied my entire morning. Regardless, my mind drifted constantly. Even as my lawyer, Asher Bradford, hashed out complex issues with union members and government members around the boardroom table.

Teddy's desperate manner the previous evening gave cause for me *to* worry. Although perplexed by the irrational behaviour, I glanced down, smiling at the photo I'd snapped barely minutes after we'd made love for the third time. The flushed skin and messy bedraggled hair epitomised her state of bliss, however, I knew differently. Behind the unguarded smile and her brightly shining eyes was a concealed pain, a secret so protected she refused to disclose for fear of the consequences; losing me was one of them.

Teddy tried her utmost best to convince me that nothing was wrong, but her demeanour presented an entirely different story. I loved that she wanted me – but, dammit, I had nothing, not a damned inkling. She did, however, show some degree of courtesy by enlightening me as we showered and dressed that morning. Even then, she masked her hurt upon sharing information, but in the same token, the details regarding her mother were relatively scarce. Her deflection and comparisons didn't go unnoticed either. Nonetheless, they were particulars I endeavoured to find out, sooner rather than later.

∞

"Scarlett and I are having dinner with our parent's tonight, so don't wait up for me as I don't know what time we'll be home. My mother's typical expectation was we're to arrive by seven, and not a minute later. I only relented as a compromise."

Confused, I frowned. "A compromise for what exactly?"

"My mother visited me unexpectantly at work yesterday, and again in her typically predictable manner, she expected me to just drop everything to have lunch with her. Never mind the work I had to do or the clients I had to see. So, I compromised purely to appease her."

"Ah, so does this explain some of last night?" I observed Teddy, awaiting a response, but she'd deliberately busied herself, making it impossible for me to read her.

"Possibly. My mother tends to bring out my insecurities with her own. It's frustrating at times." That still wasn't an answer.

"Your mother's a bully and I've witnessed it firsthand. I've always struggled to understand the disgraceful treatment of you, though. As I recall, you were always the model daughter, never putting a foot wrong."

"Unfortunately, my mother doesn't see it that way, and never will." Disheartened, her head dropped, supposedly searching for the right shade of blush. She owned one pallet, one that housed several shades. She was stalling and fighting with her thoughts. After a long minute of silence, she spoke again, the inflection in her voice conveying an envy I fully grasped, "Your mother, on the other hand, she's the complete opposite."

A smile tugged at my lips whenever I thought of my gregarious mother. "No one could ever accuse my mother of being heartless, that's a given."

Teddy briefly glanced back in the mirror at me, and gave a tight smile before continuing, "And unlike my mother, she's never had a reason to belittle any of you, even when you and Bryson misbehaved as children."

My head shook as I chuckled. "How, I have no idea, considering Bry and I ran her ragged at times with our outlandish behaviour."

Teddy's bubbly giggle rang fondly. "I agree. I remember one occasion when your mother scolded you both. If my memory serves me correctly, it was the day you and Bryson had Dominique utterly convinced she was adopted. The worst part was she believed you."

I grinned warmly at the memory. "I believe Dom was around nine years old when we did that. Mother grounded us for a week and made us do more than our fair share of chores as part of our punishment. Dominique thought she was in seventh heaven not having to do any until mum threatened to ground her too if she kept playing on it."

"Your mother's a scary woman when she's mad and can be rather intimidating at times. And I highly doubt she has any insecurities at all."

∞

Audrina Jaeger was not the type of woman you trifled with on any given day. Her acumen made her a great lawyer as she had a very polite way of dealing with certain kinds of people. Another reason I admired my mother, she loved her family fiercely and would go to the ends of the earth for them.

Whereas in Teddy's case, Therese McGovern only ever concerned herself with how others perceived her. Whenever the chance arose, which was often, she diminished her daughters' confidence. It was as if Therese hated them for their mere existence. Her son Abel on the other hand, she doted over. In her eyes, he wasn't capable of putting a foot wrong. I knew for a fact he was far from perfect and always saw right through his B grade acting.

I tenderly grazed a finger over the photo once more. "What are you hiding from me, Teddy?"

"Ari, are you still with us?"

A close friend and my lawyer, Asher Bradford suddenly interrupted my musings, making my head jerk. "Yes, of course, sorry I must have zoned out there for a minute. Now, where are we up to on this fiasco?" I replied, sliding the phone back into my jacket pocket.

12

Teddy

I WASN'T LOOKING FORWARD TO dinner one bit. Then both sets of grandparents, whom I adored, were also attending. Their presence always seemed to calm my nerves. Neither would be on this earth forever and as such, I tried to visit with them as often as possible. With that in mind, spending the evening at my parent's home was worth the inconvenience.

Horrendous peak hour traffic delayed my trip home, making me later than intended. I was just grateful Scarlett was already dressed and waiting for me. I ran into the family room and yelled out to her over the six o'clock news.

"I'm just ducking in for a quick shower, and then we'll head out as soon as I'm ready, okay?" The unenthusiastic hand waving back at me spoke volumes.

Throwing myself through the fastest shower possible, I found a set of clothes in record time, too. I just hoped that the jeans and the white blouse with a pale pink leather jacket looked presentable enough. I snorted. I could be dressed head to toe by a top designer and mother would still find a reason to fault my dress sense. Who cared, I dressed for me, not her.

I rapidly applied fresh makeup minimally before running a brush through my long tresses. With no time to throw my hair into a ponytail, I left it hanging in loose waves around my shoulders.

"Come on, Scarlett. Let's go. God forbid we're late," I muttered, rushing out the bedroom door, hopping on one leg at a time as I slipped a pair of suede, low-heeled ankle boots over each foot.

"Righto."

With barely a few minutes to spare, Scarlett and I pulled up into the driveway of our parent's Mid-Victorian terraced residence. If the place weren't so beautiful, I'd never give it a second glance. Unfortunately, when it came to the house we grew up in, the bad memories outweighed the good ones by a longshot.

Located in the swish suburb of South Yarra, the home admittedly, was beautiful. Enormously sashed windows hung either side of an oversized black front door with brass fittings, giving uninterrupted views into mother's perfectly manicured cottage gardens. Original black lace fretwork framed the outside balconies creating the appearance of a perfectly framed picture; and that's all it was – a fictional picture.

Showtime. I blew out an unsteady breath and reached for the vintage lever handle. Not so surprising was the door opening or our mother standing there greeting us in her usual chilly manner before I'd even had a chance to grab it.

Scarlett and I immediately stepped over the threshold into the foyer, the soles of our shoes scuffing against the elegantly tessellated federation black and white porcelain tiles. "Mother, here we are, and look at that," I murmured looking at my watch, "we're on time too."

"Hmph, barely," she snidely remarked, glancing at the rose-gold filigree watch wrapped around her slender wrist. Handcuffs seemed more appropriate, in my opinion.

Hanging my jacket up on a cast iron hook beside the door, I rolled my eyes – away from the disapproving line of sight. "Nice to see you, too, Mother. Where's dad?"

"Your father's in the living room, drinking more than his fair share as usual," she chided coldly, "and has done so since he arrived home."

My eyes rolled again; was there anything she didn't approve of? "I might go and join him for a drink then," I goaded, irritating my mother.

"Theodora, show a little etiquette please."

I giggled; the fish were biting well today. "Mum, geez, learn to relax and take a joke. I'm driving, so I can only have one, or was it two, I simply can't remember."

"Ooh, that means I can have a few then," Scarlett quipped giggling.

"Really girls'." Disgusted, she turned away, heading back to the kitchen to check on the progress of dinner. Good, stay there, but don't forget your chains.

Unlike our mother's frosty reception, dad wrapped us in a tight and warm embrace. "Teddy, Scarlett, you're here; marvellous. Would either of you care for some Pinot Noir or a Shiraz?"

"Pinot, please," we replied in unison.

"How's work, Teddy?" he asked, promptly pouring two glasses, and passing them to our outstretched hands. I immediately took a sip.

"It's going well thanks as I've just signed off on a rather large project, thank goodness. I can't believe Emily, and I eventually finished though; our client constantly changed her mind dragging out the process, annoying the hell out of us."

Dad flung an arm around my shoulders and pressed his lips to my temple. "That's great. I'm extremely proud of you, Teddy."

"Aw, thanks, Dad. What about you? Is everything well for you?"

"Um, yes, it's as good as it can be. Our clients are like pigs; if you keep drip-feeding their investments correctly, their bank accounts fatten, keeping them content. Now, Scarlett, how's uni?"

As my father turned his attention to my sister, I eyed him speculatively, mostly as he refilled the wine glass clasped in his hand.

I frowned; that was the third one in under twenty minutes. His speech was slurred, making me wonder just how much he'd consumed before we'd arrived. I asked if he was okay; naturally, he replied, yes. Typical.

By all appearances, he was looking older than his sixty years. Usually twinkling and mischievous, dad's cornflower blue eyes appeared lifeless and strained. His strong jawline kept ticking, and his hand kept skating over his thinning hair, indicating to me that he was quite the opposite.

Was his job as a stockbroker and financial adviser making him stressed, or was it something else entirely? Then I got a glimpse of my parent's interactions or lack thereof. The air between them so thick, it was suffocating. Not that it was anything new. I'd seen and heard it all over the last twenty-six years of my life.

Sighing and shaking my head at the tense-filled sight, I advanced farther into the living room, opting for the pleasant company of my grandmother, Violet McGovern instead. Affectionately positioning myself beside her on the red and cream floral sofa by the blazing fire, I leaned in, softly pressing my lips to the delicate skin of her cheek.

As always, she smelled of lavender, her favourite perfume.

"How are you, Gran?"

Her reply never changed: it wasn't any good grumbling as no one listened anyway, raising a hearty chuckle out of me.

Grasping her shaking hand inside the warmth of my own, I stroked the soft, velvety skin with the pad of my thumb. "You're so beautiful, Gran. I imagine grandpa still has to beat off any would-be suitors."

Vivid cornflower blue eyes sparkled as gran laughed heartily. "Oh, you're such a sweet girl. Anyway, you're one to talk." She twisted in her seat, raking ageing eyes over my blushing face.

"You're radiant, Teddy. What, or should I say whom is responsible for this glowing demeanour?"

"Don't badger the girl, Violet; she's only just walked in the door." Grandpa McGovern lovingly winked, bending down to smother me with one of his bear hugs.

The scent of wood, citrus and nutmeg drifted. I closed my eyes, breathing him in. Just like the man, grandpa's hugs were always demonstrative of his warmth and devotion to his family.

"Hello, Grandpa."

His denim blue eyes twinkled, peering down at me. "Gran's right; you do look different. Don't you agree with me, Vivienne?"

Oh boy. I inhaled sharply, bracing myself for one of my nan's wicked answers.

"It's probably a boy, meaning she has gotten laid recently."

"Nan!" My face flamed like a beacon, signifying she was right on the money.

"Must you always be so crude, Mother?" my mother admonished, gracefully seating herself beside nana on the matching sofa and crossing her legs. Acting like a lady didn't necessarily mean you were one.

Nan's hands raised off her lap as slim shoulders elegantly draped in an emerald-green silk scarf over a black blouse shrugged. Her amused gaze stared at her daughter. "Why must you always act so self-righteous?"

Whenever the time arose, Vivienne Burgoyne never behaved as a lady should and always shot straight to the point. Nor had she let the fact she was in her eighties define her. She regularly acted as if she was still in her teens. Her cropped, fiery red hair was now a darker auburn, not the salt and pepper I knew it to be underneath. Unlike her daughter's cold gaze, nan's bright green eyes had a warmth I found endearing. Loving. I just loved that she never sugar-coated anything, likewise, her husband, my beloved poppy, Benjamin.

After having heard the eloquent comment, his laughter roared, earning a deathly glare from his stick in the arse daughter.

"You don't help either, Dad. You need to pull her into line more often."

Benjamin Burgoyne was a stoic man, and characteristically, not too much ruffled his feathers. However, when it came to his daughter, they usually required a prolific shaking. Like now for instance. His hazel eyes sternly gazed at her, and his spine stiffened, adding height to his six-foot-one frame, showing he wasn't about to bow down to her either.

"Why would I want to do that? That's half the reason I love her, and I wouldn't change a damned thing. Maybe if you removed that stick from your backside, you could be more like your mother."

I hid my smirk behind my hand; it was good to know my pop shared the same sentiment.

"I'm perfectly happy with the way I am," my mother tersely responded, shooting cold daggers in Scarlett's and my direction. "Girls! Refrain from laughing as it only encourages your grandmother."

Mother's long-time housekeeper, Katrina, suddenly appeared at the edge of the living room to stiffly inform us dinner was about to be served before swiftly retreating to the safe confines of the kitchen.

When Scarlett realised our brother was notably absent, she turned to mother and haughtily questioned her, "And where is Abel? Wasn't he supposed to join us as well? It is a family dinner, after all."

Mother inauspiciously glared at her. "Watch your tone."

Unperturbed by her sternness, my sister's chin lifted defiantly. "Teddy and I made it on time, what makes him so special?"

I had to bite down the bubbling giggle before it erupted. My sister had some big brass balls standing up to our mother and calling her out; I give her that.

But shocking us all, was the lack of customary bite from mother.

Instead, she calmly and elegantly rose from the sofa, sharing with us a rare smile that fleetingly thawed her cold gaze at the mere mention of her beloved son. "Abel was held up at the office and shall be here momentarily."

Only I would choose the wrong moment to look at my nan. Her eyes rolled, evoking yet another fit of giggles. And where would I be without earning another deathly glare from my mother? I laughed even harder.

Abel showed up just as Katrina cleared the entrées, and certainly knew how to make his presence known. Mother's gushing only encouraged him. She, of course, was the first to greet him. With a gaze so full of pride, her hug was warm and affectionate, producing quite the sour taste in my mouth. Then, who wouldn't feel that way after watching such an open display of affection, when that's all I'd ever yearned for, and denied my whole life.

"Look who's here everyone, my gorgeous son, Abel, and he came bearing flowers, too. You're the best son a mother could ask for." Somebody, please grab me a bucket.

"Aw, thanks, Mum," he murmured, pressing his lips to her cheek while laying a considerably sized bouquet of mixed posies in her arms.

Suckhole.

"Thank you, my darling; they're simply divine." Her ordinarily cold green eyes sparkled like newly cleaned emeralds, more so as her adoring gaze trailed after him around the table. As he handed out two smaller bouquets to our grandmothers, she proudly observed and smiled as he used his wiles to charm them just the same.

Our father, who he ignored, was nowhere near as charmed. Nor was he smiling. Instead, he remained indifferent and rose his eyes towards the decoratively plastered ceiling, all the while refilling his tumbler with more scotch. I noticed even if no one else did. It broke my heart. Oh, dad.

Abel's hand landed on my shoulder, giving it a soft squeeze. I ignored him and his gesture. My refusal to acknowledge my absentee brother enraged my mother, resulting in her vitriol.

"Theodora! Show some manners for once in your life! Say hello to your brother!"

Setting my wine glass down with a thud, I glowered at her before twisting at the waist and looking up at the broad six-foot frame looming over me. "Hello, brother, long time and most definitely no see."

"Theodora! I won't tell you again!"

Abel's pleading gaze briefly cut to our annoying mother. He held up a hand. "It's fine. I can handle her."

"Her? I have a name, you know!"

"Yes, you do – *it's Theodora.*" Knowing I hated my name, mother smirked at me from across the table. Bitch. Then out of my peripheral, I viewed Abel waving a hand politely asking her to stop. Astonishingly, she listened.

Hazel eyes mirroring mine peered down at me. "Hey, sis, I know we haven't caught up much of late, but once the current acquisition I'm working on is secured, I'll be sure to pencil you in some time after that."

"Okay, you be sure to ring me when you're free, then I'll be sure to squeeze you into my busy life," I grimly replied turning my back on him, consequently resulting in another castigation from my mother.

"Don't get on Abel's back about making time, Theodora! He's an extremely busy man building an empire." Another adoring smile passed her lips as Abel slid into the seat explicitly reserved beside her. "And you're doing an amazing job, my darling."

My eyes rolled in defiance. I had every intention of defending myself, but as nan's hand gently squeezed mine, my head swivelled, ready to argue the point. Her head shook imperceptibly, and her eyes silently pleaded with me, indicating it wasn't worth the argument.

I let out a sullen sigh and mouthed, "Okay."

Patting my hand, she mouthed a thank you before redirecting the conversation on to another subject. Something more positive, as in my newly discovered relationship. Of course, she would.

"So, what's the name of the young man who has you smiling so radiantly, Teddy?"

Gran winked across the table. I blushed under her perceptive gaze.

"How'd you know?" I feigned innocence, sawing into the grilled lamb backstrap Katrina had just placed in front of me. I lifted the fork to my mouth and chewed, savouring the combined flavours of rosemary and mint. Mmm, flavoursome.

"I wore that exact expression when I began dating your grandfather, Benjamin, sixty years ago, and still do. Every day I count my blessings, as I go to bed each night, and as I wake up each morning beside the love of my life." Blissfully, she gazed over the table at her handsome husband quietly popping a forkful of steamed butter beans into his mouth. "I love that man with every fibre of my being."

I glanced down at my plate and hesitantly replied, ".... I'm dating Ari Jaeger."

Nan pressed a hand over her heart and gushed loudly, "About bloody time!" Her excitement earned yet another glare from my mother. I seriously wanted to poke my tongue out at her.

I refrained and reached for my wine glass, bringing it to my lips. "Only just though. Ari's the most amazing man I've ever known." Taking a quick sip, I glanced over the rim at my mother and pointedly said, "He at least treats me with nothing but kindness and respect."

Finely plucked eyebrows raised above a soulless gaze as she delicately scraped the tiniest piece of meat onto her fork and silently popped it between thin lips. Her teeth bared as she tightly scraped it clean. I had gotten to her.

Nan shrewdly grabbed my hand. "Look at me, child," she calmly whispered, unwittingly subduing me. My instinct naturally made me obey. I smiled softly with nan producing a dazzling smile in return. "Good girl." And just like that, nan kept the conversation flowing positively with the attention firmly on me.

"Ari Jaeger, eh? He's quite the catch, and if I recall, you two have held a torch for one another since you were children." Nan chuckled, waving the fork in her hand at me. "Yeah, don't think I haven't noticed the fleeting glances between you two over the years; it was hot!"

I choked on my wine. "That's a slight exaggeration, Nan. Although, if Ari were here, he'd agree wholeheartedly, and love every second of my suffering."

My father listened intently, his head nodding in approval. He then proceeded to add his own opinion, "Ari Jaeger's a lovely young man, and he'll be good for you, Teddy. He's driven, with a successful business and he at least comes from a *decent* family."

Granted, I understood the dig, but I bristled and made a point of correcting him, "No, Dad, we're good for each other. And with the way Ari's talking, we have a bright future ahead of us."

Nan lovingly interjected, "Ari sounds as if he makes you very happy, dear, and for that, I'm immensely pleased as is your grandfather, aren't we, Benji?"

Pausing his chewing long enough to speak, he gave me one of his famously lopsided smiles. "Of course, we couldn't be happier for you, darling."

My gaze briefly darted over at my mother. She too, paid attention, an interest I found highly unusual. Picking up her wine glass, she took a delicate sip before setting the glass back down. Her long fingers stroked the stem as painted lips curled into a cruel smile.

"Don't get too far ahead of yourself, Theodora. It might not last forever, as I'm certain Ari has many women chasing after him, ones who are much more suitable no doubt."

My fists clenched around my cutlery and hit the tabletop, making everyone jump. "You can't be happy for me, can you, Mother? Are you so damned miserable with your own life, you need to ridicule mine? You destroyed my life once before, and I'll be damned if I ever let you do it again! Just stay the fuck away from me you heartless bitch!" Around the table, jaws dropped, and unbidden tears sprung.

The room suddenly grew too small. I had to leave. Robotically, I pushed to my feet and stalked off. With the exception of my grandparent's and my sister, I had to escape the toxic company that was my family.

Nan typically jumped to my defence, the fury in her voice echoing as I froze in the foyer and eavesdropped on the tense argument unfolding.

"Really, Therese, do you have a constant need to feed your over bulging ego by putting Teddy down? She has found some real happiness with a man she's known and loved her entire life, and you just had to pull the rug out from under her. No amount of words can describe how I truly feel about you at this moment. And what did she mean, about you destroying her life?"

I slowly lifted my jacket off the hook, my body sagging as I sighed heavily; oh, nan, I thought you knew.

"Pay no mind to Theodora's belligerence, Mother...." That stung.

"Now that's enough!" My father irately bellowed. At whom though? "I've utterly had it!"

"For goodness sake, Evan, find some balls, if you still own any that is!" I quietly sniggered at the spiteful dig. "And for goodness sake, stand up to your bloody wife. The girls bear the brunt of your wife's unnecessary badgering while Abel continually sails through with a free pass! Quite frankly, my dear daughter, I've had enough! Benjamin, we are leaving!" Nan shouted sternly. "Violet, Barrett," she addressed gran and grandpa in a softened tone, "I apologise terribly for my outburst."

"Vivienne, please, there's no need. You stood up for our granddaughter and for that, I applaud you. A mother shouldn't ever throw such disparaging words, particularly at her children." Grandpa barely masked the grief in his voice. His distress rapidly switched to glacial as he turned on my father. "When you eventually come to your senses, Evan, only then may you see me – until then don't bother."

"Excuse me; I need some fresh air!" I heard my father's enraged voice, stomping feet and then a door slamming.

"Come on, Violet, we're also leaving, but I want to make sure my granddaughter is all right first. If she's still here that is."

"As do I. Goodbye children. And you..." Mother wasn't immune to grans wrath either. "How dare you treat my precious granddaughter in such a disgusting manner! She hasn't done a thing to earn such ire. I will never understand you, Therese, and frankly...I don't want to waste my energy trying to do so either; it's far too exhausting! Have a nice life!"

Having heard enough, I ran out the front door and over the dampened grass until I reached the large elm down the backyard, gulping in the chilly night air as grief-stricken sobs ruptured. How could my mother hate me so? What did I ever do to deserve her hatred? Why couldn't she just love me, in the same unconditional manner Audrina loved her children?

Amid the dropping temperature, the wind blew, bringing a chill and the strong stench of tobacco wafting through the air. I recognised the nutty scent of my father's cigar. A scent I once loved, but now it repulsed me.

Head down, and arms crossed over his chest, his back leaned against the stone wall of the house. A shadowy figure beneath the dim lights, he sucked on his cigar as if his life depended on it for the air to breathe.

I tentatively walked towards him. "Dad, are you okay?"

"Now's not the time!" He couldn't even bring himself to look at me and shook his head, dismissing me with a flick of the hand. Typical of him really, choosing self-preservation over reconciliation.

Between him and my mother, neither batted an eyelid if it meant letting someone else take the fall for their mistakes. I just happened to be the scapegoat who always got caught in the crosshairs.

Nothing ever changed.

Unable to mask the brewing agony felt by his rejection, I screamed, "When is it ever?"

"I'm sorry..." Regret fell over his entire demeanour, but I wasn't buying the act of contrition — not this time.

"Your apology means jack-shit to me, *Dad!*" I bolted towards the car with my father's hastened steps on my heels.

"Teddy!"

"Fuck off!"

He faltered, his mortified gaze staring after me as I jumped into the car and slammed the door. I briefly glanced in the rear-view mirror as I turned the key in the ignition and began to reverse. Guilt etched his face. He hadn't cared, so why should I?

I took off at high speed, leaving both my father and my distraught grandparents nothing more than a blur in my rearview mirror. The night had turned out to be the disaster I'd initially predicted. Emphatically finished was the relationship with my mother, as was the one with my father. Between the pair of them, they had both successfully destroyed whatever piece of me I'd had left.

My car roared down dimly lit streets until I reached my house and came to a screeching halt in the driveway. I rushed inside, running into my bedroom where I began ripping clothes off their hangers, shoving as much as I possibly could inside the numerous bags I'd flung across the floor. If I'd forgotten anything, then too bad. In a matter of what seemed like minutes, I was driving away without the faintest as to where I was headed. Anywhere had to be better than home.

My fingers gripped the steering wheel as my indecisive gaze glanced out the windscreen deciding whether to bother Ari or not. My heart clenched. I desperately wanted to run into his arms, if only it weren't for my body's refusal to cooperate. As was the fact he appeared to be busy. Clearly on the phone, I watched as he paced the living room floor above his semi-subterranean garage. His frustration with the caller evident as he ran a hand through his wayward hair.

But there was a reason behind me landing at Ari's; I needed him. His love consoled me, more than playing the piano, more than….

With that in mind, I slowly climbed from the car and trod up to the front door, the end of my forefinger hesitantly stabbing the doorbell. A charming and melodious sound rang through the house alerting Ari to my presence, his footsteps thudding across the floors as he made his way to the front door. Panic rose, forcing me to change my mind.

"No, no, this is wrong. I can't do this to Ari," I mumbled dolefully before rushing back to the car.

∞

Ari

OPENING THE SOLID TIMBER and glass panelled door wide, I craned my neck perusing the garden for whoever rang the doorbell. Huh, odd, nobody there. I looked beyond the lush palm trees and sitting in the driveway was a metallic blue Captiva, giving me my answer. Why hadn't Teddy waited for me to answer the door?

Curious, I hurried down the steps, and taking one look at her blotched face, my heart sank. What in the devil had happened at her mother's to leave her in such a distressed state?

I slowly opened the car door, and the minute I slid a compassionate arm around her shaking shoulders, the dam burst.

"Teddy, what's wrong? What has you this upset?" She collapsed straight into my arms, her battle-weary body sagging against my chest. I wrapped a hand around her head and rocked her gently. "How about we go inside, eh?"

Wordlessly, she nodded.

"I'll grab your bags later. We can't have you running around naked, can we?" I joshed, closing the door. Not even a smile cracked. "It sounds like I need to work on my jokes." Crushing my lips to her forehead, I clasped her cold hand in mine and led her inside.

I led her to the large sofa in my living room. Too exhausted to argue, she flopped her shivering body against the warmth of mine. My arms enveloping her as my cheek flattened against the glossy mane trailing around her slender shoulders. Coconut and jasmine drifted, reminding me of balmy nights and tropical islands.

As I made a move to switch the music off, Teddy quietly mumbled, "No, leave it...I love this song..."

I gave a gentle nod and increased the volume fractionally. Van Morrison's, These are the Days soothing voice filled the air, lulling her into a sense of calm. Ever so gently, my fingers trailed in a gentle caress up and down her spine, the comforting gesture wilting her further into me. With her head fallen against my shoulder, her breathing altered, blowing evenly and lightly on my neck.

I cocked my head, taking in the puffiness and the dark circles surrounding her closed eyes, indicating she was indeed exhausted. Whilst stroking her head, she snuggled in even further. Sleeping in my lap couldn't be that comfortable, surely.

Somehow, I managed to rise off the sofa and carry her upstairs, gently placing her on my bed all without disturbing her. Getting her undressed, that was an entirely different challenge, expressly as she curled up into a tight little ball. Having at least removed her ankle boots, I pulled the quilted blanket up from the end of the bed and bent down, stroking the silky strands of her hair. "Sleep well, my love," I whispered, pressing a soft kiss to her temple before quietly slipping from the room and heading downstairs. I had a phone call that required my urgent attention.

No wonder Teddy was beside herself. Dealing with Therese as a mother was like walking through a minefield – a mind fuck. How Teddy survived her childhood without cracking, I never understood. Me, on the other hand, would've lost it years ago.

The Arctic Monkey's blared, my fists pummelling the bag hanging from the rafters in my pool house with Therese's poisonous words the driving force behind each hit.

I always ran with the belief that mothers were meant to be kind, loving, and reasonably fair. Whom was I kidding? Besides Abel, her only son, Therese's maternal instincts were seriously flawed.

For years, my family was always consciously aware of the strained relationship between mother and daughter; yet I never imagined it to be this troubled. In a roundabout fashion, Teddy had warned me about her past over the weekend, and foolishly, I'd shrugged her unease off. Most people had a history they weren't proud of, then again, at that point and time, I was far too enamoured to bother with delving any deeper.

I managed a chuckle; talking was not on either of our agendas, at all.

The Teddy I knew and grew up with hadn't ever tolerated bullies. So, what had changed? I was clueless, and that bothered me above all else.

I tugged the gloves from my hands and threw them down, collecting a hand towel on the way out the door. I roughly wiped my face, my anger simmering as my determination grew. Teddy, however, was going to have to reveal all at some stage, but in failing that, I'd discover the underlying cause of the well-guarded secret plaguing our future one way or another, even if it killed me.

13

Evan

IN THE WAKE OF our so-called family dinner, Therese had remained cold and aloof. Any words uttered were only to berate our daughter Teddy for supposedly causing the divide in our family, yet again.

She stood eerily quiet in the middle of our bedroom, observing as I packed my bags. Revealing her anxiety was the constant twisting of her fingers through the set of antique double-stranded pearls hanging around her long slender neck.

I briefly peered up at her. Gone was the vivacious beauty that had once captured my heart. At one time, she had been my best friend, my soul mate, and now she was nothing more than a stranger. Any trace of that everlasting love once felt had also sadly vanished.

Ready for a fight, Therese finally spoke, breaking the awkward silence between us. That was old news, like her. "Thanks to your precious daughter's selfishness, poor Abel was forced to drop Scarlett home. Typical."

"And I'm sure it was such a hassle," I responded sarcastically.

Therese had resented Teddy from the moment she was born. To the point, she refused any chance to bond and screamed at the midwives for even daring to suggest she breastfed our newborn daughter. Therese had happily breastfed Abel; feeding her was supposedly a no-brainer. Rejecting them and her, Therese put Teddy straight on the bottle.

Rather than waste the opportunity, with every feed, nappy change or even just for a cuddle, I took it upon myself to care for our infant daughter. She was a daddy's girl through and through. My sweet, innocent little girl had me wrapped around her tiny pinkie from day dot, and I'd cherished every damned minute with her.

Whereas with our son, Therese never allowed us the chance to bond. Over the years, I tried and failed to discipline Abel for misbehaving; she overrode that, too, causing unwarranted conflict. Resigned a relationship with my only son would never eventuate, I ensured I focused solely on our daughter's needs instead. Someone had to.

Two years later, Therese's personality had transformed, and not for the better either; she was colder, harder, and more distant than previous years. Asking became futile. I was brushed off and told that Teddy was a disruptive child. Another outright lie, leading me to conclude that it had something to do with her sister's sudden disappearance. Again, whenever I broached the subject, she just brushed me off. In the end, I stopped caring.

Shortly after, she became pregnant with Scarlett, making me genuinely believe our marriage was back on track. However, that proved to be a lie the day Scarlett was born. She'd screamed God was punishing her by giving her another daughter and not another son. Understanding any of her ramblings was pointless. Not that I'd bothered asking either, I was too smitten with our newborn daughter, another fiery redhead screaming her little lungs out until I held her.

Both girls' were lucky enough to have their nanny, Alice, growing up; a warm, loving woman who'd had a hand in helping me raise them. Deprived of attention and affections by their mother, Alice lavished them with it. She kindly stayed on in my employ until Scarlett finished high school and had remained in constant contact ever since, sending birthday and Christmas cards faithfully every year. Gifts my girls' cherished immeasurably to this very day.

My heart often broke for my daughters', leading me to question why Therese wanted more children when it was apparent, she didn't love them, or me for that matter. Among other reasons, my girls' were the only reason I chose to stay in a loveless marriage. But after witnessing the hurt on Teddy's face during the evening's events, I had an epiphany. I had cruelly rejected her as equally as her mother had all these years. Well, no more.

"I want a divorce," I bluntly informed Therese. "I should have asked for one ten years ago when you sunk lower than a snake's belly by betraying our family, all for you to save face."

Therese gripped the strand of pearls a little tighter. Her one fear was becoming a reality, and it showed, flashing across her face as I trekked back and forth to the wardrobe. Having been married for thirty years, I was bound to know every little quirk and expression.

"You won't leave, Evan..."

Casting her a veiled glance, I disregarded her dig and marched into the bathroom and back out again.

A malicious smirk crossed her beautiful face. "...You don't have the guts."

Having had enough of her badgering, I exhaled sharply and dumped my toiletries into a bag before letting my anger fly, "Won't I? What am I doing now then, Therese? I'm not packing for a fucking holiday, am I?" Throwing whatever remained into the open suitcases spread over the end of our king-sized bed, I growled, "I should've done this a long time ago, and like an idiot, I stayed believing you loved our family and me enough. But that's not true, is it? Answer me dammit!"

She remained tight-lipped, barely flinching at my raised voice. Ignorance was bliss in her eyes.

"That's what I thought. It's about keeping up appearances with you; love be damned!" I savagely snarled. Zipping up the bags, I took off down the stairs with a simmering Therese closely following.

"Go on and leave! You'll come crawling back soon enough once your whore has grown tired of you."

Ignoring her rantings, I reached for the door handle.

"And I'm sure your beloved daughters' will have you..." she sneered, in a miserable attempt to antagonise me further. ".... Until the moment they learn the truth about you that is."

My spine stiffened. I dropped the bags at the door and spun around, my strides long and fierce as I stormed up the stairs, pausing at the step below my wary wife. "That's pot calling the kettle black, don't you think, Therese?" Deliberately, I kept my voice low and calm, unnerving her. Therese clung to the timber railing and paled. "Yeah, that's what I figured."

I scolded her further, "Why do you hate the girls' so much? Apart from not being more sons, what crime have they committed for you to despise them so much, specifically Teddy, huh? What did she ever do to you, for you to treat her with such contempt?"

Therese took an involuntary step back, her heel catching on the steps edge. Cold, soulless eyes glared down at me. "She was such an attention seeker, and never once was she grateful, no matter what I did for her. For her and this family," she retorted, her voice trembling. "You won't ever understand."

Astounded, I gaped. "What in the hell are you rambling on about woman? You never did a thing to help our daughter! Expressly at a time when she needed a mother and some goddamn support, but as usual, you refused her. By sweeping everything under the fucking carpet, your selfishness ended up augmenting her suffering!"

Therese lifted her chin defiantly. "Well, if she hadn't spread her legs like a little whore..."

She swiftly closed her mouth as I scowled and rose another step, my wringing hand gripping the handrail tightly. Keeping my emotions in check was growing harder by the second.

"Teddy never was and isn't a whore," I growled forcefully. "You're such a conceited bitch. You would rather others presume the worst of our daughter while you parade around acting like you are nothing less than perfect. Well, let me tell you some cold hard truths: you are far from perfect, and all you've ever done is inflict pain, damaging our daughter beyond repair. God knows how much, and by the looks of Teddy's face tonight – I would say a fucking lot!"

Her upper lip curled. "Don't be so dramatic, Evan. She and I wouldn't have a problem if she quit acting like the world revolved around her. Fantasising about Ari Jaeger is something else your precious Theodora needs to stop; they won't last, and besides, he could do so much better."

"Well, that goes to show how little you know him. The only person you'll be hearing from now is my divorce attorney. Goodbye, Therese, have a nice life. Alone." I stalked back down the stairs and straight out the front door, not even bothering to close it behind me. What was the point of looking back?

∞

Teddy

EXHAUSTION AND MELANCHOLY, that cold dish my mother served up at dinner was my timely reminder as to why I found myself tangled up in Ari's bedsheets. That tiny glimmer of hope in my life who happened to be awake, and much to my dismay, wasn't even in the bed beside me. The cold sheets a sure sign he'd been up for some time already.

Sighing, I sat up and looked around the spacious master suite. Darkly stained furniture blended with black and grey tones, the style lacked warmth. I had to question Ari about his decorator, whoever they were...they lacked taste.

Positioned above the king-sized bed was a pointlessly long narrow window with a white wall for a view. In saying that though, there was a glass sliding door to my left, which led to a small balcony occupied by two bright orange cane chairs. I frowned at the odd choice of colour on furniture that looked even less comfortable.

Curious about the rest of the room, I swung my feet to the floor, landing on soft, plush, charcoal grey carpet. The decorator got that right at least.

At the end of the room was a cavity door and sliding it open, I found a rather opulent ensuite bathroom. An egg-shaped stone bath sat under a bi-fold window in one corner while a double shower big enough to hold a party sat in the other. Situated between them was a floating timber vanity with two oval-shaped basins and matte black tapware. It was all...so modern. I inspected further, opening two more doors. One led to a separate toilet and the other a large walk-in-robe filled with Ari's expensive designer clothes and shoes.

My fingers glided over the array of suits hanging in the open racks and lifted one of the sleeves to my nose, inhaling the lingering cologne on the cuff deeply. Intoxicating.

I ventured back into the bedroom with the hope of searching out Ari, but the time on the bedside clock stopped me in my tracks. "Oh, crap! I'll be late for work!" Smacking my forehead, I sprinted back to the bathroom and quickly stripped.

I had barely worked out how to use the fancy taps on the wall and applied shampoo to my hair when Ari waltzed in wearing one of his razor-sharp grins.

He leaned against the bathroom sink, crossing both arms over a broad, naked chest. "You might as well enjoy your shower, Teddy; you're not going to work today."

Scrubbing hands stilled in my hair. "What? No, don't be ridiculous. I can't have a day off. I have to go to work," I murmured firmly. Standing under the water, I rinsed my hair thoroughly, subsequently applying a swift application of conditioner.

"I called Spencer, informing him you were sick."

Infuriation flared as I rinsed out the conditioner. "How dare you! And why would you take it upon yourself to presume what I need?"

I turned the water off and snatched the towel from his outstretched hand, speedily wrapping it around my dripping wet body. "I've never had a sick day in my life!" I spluttered, grabbing another towel from the towel rail. Bending forward, I swept my drenched hair upward, tucking in the end of the towel as I hurried past him into the bedroom.

"Work wasn't the right place for you today," Ari argued, following me and watching with avid fascination as I scrambled through the bags searching for underwear. I finally found a pair buried at the bottom and threw them onto the bed.

"You did, did you?" I asked, my agitation apparent. Not to Ari though.

He stroked his chin and wore a provocative gaze knowing full well it would leave me weak at the knees. He was deliberately taunting me so that I'd give in. Damn him, as appealing as it was, I didn't have time.

Then again, two could play at that game.

I turned around, my back facing Ari as I dropped the towel, giving him a full view of my behind. A low growl grumbled as I tugged a pink lacy thong up my legs, providing great satisfaction on my part. I snatched up the matching bra and slipped my arms through the straps. Only I ran into an issue as I attempted to connect the small clips at the back: so much for teasing him.

I twisted at the waist and glanced over my shoulder. "Do you mind, please?"

"With pleasure," he purred. Once he'd snapped my bra together, Ari patted my back and grinned. "There, all safe and secure. No chance of black eyes today!"

Unimpressed by the little joke, I glowered.

"Sorry," he whispered amidst his futile attempt to stifle the bubbling laughter with his fist.

My eyes narrowed, returning to the subject at hand. "I need to work, Ari. My job keeps me sane."

"Oh, I thought I was the prime reason?" He was so cute when he pouted. Gliding his arms around my waist, he persisted with his conquest, "Teddy?"

I sighed in exasperation. "Yes...you also keep me sane. Compared to you, work keeps me distracted in an entirely different manner."

"So, how do I distract you, Theodora?"

At the sound of my full name, my body stiffened. "Please don't call me Theodora, I hate it." Pushing out of his grasp, I resumed my search for my clothes.

"Sorry, I didn't realise," he apologised, his voice etched with regret. Then he switched tactics, making me smile. "So, Teddy, how do I distract you?" Looming closer, his voice took on an intimate tone. Fingertips skated along my spine, the light touch leaving me a quivering mess, and he knew it too. The smirk on his face spoke volumes.

I straightened and twirled, placing my hands on my hips. My chin lifted, challenging him. "You're not letting up, are you?"

He shook his head and mouthed; "No." That scorching gaze would be the death of me.

Laughing humourlessly, I ran a finger down his naked chest. Ari hissed from the bite of my sharpened fingernail as it scraped his sternum. "All right then, if that's how you want to play, I'll bite." An indulgent smile formed on both our lips. "You distract me completely. With your voice, your touch...your sex," I purred, aligning my body with his. Desire soared as the bulge inside his shorts twitched against my lower belly.

"I have no idea what you mean." Ari's hand slipped around the nape of my neck, holding me to him as he ardently crashed our lips, awakening the beast within.

"You'll need another shower..." Ari snickered smugly, propping himself up on his elbow and drawing patterns over my bare back with the tips of his fingers.

"I know," I hummed, my face turned away from him on the pillow. "You don't have to act so damned gleeful about it."

He chuckled. "Believe me; it's not an act. Are you annoyed that I successfully distracted you with my sex?"

"Yes," I grumbled.

"Are you complaining, because if you hadn't noticed – we're currently starkers, and there's not anywhere on my body that's deemed appropriate enough for me to store a pen and paper so I can write it down," he playfully murmured, leaning over me, his warm breath blowing gently on my cheek.

"That's not funny. I'm supposed to be at work, not lounging around like Lady Muck!"

"What's the problem with that?" Ari sidled up closer and attempted to kiss my cheek. I pushed away from him.

"I may have my inheritance money, but I still have to work."

"Why? It's not as if you have a mortgage to worry about."

Rolling over and reclining against the pillows, I glowered. "Irrespective of whether I do or not, that money won't last forever."

"It can if it's invested correctly," he countered as I swatted his wandering hands away from my bouncing breasts.

"It is. My father made sure of it," I sourly replied. Realising how contradictory I sounded, I produced another excuse. "But unlike you, I don't have access to millions of dollars to fall back on."

Darkening eyes narrowed. "So, what if I do. Am I supposed to feel guilty for my success and apologise for it? I still have a business to run to earn that money. But if I want to take a day off to take care of you, I certainly won't apologise for that either."

"I never asked you to take the day off to babysit me. I can take care of myself like I've always had to, and working hard proves that to people," I muttered quietly.

Ari sat upon his knees, running both hands over his face. "By people, you mean your mother?" he scoffed. "By all accounts, her opinion's worthless."

"You don't understand. Again, unlike you, I've never had the luxury of growing up in this picture-perfect family that led a charmed life. You don't ever need to prove yourself to anybody; the least of all your parents. They approve of anything you do." Swiping the falling tears from my face, I struggled to hide the sorrow in my voice. "About the house, I didn't want it. My grandparents insisted upon it, probably as a means to an end – an insurance to buy my silence." The second those words left my mouth, I wanted to slap myself, knowing they weren't aware and hadn't ever been.

Jet-black brows creased. "What do you mean, silence you? Why would they need to, Teddy? Your grandparents adore you."

"Forget what I said!" I rushed off the bed and clambered to get dressed. "I can't tell you why, and I...I shouldn't have said anything," I stammered sliding a pair of skinny white jeans up my legs, followed by the one-shouldered mint green sweater I swiftly threw over my head.

Jumping out of bed and tugging on a pair of shorts, Ari rapidly rounded the bed and tugged me into his arms.

Hysterical, I fought him off. "No, please don't."

Crestfallen by my rejection, his arms dropped to his side. He watched on helplessly as I gathered and shoved the few belongings I'd dragged out back into the bags.

An anguished Ari pushed. "Why won't you talk to me, Teddy? You undoubtedly came here for that reason. Tell me what's going on with you!" He questioned when he shouldn't.

I threw down a pair of tan flats to the floor, shoving my feet into them — quite the balancing act when you're in a hurry. "I can't! I have to think about our families."

Ari's anger swelled. "You're speaking in riddles, and what the fuck do our families have to do with anything?"

Zipping up the bags, I sighed despondently. "Ari, trust me when I say the cost to our families would be enormous. Not only that, if you knew, the repulsion you'd feel touching me again..."

He was ready to explode, and I had to leave before he did.

"Don't assume to know what I want. Whatever *'it'* is, we'll work it out together, no matter how bad; I thought I made that abundantly clear only recently when you tried to break up with me the first time?"

Slinging the weighty bags over my shoulders, I stepped towards the bedroom door. Fresh tears spilt. "It's best that I go. I love you, Ari, but I'm sorry, I can't share with you." Pivoting on my heel, I ran down the stairs and out the front door.

Ari wasn't far behind, yelling at me in frustration, "Stop shutting me and everyone else out!"

I opened the car door and threw the bags onto the back seat.

"Scarlett at least had the decency to explain to me about last night's epic dinner at your mother's!"

The pit of my stomach dropped. Slamming the door shut, I spun around. Blazing eyes glared as we faced off. "Well, if you already know, then why are you trying to force my hand? Especially if my big mouth sister has already told you everything?"

"For goodness sake, Teddy, stop with this martyr act, and let me in!" Ari desperately shouted as I climbed into my car and drove out of his life.

14

I HAD BARELY MOVED onto the freeway when my dash lit up. It was Ari. Again. For the third time, I ignored him as slow falling tears turned into full-blown sobs, swiftly forcing me off the road. Other vehicles sped past in a hazy blur rocking my car.

What had I done? Mother was right; he was too good for me.

Gripping the steering wheel tightly, I howled loudly. No one else could hear me, nor could anyone see me, or so I thought.

A firm, startling tap to the window disturbed my pitiful cries, compelling me to lift my head. I took one look and gulped. Oh, crap. A tall, burly police officer stood beside the driver's side door, his peaked officer's hat slung low. Just not low enough to conceal his hard, steely gaze. One that judged my ragged appearance; blotched face, dishevelled hair, I looked bloody beautiful.

Wiping my face with the sleeves of my sweater, I pushed the button in my door, rolling down the window. I gazed sheepishly and squeaked, "Yes, Officer?"

"Is there any reason you're pulled over in the emergency lane, Miss?" he gruffly questioned. Intimidated, I shrunk against the seat.

"I was upset and didn't want to cause an accident," I nervously admitted in a small voice.

His unblinking gaze eyed me suspiciously. "Can I see your driver's licence please?"

"Y...yes," I stammered, reaching for my purse and fumbling as my fingers slipped tugging my licence from the snug pocket. I shakily handed it to him.

He glanced back and forth studiously studying the embarrassing photo. After much deliberation and ensuring it was, in fact, me, the stoic Sergeant strolled back towards the black unmarked police vehicle parked behind me. Blue and red lights flashed inside the dash, indicative of my shame for every other driver cruising past.

As I patiently waited for him to complete the necessary checks, a much younger officer ambled around my car, checking for any visible defects; good luck finding any on my baby, buddy. As the dashing constable walked past my window, he offered a friendly, sincere dimpled smile, making my heart lurch.

Deep brown eyes twinkled, reminding me too much of Ari's gorgeous dark chocolate gaze; one he gave me unconditionally. One that had my knees trembling when we ached for one another. The one he –

The Sergeant reappeared at my window, startling me once again. "I'll let you off with a warning today, Miss McGovern. Next time you may not be so lucky," he warned, handing me my licence back. "Just out of curiosity, where were you headed?"

"Phillip Island, to my parent's holiday home in Cowes," I answered, sliding my licence inside my purse pocket.

"Good beach fishing there." The slightest of smiles appeared on his stern face before finally waving me off. "Have a safe trip."

I offered up my best smile and thanked him. Thanked him for what, catching me in a less than pleasant moment? Blowing out an unsteady breath, I restarted the car and carefully merged back into the flowing traffic. A speeding ticket or an accident would've just topped my already shitty day off.

Then I continued my morose journey to hell.

Taking a little over two hours of more tears and singing to songs which made me feel worse, not better, I finally made it to Cowes. No matter what was happening in my life, the island house always remained my go-to place.

I climbed from the car and stood on the lushly green lawn closing my eyes slowly as I deeply inhaled the fresh, salty sea air. The feel of the gusty breeze as it whipped my hair around my face, I relished in. My ears pricked at the sound of the roaring waves splashing along the shoreline and the annoying squawk of the seagulls hovering high above me. My lips quirked. "God, that's beautiful."

I opened my eyes and gazed up at the enormous double-storey. Situated on a double hillside block, the Hamptons inspired house with its beachy appearance fitted its environment rather well really. With uninterrupted views of the vast, open ocean from the first-floor windows and the wrap-around balcony, it was one of the more stunning homes on the street.

My favourite pastime whenever I visited the island was watching each wave build momentum, and finally crashing into the shoreline, its foaming water dispersing across the sand and quickly receding for the process to repeat itself. During a storm, it was even more spectacular.

To me, it was as if the ocean was singing a lullaby, a siren's call from the deep, sending me into a trance. Mother had once mocked me for even suggesting such a ridiculous notion. Regardless of how she viewed my ideals, that's how I felt.

Afterwards, I'd run up the beach to explore the shoreline or the rock pools where I'd eagerly take great delight in my discoveries.

Over the years, I had accumulated quite the collection, filling jar upon jar to the brim with the various items I scooped up. One find, in particular, had my father less than thrilled and nearly gave him a heart attack. I was a child, how was I supposed to know a blue ringed octopus was deadly? He swiftly acted, returning the angry little sucker to the rock from which it had crawled out of, possibly in the hope that I'd never find him again.

Grabbing my bags off the backseat, I moseyed up a brick-paved path past impeccably manicured gardens to the porch. As soon as I opened the front door, a warmth enveloped me. Thankfully, I'd called ahead, requesting clean sheets and for someone to switch on the ducted heating. It was far too cold not to have it on. I'd say they'd given the place a once over also, gathering by the lingering scent of the citrus furniture spray.

I made my way up the darkly stained stairs with white risers to the first floor, to the primary suite. My parent's hadn't visited the house in months, and probably wouldn't be anytime soon, so why not?

Dropping the bags to the floor, I moseyed back to the kitchen to find what there was in the way of food for me to eat. Apart from a bag of frozen peas and ice cubes, both the fridge and freezer were basically empty. The butler's pantry was equally lacklustre with nothing more than a few non-perishables on the shelves. The thought of going shopping wasn't overly appealing but living on takeaway for a week was less so. Food shopping it was.

I opened a drawer in the small study nook in the corner of the kitchen and pulled out a notepad and a pen, jotting down the basics for a start. Ari's sultry voice suddenly jumped into my head, reminding me of why I loved him so.

"Are you complaining, because if you hadn't noticed – we're currently starker's, and there's not anywhere on my body that's deemed appropriate enough for me to store a pen and paper so I can write it down."

Tears pricked the backs of my eyes. I missed him so much, yet, as much as it saddened me, deep down, breaking up with him was the right decision. I added wine to the shopping list; if I planned on being miserable for the next few days, I might as well be drunk.

Considering it was the off-season, the streets of Cowes were unpredictably busy. A few new boutiques had opened only recently, too, allowing me to indulge in my favourite diversion. Not that I needed to buy new dresses, they were something I had aplenty. Emotional shopping, Poppy called it, making me laugh. Even if it was little, it was a laugh, nonetheless.

Speaking of Poppy, she clearly had ESP. She'd tried calling me, several times, probably to rake me over the coals again. I simply wasn't in the mood for a reprimanding, by anyone. Although, I got the feeling if I didn't answer soon, she would undoubtedly drive to Phillip Island just to put me over her knee. Little was she aware, I'd actually enjoy it.

My phone buzzed again. I braced myself, answering warily, "...Hi, Poppy, how are you?"

"Teddy! About time you answered; the girls' and I have been worried sick about you! Where are you? Why did you leave so suddenly? What's with you and Ari?" Poppy shouted, rapidly firing questions. I pulled the phone away from my ear, Christ; did she ever draw breath?

Cautiously, I set it back and began my explanation hoping it was enough to satisfy her, "I'm sorry, Poppy, I truly am, but I had no other choice but to escape the city for a while." Hearing Poppy sniffling on the other end, caused undeniable guilt on my part. "And you know Cowes is the only place I can come and think clearly without any distractions." Or have anyone in my ear reminding me what a colossal disappointment I was.

"After Scarlett informed both Dominique and me about your mum's usual derogatory comments, I'm not surprised. She was downright unhappy about the entire episode." Poppy elicited a heavy sigh. "I simply can't comprehend what the problem is when it comes to you or your sister. I would end up in the nuthouse before figuring the great Therese McGovern out." She giggled, making me laugh.

"I'd be right alongside ya sister, causing chaos." I explained further, "Even dad was annoyed, not that it mattered – he turned away from me anyway." I chewed on my bottom lip, suppressing a sob. "I...I broke it off with Ari." As my face crumbled, I was grateful for my long locks curtaining my face and shielding me from the strange stares I appeared to be attracting.

"Oh dear; you didn't tell him, did you?"

Having heard the discontent in Poppy's voice, I cringed. "No, I lost my nerve," I glumly began, "I was so mad, more at myself than Ari, and rather than acting like the mature grownup I'm supposed to be, I behaved like a child and just took off. He looked heartbroken. If Ari didn't want me back, not now, not ever, I wouldn't blame him."

Poppy did her best to assure me, "You may find Ari will forgive you for just about anything."

"I doubt it." I scoffed. "Ari just kept pushing, wanting to know what was wrong. And knowing he had phoned Scarlett was the last straw, I snapped. I didn't want to talk about any of it, last night in particular."

"But why would you snap? You went to Ari, not for any other reason than you needed him, Teddy. That much is evident, and as for calling Scarlett, he did it out of concern. He cares deeply about you! Can't you see that?" Poppy barked. "He wants to help you!"

Hearing anger from my usually soft-spoken friend shocked me. Nevertheless, it wasn't enough to convince me otherwise. "I do see, Poppy, but if I start to go down that path, then that conversation leads into the conversation I'm trying to avoid with him. The chances of he and his family believing me are non-existent. They'll hate me, and then my mother shall take great delight in saying I told you so!" I argued forcefully.

"Teddy, stop! Stop right there! Your fears, your doubt...*is because of your mother*. They're her insecurities, not yours! So, stop your bullshit and be with someone who loves you unconditionally! You have earned the right to be happy for once in your goddamned life. Ari loves you desperately. If he didn't, he would have said a big fuck you and gone on his merry way. Instead, he came looking for you in the hope he'd find you at home..." she finished breathlessly.

Wiping tears away for the umpteenth time that day, I stilled in shock. "He did?"

"Yes, he did. He called me asking if I knew where you were after he'd stopped by the house."

A shuddering breath exhaled. "You're right. I do need to stop feeling sorry for myself, and before you say it; I need to stop listening to my mother's bullshit."

Poppy giggled down the phone. "Precisely! Now we're finally getting somewhere."

"Thank you, Poppy. I love you."

"I know. I love you, too. Now take care and mend those fences with Ari. He's heading to Cowes as we speak. You may feel better when you do. Until then, don't come home!" she instructed, giggling down the phone.

"Hey, it's my house," I protested.

"I know...but that's a moot point."

Laughing haughtily, I propped the pointed toe of my shoe on the bar of the trolley. "I promise to mend fences with Ari, but only so I can come back to my house."

"And all it took was a little prompting for you to see things my way." Poppy giggled. "See you when you both come home."

"Okay, bye, Poppy."

Pulling myself together enough to finish the shopping at least, I quickly wiped my face and ran down each aisle, throwing the last few items on my list into the trolley with a few added extras thrown in. Satisfied I had everything, I hit the checkouts.

Before driving out of the carpark, I gazed out the windscreen as a moment of hesitation hit me. What if revealing my past was a huge mistake and Ari decided I wasn't worth the trouble? The thought made me nauseous. But then again, what if he accepted every part of me, including my insecurities and my flaws? If he was making the trip to fight for me, the very least I could do was return the favour; the risk might be worth it.

I sped away with a renewed sense of hope.

A stab of disappointment hit me as I pulled up to the house. After Poppy informed me Ari was on his way, I genuinely believed he might've arrived by now. But the sleek Imperial blue BMW wasn't anywhere to be seen.

Maybe he'd decided to say a big fuck you after all.

Self-doubt kicked in, and as I trudged upstairs to the kitchen with my bags of shopping, and once more, those damned tears began to fall. How many tears could one person shed?

I dumped the bags on the island bench and started throwing my groceries onto the shelves inside the fridge. "Oh, for fuck's sake, just stop with the tears already!"

"Crying is meant to be good for the soul, or so I'm told."

The carton of eggs in my hand slipped and dropped at my feet, their bright yellow yolks and clear whites blending as they seeped from the box and spread over the darkly stained walnut floors. The care factor was zero as I stared at the love of my life standing in the middle of the dining room. He was with me. All that mattered was him as the shock wore off and I sprinted into his arms, clinging to him for dear life as if he was my life raft. Scratch that – he was my lifeline.

"Ari! Oh, my god. Forgive me, please?" His hands were in my hair, fisting handfuls as he held on tight and kissed me with identical enthusiasm, tasting the salty tears that coated my lips.

"Shh, please don't cry. There's nothing to forgive," he quietly assured, soothing me in between soft, languid kisses as he slowly moved to the sofa, gently sitting us down.

I shifted in his lap and let out a shuddering breath. "I didn't mean what I said. I have to explain...."

"Hey, shh," he quavered, caressing both sides of my head. "We can talk later, okay?"

"No, I need to explain." I inhaled a sharp breath. "It made for my best friend lecturing me to make me realise what an idiot I was for taking off without offering you an explanation. I behaved like a spoilt brat. I need you, Ari. Loving you is as easy as breathing; without you, I feel like I'm suffocating."

Ari crushed me to his chest and pressed a lingering kiss to my forehead. "You need to stop fighting us and whatever this issue is then. I'm not going anywhere. Ever," he affirmed cupping my cheek, his expression soft and full of love.

"I know I do. I also need to have more faith in you as well as trust." Gazing into warm, tender chocolate eyes, I leaned into him, listening as his heart thumped gently inside his chest. Ari was my balm, soothing me when nothing else could. "How did you get here by the way? I didn't see your flashy BMW parked anywhere."

He grinned. "By helicopter."

I giggled. "Now, why does that not surprise me?"

"Because you know me so well and how I operate," he pointed out, still grinning like a giddy schoolboy. "It was a much faster option than my speedster car, believe it or not. So, a friend of mine kindly gave me a lift when I explained the situation to him."

"What explanation was that?" I arched a curious brow. "Was it the 'I need to go and see my wacko girlfriend who's lost the plot' explanation?"

His head shaking, his chest rumbled with laughter. "No, I didn't give any explanation of the sort. I told him I was desperately in love with my gorgeous girlfriend, and she was distressed thanks to her bitch of a mother. Therefore, having heard my concern regarding your welfare, he happily obliged me."

"What a great friend." I smiled, chuffed by the lengths Ari took to rescue me. "But I'm beyond glad he gave you a lift. Otherwise, I'd be here all week, getting drunk while I ate shit food in my pyjama's feeling rather sorry for myself. The entire episode would've been entirely my fault anyway, not yours."

"No, I need to wear some of it, too," Ari disagreed, snaking his arms firmly around my waist and linking his fingers together. "I kept pushing when clearly, you're far from ready to share that part of your life with me. I wasn't overly understanding of the situation either. Instead, I behaved like a caveman." The corners of his mouth twitched. "See, I can admit to misbehaving when the occasion calls for it."

Patting his cheek, I laughed. "Aw, my little boy is finally growing up."

"Little boy, huh? Haven't we been over this 'little' scenario once before?" His eyes darkened. "I had better demonstrate how grown up I am then."

Oh boy, was I in trouble.

∞

Ari

WAITING FOR THE PINE kindling to catch, I tightened the blanket clinched around my waist and squatted. The logs I had lit eventually flared, bathing the living room in a muted light as orange flames crackled and glowed, dancing shadows over the soft grey walls.

Hearing Teddy's sated sigh, my head slowly turned. The serene sight of her limber body stretched across the chaise giving me cause to smile. Like me, she was rather content after an all too consuming session of lovemaking, like our love.

Our love was – unusual. Others would say it was unhealthy, but then I was never one to care about anyone else's opinions. Not when it came to love anyway, nor when it came to the stunning redhead stretching across the sofa like a relaxed cat.

The mink blanket covering her beautiful body slipped, exposing small, rounded breasts to my blatantly hungry gaze.

A ghost of a smile played on Teddy's swollen lips. "You know, if you take a photo, they last longer."

"I couldn't agree more," I attested, climbing in behind her on the chaise and spooning against the lush curves of her body. "But they certainly don't feel as good as the real deal. For instance, you can't do this to a photo." I swept her long mane to one side and trailed my lips along the smooth skin of her clavicle. "Or this," I purred, skimming a hand over her shoulder and down her breast, tweaking a puckered nipple.

She gasped pleasurably. "Your smooth-talking could charm a nun into losing her habit. She would even renege her vow of chastity in a heartbeat for you, I'm sure of it."

"Sounds like a challenge."

Giggling, she smacked my hand. "That's not what I meant."

I chuckled. "You're the only person I enjoy charming the pants off."

"And that my friend, you've succeeded there a lot."

"Ouch, the friend zone? You mortally wound me," I mocked, pressing a hand to my bare chest.

"I think we're way past the friend zone." Her fingertips skated over my forearm, the tone in her voice changing to somewhat severe. "Ari, can I ask you something?"

"Yeah sure, what is it?"

"Why didn't you wash your hands of me after my freak out earlier today?"

Propped up on an elbow, my splayed fingers lightly brushed over her shoulder. "Simply because I want to help you; you're my world, always have been," I gently reminded her. "I won't give up on us. Ever," I spoke with conviction, hoping it was enough to convey how I truly felt.

"You have no idea how much your words mean to me. But in saying that, I don't want you pitying me either," Teddy insisted, her throat tightening. "I've tried to hold my head high, to keep living. And this using my shitty upbringing as an excuse can't go on. I need to deal with this, head on; family be damned!"

Whilst toying with a lock of her bright copper hair, I felt torn and wondered whether to divulge my earlier conversation with Evan or not. I risked it. "After you left, and I was unable to contact you...I went to visit with your dad at his office. He explained your mother's tirade to me, even though Scarlett had done so already. It broke his heart."

The pain naturally still quite raw, Teddy snorted. "He certainly didn't show any sign of a broken heart when he turned me away."

"Evan's terribly sorry and regrets everything that was said and done." I explained further, "He mentioned Phillip Island and how it was your home away from home when life was getting you down. He knew this is where you'd be hiding. Poppy disclosed that piece of information also."

"They're right, it is." Her tearful gaze shifted back to the crackling fire. "What else did he say?"

"That, I must keep fighting for you and not fail you the same way he has. Therese's badgering was the final straw, so he left your mother last night of his own volition and moved into his inner-city apartment." I briefly paused before cautiously continuing, "He's asked your mother for a divorce."

Teddy's glazed eyes jerked back to me. "Oh. Dad best be prepared for a fight then. Knowing my mother, she'll try to take everything from him. I got the feeling he wasn't happy when I was there the other night at dinner. Dad seemed-" Her hand waved as she searched for the right words. "I don't know, out of it. And don't get me started on the tension between them...."

"I imagine it wasn't pleasant. Your father spoke of his regret, muttering something about not leaving ten years ago when Therese betrayed the family." Teddy tensed against me, piquing my curiosity. Not that she gave any hints as to what he meant, nor did I push for an answer, mainly if I wanted to avoid a repeat of the morning's debacle.

"I'm convinced dad only ever stayed because of us. Perhaps now, he'll have a real chance of finding true happiness," she speculated, shuffling onto her back. Brightly shining eyes stared up at me. Stunning. "Change of subject: are you hungry, because I am?"

"Hmm, now you mention it, I am indeed." I peered down, giving her a lop-sided grin. "You weren't planning on cooking eggs for dinner by any chance, were you?"

Her face scrunched impishly. "No, not particularly. I had better clean up the mess I made then, hadn't I?" Reluctantly she sighed and slowly rose her gloriously naked body off the sofa and out of my reach. I watched as she redressed, admiring the flawlessly creamy skin illumined by the glowing flames from the fire.

I scooted across the sofa and bent down, grabbing my skinny chinos and long-sleeved shirt off the floor, dressing as I wandered over to the kitchen to investigate. I opened the fridge, my eyes lighting up at the fat, juicy scotch fillet steaks on the shelf in front of me. "These look good." I grinned holding up the plastic package while Teddy scraped dried eggs off the floor below me. "You most definitely knew I was coming." I raked through the rest of the fridge: mushrooms, spring onions, white wine, cream. Perfect.

"A big fat steak is a dietary requirement for a caveman, no?" Teddy giggled, her eyes glinting playfully. "Protein from red meat keeps you vigorous."

I growled. "You just wait until after dinner, and you'll see just how energetic I can be." Her eyes flickered to something darker; the craving for something more was unmistakable. Well, I'd hate to disappoint her. Let the games begin.

15

Teddy

IF IT WEREN'T FOR the sound of the rolling waves crashing against the beach only a few metres away, I might have forgotten where I was. My body, on the other hand, told an entirely different story.

Ari made right on his promise and took vigorous to an entirely new level. Every inch of my body ached. How many positions had we tried? I hadn't the foggiest; I'd lost count after the first few.

Hearing Ari's soft snore, I couldn't help but smile. After working up quite the sweat in his mission to fuck me like a maniac, he'd worn himself out, my poor love. A bath later should surely soothe our stiffened muscles.

I felt so blessed. Just knowing Ari loved me unconditionally was enough to melt my heart and tear down my carefully built walls. Then there was the small fact he'd followed me to Phillip Island, a sure sign of love if there ever was one. A love that gave me a renewed sense of hope for my future. Our future.

Walking away from him was the worst and first mistake. Causing him untold pain was the second. They were mistakes I never planned on repeating.

And if I weren't desperate for the toilet, Ari would've received quite the thank you for reigniting that dying fire already. Speaking of fire, I needed to check the one in the living room.

I bounded out of bed, the fresh morning air hitting my warmed skin, producing a shiver. I seized the faux minx dressing gown off the back of the door and slipped it on. Much warmer.

Once I'd taken care of business, I quietly padded from the bedroom and into the living room. For hours, such beautiful lovemaking had materialised in front of the open fire, and I wanted to keep it alight. Only a few red-hot coals remained, glowing brightly amongst the blackened ash. The wood basket placed atop the stone hearth was also in need of restocking. I hurried downstairs into the garage and loaded my arms with as many logs as I was capable of carrying. If we needed more, I'd send Ari.

As I trudged back upstairs and re-entered the living room, I received the most pleasant shock of my life – Ari, in the kitchen – unashamedly naked. I homed in the delicious package swaying between his legs, paying no mind to the cumbersome logs nestled in my arms. Nor as each one rolled, hitting the immaculate timber floor with a resounding thud.

Dark eyes salaciously gazed. "Good morning, gorgeous. I was rather lonely without you."

"I had to go and get more...um...wood." I gulped. Oh, the irony. "The fire was dying and I... I didn't want us getting cold," I stuttered, my heated gaze clamped on Ari's expanding cock. He stalked towards, me with the wide crest bobbing towards his navel. Each step measured, matching the predatory glint in his eyes.

My mouth dried in anticipation.

"I'll always keep you warm," he rumbled, demurely loosening the sash of my dressing gown, and pushing it over my shoulders. "In more ways than one."

"I'm feeling warm already, sex fiend."

Ari's mouth twisted in amusement as he palmed my stiffened peaks. "A sex fiend and a caveman, what an interesting combination." His hand skated down my abdomen to my aching cleft, his fingers probing my silky folds. "Hmm, so you are."

I was mindless with pleasure and lost in the slow thrust of his massaging fingers. The way they moved in and out of me, stroking my inner wall while his thumb methodically brushed over my clit, bringing me closer and closer to the edge. I wasn't far off. My legs stiffened as an orgasm abruptly rippled, my cries echoing through the walls around us.

I was barely over the last orgasm when Ari repeated the cycle. Thrusting, circling, stroking. Sweet Jesus. Once more, everything inside me tightened until I trembled around his fingers. I came so hard, I thought I would die from the pleasure alone. And just when I thought Ari had finished with me, he wasn't.

I lifted my weary head, meeting his unwavering gaze. Sculpted lips curved decadently; by that smile, I knew I was in for more. He would have to carry me if that was the case.

He appeared to read my mind. Without any warning, he'd thrown me over his shoulder and back onto the bed, my ankles grabbed and tugged towards the edge of the mattress. My back arched off the mattress as he plunged his cock balls deep inside me.

My curling fingers fisted the blankets, holding on tightly with each savage thrust. Each lunge was long and hard with rhythmic blows, then in one fluid movement, he rapidly pulled out. His fingertips dug into my hips as he flipped me over and dragged me to my knees, drifting a finger along the seam of my behind. He paused and began circling my tightened rosebud.

That felt so good. I moaned and nudged backwards. "Ari, touch me, please..."

"If you're sure?" I was sore there, yes, but at this point, I refused to care.

"I'm sure...just do it..." He stalled. "I can handle it."

I groaned as he finally obliged, rubbing moisture from my drenched sex over the puckered hole before gently inserting his finger and pushing way past the knuckle. I clenched. The tightness was euphoric, even more so when his hardened length nudged back into my trembling sex.

Grabbing my shoulder with his free hand and hanging on, our hips rolled in an erotic dance as I reached between my thighs, frantically rubbing my clit with my fingers. Everything inside me began to tremble, compelling Ari to flex harder, and faster with each thrust of his cock in sync with his plunging finger.

I buried my face into the blankets and let out an enormous scream, my orgasm overwhelming me as my body tremored, and my inner muscles squeezed around his swollen length.

"Oh, sweet Jesus..." Ari grunted, his hips pumping hard and fast until he stilled, spilling his warm seed deep inside me.

I collapsed spreadeagled onto the mattress. Ari landed with a thud over my back.

"Well fuck, that was fucking amazing."

"Mmm..." I uttered incoherently, "It was, and now I can't move."

"I need a shower after that," he puffed, rolling off my back, and off the bed. "Come on, shower," he insisted, dragging me with him.

∞

Ari

HAVING EMERGED FROM THE BEDROOM, I waltzed into the kitchen, a smirk forming as I opened the fridge. "Oh, that's right. If my memory serves me correctly, you dropped the entire carton of eggs on the floor." My amused gaze darted across the living room to Teddy as she plumped a cushion on the sofa.

She feigned innocence; I knew better. "That's not my fault. You scared me....so if you want eggs, you'll need to purchase more."

I snatched up the car keys and growled. "Fine, if I must."

Teddy smiled sweetly and blew me a kiss, her attempt at placating me. It worked.

"I love you, too."

Upon my return, I was immediately greeted by Zella's, Hypnotic, blasting through the house. I quietly chuckled and trundled up the stairs, my steps slowing as I reached the landing on the first floor.

Damn, what that woman did to me, and those narrow hips, provocatively swaying in those tight jeans. Positively hypnotised, the moment burgeoned, urging me to take full advantage.

Silently, I slid up behind her, pressing my lips to the soft skin at the base of her slender neck. "Hello, gorgeous."

Alarmed, she screamed, and her arms flailed, which in turn, sent the new carton of eggs clutched in my hand crashing to the floor.

Howling laughter swiftly followed.

I raised my eyes upwards and sighed. "That's a sign we should just go out for breakfast."

"What an unusual name for a café," I noted about the name whilst taking in the unusual décor surrounding me. Situated on the Esplanade in Cowes, the Mad Cowes Café with its rich timber floors and tables was warm and inviting – it also had a fully stocked bar. Regrettably, even for me, it was far too early for a drink of the alcoholic kind.

"I always come here when I visit," Teddy explained, looking around and pulling up a chair. "It makes me feel right at home."

"Well, if the shoe fits!" I taunted, sliding into a seat and hiding my laughter behind a menu. Teddy's foot abruptly connected with my shin beneath the table. "Ow! You're a bully. You know that?" I scolded light-heartedly. "I don't know what you're going to eat, though; they don't seem to have grass on the menu."

"Well, I don't know what an arsehole eats, but there's nothing on the menu for that either!"

"Ouch." I clutched at my chest, feigning offence. "You wound me so."

"Aw, would you like me to call the wambulance?" Teddy retorted mocking my pout.

"No, I do not need a 'wambulance' thank you very much...just a Band-Aid."

Stirring the sugar into her vanilla latte, Teddy coyly peeked out from under a fan of copper lashes. "We have a lot of sex, is that normal?"

My gaze glinted across the table at her. "Probably not. Why, are you complaining?"

"No, I'm not complaining. It's just with the limited experience I've had, I've never had this much sex before."

My brows raised questionably. How was that possible? Teddy was so skilled in the sack, at times, she even gave me a run for my money.

"Well, sex fiend? Are you going to answer my question?" she murmured, eyeing me salaciously, her tongue darting to lick the foam covering her spoon. I groaned tightly as my cock twitched, responding to the audaciousness.

My eyebrows shot up. "I'm the sex fiend? Pot. Kettle. Black. And stop licking the damned spoon, will you! It's bloody distracting."

"Why? Is it making you all hot and bothered?" The fire in her eyes and flushed skin spoke volumes as she deliberately swept her tongue around the spoon's shallow bowl, antagonising me.

I growled and ripped it from her hand, slamming it down on the saucer. The ruckus caught the attention of the surrounding diners. I purposely ignored their stares. "Stop it! You truly are naughty," I tightly simpered, staring wildly at her. God, she drove me crazy.

"If I'm so naughty, then perhaps you should consider spanking me?" she purred, leaning across and biting down on my lobe.

"Hmm, behave," I hissed. "You have no shame whatsoever."

"No, I don't." Sitting back to give the hovering waitress room to set our plates down, Teddy winked. "This looks yummy and tastes even better."

Picking up the salt grinder, I shook my head and chuckled. "As I said – naughty."

"You didn't answer my question before either," she casually reminded me, sawing through the toast, and lifting a blend of eggs and salmon to her delectable mouth. Plump lips closed over the fork.

"I wasn't given a chance thanks to your little games. I'm beginning to believe you're rather adept at driving a man to distraction." I smirked, taking great delight in turning her words back on her. Her tongue poked out at me. "Touché."

I took a sip of my coffee and gazed thoughtfully. "But to answer your previous question, no, I've never had anywhere near as much sex with anyone else before you. I never really had that much interest in doing so either," I replied earnestly. "I'm aware of how cold that sounds, but that's the truth. I cared fractionally if that's any consolation." I took her slender hand in mine, stroking her long fingers. "...They just weren't you."

After my blushing declaration of love, we finished our breakfast in respective silence. I paid the bill and clasped her hand inside mine. "Let's go for a walk along the beach, it's a glorious day, far too nice to waste inside." Sensing Teddy's uncertainty, I gently tugged her towards me. "We don't have to talk about your past if you don't want to."

She met my concerned gaze and visibly relaxed. "Okay."

Pulling her towards the beach, I squeezed her hand reassuringly. "Come."

Carting our shoes in our hands, we leisurely strolled along the sand, the soles of our bare feet sinking into the unforgiving grains. Besides the cool, shifting winds, it was one of those rare, perfect days with vividly blue skies and a gently warming sunshine. We ambled past piles of scattered seaweed, the offensive smell making Teddy gag. She pinched the end of her nose.

"Ugh! That's rank!"

Unable to help myself, I swept up a clump in my hand and began chasing her through the waves along the shores edge. Her squealing laughter echoed. "Why are you complaining? It's not that bad; perfect for making sushi too."

"No! Go away! It's slimy and smells disgusting!"

I laughed loudly and waved one of the leaves at her. "Be daring!"

"No! Throw it away!"

"Spoilsport," I playfully scorned throwing it down with the rest of the debris, and only after washing my hands in the chilly seawater was I allowed to hold hers again.

Walking farther up the beach, we debated, and disagreed, shared our love of the arts and our philosophies on life. That we discussed in-depth; our hopes, our dreams, but mostly we talked about our achievements. Mine, of course, was starting JPD. For Teddy though, hers was the recent promotion at Bricks and Mortar.

I looked at her in wonder as she described several of Victoria's oldest buildings, around Melbourne and the Goldfield regions predominantly, in fascinating detail. Her love of timeless architecture shone through in its entirety as her face lit up. That love quickly turned to dismay, leaving me in raptures of laughter.

"I get so frustrated when clients want to modernise...homes, especially!"

"Oh, the horror!" I mocked, earning me a playful shove to the shoulder.

"Don't laugh. It's such a crime! A mandatory jail term should be handed out to anyone who destroys these old beauties!"

My laughter intensified as she proceeded to inform me about her little victory dance, one that was performed in secret, *after* she'd won her clients over with her ideas. "Preventions better than the cure, right?"

Flaming hair billowed around slender shoulders as amused hazel eyes rolled. "You don't understand. Changing the look of these houses means stripping them of their identity, not to mention all that history! Regardless of the era of the home, they each tell their own story, whether it's about the families that lived there, or the materials used to build them." Her passion was evident as she continued, "I'm an avid supporter of the Heritage Council, and the goals they're trying to achieve in preserving Australia's history. We must pay homage to what we have left. I believe we should anyway, even if others don't."

After what seemed as if we'd walked for miles, we finally took shelter from the fresh breeze behind one of the dunes and settled into each other's arms. The easy-going chatter flowed as it took on a new direction. Before we knew it, we were comparing notes on who was more the diva, Scarlett, or Dominique. Neither of us could decide.

As I gazed out at the whitecaps, an awkward and eerie silence drifted over Teddy, causing speculation; was she about to disclose her past to me? Finally?

∞

Teddy

AS I RELISHED IN THE SOFT rasp of Ari's voice, an epic proportion of envy washed over me, more so as he fondly spoke about his family. At least they loved each other, unlike mine.

A cold, southerly wind blew off the ocean and over my face as I leaned into his chest, basking in the warmth of his body and the strength of his firm arms wrapped around my shoulders. I breathed him in. He was the epitome of masculinity: his scent, his clothes, his body, and the way he held himself. In one breath, he could act like a primal male, exerting his authority and territory by savagely beating his chest. Then in the next breath, he morphed into my soft, sometimes dominating, attentive lover. I adored that part of him. But both were a significant turn on either way.

I reflected on my past and the possibility of the ripple effects if I decided to tell Ari, a thought that made me shiver mostly out of fear.

Ari peered down at me. "Are you cold, Teddy, we can go back to the house if you prefer?"

"No, it's fine." I shook my head and pulled my woollen cloak tighter.

"Okay, if you are sure."

His concern for my welfare made me love him all the more. I rewarded him with a token smile whilst lying through my teeth, "I'm sure." My hands trembled as I toyed with the white gold locket dangling at the base of my throat.

My past gnawed at me daily, and in addition to Poppy, if I didn't tell someone else about it soon, it would continue to eat me alive, and eventually, drive a wedge between us. Realistically, how long would it be before Ari tired of my ever-fluctuating moods simply because he triggered a memory? Through touch, through sex? I despaired inwardly. Either way, he might run regardless.

My heart pounded as if it might explode from my chest at any second. I inhaled deeply, my breath shuddering as I took a giant leap of faith. "Ari, I need to tell you something, and if I don't do it now, then it may never eventuate."

Puzzled by my rushing words, his brows furrowed. "Okay..."

"Do you remember when my father mentioned about those ten years ago – when he should have left my mother?

"Yeah, I do," Ari slowly replied, his breath faltering. "What about it?"

Taking another deep, shaky breath, I launched into the unknown. "Well, the reason for that is...is because I was raped, and rather than seeking justice for me, my mother covered it up." I closed my eyes, waiting for the explosion.

Nothing but an unnerving silence followed. Ari's quiet and tense demeanour had formed a constricting knot inside my stomach. I needed to know what he was feeling and cautiously rose to my knees, spinning around to face him. Tentatively, I removed his sunglasses. Desolate, darkened eyes brimming with tears flicked up at me.

I spoke quietly, touching the side of his stubbled face, "Ari, please say something, anything, please?" The muscle in his strong jaw twitched beneath my palm.

"How old were you, Teddy, when this happened exactly?" he finally asked, his lips drawing back in a snarl.

My nervous gaze lowered as I sunk onto my haunches. "I was fifteen," I tentatively whispered, "just shy of my sixteenth birthday."

"Did you know the person who...raped you?" he queried, saying words he naturally found difficult to swallow.

"Yes, I did...do – but I can't tell you." I blanched at the glowering stare, but quickly found a way to mollify his anger. "That part, I'm not quite ready to disclose yet. Please don't ask that of me."

Ari's hands balled into tight fists. "Okay, I respect your decision, for now. But I'm guessing the reason you aren't passing this information on is that we both know this person, right? At least give me that so I can understand a little more."

Heat crept into my cheeks; he was so intuitive. I inwardly pleaded, please don't push me to tell you. As opposed to answering him, I stared down at the ground, blinking my falling tears away.

"I gather by your silence, that's a yes. Hmm, I thought so. Okay, another question then: why did your mother not report it?" Ari asked indignantly.

"Because it would ruin her life," I muttered bitterly.

His jaw clenched. "Say again. I'm not quite sure I heard you correctly."

"According to her, one never airs their dirty laundry for all to see. Her words were, and I quote, *'Reporting this would be pointless, and why would you? Imagine the scandal, not to mention the untold shame it would bring on our family.'* So, there you go, that's my mother's way of showing she cares."

Ari gaped. "She was worried about *your rape ruining her life?*" He pushed off the sand and stalked to the water's edge, the softly rolling waves lapping at his bare feet as the breeze rustled the spiky tips of his hair. "I just don't get it!" he shouted, making me jump. "A mother is meant to protect her child!" he strained, his arms flinging around before thrusting his hands back through already dishevelled hair. "Not ruin it further!"

He was angry; I got that, so why did it feel as if he was projecting that anger out on me? Regardless, he had to hear the rest.

I rose off the sand and nervously brushed off my jeans, joining him by the shore. Tentatively, I reached out to him. "That's not all of it...it gets worse."

"Worse? How could it possibly be any worse than it already is?" Ari furiously choked.

Grasping his flexing bicep, words I'd once dreaded hesitantly stumbled from my mouth, "I... I became pregnant as a result."

"Pregnant?" he repeated. "The bastard who raped you also got you pregnant?"

Swallowing the bile that threatened to rise, I stiffly nodded. "Yes." Ari's throat bobbed profusely fighting the same urge. "Tell me you didn't keep that bastard's child, Teddy?"

I closed my eyes like a coward and sighed heavily. "No, but I didn't get an abortion either," I informed him quietly, and pensively. When I reopened my eyes, Ari's reproachful gaze stared. Shame spiralled.

"Oh, dear god." Swallowing hard, he stiffened. "What happened to the...child?"

"I was told she died not long after she was born, breathing complications they told me." Fresh tears streamed down my cheeks as Ari opened his mouth to say something, but I held up a hand and shook my head. "I didn't have any other choice but to go through with the pregnancy. However, before you judge, let me explain."

His head slowly swivelled, his widened, watery gaze darkly staring. "I'm not judging you, Teddy. It's a helluva lot to take in."

"I'm aware of that but put yourself in my shoes for a minute and imagine what I've been made to feel all these years," I barked defensively, crossing my arms over my chest.

Ari glared. My expression softened. "I'm sorry, that sounded harsher than I meant it to." He acknowledged with a curt nod. I guess I deserved that.

"I had no idea I was even pregnant until I was well over the twelve-week mark. My periods were always erratic, and at the time, I thought stress was the cause as to why they'd stopped. You'd think vomiting up nearly every meal would clue you in. But again, I blamed the emotional trauma," I explained, gazing out at the ocean.

"So, what did your mother do? No, let me rephrase that – *what did she make you do?*" Ari seethed through gritted teeth.

"She pulled me out of school and sent me away to live somewhere in New South Wales. That's where I remained until the baby was born. In the meantime, I kept up with my schoolwork; I didn't want to fall behind for obvious reasons."

"What did you have?" he asked tightly.

The vivid memory formed a lump in my throat. "A little girl; she was beautiful, I remember that much," I recalled, smiling weakly. "I wasn't allowed to name her as Mother informed me yet again, *'It would have been a waste of time; I'd never see her again anyway.'*" I began to weep. "Twelve hours of intense labour only gave me one pathetic minute to hold her. I remember screaming at the midwife who came in and ripped her from my arms, while my mother idly stood by, telling me again, *'It was for the best.'*"

The image of my child was committed to memory; her dark almond-shaped eyes, the mass of thick, dark hair, plastered to her tiny head and body. Both still covered in blood and white vernix from the delivery.

"After that, all I felt was emptiness. For weeks on end, I cried nonstop pissing my mother off even more. Then this doctor, I can't recall his name, prescribed anti-depressants and sleeping tablets. He too, informed me it was the best course of action to aid in my recovery. Mother made certain I took them, every damned day by checking the inside of my mouth afterwards just to ensure I'd swallowed them." I shuddered at the terrible memory of her forcing the tablets to the back of my tongue, preventing me from spitting any out. "Mother kept telling me it was…"

"For the best? I got it! She knew what was best!" Ari threw down angrily, his words pissy and clipped. Before I realised what was happening, he was swiftly hauling me hard against his chest, and safely enveloping me within the confines of his arms. We held each other tight, mostly in silence with few words spoken between us.

But the quieter Ari remained, the heavier the weight that settled in my aching heart.

He was brooding; I understood that. I just wished he would tell me what was running through his mind. Not one more word was uttered, even when we arrived back at the house. Adding insult to injury, he chose to stay outside on the balcony. Once he'd polished off half a bottle of bourbon, only then, did he come inside to sprawl across the sofa and pass out.

Heartbroken, I left him there.

16

Ari

BLINDSIDED BY TEDDY'S CANDID confession I selfishly took to the bottle, upsetting Teddy greatly. Regardless of the insight behind her insecurities giving me a greater understanding, I dwelled on the pain inflicted upon her. The booze merely fuelled my anger. Likewise, her mother's actions. A mother who habitually made her feel unloved and unworthy, and still did. I swore at that moment she'd never have to feel that way again.

Her mother was going to pay dearly for her misdeeds.

The spicy aromas of dinner wafted under my nose, stirring me from my self-absorbed alcohol-induced coma. Lifting my head, I winced. Only a shower, a large glass of water and painkillers might possibly ease the jackhammer pounding inside my head. The urge to throw up also rose, compelling me to clap a hand to my mouth as I dashed for the bathroom.

The door flung open shortly after.

Having flushed, I closed the lid and silently perched on top of it, observing a stony-faced Teddy wet a face washer beneath the tap. In the same curt manner, she tossed it to me.

"Thank you."

She glared reproachfully at me through the mirrors reflection as I wiped the warmed washer over my sweat-lathered face. "Wasn't so smart to drink a ludicrous amount of bourbon, was it?" she spat caustically.

My head hung in shame.

"Well, once you've finished acting like you're the wounded bull, come and join me for dinner! You need something to soak up all that damned alcohol!" On the verge of tears, she stormed out, slamming the bathroom door behind her. Ouch.

Listening to Teddy's irate scolding ought to have woken me up, however, I lacked enthusiasm. In the end, I forced myself to strip and climb into the shower. During which, I used the time to admonish myself for my reprehensible behaviour.

Teddy was highly upset with me and had every right to be. As opposed to offering her a sympathetic shoulder to cry on, I took to the bottle and drank enough for both of us, and then some. My self-centred behaviour served no purpose. It was selfish and only added to her stress.

I leaned my head back and closed my eyes, enjoying the spray of the water over my aching head. The sound of a door slammed, and another, both a swift reminder that I needed to finish up; it was time to face the music.

Emerging from the bedroom, I halted in the doorway and took in the transformed living space. Whilst I wallowed in self-pity, Teddy had clearly spent ages setting up for a charming night ahead.

From the fierce blaze licking the logs in the open fireplace to the scattered pillar candles, their shadowy flames flowing in an erotic dance across the white vaulted ceilings high above us, the room was lit up in a romantic glow. A gentle concerto compilation also played, adding to the allure.

Out of my peripheral, a gliding movement caught my attention. An enticing vision dressed head to toe in black, Teddy's glossy copper mane glowed in the flickering light as she inched towards me with the two of us meeting in the middle of the room.

Her breasts pushed against my chest, Teddy's long fingers grazed over the stubble on my unshaven jawline as shining eyes lovingly searched my face. "Hi there. Do you feel any better?"

My brows furrowed; I had the distinct impression all was forgiven for my thoughtless indiscretion. Better to go with the flow rather than raise questions and cause yet another disagreement. "Much better. You look...gorgeous."

"Thank you. The dress is new. Do you like it?"

My enchanted gaze wandered with my hands over Teddy's luscious curves, admiring, for the most part, the long and explicit slit in her dress, showing off one of her shapely legs to absolute perfection. "Hmm...stunning."

Teddy smiled serenely. "Wine?"

"Please."

As she spun on the spike of a black strappy heel, my roving gaze trailed her to the wet bar, surveying her swishing hips in the form-fitting dress. Wry amusement fell over my face. My temptress was full of surprises tonight.

I stroked my chin, a smile flittering at the possibilities.

Handing me a glass of Pinot Noir, Teddy eyed me speculatively but said nothing. "I was hoping to go out for dinner...but thought this would be much nicer. And private," she purred. Well, fuck me.

"I couldn't agree more."

"Let's have our dinner before it gets cold." She grasped my hand and led me to the dining table. With the white linens, candles, and the softly hued pink roses from the garden in a fishbowl vase, she had truly outdone herself. Also awaiting us were two warmed plates. They smelt equally heavenly.

Throughout our meal, Teddy consistently flirted with me, raising the bar with each brush of the fingers and her heeled foot, literally.

Living with the knowledge, that she was indeed naked underneath that dress stirred up wanton thoughts and my cock, which grew increasingly harder with each painfully passing minute. The white macadamia mousse with balsamic strawberries was going to have to wait until later. This dessert had my mouth watering for an entirely different reason.

An intriguing smirk formed over Teddy's luscious lips as I wiped my mouth with the linen napkin and pushed the chair back. The little minx was on to me.

I rounded the table and roughly hauled her from the chair, my nose burrowing in her thick locks to breathe in the sweetened scent of the beguiling woman who lived to drive me wild. The air around us irrefutably suffused with a magnetism that only we understood, forever drawing us together.

The soft skin of Teddy's cheek nuzzled as her mouth silently sought out mine. One hand wrapped around the back of her head as my head leisurely dipped ready to take her in a slow, gentle kiss. The other dextrously slid up her naked back, unfastening the singular button holding her dress up at the base of her neck.

The dress sedately curled to the floor and pooled around the sky-high heels at her feet. My mouth dried; she was unashamedly naked, just as I'd suspected all along.

But as my fiery gaze greedily travelled up and down, taking in the luscious body that brazenly stood before me, my confidence of earlier evaporated.

I was that awkward teenager again, when I thought of no one else but Teddy. Day and night, she'd consumed my thoughts. Nonetheless, taking advantage of someone so young and so vulnerable was never my style – unlike…, reminding me of the cruel joke that kept us apart for so long.

The lines blurred, conjuring emotions unlike anything I'd ever experienced before. I lunged, our lips colliding fiercely. Her groan rumbled as she tore at my shirt, sending buttons flying before fumbling with the zipper on my dress pants, leaving me in a state of partial undress. Crazed and burning with desire, I hooked my arms under her thighs and carried her to the soft Flokati rug in front of the fireplace. We crashed to the floor, and gazed at one another, the dancing flames accentuating the green flecks in Teddy's eyes as they stared up at me.

Despite the tender gaze, there was a hidden uncertainty, evoking a torrent of raw emotions within, which in turn spilt into our lovemaking. Without thinking, I slipped both hands into Teddy's, pinning them above her head as I plunged into her warmth. Her sharpened breath hissed in my ear.

I battled to contain both my self-control and my thoughts. Each thrust was hard and deep, indicative of my despair. My momentum shifted as I strained, trying to find my release. I lunged harder, faster, until that familiar build cascaded through my core into my stiffening legs. I cried out, collapsing against Teddy, my apologetic sobs for my animalistic behaviour muffled in the crook of her neck, "Oh god, Teddy. I am so sorry. I love you so, so much."

∞

Teddy

I STARED AT THE FLAMES blazing from the lit fire and shuddered, prompting Ari to lift his weighty forearm as he shifted closer, aligning his body with mine.

"Are you cold?" Rather than wait for my reply, he tugged at the blanket, covering my bare shoulders anyway.

"No. Maybe. A little." For the life of me, I grappled with my mind. My head was spinning. I wasn't sure which way was up. I raised my thumb to my mouth and anxiously chewed on my thumbnail.

Ari's hand glided over my shoulder. "Are you all right? I mean, after today's disclosure."

No, I'm not. "Yes and no. Yes, because I feel relieved for telling you, and no because it's clearly affected us already."

He tugged at my shoulder and rolled me to my back. I looked up at him. Confusion and concern had etched over his handsome face. "How has it?"

I sucked in a deep breath. "For starters, you shut down and barely spoke to me once I told you. I realise you needed a moment to process it all; it was a lot to take in. Secondly, you came home and got blinding drunk until you threw up. Then when we made love, if that's what you'd call it. Your emotions ran higher..."

He held up a hand, interrupting me, "How was it different?"

"Well, initially, you were reticent but attentive. Then something shifted, and it's like, ugh, how do I say this?" I paused for a minute, choosing my words carefully before conveying them; he was fragile enough as it was. "At first, it felt as though you were desperate, then all of a sudden, you were angry. Then you broke down and apologised as if you were the one responsible for hurting me. It was rather...confusing." I frowned, running a splayed hand over his shoulders and down his biceps, both tensing under my touch.

"Ari?" His silence worried me. "Ari, please tell me what's wrong!" The more I pressed, his agitation grew ostensibly apparent.

"Teddy, please stop asking!"

"I'm concerned abo...."

"Stop! Just stop, please!" Out of the blue, he pushed away from me and bounded off the floor, glowering as he attempted to do up any remaining buttons on his shirt. He gave up and slapped his hands to his sides, zipping and rebuttoning his pants instead.

"What are you doing?"

"I need a minute to clear my head!"

"What is it you need to think about; I thought we were okay," I whispered, my hopes crumbling right before my eyes. Ari at least owed me the decency of an answer, so I pressed him further, "I don't understand. Tell me why!"

"Just stop! I need a fucking minute to breathe! Is that too much to ask?" he roared, scaring me, and realising his mistake, he rapidly apologised, "I'm sorry..."

I blanched and recoiled from his outstretched hands. "Get the fuck away from me."

Crestfallen, he dropped them back to his sides. "I'm sorry, I didn't mean..."

His raw attitude threw me. He'd just ripped my heart right from my chest with his bare hand and thrown it to the floor, crushing it with his size ten boot.

With hot tears streaming down my face, I scrambled off the floor and wrapped the blanket tightly around my naked frame. "No, you go and have your fucking minute!" I shouted as I clung to my dignity. "I knew telling you would be a mistake!"

Ari's head shamefully hung, and once more, he tried to reach out to touch me. I stepped back. "Teddy, I'm sorry."

"No! Go! Now!" I screamed, choking on my rage. "And while you're at it...go to fucking hell!" I stormed off to the bedroom, banging the door shut behind me. As I slumped onto the bed and curled up into a ball, wishing I could take every word spoken back, the front door slammed.

∞

Ari

I WAS IN HELL, and I deserved to be. I had no right to be angry; it wasn't my life destroyed, Teddy's was. I had failed her again.

Immersed in guilt, I ran along the shoreline until my legs and chest burned, and the muscles in my body ached. I collapsed in a heap onto the sand with the chilly water lapping at my toes. My reaction was wrong, and I hurt her immeasurably, and for that alone I was inevitably ashamed. My tears shed as a guttural cry escaped, mourning for all that my beloved Teddy had lost.

By the time I re-entered the house, any evidence of our romantic dinner was cleared away. The muted lights over the kitchen island had since replaced the soft glow of the burning candles. The table, with the exception of the vase in the centre, its linens were also packed away. Whilst the dishwasher hummed lightly, completing its cycle.

Upon hearing a mournful whimper, my head swivelled in the direction of the sofa and skimmed my gloomy gaze over a sleeping Teddy. While I was off sulking, she had redressed, opting for a pair of black leggings and an oversized baby pink woollen sweater. But consuming me with yet more regret was the sight of the red-rimmed eyes and the swollen lips.

Thrusting a hand through my hair, I sighed and ambled over to the sofa, lightly skating a knuckle over Teddy's soft cheek. "I'm so sorry, Teddy. I'm so sorry for being such an insensitive arsehole." Apologising whilst she slept was a cowardly move and ridiculous to boot, it wasn't as if she'd hear me. "Let's get you to bed at least," I whispered, scooping her up gently into my arms.

At first, she rolled into me, then without any warning, her fist unexpectantly connected with my jaw. Knocked off balance and in a clear state of shock, I unwittingly dropped Teddy in the process. She thudded against the floorboards, the shock equally startling her.

Dazed and blinking, she jolted upright and scrambled backwards. "Wh... What happened?"

"You punched me, that's what!" I barked, swinging my jaw side to side. She hadn't broken it thankfully.

Her brows knitted. "How'd...how'd I manage that?"

"I simply picked you up with the intention of carting you off to bed; only we didn't make it that far, obviously," I grunted, sliding down beside her.

"I didn't mean to hit you."

"It's fine, really."

Teddy grasped my chin and inspected my face for any further signs of damage. "It doesn't look like it."

I chuckled. "I probably deserved it for being such a jerk to you earlier."

She scoffed. "I can't believe you're laughing."

I shrugged. "Well, what else can I say?" A smile danced on my lips as I rubbed my tender jawline. "I tell you what, though; you have a mean right hook."

"It's starting to bruise; it needs an icepack," Teddy muttered, unfolding herself off the floor and making her way over to the kitchen. Taking an icepack from the freezer, she rolled it up inside a tea towel before stiffly patting the barstool with her free hand. "Sit."

Behaving like the dutiful boyfriend, I obeyed, wincing at the pressure as she applied the icepack to my face. "Ow."

"Don't be such a baby." Much to my dismay, she swiftly removed her hand and stepped away from me. Then wordlessly, she wandered over to the French doors and stared out at the blackened sky, her arms circling protectively around her upper body. Apart from the drawn-out heavy sigh, a depressing silence remained between us. I couldn't stand it any longer.

"Teddy, I..."

A hand flung up. "Don't, please," she begged, her back still facing me. "I can't do this now, Ari. I'm far too tired for this conversation."

Dejected, my shoulders slumped. "Can we at least talk about this tomorrow?"

"Fine, tomorrow it is." Pirouetting on her bare feet to face me, she motioned to the cold tea towel on my face. "Let me take another look."

I removed the icepack and sat it on the counter beside me, my eyes following her as she checked the bruising.

"Hmm, it may still bruise, but it shouldn't be overly bad, so no long-term damage to your handsome face." She gave the briefest of smiles. If only it reached her beautiful eyes.

"Well, that's a huge relief then."

With a contemptuous roll of the eyes, Teddy snatched up the icepack and opened the freezer door, throwing it back onto the shelf. "I'm off to bed. What about you?"

Aware of the icy wall, I slid off the stool and tentatively walked towards her. "I'll do the same...if I'm still welcome that is?"

She eyed me reproachfully. "I'm still mad at you." Her arms wrapped protectively over her chest, she took a step back, widening the already extensive gulf between us.

"I do love you. You know that, right?"

"Do you? I'm starting to doubt that, largely after today..." Her throat bobbed tightly. ".... And tonight."

"Please don't," I replied quietly, sighing despondently. "The way I reacted...it was completely out of line; I'm sorry."

Teddy closed her eyes and sighed, raking her long fingers through her curls. "Can we just go to bed, please, and talk about this tomorrow?"

Smiling bleakly, I stiffly nodded. "Of course."

Following her to the bedroom, I looked on miserably as she slid a nighty over her head and slipped into bed with her back facing away from me for the first time, ever. I wasn't about to be forgiven that easily this time around.

Consequently, my sleep was the worst, making the next morning a struggle to peel my weighty eyelids open. A tight band also gripped my head; long-lasting side effects of my binge clinging to whatever brain cells I had left I suspected.

I rolled my head on the pillow and sighed as I peered over at Teddy's side of the bed, which, of course, was empty. Rather than speculate, I flicked the blankets back and slowly made my way into the kitchen. With any luck, I'd find a clue as to where she'd disappeared to in there.

Propped against the fishbowl vase in the centre of the dining table was a note, my name clearly marked on the front in Teddy's elegant handwriting. I picked it up, scanning the short note just as swiftly.

Ari,
Gone for a run. Back soon.
Teddy.

Wow, talk about indifferent, not even a kiss. At least Teddy hadn't left, that's one consolation; I think. In a reflective mood, I threw the note back onto the table before heading to the bathroom.

I needed a shower.

∞

Teddy

A TEN-KILOMETRE RUN UP the beach had given me ample time and space for regrouping my thoughts, and, likewise, my feelings after the previous day's hellish turn. The morning had begun flawlessly, and once I opened up to Ari, it became the catalyst for the rest of our day, turning it into our own private hell.

Had I made a mistake telling Ari? I was inclined to believe it was, gauging by his reaction. Could we survive as a couple? Because if we couldn't, then we were better off going our separate ways before our relationship imploded. Discussing our feelings and whether my disclosure had changed his or not was a conversation to be had, sooner rather than later.

The shower was already running when I returned to the house, and the moment I strolled into the bathroom and took one look at Ari, my heart just dropped. He looked broken. Downhearted even as he scrubbed his well-defined body brusquely.

I had to fix us.

I quietly stripped and slid in behind him, aligning the length of my body firmly against his. The taut muscles flexed beneath the skin as I pressed my cheek to the broad width of his back. I greeted him softly and tentatively, "Hi there."

He peered over his shoulder, giving me the briefest of glances. "Did you enjoy your run?"

"I did. The sunrise was particularly stunning this morning, too," I murmured, nuzzling my nose against his soft skin. "The landscape changed right before your eyes."

"Back please." His tone brisk, he handed me the loofah. "Are you still upset with me?"

Gliding the sponge over his shoulders, I shook my head and whispered, "No, I'm not, and despite everything that went down last night, I was angry, more at myself than I was with you."

"Why would you be mad at yourself? If you're going to be mad, be mad at me, expressly for my insensitivity and for taking off, leaving you in a distressed state once again."

"Everything I disclosed was a lot for you to take in, and by not anticipating your reaction was wrong on my part. I took you for granted, and doing so, took your love for me for granted," I explained dolefully, gliding the loofah across the blades of his broad shoulders and down the gentle curve of his spine. "The selfishness in me had me scared...scared you wouldn't want me anymore. And honestly, I wouldn't blame you if you didn't."

Ari scowled and spun towards me, snatching the loofah from my hand. He hung it over the tap before pushing me towards the tiled marble wall, his palms flattening either side of my head. "Would I still be here if I didn't want you?"

Staring up into his darkened eyes, I slowly shook my head at him. "No," I admitted flatly. "You wouldn't."

"I love you, Teddy, and I'm not sure how much clearer I can make it. Yes, I admit I did lash out – only because I was appalled. Not with you, but with your mother and the person who attacked you. And with whoever else was complicit in this heinous crime. Who wouldn't be? It's a natural reaction for one to be outraged by such repulsive transgressions," Ari clarified tightly. Straightening, he ran his hands through his drenched hair. "What happened to you was abhorrent, and quite frankly – I felt overwhelmed, I won't deny that. I shouldn't have yelled at you either, and nor can I apologise enough for doing so." He gripped my chin, our sobering gazes meeting as he tipped my head. "We need to have a little faith and patience with each other. It's the only way we'll survive this."

"Can you at least explain why you made love to me the way you did, please?"

"I was hurting...in here – for you," he expressed, pressing a hand over his heart, the regret evident in his voice as he slowly lowered onto the bench seat. He leaned against the tiled wall and gently urged me between the widespread of his legs. "I desperately wanted to take away your pain. I felt angry because I wasn't there for you that night and if I'd been home..."

My heart wrenched. "Please don't go beating yourself up over this. You were away at university and getting your life in order. Nothing can change what happened."

"But if I had, I could have stopped the bastard from raping you! I could have prevented all this pain, all this anger at least!"

"Ari, stop it, please!" I cried out, catching his face between my hands. I tipped his head, forcing him to look up at me. "Nothing could've prevented any of it! I was at my family's home; the place where I always assumed I was the safest. I never expected someone I'd known my entire life, to attack me in the sanctity of my bedroom."

Ari's brows snapped together. "You didn't tell me that bit yesterday. How did it happen?"

I sighed regretfully. No, I hadn't and for a good reason. Now I had no choice but to reveal a part I'd deliberately left out.

I smoothly sat in Ari's lap and began to explain, "Mum and dad were throwing one of their frequent dinner parties, and I was upstairs in my bedroom, attempting to finish my English homework.

I was also listening to music through my headphones to drown out the noise downstairs." A grim smile marred my face. "But it also meant I was unable to hear my door opening and closing. Only when *he* stepped into view, did I realise he was there. Initially, I wasn't alarmed; until he turned and locked the door..." I shuddered and moved closer into the proximity of Ari's open arms, welcoming the warmth and the security it gave me.

"It's okay; we can leave that conversation for another day." Skimming a hand over my back, he pulled me tighter and rested his cheek against the crown of my head. Assured I was indeed safe and loved, the irritation of earlier, was swept away in an instant.

∞

Ari

SINCE OUR SHOWER and further disclosure about her past, I'd observed Teddy's plummeting mood from afar. It was as if a dark cloud had overshadowed what was turning out to be a beautiful day. We'd ventured outside onto the balcony to bask in the warmth of the sun, well, I was even if she wasn't, whilst eating our breakfast.

"Are you going to finish that?" I queried, pointing at the two uneaten pancakes on her plate as her blank gaze remained riveted to whatever she'd been staring at for the last five minutes.

"No, you have it." Even her response was robotic.

"You sure? You've barely eaten anything."

Her fingernails timely drummed on the bone China cup in her hand. "I'm not that hungry." She pushed the plate across the table.

"Your loss," I murmured, stabbing each one with the fork and dropping them onto my empty plate.

"You do realise, dealing with my past won't be easy, don't you?" Teddy suddenly blurted.

I mopped up the remnants of the mixed berry sauce with a slice of the pancake before popping it into my mouth. Chewing, I nodded. "I know what to expect, and yes, I do realise the journey won't be all sunshine and roses."

Teddy's eyes raised questioningly to meet my steadfast gaze. "You must be a masochist."

I found myself laughing at the ridiculous question. "No, I'm no such thing, but if I've given that impression, I'm awfully sorry."

Not impressed, she threw a blueberry at me, and much to Teddy's chagrin, I laughed harder. "It's no laughing matter, Ari Jaeger!"

"What on earth was I thinking, getting involved with a redhead? They're so fiery. That must make me a masochist after all!"

"Stop it!" she growled, hurling more blueberries across the table. Perhaps I had better stop with the jokes, or I'd end up looking like an oversized grape, or worse – a smurf.

Holding both hands in the air either side of my head, I relented, "Only if you stop throwing blueberries at me?"

Teddy raised a well-shaped eyebrow. "Only if you stop being an arsehole?"

I smiled. "Fine, anything to put a halt to the name-calling." I chuckled and had to hold up my hands again as the threat of more blueberries loomed. "You are strong, tenacious and if I forget to mention, a wilful young woman, you know that?" She snorted and rolled her eyes, making me chuckle. "I have more faith in you than you do of yourself; surely the strength you have shown thus far would tell you that?"

Her head shook, disagreeing with me. "Why would you say that?"

"Well, regardless of your past, you've shown quite the resilience. For starters, you completed high school, as DUX I might add, and then university to become a brilliant architect. You haven't let your mother, or this bastard stop you from achieving any of your dreams when you could've easily given up, although I don't doubt that you probably had days where you wanted to do so. However, you didn't, and for that, I'm immensely proud. Your strength, Teddy, is your power, of you taking control. Even if you don't realise this, it's the truth."

"When you put it that way, I can see your point," Teddy agreed, slowly relaxing back into the chair and drawing her knees up. "Honestly though, I've never thought to look at it in that context before either."

"You've been healing in some form or another. Has anyone ever bothered to point it out to you?" I added, leaning back in the chair, an ankle coming to rest on my knee.

"No, nobody has, not even my shrink," she scoffed. "My dad's right, you are good for me. Although, my mother says otherwise. In her eyes, I'm not worth loving apparently."

"You should listen to your father more and your mother less. In fact, do yourself a favour and don't listen to her at all. She fills your head with self-doubt, killing your self-esteem and self-confidence," I interjected abruptly. "You are extremely easy to love, despite what your bloody mother says." I blew out a frustrated sigh. "Let me point out all the positives to you. One: You're intensely passionate about everything you do. Two: You care about other people and their feelings. Three: Considering the shit, life has dealt you – you've handled yourself with nothing but grace and dignity. I also understand trust is a big issue, and it's not without reason. I am determined to spend my time helping you overcome them." I passed my handkerchief to a weeping Teddy.

"Thank you. Your mother would be so proud."

I cocked my head. "What, for the hanky?"

She laughed. "No, not for the hanky, ya wally – for the advice and for honourably choosing to stand by me."

Leaning across the table, I gave Teddy a soft, lingering kiss on her plump lips. "Oh, but you are most welcome."

17

SEATED ACROSS FROM ONE another on the floor, we eyed each other, the tension slowly building as Teddy added the numbers of her letters on the board. She sniggered, jotting down our final score.

"Woohoo! I beat you again!" Then further adding salt to my wounded ego was the waving of the score sheet in my face.

"I can't believe I lost by fifty points!" Wailing, I snatched it from her hand to check for myself, among other things.

"I didn't cheat if that's what you're thinking."

I scowled and glanced up at a smug Teddy, her chin resting in the palm of her hand. "I wouldn't dare imply such a thing."

"Aha." She knew me well.

"The best out of three?" I challenged, raising a brow sharply. She automatically began clearing the board, not without another merciless dig to my ego.

"Aw, can't stand losing to a girl?"

A smile tugged at the corners of my mouth. "No, not at all. I'm just not a fan of losing, and I want to see how good you claim to be Miss Smarty Pants."

Teddy dug inside the tiny pocket of her super short, ripped denim shorts and pulled out a fifty-cent piece sliding it across the lowline coffee table in my direction. Preoccupied with the impressive cleavage bursting out of a lacy bra beneath a sheer blouse, I paid no mind to the now dulled coin.

I frowned as my distracted gaze finally dropped to the table. "What on earth do I want that for?"

"To go and call someone who cares." She shovelled her hand back inside her pocket, her nose playfully scrunching as she tugged something else out of there. Please don't let it be another coin. Thankfully, it was just a lollipop. But then again…. Mischievously glinting eyes peered up at me from underneath fluttering lashes; I'd say she was up to no good.

My brows shot up knowingly. "Have I ever told you, you have such a smart mouth to go with those extremely short smarty pants?"

"No, you didn't," she murmured, salaciously swirling her tongue around the strawberries and cream flavoured lollipop. She was using that thing as a distraction. The problem: it was working.

I raised my brows and chuckled. "Now let's concentrate, and no distractions!"

What the…? Defeated again! I threw my head back and cried out, "Oh, my god!" Teddy giggled mercilessly at my pouting. "I can't believe I lost…three fucking times!"

She crawled over the floor and into my lap, straddling my thighs with her slender legs. "I can't believe you're pouting about losing. Would you like another fifty cents?" Hazel eyes danced with laughter.

"You find this amusing do you, me losing to you?" I smacked her firmly on the behind.

"Ow, what was that for?" She feigned pain, but the fire igniting in her eyes told me differently.

"For laughing at me, and for distracting me with your exquisite lollipop sucking skills."

Her mouth twitched with suppressed amusement. "Hmm, well that truly shows where men's brains truly are. How do you manage at work?"

"I manage perfectly well, thank you very much," I murmured indignantly, my hands sliding beneath Teddy's lightweight blouse to plump and knead her breasts over the top of black lace. "Do you require a demonstration of how?"

"Oh, I'm fully aware of how, Mr Jaeger," she replied decadently. "But I may need reminding."

"Far be it for me to deny you." Pushing the coffee table away with my feet, I tipped us to the ground and hovered over a writhing Teddy. Such a greedy girl. Lust filled eyes gazed upwards, and plump lips parted, panting with want... Let's play.

With the tips of my fingers, I traced over plush lips, her mouth delectably sucking on each digit before firmly clamping down with her teeth. Damn, that went straight to my groin.

"Naughty girl," I growled, jerking my fingers from her tight grip.

"I am so," she hummed, weaving her fingers through my hair and tugging at the roots, dragging me towards her gaping mouth.

"Oh, no." My head shaking, I grabbed her wrists, pinning them both above her head. "This is mine, remember?" I smirked at her pouting. "Sorry, love, that won't work either."

Dipping my head, I grazed the rough stubble covering my cheek along the soft skin of her jawline. Teddy squirmed in anticipation as my free hand deftly popped the buttons of her cotton blouse.

I gripped her wrists tighter, holding them steadfastly to the floor as I pushed the flimsy material apart. Beautiful breasts strained against the black cups, and stiffened pink nipples poked through the see-through lace just begging for freedom. I nipped with my teeth and teased one whilst reefing the cup down on the other, plumping, and kneading, rolling, and tugging until I reached my goal.

Hearing a pleasurable gasp brought my teasing to an abrupt end. I jumped up, leaving a confused and half-naked Teddy behind on the floor.

"Why'd you stop?" she whined, squeezing her thighs together.

"I'm starving. Are you?" I strolled over to the kitchen and hid my wolfish grin behind the open door of the fridge. Teddy's jaw gaped in disbelief.

"Wow, you certainly know how to ruin a moment," she uttered, sitting up and tugging her bra back into place. Buttoning up her blouse, she flared with exasperation. "You've left me hanging!"

I began raking through the pantry, taunting her softly, "I can't help it if I am hungry, or you are horny for that matter."

"Well...I hope your balls turn blue, and they wither into tiny little raisins then." Studying her nails, Teddy tried her hardest to appear unruffled.

"I'll just have a wank then, so that solves that 'little' problem."

"Grr, you are so...frustrating."

"Paybacks are a bitch, aren't they? Remember the café the other day, hmmm?" I droned.

"All right, you win," Teddy petulantly mumbled. "If you order me the deluxe supreme pizza from George's Pizzas, I may consider forgiving you."

"You're so generous," I murmured dryly, retrieving the menu from inside one of the top kitchen drawers. "Pizza it is then. Does madam want garlic bread with her delicacy of pizzas?"

"Yes, please. I need something tasty and satisfying," Teddy implied suggestively, winking at me and my gaping mouth before disappearing to pack up the scrabble.

I ended the call and leaned on the island bench counter, admiring the soft curves of Teddy's delectable arse poking out from the edges of her cut off shorts as she bent over. "The pizza will be delivered in about twenty minutes. I might fade away, waiting."

Teddy snorted. "You're seriously exaggerating, even if it is just a little. There's not a chance of that ever happening."

"Are you suggesting I'm obese?" I attempted to push out my well-toned abs.

"That's exactly what I meant," she taunted, pushing the board game back into the low cupboard with a wiggle of the hips. A deliberate move, I'd say, to get back at me for leaving her sexually frustrated. Well, my cock surely noticed and immediately stood at full mast waving a white flag in her direction.

I growled and repositioned myself behind her. Grinding my aching crotch against her denim-clad cheeks, I breathed huskily, "I know what you're doing."

"I haven't the faintest," she demurred, feigning innocence. "If you keep growling like that, someone may begin to wonder if an agitated bear lives here."

I held Teddy around her slender waist and yanked her hips, drawing her body closer. She smelt divine, and I wasn't just referring to her perfumed scent either. "I thought I was a caveman?"

She quivered as my splayed hand wrapped around her throat, and my fingertips lightly stroked along her smooth jawline.

"Damn straight, you are..." She moaned as I pinned and took her against the wall.

"I had a thought; although it's been peaceful here, we should think about heading home tomorrow," Teddy suggested chewing on her fifth slice of pizza. A workout like we'd just had it wasn't surprising she had the appetite of a horse. I'd taken her like a prized stallion, too, throwing in the occasional spanking on her bare derriere as I took her from behind. The thought made me smile; Ari, one, Teddy, zero.

We sat out on the balcony, enjoying the delightful streaks of the sunset whilst listening to Teddy's playlist in the background. Chris Isaak presently crooned over the speakers, drowning out the hovering seagulls circling around us.

Noticing her hesitation, I gazed thoughtfully. "I take it you really don't want to?"

She groaned. "No. But we have been here for days, and as much as I wish to stay in our little bubble, we really should go home."

Yeah, the thought of leaving saddened me, but I reluctantly nodded in agreeance. "We should, and undoubtedly, an inbox full of emails along with a pile of messages shall be waiting for me. My assistant has probably torn out her bleach blonde extensions due to my unexplained absence. Bless her little cotton socks." Teddy didn't miss the sarcasm or the rolling of my eyes.

"Don't you like your assistant much?"

No, I despised her. "Lila's good at her job I give her that..." When she wasn't flirting with me.

"But?"

"Yeah, hers when she 'drops' papers trying to get a rise out of me."

The pizza in Teddy's hand paused at her lips. "Oh, she does, does she? Perhaps I should pay a visit to JPD, mostly to kick her flirting arse out of your office."

I chuckled as she glowered and leaned in to kiss her cheek. "Jealous much?"

"Yes, I am. What's wrong with that?"

"Absolutely nothing." I smiled indulgently. "Who doesn't love watching a good catfight?"

Her eyes rolled. "Of course, you would." I stilled as her hand snuck into the leg of my shorts and grasped my cock. "So, tell me; does she get a rise out of you?"

"What?" Squeezing fingers encouraged me gently to find the right answer. "No, I would never. I only rise and stand to attention for you."

"That's good to know then." She grinned and chomped down on the slice of pizza in her hand with an exaggerated bite. A worrying move that compelled me to cross my legs.

∞

Teddy

THE LITTLE GAMES in the living room were merely a ruse, a prelude for what was to ensue, and once dinner was over, Ari practically mauled me.

Starting in the kitchen, we ended our sensual lovemaking at some ungodly hour in the bedroom. Long drawn-out erotic play that had me begging in the end, not only for my release from the bonds around my wrists and ankles but also an orgasm. One that left me pleasantly satisfied and completely wiped out. Every muscle ached, and every orifice was tender, and I had relished in every part of the pleasure Ari had given me.

So, when he offered to drive the two-hour journey home, I hadn't objected; I was too exhausted to drive the bustling freeway anyway.

The relaxation wasn't proving useful though, even with Ari stroking my hand in the warmth and safety of his lap. After hours of mindless fucking, I thought I'd be relaxed and my mind somewhat clearer. Alas, that wasn't to be the case due to the disturbing occupation of our recent conversations this past week in my head. I just wished they'd pack up and leave already to let me live in peace.

Music, I needed music. The soft, mellow sounds of a piano always calmed me, even on my worst days. Letting out a deep, shuddering sigh, I deftly rolled a finger over the screen searching for my favourite piano playlist and pressed play. Much better.

The change in mood had Ari briefly taking his eyes off the road and glancing in my direction.

"Eyes back on the road, Jaeger. You get distracted far too easily."

He tutted, "Such utter tosh. I am watching the road Miss Bossy Boots."

My head shook as I let out a humourless laugh. "Speak English, please."

"Oh, and here I thought you got off on my British lingo, and accent?" he murmured, acting offended while thoughtfully stroking the stubble along his strong jawline.

Everything about him turned me on; his scent, clothed, unclothed, his accent. The list was long. He knew what buttons to push and exactly how to push them, and right now, he was toying with them.

"Oh, you know, I do. Please behave. I am far too sore from last night or this morning's rather brutal attack on me." His smiling face swiftly dropped and returned to the road in a flash. My face dropped. Oh, shit, talk about insensitive.

Sitting upright and twisting at the waist in my seat to face him, worry washed over me. "No, no, Ari, that's not what I meant. What I meant was...you made love to me in a fashion I enjoyed, not in the other..." Agitated by my stupidity, I scrubbed my hands over my face. "I'm such an idiot," I whispered.

Ari reached across and tucked my hand back inside his. "I'm aware that's not how you intended for it to sound. It's just..." He let out a grim sigh. "...after your disclosure, I guess your words hit a nerve. Processing everything is going to take some time, is all."

Time. Ten years wasted simply because I refused to deal with my past and going home meant facing it head-on. Eventually. Telling Ari was a huge enough step as it was.

I swallowed hard and slowly settled back into my seat. "I know. I also realise talking about my past openly with others, and in particular, your family.... that won't be easy on any of us. For that, I apologise as I dread it the most." Unfortunately, my attitude now matched the soft drizzle falling from the ominous grey clouds floating overhead.

Ari glanced sideways and soothingly ran his thumb over my knuckles. "Baby steps, remember? There's no need to go ripping that Band-Aid off just yet. So, when you're ready, I'll be right there beside you, okay?"

"I know that, too." I smiled softly at him as a tear rolled down my cheek, splashing at the breast of my white knitted sweater. "Thank you."

"You're welcome," he whispered, and in a sweet gesture, he raised my hand to his lips, pressing a soft, tender kiss to the top of my hand.

With Ari by my side, what could possibly go wrong?

Barely back at the house or in the door for that matter, Poppy latched onto me like that annoying fly on a sheep's behind. Following me to the bedroom, she zealously buzzed about for information regarding my trip away.

"Did you tell Ari about your past?"

"Obviously, or you wouldn't have let me into my own home," I muttered dryly, dumping the bags onto the floor before collapsing onto the bed.

"And?" she impatiently prompted, flopping down beside me.

"Actually, it went better than expected. Well, apart from one night...." Poppy's worried expression evoked my laughter. "Don't stress, we worked things out, so we aren't here under false pretences."

"Oh, thank goodness." Relieved, she pressed a hand to her chest. "I was worried the entire time."

"Yeah, you're not the only one. I had expected the worst."

"But...?"

My nose scrunched sheepishly. "...But you were right, about everything. He wants to be with me, regardless. Still, I can't afford to be naïve about the journey ahead; it won't be pleasant, for anybody."

"With a little faith and patience in each other...you will get there."

"That's precisely what Ari said."

"Well, Ari's a man of wisdom then."

"Did I just hear my name mentioned?" The man of the hour grinned as his handsome face peered around the door. "Can I interest either of you ladies in a cup of tea?"

"You must have read my mind. I'm dying to have one after someone sucked any energy I had away." Rising off the bed, I lovingly patted his perfect behind passing him in the doorway. "Hmm, very nice."

Poppy giggled leading the way to the kitchen. "Oh my."

"I'm sorry for taking off without telling any of you where I was headed," I apologised as the five of us sat around the dining table enjoying a late lunch, once they'd finished berating me first. "I caused you all to worry unnecessarily."

Scarlett's hand waved frivolously. "Oh, forget it, sis; you needed a break. Especially after mum's little tirade the other night," she sympathised. "Her comments were totally uncalled for and completely unfounded."

"But at least it's giving you a chance to iron out some creases." Poppy smiled softly.

Ari nodded, reiterating, "There are a few matters that require ironing out, but for now, we've agreed on baby steps."

A perplexed Scarlett's fork clattered on the plate. "What's going on? Have I missed something here? Has something happened? Teddy?" When I hadn't answered, her anxious gaze turned to my best friend. "Do you know what's going on?"

"Sorry, it's not my story to tell," Poppy defiantly responded, leaning against the back of the chair.

She turned to Ari. "Ari? What about you? Are you going to give me the same vague response?"

He glared at her. "As a matter of fact, yes, I am." Ari twisted in his seat and reached out to me. "Teddy? It's entirely your decision."

Frozen with fear, I whispered, "I need to rip that Band-Aid off." Shaking, I set the cup I nursed between both hands onto its matching saucer.

He eyed me sceptically. "If you're sure?"

"Without the full support of everyone around me, how am I supposed to heal?"

Through a taut nod, Ari reluctantly agreed, "Fair point."

Heat stained my cheeks as I blew out a shuddering breath and began my disclosure about my horrific past, each word seamlessly flowing one after the other and without interruption.

My fingers twisted nervously in my lap as my sister and Dominique sat glued to the chair, their brows furrowing as they attempted to process every last word I'd painfully shared. Likewise, with Ari, I agonised waiting for their reaction. Scarlett, in particular, having heard me talk about our mother in such an undignified manner must have been upsetting for her. However, in my naivety, I expected her response to be a little less explosive.

"This is entirely fucked up!" she fumed, her head jerking angrily, making both Ari and I flinch. "But mum? I always knew she could be a first-class bitch, but this? Surely, sinking this low would be beneath her, wouldn't it?" Questionable doubt hung in the air.

"As hard as it is to believe, Scarlett, she did sink that low," I sadly informed her. "Her betrayal's unforgivable. So now you understand why we can't have the usual mother-daughter relationship most people do."

"But what she did...it's just not right!" Scarlett vexed, relentless tears brimming. "What did dad do about it? Does he even know what happened?" Naturally, she was inquisitive, but as I was unsure myself, how could I possibly answer her?

I gave her a lacklustre shrug. "Honestly, I don't know." I left my chair, coming to kneel on the floor beside my sobbing sister. "Everything will be fine, I promise."

Scarlett gaped disbelievingly. "How can you say that? Mum and this person who raped you are still walking around as free as a bird when neither should be!"

"I need to do this right...baby steps, sis, and as much as I want to dive in headfirst by confronting mum, it won't do any good. She would only deny everything and then lay the blame squarely on me."

Blazing blue eyes widened in anger. "No! Surely not? How can she blame you? You didn't ask to be raped, or have your baby taken away." Her teeth clenched. "You. Didn't. Ask. For. Any. Of. It."

Anger was good. "I know, but unfortunately, it's mum, she won't care." So much so, it was upsetting. I winced as a sharp pain lanced my head. "I need to go and lie down for a while. I'm exhausted. Are you going to be all right?" I asked, rising to my feet.

She snorted. "I can't believe you're asking if I'm okay, but yeah, I'll be fine. It's just a shock is all, and it's a lot to take in."

I lovingly squeezed her hand. "I know. Ari felt the same way." "I love you, sissy."

"I love you, too."

18

Ari

"POOR TEDDY," Dominique commiserated, sagging against the cushioned sofa in the formal living room. "How in the hell has she managed to keep this to herself all this time?" she queried. "If it were me, I would've lost it yonks ago."

"She felt she didn't have any choice thanks to her mother. Therese led her to believe no one would accept the truth," I uttered dryly. Retrieving the decanter of bourbon from the buffet, I poured each of them a much-needed glass. "Telling me was a huge step for her as it was."

"Did she disclose her rapist?" she probed, accepting the tumbler from my outstretched hand.

Gulping my drink down, I refilled the glass and shook my head. "No. She didn't. All I can tell you is that it's someone amongst our social circle."

"Oh, great. That narrows it down, doesn't it?" my impetuous sister argued, waving a hand around. "That could be any one of our friends or relatives." Her head jerked towards Poppy. "Do you know who *he is*?"

"Unfortunately, that piece of information was never given to me either, and even if I did know, it's not my secret to tell; it's Teddy's," she reiterated.

"We should know, just in case he tries to attack one of us!" she irately whined. I had to shut her down.

"Poppy's right, Dom, we can't force Teddy to tell us. Be a little more understanding, please. She'll be the one to tell us of her own accord when she's ready."

"Okay, fine!" she huffed, her face growing crimson from my hardened expression.

"Please respect Teddy's wishes, Dominique. If I hear of you pressuring her, you'll have me to deal with, am I clear?"

She glared frostily across the room at me. "Yes, Ari, crystal clear."

It seemed like Deja Vu with everyone around the table, silently enjoying the fresh mango and prawn salad Poppy had assembled in front of us. Although, observing the vicious jabs my sister gave to the food on her plate, it compelled me to question her mood.

"You know the prawn's already dead, don't you?" She shot me a deathly glare. I took a sip of my beer and chuckled. "So, ladies," I remarked, setting my stubby in front of me, "what have I let myself in for, hanging out here with all of you?"

A loud giggle erupted from Teddy, and I couldn't help but laugh with her. Or at her? I was amused either way.

"Aw, my poor baby. You wanted to stay here, so suck it up, princess!"

"I'm a princess now, am I?"

"Yep, you... are... a... princess," she slurred, poking at my chest with those talons she called nails.

Grinning madly, I caught her finger between my teeth and bit down. Payback.

Teddy smiled salaciously. "Ow! You're such an animal, but I love it."

"I know."

"Um, can you two get a room please?" Poppy's nose wrinkled at our less than charming display. "We don't particularly want dinner and a show."

"You, Popsicle, are so funny." Teddy laughed hysterically. "Dinner and a show, that's a good one. Ari loves the idea, don't ya, babe?"

A ghost of a smile danced on my lips. "You need to go to bed and get some sleep; it's been a long day. Come on, Teddy."

"But I don't want to go to bed." She childishly pouted. "I want to drink more wine."

I suppressed my laughter and growled, "No, you've had enough. Let's go."

"Oh, there's that bear again. I swear your brother's a bear, Dom; he's always growling like one." Teddy giggled and pushed to her feet, her legs wobbling beneath her. Her housemate's laughter at the drunken antics certainly weren't helping matters either, each of them failing to notice the glowering stare raining down on them.

"Right, that's it," I barked, scooping her over my shoulder and smacking her behind. "We're off to bed! Goodnight girls'!"

"What about my strawberry cheesecake?"

"Have it tomorrow." I had hoped to take a slice to bed and use Teddy as a plate, but as she was drunk, another night would have to suffice.

Ignoring the protests, I carried her into the bedroom, dropping her on the bed with a thud.

"I could've walked, you know! I am perf...ectly cap...able." She hiccupped, bouncing off the mattress. I watched with wry amusement as she swayed and fumbled her way to the bathroom.

"Of course, you are," I uttered, tossing the countless pillows off her bed to the floor.

"Fuck!"

At the loud expletive, I quickly spun to find myself viewing a shell-shocked Teddy sprawled across the floor, a hand nursing one side of her head. "Ah, Jesus, Teddy. Let me see. What have you done to yourself?" With an exasperated sigh, I sat her up and gently brushed the flopping hair from her face. "I'll need to go grab a cold pack; you have an egg forming on the side of your head, and it's starting to bruise already."

In a fit of giggles, Teddy rolled back onto the floor.

My bemused gaze stared down at her. "What is so funny about this, may I dare ask?"

"We have matching bruises, we can be twinsey's!" she blurted, her giggle turning into a full-blown cackle.

My eyes raised to the heavens. "What did I ever do to you?"

∞

Teddy

DELIGHTFUL SMELLS FROM THE kitchen drifted, making me stir. I slowly sat up, wincing at the dull ache in my head. "Ow, so much for never drinking again." I sifted my fingers through my tangled hair, grimacing at the formed lump on the side of my head.

A warm buttery aroma wafted under my nose, compelling me to clap a hand to my mouth. I leapt from the bed and into the bathroom; two bottles of wine on an empty stomach with a headache wasn't one of my brightest ideas.

I had barely finished heaving when a widely grinning Ari entered the bathroom. Ironically, our roles were reversed. The only difference being, we weren't mad at one another this time.

"How are you feeling?" he quizzed, propping a shoulder on the doorframe.

I grabbed the mouthwash from the vanity and threw back a capful, swilling it around inside my mouth. I spat it back into the sink and wiped my mouth with the back of my hand. "Like shit."

"I bet." Smiling roguishly, Ari moved towards the shower. "Let's get you cleaned up," he ordered, opening the door and flicking the tap on, "and then you can eat. Arms up." I complied, raising my arms above my head. "I've cooked one of your favourites, buttermilk pancakes, whilst Poppy made a summer fruits sauce to have with them," he informed me, hauling the white cotton singlet over my head.

"Ugh, I don't know if I'm capable of stomaching food right now." "You need to eat. Everything you ate last night is probably swimming its way to the sewerage farm by now."

"Are you trying to make me vomit again? Because if I do, it'll be all over you!"

"Someone's a cranky puss this morning." Gentle persuasion pushed me against the vanity and slid my cotton panties down my legs. "I might start my breakfast right here," he purred, peeking upwards from beneath dark lashes. He pushed my thighs apart and buried his tongue deep inside me — each lick soft, slow, arousing, leaving my silken folds drenched.

Ari hummed appreciatively, an erotic sound that reverberated exquisitely through my entire body. I greedily wanted more and lifted a leg, setting one foot on his shoulder, pushing my cleft further into his mouth. My fingers gripped his hair as he hooked an arm around my thigh, the savagery making me moan softly and my insides quiver as his thumb pressed against my sensitive nub.

I quickly became a shuddering mess and cried out, my hips bucking against his lips. The savagery ongoing until the insides of my thighs became slick, and I cried uncle.

A harshly breathing Ari slid up my sated body, peppering kisses along my dampened skin. Beads of sweat dripped over his brow. "The bathroom's steamy, in more ways than one."

"Join me for a shower, then you can finish what you started," I challenged, tugging at his clothes. Ari quickly hauled his T-shirt over his head, throwing it to the floor.

"I'd be a fool to refuse such a tempting proposition."

A slight breeze caught wisps of my hair, blowing it across my face as we stepped off the number nine tram in front of the Queen Victoria Markets. I beamed. The sight and smells alone made my mouth-water. Ari was less than enthused.

"Couldn't we have just stayed at home rather than being surrounded by these wretched people? And for the record, it would've been quicker to drive."

I rolled my eyes at him. "Come on grumble butt." Clutching Ari's hand in mine, I dragged him towards the buzzing markets. I was enjoying myself, even if he wasn't. Particularly as a variety of music materialised from the buskers scattered around the outside on the footpaths. Each one manifested hope, wishing to make a sale on their self-produced CD's or just a quick buck from the coins and notes onlookers threw into their guitar cases.

Stretching two blocks between Victoria and Peel streets, the famously historical market was notoriously busy. Parents with overexcited children attempted to trudge through the masses trying to complete their shopping, likewise, couples similar to us, casually strolling without a care in the world. Well, I wasn't for the moment anyway. Ari was the only person out of hundreds acting as if he had the entire weight of the world on his shoulders.

Whether you were shopping for the clothes or the food, Queen Victoria Markets knew how to cater to the masses. Each stall varied from the last as were the smells, mostly as we passed the food court. Various aromatic scents drifted, making my stomach growl loudly much to Ari's amusement.

As it stood, I was after the fresh produce. We had filled several bags with meat and seafood as it was already, which Ari was dutifully carrying much to his chagrin. He was also growing impatient, his consistent huffing making me laugh whenever we paused to look at something else. I told him to stop being a cranky arse and dragged him to a café, leaving him somewhat amenable after having a bite to eat and a coffee.

Vendors yelled around us, their loud voices echoing as they attempted to lure the slow-paced buyers to their stalls with their competitive prices, each wanting to make enough sales by the day's end.

"What an amazing place, don't you agree, Ari?" I asked, sampling a fresh grape. It's sweetened taste bursting inside my mouth. Perfect. The obliging vendor swiftly piled two generous bunches into a brown paper bag.

"Why did I bother coming here, particularly on a Sunday morning?" he retorted, chewing on the sweet grape I'd just popped into his grouchy mouth.

"You get the best bargains on a Sunday, that's why," I countered, handing the vendor my cash.

Ari gestured to the numerous bags hanging from his hands. "Do you think you have enough now?"

I looked down at the hessian and cold bags gripped tightly in both hands and crinkled my eyes in delight. "Are you tired you poor old dear, and in need of a nana nap?"

Irate, he growled as I took one bag off him and slipped it over my wrist. "I'm only thirty, so no, I don't need a nana nap. I've just had enough of shopping and all this bloody noise."

"Okay, old-timer, let's go home then." My giggling turned into a yelp as his free hand connected with my backside.

Walking back towards the tram stop, he grunted in my ear, "I'll show you old timer later."

Having learned my roommates had gone to the movies for the afternoon, I collapsed onto the sofa and lifted my aching legs, plonking my sore feet directly into Ari's lap the moment he joined me. "Rub please."

Ari looked down at my feet and screwed up his face only to oblige me anyway. "Cheeky little bugger, aren't you?"

"Thank you; they're aching a lot." Lapping up the tender massaging, I rolled my head against the padded arm and closed my eyes for a minute or two.

"Are you going to sleep?"

"No, I'm just resting my eyes. Someone kept me awake all night with their snoring."

"I do not snore!" he retorted indignantly. "After your guzzling last night, you were the one snoring!" Ari smirked, tickling the bottoms of my feet. He grabbed my ankles as they thumped a little too close to his groin. "Can't have you ruining the family jewels now, can I?"

"No, most definitely not."

The toasty warmth of the sun unexpectedly disappeared behind some very sketchy black clouds. Torrential rain subsequently followed, blustering against the sashed windows, turning the day depressingly chilly. As a result, Ari and I spent the rest of the afternoon snuggled under a blanket, sipping on hot chocolates, and binge-watching one of my all-time favourite sitcoms. He, of course, shared his displeasure.

"Do women actually think and behave as they do?" he quizzed, pointing to the flat screen on the wall above the lit fireplace. I snorted as I licked the last of the melted chocolate and gooey marshmallow off the spoon. "No, not all."

"No, only most of the Victorian population do," he argued pointedly. "You women are complicated creatures."

I couldn't help but laugh at his musings. "Speaking from experience, are we?"

"I shall neither confirm nor deny," he demurred quietly, giving me a lopsided smile.

"Ooh, how diplomatic of you. I imagine you learnt that clever tactic from your mother."

"No, my father," he freely admitted. "That's what he tells my mother anyway, mostly when he's trying to avoid a scolding."

"So, if you misbehave, and say the same thing — I could make all kinds of assumptions," I quietly reasoned, straddling his lap. The hem of my short skirt lifted as I rocked back and forth, rubbing my lace panties against his denim-clad crotch. "Couldn't I?"

"I had better behave myself then, now that I've unwittingly opened that frightful can of worms," he addressed, gliding his splayed hands along my bare thighs and underneath the skirt. He tugged at either side of my panties, tearing the lace. Its thin elastic snapped against my skin.

"You'll open a can of whoop arse if you don't," I confidently added, stroking his stubble with the tips of my fingers.

"Bring it on," Ari dared gruffly, fisting my hair, and capturing my mouth in a hunger filled kiss.

He groaned against my lips as I reached down, undoing the zipper and the button on his shorts to free his rock-hard erection. He instinctively acted, his palms skating over the curve of my behind and cupping each cheek before lifting me to slam me back down over his engorged cock.

I cried out. Filled to the hilt so abruptly, my back arched, and my nails dug into Ari's muscular shoulders. Frenzied, we tore our clothes off, leaving them scattered over the floor as our mouths met in a hot, sensual kiss. About to roll my hips over his rigid length, Ari grabbed me and took complete control.

I happily let him.

19

Ari

AS I CRUISED ALONG the busy freeway in the direction of work, my mind grew preoccupied with the past weeks events. Everything about Teddy was mesmerising, and my appetite for her was insatiable. Monday morning had sadly loomed too fast.

Arousing thoughts of Sunday afternoon sprung to mind. The session so intense, neither of us were surprised that our screams alone hadn't sent the neighbours scurrying up the footpath and banging on the front door. Although, at one stage during the afternoon, I swore I spotted a male figure peeking through the open window of her bedroom. Not wanting to alarm Teddy, I checked while her sister kept her otherwise occupied. After discovering two footprints embedded deeply in the garden bed below, I was glad I had.

Thankfully, Teddy had remained none the wiser.

The shrilling sound of the phone rang through the car's speakers. rudely interrupting my illustrious thoughts. Sighing, I hit the call button on my steering wheel. "Ari Jaeger speaking."

"Lose the formalities, son," my mother playfully scolded.

I grinned. "Hello, Mother."

"Ari, darling, how are you? Where have you been hiding? I've been trying to get ahold of you all week," Mother softly complained.

"Can I get a word in please, Mother?"

Her raspy laugh rumbled through the speakers. "Oh, I'm sorry, darling."

"I'm well, thank you, and the reason behind my absence was because I was away..." I braced myself for the inevitable screech. ".... with Teddy."

"Yes!" There it was. I jumped back in the seat out of fright.

"Fuck me!"

"Language son," she admonished, and barely taking a breath, her delighted demeanour quickly returned. "I knew it! I knew you two had finally come together."

"Yes, indeed, we have." In more ways than one, I mused inwardly.

"Dominique remained mum on the subject, too. You know, she churlishly deflected or changed the subject whenever I broached the topic. So unfair, keeping me out of the loop," she informed me irritably. "But despite her evasiveness, I guessed anyway. Unfortunately, it's a habit she's learnt from me."

I rolled my eyes at the dramatics.

"Don't roll your eyes at me either, Ari Jaeger!"

Disconcerted by my mother's intuition, I frowned worryingly; how did she do that? I thought I was safe, apparently not. Note to self: check the car for cameras. "I apologise for not informing you sooner. However, we had planned on surprising you by hosting a dinner party at my house one night." I had no idea where that came from, but thankfully, my mother believed the little white lie that had just rolled off my tongue.

"Hmm, I'll let you off the hook this time," she cautioned dryly.

Raising a brow at the polite response, I chuckled. "Why, thank you for being so gracious, Mother."

She snorted. "You have a smart mouth; you know that?"

"I only learnt it from the best," I retaliated, grinning.

"I can't argue there," she acquiesced. "So, when can we get together for this dinner?"

"You're bloody persistent." I smirked, mentally checking my hectic schedule. "Let me confer with Teddy, and we'll check both our calendars, then I'll get back to you later today. Shall that be enough to quell your unquenchable thirst for now?"

"Don't be so dramatic! Of course, it is darling. I can't wait to tell your father; he'll be as ecstatic as I am."

"Or end up equally deaf." I chuckled. "Mother, I have just arrived at work, and as much as I've enjoyed this little chat, I really must go."

"Okay, darling. Love you and have a lovely day. Pass on my love to Teddy, too, won't you?"

"Of course, love you, too, Mother." Regardless of that small fact, my ears were still ringing. The dinner invitation and mother's annoying, but loving enthusiasm reminded me I needed to contact Teddy, preferably sooner rather than later. Knowing my mother, she'd have the champagne on ice and a three-course menu set by midmorning.

Climbing from the car, I reached into the pocket of my jacket and tugged out my phone. The call proceeded directly to message bank with Teddy's melodic voice speaking to me just as I entered the lift.

"Hey, it's Teddy. Leave a message, and I'll get back to you."

"Hey, gorgeous, can you call me when you have an opportunity to do so. I love you." I stepped off on my floor and traipsed by Lila's desk. Much to my annoyance, she was practically on the threshold of my office waiting for me. I beg of you, Lila, please don't drop any of the damned messages clasped in your hand.

"Is there anything I can get you, Mr Jaeger?" she purred, nipping at my heels in a ludicrously tight-fitting pencil skirt and six-inch heels.

Hanging my jacket on the coat rack, I stopped and turned towards her. Right, it was time to squash her little fantasy. "Yes, there is actually."

Lila's false eyelashes battered feverishly at me as long bleach blonde extensions twirled through her bony fingers. "Yes, sir?"

"Are you able to grab me the number for Fleur's florist please?" A task I knew I could've easily managed, but her constant flirting had grown beyond bothersome.

Confused, her brow furrowed. "A florist, sir?"

"Yes, a florist, Lila. I want to purchase a bouquet for my girlfriend."

Staring in disbelief, she stuttered, "G...Girl...f...friend...sir?"

In a flare of exasperation, I openly rolled my eyes and repeated myself, slowly, "Yes, Lila, my girlfriend. Now, the florist, please, and I'll order them myself." I briefly glanced up from my computer and had to bite my bottom lip as laughter bubbled at the crestfallen expression.

"Yes, that's all for now, thank you, Lila." I waved a dismissive hand before pausing. "Oh, and one more thing, Lila...."

In an annoying huff, she spun back to face me, her teeth clenched as she responded, "Yes, sir?"

"If my *girlfriend*, Teddy McGovern, happens to call, please direct her call straight through at all times," I clarified, smiling brightly. "The same rule applies if she drops by. Are we clear?"

"Of course. Is that all, sir?"

"Yes, for now." Deliberately, I turned my attention to the computer, chuckling as Lila closed the door, a little too hard for my liking.

∞

Teddy

I BRIEFLY GLANCED ACROSS THE DESK at my buzzing iPhone and picked it up, instantly rejecting the call. I had no desire to push the issue. Spencer had acted incredibly gracious about my sudden week away as it was, particularly without explanation. Besides stopping in to check in on me, he at least possessed the grace not to pry into my private life.

The hours since I'd settled at my desk had flown by, and only realised it was lunchtime when I heard my name squeakily called out.

"Excuse me; is there a Teddy McGovern here?"

I swung the chair around to acknowledge the bored courier flanked by a large bouquet of two dozen deep pink roses, impatiently shuffling in the centre of the hallway outside my cubicle.

"That's me," I simpered, rising from the chair, and striding over to remove the fragrant flowers from skinny, sweaty hands. "Thank you; they're beautiful."

Disinterested by the gushing, the weedy courier took off just as quickly as he arrived.

"Wow, he was excited. Maybe he wished it was him receiving flowers instead?" Emily jibed, eyeing the flowers enviously. "So, are they from the infamous Ari Jaeger?"

Happiness bloomed undeniably bright, matching the bouquet laying on the desk. I grinned as my excited gaze scanned the handwritten card found hiding amongst the soft, delicate petals. I read it aloud,

'My beautiful Teddy,
These roses reminded me of you.
Stunning and delectably sweet.
Love you, infinity,
Ari, xxx.'

"He's a keeper, Teddy." Emily sighed. "I hope I find someone like that one day."

"Don't fret, Ems. You never know, the right guy may just come along and sweep you right off your feet when you least expect it."

"That's all well and good as long as he doesn't trip me over."

I giggled and checked the time on my watch. I had plenty of time to thank Ari in person for his gift. His building was conveniently within walking distance after all. A naughty smile flittered on my lips as I reached for my handbag beneath the desk; perhaps I ought to show my appreciation instead? With a plan in motion, I rushed out the door.

Tilting my head, I looked skywards and scanned the modern thirty-storey, rectangular building encompassed by nothing more than steel framework and walls of tinted glass.

As soon as I stepped through revolving glass doors into a striking lobby, two burly bodyguards situated behind a large circular desk eyed me with their steely gazes. Their size alone was intimidating, enough to frighten anyone away with unclear intentions at least. Although, I suspected lying beneath that harsh exterior they were undoubtedly nothing more than marshmallows, not that I intended to stop to ask them. The thought of having them tackle me to the ground wasn't exactly appealing, nor was it on my agenda that day, something else was. So, as I sauntered past them on my way to the bank of lifts on the far wall, I made a point of smiling cheerfully. In return, they mustered a curt nod, barely. Nope, they're most definitely not marshmallows. Oh, well, couldn't win 'em all.

I pressed the inset button on the wall and patiently waited, using the time to admire the lobby's timeless elegance. Sunlight shimmered through high paned glass windows, bouncing light across large grey and white veined marble tiles, highlighting the lush greenery of the urban garden wall hanging behind a row of caramel leather bench seats. A rush of men and women alike in their expensive suits or dresses scurried in an antlike manner from all directions, and except for a mere few, most had their eyes glued to their iPads or phones. It seemed interacting with others was outdated these days, quite sad, really.

When the lift eventually arrived on the ground floor, I stepped into the car and pressed the button for the thirtieth floor. My gaze glinted, carefully examining the printed silk shift dress in the mirrored walls as the doors slid closed, ensuring my arrival was that of perfection — nothing more, nothing less.

Before I knew it, the lift dinged, and the doors opened.

Showtime.

I confidently strode from the elevator, my heels clicking as I stepped onto matching marble tiles. I peered around the large lobby, scrutinising the stylish layout, noting that the colours and furniture were highly similar to Ari's house. I rolled my eyes: he'd clearly hired the same designer. As I approached a smaller version of the semi-circle desk downstairs, a knowing smile crossed my lips upon examining Lila. What on earth had possessed Ari to hire her? An outstanding résumé perhaps? That surely had to be the reason as she certainly had nothing else going for her.

I cleared my throat, drawing Lila's attention away from the fashion magazine spread before her. "Lila, is it? I'm Teddy McGovern, Mr Jaeger's girlfriend; is he free?"

Her heavily made-up eyes narrowed up at me as red-painted lips curled into a tight, phoney smile. "I will ensure Mr Jaeger's not busy first," she rudely replied, picking up the receiver and dialling his office. People skills weren't one of her greatest assets, that's for sure.

"Mr Jaeger," she purred. Seriously, grab me a bucket. "You have an unscheduled visitor. They wouldn't say. Of course, Mr Jaeger."

Annoyed by the blatant lying, I drummed my French manicured nails on the desktop, earning a deathly glare from Lila.

Good.

Having hung up, Lila cleared her throat and greeted me with a cold stare.

Willpower, Teddy, willpower. A tight smile graced my face as I responded, "Yes, Lila?"

"Mr Jaeger informed me that you'll need to make an appointment like everybody else as he's far too busy to see you," she informed haughtily.

I raised a brow sharply; oh, we're playing that game, are we? "That's fine," I murmured as she rapidly tore her lying gaze away and turned her attention back to her magazine. That was short-lived as I dug into my tote and grabbed my phone.

"Um, what are you doing?" Her high-pitched voice resembled scraping nails on a blackboard.

In exasperation, I rolled my eyes. "Oh, for goodness sake – I'm just leaving Ari a message. After all, you only just informed me he's far too busy to see me." I smirked, holding it up to my ear. "Hi there. What are you doing now? Oh, I see. Hmmm, I am. Okay, no worries." Hanging up, I chucked it back into my bag and smugly folded my arms.

Three, two, one.

Disguising my satisfied grin wasn't easy as the door to Ari's office flung open and Lila's jaded expression swiftly turned to terror. His loud hurried footsteps distinctly heard as he strolled straight into my open arms and hungrily devoured my mouth, intensifying my need for him.

We finally came up for air, pausing long enough for a breathless Ari to speak. "What a pleasant surprise. Now, what do I owe to this unexpected but welcome visit?"

"I came to thank you personally for that gorgeous bouquet of roses you had delivered this morning."

"You are most welcome," he murmured, tenderly brushing a fingertip along my cheek. He tilted his head, planting a soft kiss to my parted lips. Suddenly, he yanked me closer, his tongue darting to languorously coax my mouth open. Not that I needed any provocation. Aware that a gaping Lila's beady eyes stared jealously, I deliberately weaved my fingers through his unruly hair and arched my back, curving us together perfectly. I could kiss him endlessly but ultimately, we had to stop.

"Wow, you are indeed welcome. I might send flowers more often if this is the thanks I receive," Ari breathlessly whispered, clinging to my waist.

"Perhaps the next time I'll give you a blowjob instead, how about that?" I purred, biting down, and sinking my teeth into his bottom lip.

His eyes lit up like the fireworks on New Year's Eve. "I'm up for anything you offer."

"Likewise."

He chuckled. "Oh, I know. However, before we go shagging on the floor, another matter requires my attention," Ari muttered, thrusting a hand through his thick hair. "I apologise ahead for what you're about to witness."

I silently nodded whilst observing his soft expression morphing from Jekyll to Hyde in a nanosecond. The searing gaze grew harder, darker. I was instantly aroused.

His narrowed gaze zeroed in on his defiant assistant. "You," he roared, wagging a stern finger at Lila, "are fired! You have ten minutes to pack up your belongings and leave."

Lila shrunk under Ari's frightening glare. "But, Mr Jaeger sir, you told me no interruptions, and everyone must have an appointment!"

Her horrid whining wasn't helping the situation, nor were the lame excuses.

His darkened gaze flared as his intimidating frame leaned over the desk. "Not only were you rude to my girlfriend, but you openly lied to her as well! I informed you only this morning that she was always to be let through without hesitation!" he bellowed. "You can thank your petty jealousy, and ridiculous fantasising for the loss of your job. Oh, and for the record, don't expect a glowing reference from me either! Now get the fuck out of here!"

He picked up the receiver from the phone on the desk and dialled security, informing them of Lila's termination with the request they escort her from the building. "Make sure she hands in her security pass too. Thank you." I flinched as the receiver slammed against the cradle. "Sorry."

"It's all right," I assured, walking into his outstretched arm, my empathy flowing as I observed a miserable Lila packing a handful of personal belongings into a cardboard box. Tears flowed, producing blackened streams as her mascara ran down her reddened cheeks.

She looked up and shot me a deathly glare, dissipating my empathy instantly. Especially as her scowl darkened as the two burly guards Ari requested stepped from the lift, escorted her out.

"Now this unpleasantness has been dealt with, let us go into my office for a spot of lunch," Ari offered, turning back to me, his hard expression gone. "There's enough for the both of us." Placing a hand on the small of my back, he guided me towards his spacious office.

My mouth gaped as Melbourne's vast skyline drew me in. "You have a beautiful view of the city from up here," I remarked, leaning my forehead on one of the floor-to-ceiling windows and peering down at the ant-sized people scurrying about their business on the busy streets.

"If you look beyond the skyline, you should be able to view Port Melbourne quite clearly from up here." Ari's hand signalled in the port's direction. "I have the perfect ocean view."

"So, you do," I murmured, spinning around to eye the mini feast laid out on the black, ultra-modern coffee table, the delicious aromas making my mouth water. "What's on the menu? Besides you?"

Ari chuckled motioning to the mahogany leather sofa situated in the corner of the room. "Shall we sit? We have spinach and ricotta ravioli," he began, scooping pasta out of a plastic container and onto a ceramic plate, passing the dish along with a set of cutlery, placing both into my outstretched hands. "Help yourself to the Greek salad, too. There's plenty there."

Using the small tongs to grasp a handful, I grinned suggestively. "I'm pretty adept at helping myself."

Ari shook his head and snorted. "I'm well aware," he responded, pushing back to his feet to retrieve two bottles of water from a bar fridge beneath the wet bar.

I playfully scrunched up my nose and giggled, my gaze upon his handsome face as he strolled towards me. "Thank you, but I wasn't expecting this. I only came to thank you for the roses." I lifted a forkful of pasta and salad to my mouth and chewed, enjoying the perfect marriage of flavours thoroughly.

"You certainly showed your appreciation for those." He winked playfully, setting the bottles down on the table before lowering into the seat. "I wanted to ensure my girl's day stayed bright."

"Well, I can happily inform you, Mr Jaeger, that you most certainly brightened my day. I could return the favour and brighten yours a little more if you like."

Ari's fork clattered back onto the plate. "You have an extraordinary sexual appetite considering."

Unconcerned, I shrugged my shoulders. "Considering what? My rape? Why should I let that stand in the way of my fucking you?"

His jaw dropped. "As much as I would love to take you up on the offer, and I can't believe I'm saying this, but I must decline. Blame the run of scheduled meetings, all of which shall be held in my office."

I tried pouting. "You know how to be a party pooper."

"Does returning to work smelling like sex turn you on, Teddy?" Ari's voice rasped. His Adam's apple bobbed profusely as he carefully observed me setting my plate down on the coffee table and rising off the sofa, positioning myself between his widely spread legs. I raked my fingers through his gorgeous hair.

"You turn me on – all the time. I think about you non-stop, and your amazing – cock."

The front of Ari's pants tightened as his widened gaze drifted to the rising hem of my dress. "You're pantiless?" He gulped, sliding a hand towards the zipper of his trousers, and springing the erection he now sported free.

My lustful gaze swept downwards, staring hungrily at the hard and swollen length firmly nestled inside his stroking hand. "Yes," I breathed huskily.

With his free hand, Ari drew me closer, the tips of his fingers grazing the curve of my buttocks as he guided me over him. Our gratified moans reverberated as I slowly sank down, inhaling sharply as his wide girth stretched, while his impressive length filled me. I inhaled sharply. Christ! His intense arousal made him feel larger than normal, compelling me to adjust my hips just to ensure he fitted all the way.

He sensed my struggle and leaned back, warning me to grip his shoulders. His hips flexed, and I cried out before slowly rising and easing back down, again, and again, feeling every exquisite inch of him.

Aware he was entirely at my mercy, Ari succumbed to my desires; the carnal call between us was too strong to deny. I began soft and slow, enjoying the sensation of his velvety length inside me. His breath hitched as each tantalising stroke of his swollen head hit that sweet spot, building towards an even sweeter climax.

Ari gruffly urged me to ride him harder, and faster, his fingertips digging into the soft flesh of my buttocks as our honied moans echoed around his office, flowing out and under the closed door.

"Now that wasn't so bad, was it?" I breathlessly murmured, sliding both hands beneath the soft fabric of his shirt to caress his heaving chest.

"It was –," Ari winced as I tweaked both nipples. "Ah, gently – amazing. You are incredibly gifted at seduction."

"I told you – I can't help it. You turn me on constantly," I whispered, grazing his lips.

He gingerly grasped my nape and took my mouth, deepening the kiss, his tongue exploring and tasting me. Our hips undulated against one another, stirring his semi-hard cock to life as unmistakable desire sinuously soared through our veins.

Ari swiftly switched our positions and tugged my dress over my head, tossing it aside. In the next breath, he wordlessly flipped me over, embedding my knees deeply in the cushions with my head facing the windows — an indulgent groan producing as he slammed into me. I reached out for the arm on the sofa, my grip tightening with each unyielding thrust he pounded into me.

He leaned forward and snaked his hand towards my cleft, pinching my swollen nub. My body quaked, squeezing his long shaft as an intense orgasm rippled, eliciting a pleasurable grunt from Ari. His body shuddered, grazing my bare cheeks before stilling and collapsing over me.

"I am well and truly fucked!" he breathed erratically, nuzzling the crook of my neck. "My colleagues shall undoubtedly guess how I spent my lunch hour."

I giggled as he straightened. "At least they'll now know I'm a bona fide person." A hand landed firmly over my exposed cheek with a resounding slap. I moaned…. I was in the mood for a good spanking too. Aware of my arousal, Ari rapidly eased out of me and pulled up his trousers.

"No more time for that, we need to get cleaned up!"

With jellied legs, I pushed off the sofa and grabbed my dress along with my purse to retrieve the missing panties. Clutching both in my hand, I headed into Ari's private bathroom where my eyes dipped, avidly watching him wash and dry off his cock.

His gaze darted, a smile tugging at his beautiful lips. "Don't get any ideas."

I smiled coyly. "I wasn't. I was simply admiring."

He threw the face washer into the hamper beside the sink and smirked. "Oh, I nearly forgot thanks to your sexpertise, my mother phoned me this morning with an invitation to dinner one night this week."

"She obviously knows about us then." I chuckled, unsurprised by the news.

"Clearly." He glowered, tucking his shirt back into his pants.

"Mother was annoyingly insistent; she just about deafened me, too."

I frowned. "Why was Audrina screaming at you?"

He leaned against the wall and folded his arms across his chest, his mouth twisting wryly. "Let's just say mother overshared her excitement... It's not funny!" he chided as I laughed, his tickled gaze on the lacy panties sliding up my legs. "I swear my ears haven't quit ringing since then."

"Oh, this is priceless. I'm sorry for laughing at your suffering, Ari, but it's adorable to know your mother's excited for us," I gushed, biting down on my bottom lip in an attempt to stifle my bubbling laughter.

"I can tell you're extremely sorry," Ari scoffed.

"Really, I am. But dinner would be lovely. I love your mum. She's fun." I threw the used towel into the hamper and slipped my dress back over my head. "So what night are we going?" I quizzed, giving my hair a quick brush.

"I'll call her back shortly to find out the rest of the details, okay, love?"

"That's fine." I glanced down at my watch, noting the lunch hour was nearly up. "I need to return to work. I'll see you later?"

An indulgent smiled formed. "What about you...come to my place and stay for a few days? Give the girls' a break from our love fest; what do you say?"

I grasped the collar on his shirt and leaned in, kissing him softly.

"I'd say that's affirmative," Ari mumbled against my mouth.

I smiled coquettishly and slowly stepped back, pressing a fingernail into his firm chest. "Well, I guess we'll be seeing each other later then."

"Well, I guess we will."

I pirouetted and strolled through his office, his darkened gaze trailing me. Smirking, I paused in the doorway and pointed towards the empty desk in the foyer. "Um, don't forget you're in need of a new assistant too." He scowled, making me laugh.

"I thank you for the reminder," he retorted dryly, following me to the lift. He leaned across me and pressed the button on the wall with the bell dinging, and the doors gliding open soon after.

I stepped inside. "Thanks for lunch; it was fun." I lifted the hem of my dress and flashed my panties, his chuckling resonating just as the doors closed.

∞

Ari

ONCE THE DOORS SLID CLOSED, no longer could I hold back the laughter. Teddy's unpredictable antics certainly kept me on my toes. Nevertheless, she was my siren, my temptress and I refused to change a thing.

As I made my way back to my office and sat at my desk, I leaned back in the chair and sniffed the air. The scent of Teddy's sweet perfume and sex lingered, two aphrodisiacs guaranteeing a distracted afternoon. I chuckled and shook my head before turning my attention back to where it ought to be; putting the word out that I required a new assistant, ASAP.

20

Thomas

WITH A HAND RAISED ready to knock, I stood in the open doorway, my jaw on the floor. The angry expletives coming from inside Mr Jaeger's office shocked even me. Me; the usually unflappable Thomas Garcia was stunned, and it had me wondering if applying as his PA was a great idea after all. I spun around to leave.

"Mr Garcia, to what do I owe the honour?" Mr Jaeger enquired, his voice clipped as he briefly glanced up from his desk, catching me off guard.

Grimacing, I slowly pivoted and nervously stepped through the open doorway, adjusting the large, black-framed glasses on my face. "If this isn't the right time, Mr Jaeger, I can come back later if you like?"

"No, it's fine. I'm between meetings anyway. Besides, you're here now, so please, come in and take a seat," he offered, gesturing to the chair adjacent to the desk.

As I strolled further into the room, my sensitive nose caught a whiff of a woman's perfume; one I believed to be of a floral nature mixed with the musky scent of sex. I didn't know what shocked me more; the fact my boss had lunchtime sex in his office or the expletives I'd heard. Either way, if this was what I had to look forward to, then I might just quit now before giving him the chance to hire me.

"Mr Jaeger, I hope you don't judge me too forward, but when I saw your internal email about needing a new assistant, I immediately knew I had the qualifications required to fill the position," I confidently informed him, positioning my lanky frame on the mahogany leather chair. Please tell me they didn't have sex on the chair. Too bad if they did, I was already seated.

I unzipped the folder in my lap and was mid-way pulling out a résumé when Mr Jaeger held up a hand.

"No. I want you to tell me about *you*. Anyone can read a CV," he asserted. He's rather astute, I noted inwardly. "If you want the job, you need to sell yourself to me."

Stiffly nodding, I gulped and met his unwavering gaze. I'd be lying if I didn't say he slightly intimidated me. More so as he leaned forward, resting his elbows on the desk and steepling his hands in front of him.

"Please, begin."

I cleared my throat and commenced, informing Mr Jaeger of my qualifications. "I have a Diploma in Business Management, including a Certificate in Leadership and Management. I'm up to date on all computer programs, like Excel, Word, and Data." I paused briefly before continuing, "Not only am I adept at dealing with the media or other HR departments, but I'm also discreet – when the need calls for it." My boss smirked arrogantly. "Most importantly, I'm well equipped to deal with...your less than pleasant moods." Sensing my discomfort, another smug smile tugged at Mr Jaeger's lips.

"My reputation precedes me, I, see?" He leaned back in his chair, his amused gaze eyeing me as he let out a small chuckle. I sagged in relief. "Are you not happy with Human Resources?"

"I am, but I wouldn't mind a change of scenery. Being employed as your PA would offer something fresh and exciting, as well as some new challenges."

"Working for me would indeed offer you those, and as your boss, I do have elevated expectations." Shifting papers around on his desk, he impishly smiled. "Quite honestly, I'm in desperate need of a new personal assistant as I fired mine this morning for reasons I won't divulge." I daren't ask why. "When can you start?"

"Tomorrow if that would suit you? Or even today, given the fact you are in a bind." Either I had seriously bad verbal diarrhoea, or I was just desperate. It was most definitely the latter. I needed the extra money, as I knew from Lila's fat mouth, Ari Jaeger paid well above award wages.

"No, tomorrow's fine, thank you. I shall inform HR shortly that as of tomorrow, you are up here working for me," he offered as a substitute, pushing to his feet.

"Thank you, sir; I appreciate you giving me a chance." Excited, I swiftly stood to shake his extended hand. Damn, what a grip.

"You're welcome, and thank you for taking the initiative to see me. I'll see you first thing, then." Ari nodded and picked up his phone. I guessed I was dismissed.

∞

Teddy

A FAMILIAR ACHE STIRRED between my thighs; I wanted more, even after the lunchtime rendezvous in Ari's office. His cologne, the musky scent of sex, both still lingered, causing my concentration to wane often throughout the afternoon. Mostly, I'd wondered about Ari and how he'd handled himself afterwards. Unreservedly, the same, no doubt.

The moment I arrived home, I quickly changed from my dress into a pair of yoga pants and running shoes in the hope a run would temporarily curb the craving; until later at least. I strolled out the front door and stretched before hitting the pavement. If I planned on seducing Ari after dinner, then a strain just wouldn't do.

∞

OBLIVIOUS TO MY LINGERING PRESENCE, I viewed Teddy from afar, my eyes following her as she jogged straight past my car. I highly doubted she'd see me through the cars darkly tinted windows. I lifted the camera in my hand, snapping a picture to add to my extensive collection. She looked spectacular with her luscious figure emphasised by skin-tight leggings and a tight T-shirt. It appeared she was home on her own, an opportunity one couldn't miss.

Before I got the chance, however, her annoying sister arrived home, followed by Ari, a short while later. Well, aren't you looking as fresh as a daisy?

Strangling the steering wheel in a vice-like grip, jealously irrationally bloomed. I desired Teddy above all others, but since she and Ari were inextricably involved, my chances were slim. According to my father, patience was a virtue, and good things came to those who waited. I'd waited for years, and my patience was wearing thin.

I waited a little while longer and observed the lovebirds strolling back outside with a suitcase in tow. Interesting. I snapped more pictures as Ari helped Teddy into his precious BMW before placing the suitcase in the boot. I had to find out more, and I knew just the person to ask.

∞

Teddy

WRAPPED IN A LARGE BATH SHEET, I scanned the rows of clothes in the spacious walk-in-robe trying to find the right outfit to wear to dinner, one that became a small mission. The short notice hadn't helped either. Everything I looked at was decidedly the wrong choice. Eventually, I chose a navy and white chevron dress, with elbow-length sleeves and a sash belt around the waist. I twirled around in front of the mirror and checked the length, ensuring it wasn't too indecent for a family dinner at the Jaeger's.

"Just to be certain, you are wearing underwear?" Ari playfully enquired upon entering my room, his dark eyes gleaming. A lunchtime romp would do that to a man.

My face turned a deep crimson. "Yes, I am. Why wouldn't I be?" I murmured, twisting my long hair into a stylish knot.

"Why she asks?" he implied indignantly. "Do you not recall my office today when you turned up without said panties?"

"Of course, I do." I swiftly kissed him on the lips before placing a hand on his shoulder to balance myself as I stepped into a pair of glittery white heels with gold stilettos. "We're going to your parents, not your office," I remarked, feigning indignity of my own.

"Okay. Then could said panties possibly be removed before we go home?" With a hopeful and lustful glint in his eyes, he rocked on the heels of his Italian leather shoes.

"If you behave, I might."

He snorted and pointed to his chest. "Me? I'm not the one who turned up to your office without their panties."

"I'm not sure how Spencer, or my co-workers for that matter, would feel about that?"

"It certainly would give them something to talk about." Ari chuckled, taking the suitcase I'd packed immediately upon my return from my run from my hand.

The thought made me giggle as I followed him out to the car. "Well, let's not."

"Ari, darling, I'm so thrilled you could finally make it for dinner," Audrina articulated, her crushing embrace greeting us at the front door. "And with an exceptionally marvellous date, too."

"Biased much, Mother?" She chuckled as Ari responded dryly, kissing her on the smooth, fragrant skin of her upturned cheek. "I also brought two bottles of Shiraz for the occasion."

Both bottles were eagerly removed from my hand. My mother's chocolate brown eyes glistened upon reading the labels. "Lovely, these should go perfectly with dinner. Thank you, Ari, you know your mother well." He quietly chuckled as she tucked a bottle in the crook of her arm before turning her attention to me. She linked her free hand with mine, gushing, "Teddy, darling. It's so good to see you; you look beautiful."

"Thank you, Audrina. I was worried my outfit was a bit much."

"Oh, nonsense." She waved dismissively. "That dress looks positively perfect on you. Now enough of this dreary entryway, please come through to the living room. Everyone's already into the champagne."

"How unusual!" Ari uttered, rolling his eyes.

"I saw that, Ari!"

"I swear she has eyes on the back of her head," he whispered, taking my hand. I giggled at his displeasure; he responded by swatting my behind. The rough foreplay had better continue later.

"Ari, Teddy, welcome to both of you." Jaxson's warm smile first greeted his son, their hands shaking, and then me, his lips pressing a gentle kiss to my cheek. "So glad you could make it. Your mother has raved non-stop about the pair of you since she found out. It was like listening to a broken record."

"Oh, don't exaggerate dear, I wasn't that bad. I was just a little excited is all," Audrina scoffed, handing us each a glass of champagne.

"Excited? Don't *under exaggerate* dear? My ears haven't stopped ringing since you phoned me at work this morning." Jaxson groaned placing a finger inside his ear.

Ari hid his grin behind his glass. "See, I'm not the only one." He smirked, taking a sip of the crisp Moet.

Ari's eldest sister, Carys Jaeger hugged us a little more delicately than their mother did. "Hopefully, mother can now settle down over you two."

"I can't win, can I?" Audrina objected. "I only want my children to be happy, and there's nothing wrong with that."

Placing an arm around his mother's shoulders, Ari chuckled. "We all know you do, Mummsy."

She narrowed her eyes up at him. "Now, you're trying to sass me, Ari Jaeger!"

"Who me?" He pointed to his chest, feigning innocence. "Mother, I'm appalled. You should know your favourite child's not capable of such an atrocity."

"Now I know you are mocking me, Ari. Besides, I have never claimed to favour any of you," Audrina stated impassively. "Except Dom, of course."

"You seriously know how to wound someone." He feigned hurt. "We are, however, all aware it's your life's mission to marry us off in the hope we'll provide you with grandchildren to carry on the family name. For that, we love you, dearly."

She scrutinised her son over the rim of her champagne flute. "Now you're just an arse." Mockingly patting his cheek, she let out a small laugh at Ari's gaping mouth. "Close your mouth, dear, before you catch a fly."

Audrina elegantly swanned towards the cream three-seater art deco sofa and settled against the cushions crossing one leg over the other. "Carys, darling," she expressed lovingly, directing her warm gaze towards her eldest daughter, "tell me about your day."

"It was the same as always, Mother. Taking care of hospital business isn't easy on any given day," she answered aloofly.

I settled beside Ari on the matching sofa opposite and listened intently to Carys recounting her day. Highly astute, she didn't take fools lightly, a sure trait replicated from both parents.

At thirty-two, Carys Jaeger was the oldest of the four siblings and undeniably stunning like her mother, only slighter and taller. Besides Carys and Ari sharing their mother's distinctly deep chocolate eyes, there was no mistaking the resemblance between their children with their fair skin and jet-black hair. Bryson and

Dominique were the contrasting exception, having inherited their father's intense blue colouring. Characteristically, they each too displayed their parent's strong personalities.

A Senior Barrister, Jaxson's astuteness and business savvy had played a valuable part in establishing the law firm of Jaeger and Associates with his younger brother Garrett, also a Senior Barrister. Highly sought after due to an impeccable record that accounted to their due diligence, the brothers rarely lost a case as neither ever ventured into any meeting or courtroom without ascertaining the facts first.

Audrina was equally successful, and as a corporate lawyer, she was capable of swaying any favour or transaction her way. Ari had always stated that his mother was incredibly clever. I never doubted his word after having witnessed it for myself on numerous occasions.

"Mum, I'm starving. What's the great chef cooking for us tonight?" Bryson asked, relaxing beside his girlfriend, Olivia on the sofa, his arm outstretched across the back, while patting his stomach with the other. "I've had a long rough day, and I need to feed these worms that are biting."

"Combantrin is what you need, not food," Audrina coolly retorted, moving from the sofa to elegantly seat herself on the navy-blue wingback chair beside the open fireplace. She never sat still, just like someone else I knew.

Olivia laughed haughtily. "Your family probably thinks I never feed you."

"Well, that's the truth."

Insulted by his remark, she slapped his thigh. "It's not my fault you have a bottomless pit."

"Oh, don't worry, Livvy; I'm aware you feed my son extremely well," Audrina countered, waving her glass around, splashing wine over the patterned Persian rug. I speculated they had the carpet cleaner on speed dial. "He's another who likes to exaggerate."

"Lifting a pen all day must be extremely tiresome, brother," Ari jibed gleefully. "You may want to get that wrist checked for carpal tunnel at your next check-up."

"So is using your brain; how do you feel now you're over the hill. Do tell, brother. Or can't you remember?"

Their banter was hilarious, and for as long as I'd known the Jaeger's, a visit with them always guaranteed a good laugh. One I'd vastly enjoyed growing up before... No, I wasn't going there. Lovingly squeezing Ari's knee, I quickly shifted my focus onto something lighter. "You and Bryson are two peas in a pod when it comes to food. Both of you seem to have bottomless pits."

"I need the extra sustenance just to keep up with you," he expressed quietly, skimming a hand over my exposed thigh. Delicious shivers curled around my spine.

"You're all so hard done by, aren't you?" Audrina simpered, rising from her chair and disappearing into the kitchen to check on the progress of dinner. She returned, announcing dinner was ready. "We need to ensure we feed Bryson's worms before he scrapes his arse, ruining perfectly good floors."

"Are you listening to any of this, Ari?"

Ari laughed mirthlessly. "Don't look at me for sympathy, little brother. I cop the same from mum, and dad, likewise."

"Don't involve me, Bry, I am staying clear of this argument." Jaxson mimicked drawing a finger across his throat, erupting fits of laughter from everyone, including me.

"How diplomatic of you, Dad."

Smart move Ari, I thought quietly. His head turned my way. A brow raised, indicating I needed to take note. Oh, don't worry sunshine; I was indeed taking notes.

Following everyone into the dining room, Jaxson continued his advice in a hushed manner, "I learnt a long time ago to be where your mother's concerned, son." He placed a hand on Ari's shoulder. "As a Barrister and your father, I advise you to do the same."

I unequivocally heard that little piece of advice.

"Duly-noted, Dad." Ari grinned, shoving Bryson when he hurried past him.

Bryson promptly returned the favour, sending Ari flying into a 19th Century Royal Doulton vase. Audrina reacted swiftly, diving and seizing the priceless antique before it took a swan dive to the floor, with both boys earning her ire in the process.

"Boys! Enough!" she growled, glaring frostily. "You're both behaving like a pair of buffoons!"

"He started it," Bryson blurted defensively, pointing a telling finger at his brother.

"Oh, for goodness sake, Bryson, how old are you? And don't even think about being smart with me, young man!" Audrina warned, wagging a finger, her narrowed eyes watching as his raised hand slowly and wisely drifted back to his side.

Ari and Bryson apologised in unison. "Sorry, Mum." Beaten into submission, they promptly took their seats at opposite sides of the table, away from each other.

Holding in my laughter was impossible as I watched two grown men shrink under their mother's intimidating glare. "Now I know who to call when you're misbehaving," I whispered in Ari's ear as I took my seat beside him.

"I am not a child who needs reprimanding, but I might need a good spanking once in a while," he chirped, his eyes mischievously glinting.

"I'm sure your mother has a large wooden spoon I can borrow."

"No, I don't," Audrina responded, winking across the table. "I broke it spanking Jaxson."

Mortified groans echoed throughout the room. "Mum! Ew, gross!"

"Well, it seems I'm not the only one who had worms to feed," Bryson protested, his hand waving in my direction as I devoured the last of the roast lamb and the melody of vegetables on my plate.

"A hectic day was bound to make one famished," Audrina lovingly stated.

I giggled as Bryson's jaw fall open.

"What's the bloody difference?"

"How on earth does one become hungry when he sits on his arse all day behind a desk?" she argued, winking across the table at me.

"So does Ari, but you aren't picking on him." Defeated, he slumped in his chair and pouted.

Ari leaned into my ear and murmured, "Worked up an appetite, did we?"

"The run after work was the cause." Winking at him, I licked my finger clean of the red wine gravy.

Sliding a hand under the table, Ari squeezed my inner thigh and growled, "You are in big trouble when we get home."

I picked up the wine glass, taking a sip to conceal my gasping as Ari's fingertips brushed the inside of my panties. I squirmed and hoped nobody else was paying attention. "There's that bear again, and for the record, I'm expecting you to."

"Be prepared not to walk tomorrow then."

Once dinner was over, everyone relocated back to the living room for more drinks and coffee. The gleaming grand piano in the corner of the room caught my eye, and shyly, I approached Jaxson, asking him if he'd mind me playing something on it.

"I had no idea you even played, but we'd be utterly delighted if you would." Pleased, he motioned towards the low bench seat. "I just hope it's tuned," he murmured, his blue eyes twinkling.

Taking a seat on the stool, I floated my fingers over the keys and began playing. My mind and body relaxing with each note, an inner peace, my inner sanctum, washed over me.

∞

Ari

MY DISCUSSION with Carys about a project for the hospital unexpectedly drew an abrupt end before we'd barely begun. I frowned; when was the last time anyone had played the piano? My head turned towards my mother's beloved Steinway in the corner of the room, leaving my astonished gaze riveted as I watched Teddy effortlessly playing Hallelujah. Her every emotion lovingly poured through each note of the melodious but sad requiem. Possibly, she was obliquely trying to send me a message about disappointing people.

Also only then, did I realise the power behind her love of music. It calmed, taking her away from the dark, and into the light. She had played a similar piece in the car during our trip home from Phillip Island due to her feeling tense. So, why hadn't I connected the dots then? She impressed me further and smoothly segued from one compilation to another without missing a beat.

A tear trickled down my cheek; ah, that explained the strange look I was receiving from Carys.

When the last compilation eventually ended, Teddy slowly spun on the seat, blushing profusely as everyone around her clapped.

"Um, thank you." Humbled, she pushed to her feet and shyly glanced across the room at me from beneath long lashes.

My heart gushed; she looked adorable.

"Teddy, you played beautifully. I had no idea you were so talented." Mother proudly smiled, hugging her warmly. "Ari, did you know?"

"No, I had no idea." Gazing admirably, I planted my arm firmly around her waist, stroking her with my fingertips over the top of the dress. She shivered against me. "You played beautifully."

"It's not a talent I usually like sharing, and honestly, I never thought I was that good," Teddy confessed bleakly. What?

I shook my head, disagreeing with her. "Don't doubt yourself. You played flawlessly. Now you've made me aware of this little secret, I look forward to hearing you play more. Don't you agree, Mother?"

"Of course, we'd love nothing more," she concurred, "and I'm sure your parents are naturally proud."

Teddy forced a smile on her face. "Of course."

Perplexed, I stared at her before politely returning my attention to my mother. "Would you excuse us for a minute, Mother?"

"I need a top-up anyway." She held up her glass, flashing a bright smile before sauntering back to the bar in the corner of the living room.

Placing a hand on the small of her back, I steered Teddy towards the French doors, leading us to the patio. "Why, of all people did you lie to my mother?" I brusquely asked, stepping outside, and settling into one of the wicker lounge chairs, hauling her into my lap.

Teddy snuggled into me, seeking warmth against the bitter chill that had fallen. "I'm sorry, but I'm too ashamed to admit to anyone that my mother never encouraged me to play, even when I showed an interest. If it wasn't for nana, then I never would've learnt," she sadly explained. "Even then, my mother despised the fact she openly encouraged me. Whenever I practised at home, she would yell at me to stop. I was making a terrible racket, and my playing the piano gave her a headache apparently," she expressed bitterly. "But when Abel was learning guitar...that was exciting, and he was wonderful."

I snorted derisively, recalling the one time I'd heard Abel play. "He was terrible, and although I tried to teach him, he wasn't interested in learning. The only reason he attended lessons was to appease your mother."

"And everyone must please my mother!" she uttered. "To keep up my learning, I had to either practise at school or nanas. Both she and poppy were always more than happy to listen to whatever piece I was learning at the time. Poppy Benjamin always sat right beside me, encouraging me, even when I wanted to give up." Teddy suddenly changed the direction of the conversation. "Do you still play your guitar?"

"Sometimes, but I'm a little rusty these days." I redirected the conversation back to her. "What was that last piece you played?"

"Metamorphosis Two; ironic, though don't you think?" Staring at me, her usually bright eyes filled with sadness.

My brows knitted together. "I'm not exactly sure what you mean?"

"When I taught myself that particular compilation, it felt like…like it was speaking to me. Over the years, I've had to adapt, mostly because I was…am, made to feel like a freak. Eventually, you start to believe that to be the case. For once in my life, I wanted to be seen as normal, even if it meant wearing a mask of sorts in front of certain people."

"Your mother predominantly, am I wrong?"

"No, but then, are you ever?"

He chuckled. "Only on the odd occasion." Resting a cheek against the crown of her head, I laced our fingers together. "You're beautiful, Teddy, inside and out; never doubt that."

She reached up, stroking the side of my stubbled cheek. Tenderness had replaced the sad expression of earlier. "You always know what to say to me."

"It's not a chore, believe me," I articulated, pressing a tender kiss to her knuckles.

"I believe you. You're the only person who's made me genuinely believe that I'm worth loving."

"And I shall continue to do so – every day," I assured truthfully. "Now, shall we go back inside and say our goodbyes?" Teddy climbed off my lap, and as I straightened, I tugged her closer, my head lowering to possess her warm, soft lips. "I love you," I declared. "Always have, always will."

During Teddy's stay, we spent countless hours candidly talking, extending on the conversations we'd had during our stay at Phillip Island. All but one detail, she reflected on her past, admitting the rape had left her damaged, possibly beyond repair. I naturally disagreed with her. Surprisingly, she didn't argue back. From then on, we only existed for one another. So much so, with the exception of work, we scarcely left the house.

One love she communicated freely was the fundamental joy music brought her. Solace too, and as such, I encouraged Teddy to utilise my Fazioli Grand Piano at her leisure. She willingly accepted and played frequently, pleasing me immensely. The exuding bliss was thoroughly worth the experience. In addition, and regardless of our activity, her ever-present music played in the background, distracting me from my tasks. My gaze would wander, pausing to observe the graceful fluidity of her fingers dancing over the furniture. Like now, for instance.

Having caught me in my apparent daze, Teddy slipped me a curious glance. "What are you gawking at?"

"Only you," I simpered.

"Why?"

"Because I can."

"Perver."

Lucky, I understood and spoke French too. "Avec Vous, Toujours." With you always.

21

I RECLINED AGAINST the pillows, my amused gaze observing a cheery Teddy bound out of bed. Her slender hips swayed as she sauntered towards the ensuite bathroom, and pausing in the doorway, she wagged a crooked finger. "Come on big boy, you know ya wanna!"

I laughed heartily. Sharing in Teddy's excitement was the anticipation of spending the day poolside with my family. Her joy was infectious, and as such, I playfully flicked the sheet back. "Look out, here I come!" I growled, rushing towards her, and flinging my arms around her narrow waist, lifting her feet off the floor. "You're in trouble now, Missy."

She wrapped her lean, naked body around me like a vine and whispered huskily, "Ooh, yes please."

"You're feisty this morning."

"I'm extremely feisty, so watch out."

"I love feisty Teddy in the morning."

She pouted. "Only in the morning?"

"I'll take you morning, lunchtime, dinnertime," I retorted, carrying her into the shower. "But I prefer anytime."

"As do I," she moaned as I pushed her against the shower wall, my thrust hard and deep, precisely how she enjoyed it.

"One is a caramel slice made with treacle, and the other is a chocolate mud slice laced with bourbon," Teddy explained, handing the slice containers over to my mother. Her mouth quirking in amusement as my mother raised the lid, inhaling the bourbon deeply.

"I may have to hide this one from Jaxson," she quipped, sliding the containers onto a shelf inside the fridge for later. "Come on. We're out by the pool already."

Strolling outside, I noted that my siblings had made themselves quite comfortable already, as had their partners, all of them lazily lounging beside the pool with my father's cocktails nestled firmly in their hands. God help us with those.

Carys fiancée, Michael wobbled towards us. "About time your ugly mug showed up."

"Speak for yourself." I laughed, shaking his hand firmly. With his dark hair bleached from the sun and glistening blue eyes, Michael's intoxication was apparent already. "You're sparkling, or is your sunburnt complexion the culprit?" I asked as he greeted Teddy with a peck to the cheek.

"Blame dad's cocktails." Carys giggled, sliding an arm around Michael's waist, her pale skin glowing from the biting sun. "Dad's been a busy little bee mixing all sorts of concoctions," she informed us, raising her empty glass.

I grinned listening to my father's voice warbling over the music blaring in the background. "By the sounds of his glorious singing, I'd say dad's sampled every single drink." My suspicions all but confirmed as his eyebrows rose, tasting the fresh cocktail in his hand. He was blotto already.

Upon noticing our arrival, he waved us over. "Ari, Teddy, come and grab one of these, they're delicious!"

I let out a low growl. "I'd rather have a bourbon over one of those lethal brews any day."

Alight with mischief, Teddy grabbed my hand and dragged me towards the bar. "Come on Mr Bear, let's go live a little."

I attempted to caution her. "Dad's cocktails are lethal, and you'll be bouncing off the walls in no time once you've tasted them."

It was to no avail. Before I knew it, dad was zealously shoving a hurricane glass into our hands, the inside layered in a multitude of bright colours.

"Here we go you two, wrap your lips around these; my rainbow cocktails."

We both took a tentative sip and immediately began coughing from the deathly strength of vodka.

"Whoa, Dad! Have you added the entire bottle of vodka?" I spluttered, my face screwing up upon swallowing the smallest mouthful.

"Says the man that drinks straight bourbon," Dad countered dryly.

"We'll all pass out before lunch at this rate."

Teddy gingerly sipped on hers and grabbed the lemonade, pouring quite liberally to water the drink down. Giving it a quick stir, she lifted the glass and took another small sip. "Mmm, much better; it's not as strong."

She passed me the bottle. If I wanted to survive the day, I'd better follow suit. "Perhaps we ought to consider making dad's and slip lemonade into his? With any luck, he won't even notice," I suggested, ruefully twisting my lips as we moseyed towards a two-person sunbed. "But I must say I'm pleased mother has Frances cooking the barbeque because Lord knows what we would end up with if dad cooked."

She giggled, setting her drink down on the low table beside the chair. "Your dad cooks a mean steak."

"When he's not drunk, he does..." I trailed off, observing Teddy strip down, my eyes popping out of my head as she tossed her blue and white striped boho shirt onto the cream-cushioned chaise. The tiny triangles on the black ruffled bikini barely covered her striking figure; if I'd realised the outfit she called bathers was what she was wearing, I would've ordered she changed.

I resisted the urge to cover her up with a towel. Having my pervert brother drooling beside her was something I'd rather avoid. Too late. If Bryson's jaw dropped any further, he'd trip over it.

I pointedly shot him a deathly glare whilst mouthing at him to fuck off.

At that point, I was grateful for the sunglasses covering my eyes, and for the shorts covering my growing bulge.

Oblivious to the fuss, she passed me a small tube of sunscreen and lay face down undoing the flimsy shoestring straps holding her bikini top together. "Would you mind applying some sunscreen to my back and shoulders please, Ari?"

"Um, sure." I groaned and began lathering her fair skin in lotion. "Teddy...."

"Yes, Ari?"

"Is there any chance you could put your shirt back on?" The glare over the top of her sunglasses spoke volumes.

"Oh, wowsers, I am so full! I'll be rolling out of here later," Teddy complained, strolling back to the pool after having gorged ourselves silly with the delicious lunch Frances had served.

"I know what you mean," I grumbled, rubbing my belly. "But we can always work it off later," I added, winking mischievously.

"Oh, god no," she squeaked, settling back onto the wicker lounge. "That would be impossibly uncomfortable right now, even as a starfish while you did all of the work."

"Ew, you two, that's gross!" Bryson piped up beside us. "You're making my virgin ears sting from the yuk factor!"

"Says he with a mouth that's pottier than mine," I shot back, crouching to apply another coat of sunscreen to Teddy's burning shoulders.

"I happen to have an innocent mouth I'll have you know!"

"You've had too much sun and one too many of dad's cocktails; that's an indication of sunstroke, brother. You must be hallucinating, bro," I dryly murmured, standing up.

My joker of a brother suddenly launched out of the chair, his intentions clear as he came at me with outstretched hands, except he misjudged his steps and caught his foot on the leg, tumbling headfirst into the pool.

"See, too many cocktails!" I laughed hysterically from the safety of the water's edge only to have my rascally sister Dominique turn the tables on me. I swiftly spluttered back to the surface and bellowed irritably, "Just wait, little sister; I'll be sure to get you back for that when you least expect it!" I turned my glaring gaze on a giggling Teddy and hightailed it out of the pool.

"Laughing at me and my misfortune, are you?" I growled, squeezing the icy water from my wet T-shirt over her sun-warmed body.

"No, not at all!" she squealed.

"You look a little hot sitting here..." Leaning down, I rubbed my drenched hair along her neck and over the perky swell of her small breasts. "...and in desperate need of a cool down." I snaked my cold arms around her narrow waist, and holding on tight, I picked her up. Her legs kicked in protest as she screamed at me.

"What are you doing?"

"Never you mind!" I muttered moments before I jumped into the pool. Teddy hurried back to the surface, breathlessly spluttering her discontent.

"That's twice now!"

"Paybacks are a bitch."

"Your sister pushed you into the pool, not me!"

"Laughing makes you equally guilty." I pouted, sliding my hands inside the barely-there bikini bottoms, and kneading her behind.

She giggled, slithering her arms around my neck. "Aw, don't go acting like a big baby and just suck it up."

"Aw, the poor whittle boy can't handle being teased. You better see mummy for your dummy," Bryson mocked from the opposite side of the pool.

"I'll be right back," I grunted, pushing away from Teddy to lunge at my squealing brother. "You're a goner bro!" I warned, shoving his head beneath the surface.

Taking turns dunking each other, we continued to wrestle much to our mother's displeasure.

Her hands on her hips, she yelled from the edge of the coping, "Boys, cut it out! You're both acting like a pair of five-year olds!"

Both of us came up for air, and grinning wolfishly at one another, we each grabbed a hand, pulling our objecting mother into the pool.

We watched with trepidation and fascination as she calmly swam to the surface and over to the ladder climbing out. Her legs swivelling in front of her as she adjusted the backrest on the sun lounge before pulling a wide-brimmed floppy straw hat over her soaked hair and eyes. I got the feeling she was not the least bit impressed with either of us.

Bryson was similarly shell-shocked. "Should we be worried, bro? Mum didn't even yell at us."

"Quite possibly."

He waved a dismissive hand. "Nah, she won't do anything; she loves us."

I shoved his head back beneath the water.

∞

Teddy

LUNCH AND SWIMMING LATE into the afternoon turned into us staying for dinner. Before which, Ari and I found a quiet moment to take off upstairs, satisfying urges brought on by hours of constant touching and heated kisses, starting on the bed, and finishing during a nice long shower.

As I slid a strapless dress up my torso, I strolled around the room taking in the décor. I reminisced about Ari's teenage years when he had it filled with everything and anything soccer related. Along with the glass cylinder lamps on the bedside tables, and soft, flowing curtains covering the double-hung windows, dark timber boards and furniture with teal blue walls, the room now had a soft, yet elegant touch. Other than that, not much else had changed.

I peered up at the wall above his desk and smiled looking at the prized soccer boots hanging off the hook by their filthy, tattered laces. A pair signed and given to him by one of his favourite players after his beloved Chelsea defeated Middlesbrough, two goals to zero. Since he was a child, Ari had always been soccer-mad, or football as the English called it, he'd irritably and regularly inform me; still did. While he was away at university, I would often sneak into his room and curl up on his bed with them securely held in my hands. I just wanted to feel close to him.

My dirty little secret: I smiled warmly at the memory.

"What are you smiling about?" a curious Ari asked, sliding the zip of my strapless sundress up my back, his fingers brushing lightly against my bare skin.

I gasped at the connection. "...Nothing."

Ari's hands leisurely glided around my waist as his lips softly trailed, planting seductive kisses along my sun-kissed shoulders. "What had you smiling like you had a secret?"

The back of my head rolled over his shoulder as his hand slid into the front of my panties. "Never – you – mind," I mewled as he teased my already sensitive clitoris.

Holding my bucking body tightly around the waist, he deliberately taunted me, "Do I need to torture it out of you?"

"No. But please don't stop," I begged, whimpering as the warmth spread throughout my body.

"Tell me..." Ari demanded, rubbing my swollen nub.

Panting, my back arched. "No..."

"No?"

"No," I repeated, my head shaking furiously against his shoulder.

"Your loss then," he modestly stated, withdrawing, leaving me highly aroused and bereft. "You want torture..." Ari shrugged his shoulders and calmly adjusted the bulge inside his cream chino shorts. "Then you have it – All. Through. Dinner."

"That *is* torture," I whined, rubbing my thighs together in an attempt to suppress the ache.

He snickered, and his eyes danced. "I know," he freely admitted, strolling from the room. I threw the white sandal in my hand across the room, barely missing his head. He turned in a leisurely pivot in the doorway, murmuring, "I love you," before dashing down the stairs as another sandal narrowly missed him.

Narrowing my eyes, I formulated a plan; one guaranteed to evoke his dormant dominant side. I chuckled quietly, and putting on my best poker face, I casually waltzed down the stairs joining him, and the rest of the family in the dining room.

∞

Ari

MIFFED BY TEDDY'S ALOOF COMPOSURE DURING the rowdy dinner I attempted to whisper in her to find out why she was consciously ignoring me. Hoping to provoke an answer, I slid a hand beneath the skirt of her dress, which she discreetly thwarted, pushing me away. My discontent shared as I growled in her ear, making her giggle, which in turn frustrated me further.

I slipped her a curious glance wondering about the devious smirk on her lips, expressly when she excused herself from the table. The seductive sway of her hips merely increased my curiosity.

About to resume my conversation with Michael about the latest in cardiothoracic surgeries, my gaze inadvertently dropped to her vacated chair. And upon noticing the lace panties casually strewn across the seat, my eyes widened: that naughty little minx! I snatched them up, shoving them into the pocket of my chino shorts hoping that neither Michael nor Carys caught a view of them before I had.

"Excuse me a moment will you, but I need to check on Teddy. She may have had too much sun today." A polite smile graced my lips as I hastily made a beeline for the downstairs powder room. Where, with a closed fist, I banged on the locked door.

Hearing her drunken giggle just wound me up even more. "Teddy, open the bloody door!" I listened as the lock disengaged and leaned against the wide doorjamb, swinging the misplaced panties off my forefinger. The door slowly opened with a rather pleased Teddy meeting my bemused gaze.

"Oh, there they are!"

I snorted contemptuously at the feigned surprise. "Please, you purposely went without."

"Who knew underwear could simply fall off like that? Slippery little suckers, aren't they?" She giggled, slipping them off my finger. As she hitched her dress up to her waist, I let out a lowly groan. The sight of her naked behind made it awfully tempting to take her now. When in reality, all I wanted to do was spank the little daredevil's arse. Either way, she'd enjoy it, so I settled for a good old-fashioned verbal scolding instead.

"I can't believe you left them on the bloody chair! What if Carys, or worse, Michael, discovered them — he was right beside you if you hadn't noticed!"

"How? They're as drunk as I am," she slurred dismissively. Then her hands flew to her hips. "Besides, you left me all hot and horny, so I had to get back at you somehow."

I scrubbed my hands over my face and groaned; she would be the death of me. "I'll let it slip — just this once."

She clapped gleefully. "Does that mean you'll spank me if I do it again?"

"Bloody hell, Teddy, you're impossible!" Tightly grabbing her hand, I led my profusely giggling girl away from the bathroom.

"We're saying our goodbyes. Then we're going home just so I can fuck you senseless, with a spanking on the side."

"Ooh, I like that idea."

"Don't get too excited," I firmly cautioned. "The spanking shall act as a reminder not to behave in such a risky manner, especially within the confines of my parent's home." The smile that graced Teddy's face might have temporarily slipped away, however, I was acutely aware of the ignited fire searing away inside her. Likewise, I suffered the same affliction.

Thus, the swift reuniting with my family in the dining room where we began the tedious round of kissing cheeks and handshaking. Seconds later, Teddy informed me she was in dire need of the bathroom once again.

Frustrated with her, I groaned.

She shrugged nonchalantly. "What? I broke the seal."

"Don't be long," I warned gruffly, holding her firmly around the waist.

With a mock salute, she giggled. "Yes, sir!"

Exhausted, I ran a hand through my hair, watching on in disbelief at the antics. Dad's cocktails were undoubtedly the primary cause, and I had warned her. However, she refused to listen, and kept on drinking, throwing them down as if they were lolly water.

What in the devil was taking her so long? Anything was possible, but after today, perhaps I had better check on her.

∞

Teddy

AWARE ARI LACKED patience, I intentionally dawdled during my umpteenth trip to the bathroom and paused in my travels to admire the wall of family photos in the hallway. I reached out, picking up a silver-framed baby photo of Ari; as an infant, he was adorable. I imagined our son – if we had one, he'd undoubtedly resemble his handsome father to a tea. I sighed; someday, just not yet.

As I set the frame back in its original place, my eyes blurrily scanned over the long hall table. A delightful smile formed upon admiring several school photos, university graduations, family portraits, holidays, and Christmases. Apart from their physical appearances, nothing else had altered.

The admiration derived from looking at their smiling faces gradually slipped away as envy for the charmed life I'd wished for growing up grew – without the monster that unwittingly kept company amongst them. A sickening thought that forced my gaze upwards to the newest portrait hanging centrally amongst the rest. Why was it even up there, with *him* included?

Those beady eyes, I despised, always had. They watched and leered over me, crawling into my private space at any given opportunity. He'd help me with my homework, even when I refused his damned input, or his eagerness to team up with me during board games...they were nothing more than a means to a horrific end. I was so fucking naïve! How was I so blind to his ulterior motives? Anxiety and resentment bloomed.

How was it, *he* was allowed the privilege of living contently while I quietly suffered in the darkness? Surrounded by his wife, adult children, and extended family, he smiled innocently as if everything in his life was perfect, rubbing the salt into my wounded soul. All I visualised was pure unadulterated hatred, a reminder of what he and my mother had painfully inflicted upon me. He might not have been present physically, but the sickening scent of his cologne seemed to leach from the photograph, a horrific trigger that sent me scurrying back to the bathroom.

∞

Ari

AS I ENTERED THE HALLWAY, the bathroom door opened and abruptly slammed shut. Alarmed, I picked up the pace. "Teddy?" I banged on the door with my fist. My concern mounted upon hearing her heartwrenching sobs. "Teddy, is everything okay in there?"

"I'm fine!"

"May I come in?" I attempted to turn the locked handle, prompting again for an answer, "Teddy?"

"No, don't! I'm a mess...." Her panic dissipated as quickly as it rose, her voice softening to a reassuring tone. ".....I'll be out in a moment."

"Okay, but the moment you do, we're heading home." Reluctantly, I backed away from the door when all I wanted to do was break it down.

"There you are!" my mother simpered sauntering towards me, her brown eyes twinkling brightly at me. "I thought you had slunk off without saying goodbye."

I gave a disparaging shake of the head. "No such luck, Mother. Teddy's still in the bathroom puking."

"Oh dear," she tutted disapprovingly. "Too much sun and one too many of your father's cocktails, I imagine."

With a shrug of the shoulders, I sighed. "I don't believe Teddy drank enough water either." Hearing the click of the lock, I turned as the door finally opened and frowned at the distressing sight of Teddy's ashen face. Also somewhat alarming were her downcast eyes as she unsteadily ambled towards my outstretched arm.

"Are you all right?" Noticing the apparent agitation, my brow furrowed, and my eyes dipped, checking her over.

"No, not really," she mumbled. What had gotten into her?

"Let us get you home, eh? Can you finish saying our goodbyes, please, Mother?"

"Of course, I'll call you tomorrow."

"Yeah, sure."

∞

Teddy

MY GLOOMY MOOD cascaded. To the extent, I rejected Ari's usual gentlemanly assistance into his car. His hurt was undeniable as he walked away from me. More so as he slid into the driver's seat and I twisted in my seat away from him, tucking my arms tightly around my waist. He couldn't possibly understand how I felt. I needed space to wallow, alone, away from him and away from a world that filled my head with nothing more than self-loathing and hatred. Why was the twenty-minute trip to Beaumaris taking longer than usual? I wanted out, now, but that was impossible when we were only halfway and travelling along a chaotic freeway. I struggled to breathe, my anxiety rapidly rising as the small interior of Ari's BMW closed in on me.

Concerned, Ari attempted to reach out to me; I abruptly reacted and recoiled closer to the door, slapping his hand away.

"Don't touch me!"

He swiftly restored his hand to the steering wheel as confusion marred his handsome face.

My face sank into my palms, hiding my shedding tears until I sensed the car turning onto Olinda Way. As he pulled into the driveway, the relief was immediate, as was the opening of the car door.

Ari cursed, slamming on the brakes. "What the fuck, Teddy?"

I ignored him and ducked beneath the barely open roller door, sprinting inside through the connecting door into the kitchen. My legs on autopilot, I dashed up the stairs and into Ari's bedroom, locking the door behind me. Likewise, the bathroom door before jumping beneath the scolding shower spray, ensuring my skin turned raw. Like I felt on the inside.

Ten years of harrowing silence came flooding back in its entirety; the pain malignant. I just wanted the agony vanquished; to feel free. My only solution lay on the niche shelf beside me. I wasn't thinking about the consequences as a sense of peace and bliss washed over me. To the point, I barely heard the crash or felt as a hand came down grabbing my bloodied forearm. Ari was too late.

"Teddy, what have you done?" he cried.

Everything went black.

22

Ari

ANXIETY COURSED THROUGH MY VEINS as each second that passed without any news, likewise, the hours since the paramedics had rushed Teddy into emergency. I hadn't spoken to another soul. Not a doctor, a nurse, or even a family member for that matter. I'd left enough bloody messages. I held out hope that at least one of the girls' would return my numerous calls, and soon.

Teddy needed them, and truth be told, as did I.

The longer someone kept me waiting, the edgier I grew, pacing the small waiting room as though I were a caged lion, giving me legs that ached like buggery. In the end, I gave into my fatigue, sagging into one of the plastic chairs lined up against the wall. My head rolled backwards, and my eyes drooped. I swiftly forced them back open.

Closing them meant hearing her petrified screams as I attempted to break down the door or viewing the haunting images of Teddy on the shower floor, helpless and bleeding with *my* razor in her bloodied hand. I'd fought for her, for her life using every towel in my bathroom. I had to do whatever it took to stop the bleeding.

I'd spent countless hours wracking my brain, surmising the possible triggers behind her heartbreaking decision: had something happened at my parent's house? No, that couldn't possibly be it. Leading up to the barbeque, Teddy remained perfectly content.

Until after dinner, anyway. Other than that, I was clueless, and until she relinquished that piece of information, I was powerless to do anything about it. Again.

Now and then, as the doors to the emergency room swung open, a tiny ray of hope that it was the doctor with some news bloomed, even the nurse I'd openly berated on arrival. Only afterwards, as I watched her scurry off in tears, did the guilt set in; she was only doing her job after all.

As were the police who followed the ambulance to my house, their insinuation that I had something to do with Teddy's suicide attempt, I hadn't taken kindly to and arced up at the officer. He attempted to mollify me by sternly informing me they were only following protocol. Why didn't he say so initially instead of leading me up the garden path?

Christ, my head was pounding, and my weary eyes were stinging. Not helping my irritation were the offensively bright fluorescent lights flickering overhead. I flanked my head between my hands, seeking respite. That was short-lived as my phone began buzzing in my shorts pocket. I scrambled, trying to yank it free. I didn't even attempt to read the ID before finally answering, albeit I snapped, "Ari Jaeger!"

"Ari, it's Poppy…" Oh, thank goodness! I sagged in relief. "Is everything all right, Ari? Your message sounded rather strained."

"No, everything has gone to pot…" Through my sobs, I did my utmost best to explain, and by the time I finished, she was equally upset.

"Oh, my God, Ari, this is devastating! We'll leave immediately and should be there as soon as possible."

"I appreciate it more than you know," I sniffled, hanging up shortly after.

Their impending arrival offered mild relief, but it simply wasn't enough. I needed a different kind of support.

"Oh, Ari…"

The sympathetic sound of my mother's soft voice awakened me from the depths of my deepened slumber. I probably looked like hell compared to my usually polished self.

"Mum…" I managed to croak out right as the dam broke.

Hurrying over to me, she immediately enveloped me inside the loving warmth of her arms. "Oh, my darling, I'm here now."

"It's so awful. Teddy…."

"Shh, everything's going to be fine now, son."

I genuinely thought a good cry might have offered catharsis. Instead, I was drained, more exhausted than I'd ever encountered in my entire life. About to drop back to sleep, that ray of hope I'd prayed for earlier unexpectedly walked through the doors.

Dressed in dark blue scrubs, a beefy young blonde entered the waiting room, his weary bloodshot gaze zeroing in on us.

"Theodora McGovern's family?"

I swiftly jumped to my feet. "Ari Jaeger, Teddy's boyfriend."

"Dr James," he stated, shaking my outstretched hand. "I was the attending doctor when Theodora first arrived."

"She prefers Teddy," I corrected him. He eyed me quizzically. "It's mostly due to an intense dislike of Theodora."

"Ah, my apologies then."

"How's Teddy, and is she going to be all right?"

"Mr Jaeger…." The doctor rubbed the back of his neck, blowing a hesitant sigh. "I'm afraid since you aren't her next of kin, I'm not authorised to relinquish any details regarding Teddy's afflictions to you."

Rage boiled. What the fuck? Just like the pain in my head, my temper exploded. "Teddy is my girlfriend and was at my house when she attempted suicide!"

The doctor unmoved by my plight, regarded me impassively. "I'm sorry, Mr Jaeger…"

I held up a hand, silently requesting he stop right there. My irritated gaze dropped to the hand pressed to my arm: my mother's feeble attempt at trying to keep me calm.

"Is there anything you can tell us, anything at all?" she asked ever so politely.

"No, unless there's a next of kin like a parent or a sibling present I can't. I'm sorry, but it's hospital policy," Doctor James insisted, raising his hands in defence as I furiously shook my head.

"It's bloody ridiculous! Just tell me! Please!"

With impeccable timing, my saviour walked through the door, accompanied by my sister Dominique. A similarly sombre Poppy trailed not far behind, dropping her coat onto a chair.

Scarlett quietly strolled into my arms, embracing me tightly before slowly spinning to face the doctor. Her hand desperately clasped mine and squeezed, her bottom lip trembling as she pleaded with the doctor, "Just tell Ari what's happening with Teddy, please?"

"Who are you?" the doctor quizzed, eyeing her suspiciously. Fucker.

"Scarlett McGovern, Teddy's...young...younger sister," she stammered through her tears. "We have to know if my sister's going to be okay. We *all* do, including Ari," she emphasised.

The doctor crossed his arms and rocked on the balls of his feet. Sighing heavily, he finally relented. There was a God; it just wasn't him. "The left laceration was profoundly deeper than the right, and thankfully, she cut across – not upwards, meaning she missed the arterial veins. Our surgeon checked to be sure before we stitched and bandaged the wounds, both wrists needing a dozen stitches or so each."

I made my frustration known as he paused and wound my arm, motioning for him to continue. "Please don't keep us in suspense, Doc!"

"Ari, shush!" my mother quietly scolded. "Let him speak."

Reserving a dashing smile for my mother, the doctor openly glared at me. "Our resident psychiatrist, Doctor Montgomery, will visit with Teddy tomorrow to conduct the proper assessments. With any luck, she'll open up to him." He placed a sympathetic hand on my shoulder. Induced by the magnitude of the situation weighing me down, I resisted the urge to shake him off. "Go home and try to get some sleep. The sedative we administered may keep her knocked out until tomorrow morning anyway, and all being well, you can see her then."

I managed a stiff and curt nod.

"Teddy was being moved upstairs to our psych ward as we speak. Depending on how she responds to treatment could determine how long she stays. That's all I can give you for now."

Ever gracious, my mother held out one of her slender hands for the doctor to shake, which of course he eagerly took. "We appreciate your time, Doctor James, you have been most helpful."

I raised a contemptuous eyebrow as he made eyes at her.

"I try my best," he murmured, hanging onto her hand a little too long for my liking. I needn't be concerned; she'd eat him for breakfast and spit out the leftovers if he made a move on her anyway.

Once the ogling doctor tore himself away from my mother, she gravitated her attention back to me. "Driving in your current state isn't ideal, so I'll drive you home."

I glowered. "How do you think I got here?"

"Fine, I'll follow you then."

I rolled my eyes in exasperation, earning a glare that dared me to argue.

"I just want to ensure you make it home safely, okay, son?"

I exhaled sharply. "Fine."

With an annoying tut, my mother turned to Teddy's roommates. "If you girls' need anything, anything at all, please do not hesitate to call me. I don't care what the time is," she reinforced, firmly hugging each of them. "Teddy's a strong girl, and with everyone's love and support, she'll come through this," she reassured, her throat tightening. "Now go, go home and get some sleep."

Fishing a handkerchief from her purse, she dabbed her eyes. "Now, Ari, let's go before you fall asleep again in those god-awful seats."

Too late.

Having wandered inside my house, I regarded the deathly silence that contemptuously greeted me and headed straight for my favourite tan leather chair. With the fire lit beside it, my chilled body gradually warmed. Yet, regardless of the radiating temperature, no amount of heat could quell the lingering ache in my heart.

Staring darkly into the flames, I raised my feet off the floor and set them down on the footstool in front of me as images of Teddy on the shower floor flashed. As were the muddled words she spoke whilst drifting in and out of consciousness: *'His eyes, I hate his eyes.'*

But whom was she referring to? Her rapist? Again, I was clueless.

I frowned; what was that noise?

"Are you hungry, Ari? I could make you something if you are." Oh, it was my mother. I'd completely forgotten she was even here. "Or tea, I could make a pot-"

"I don't want fucking tea!" Irritated, I pushed to my feet. "I want Teddy!" My shoulders sagged at the sight of my mother stiffening. "Mum, I apolo..."

"Don't," she cautioned, holding up a hand and glaring at me. "I appreciate that you're upset and angry, but don't you ever raise your voice to me again! Do you hear me, son?" Her tone was absolute, making me feel like that small boy again.

I was mortified. Never in my thirty years had I ever raised my voice to my mother, the one person I respected more than anyone or anything, even life itself. The anguish crossing her face was more than I could bear.

I slumped back into the chair, tears welling. "Again, I apologise. Yelling at you was downright disrespectful."

She sighed and plopped into the sofa beside me with a thump. "There's a lot more to this anguish than you're letting on."

I sniffed quietly at my perceptive mother. "That, there is."

Her forehead creased. "Well, what is it then?"

The desire to reveal Teddy's secret weighed heavily, as did the conflict not to. She had bravely entrusted me. Yet here I was contemplating a decision I knew once divulged, there was no turning back. Mum was a lawyer; discretion was of utmost importance. However, she was my mother first, and if I couldn't trust her, then who could I?

I leaned my elbows on my knees and took a chance. "What I'm about to tell you, I'm telling you in confidence." Once she nodded prudently, I began, my heart breaking as each sordid detail spilled from my mouth. "Ten years ago, someone raped Teddy, and her darling mother Therese covered it all up into a nice, neat little package...."

It was no surprise that my mother's jaw dropped to the floor as I reached the end. "What on earth were her reasons for covering up such an abhorrent crime?"

"One was Teddy's age, and the other was mostly for selfish reasons. Therese," I spat venomously, "believed making Teddy's rape known to the authorities would disgrace the family and make them social outcasts."

Scoffing, my mother's hand flew to her throat. "That's ludicrous! It's the twenty-first century, not the nineteen fifties for goodness sake! As for her social status, she's not exactly that high up in the community." Toying with the diamond heart at her throat, she snorted. "Were you aware she heads a charity for abused women and their children?"

Incredulously, my jaw fell open. "What a bloody hypocrite!"

"Our families have known each other for years. so how was I not aware?" She frowned. "Has Teddy enlightened you to the culprit responsible for this heinous crime?"

I ran my hands over my face in frustration and grumbled, "No, she hasn't, nor will she tell me." Levering out of the chair, I wandered over to the bar and snatched the bourbon off its tray. "Do you want one?" I asked, holding up the bottle.

"Yes, please."

At the indignant response, I poured our drinks, choking on my laughter. Why'd I even bother asking?

My mother's gaze drifted from me to the fire. "Words fail me," she demurred quietly.

"You and me both," I grimly concurred, handing her one of the half-filled tumblers and settling back into my chair.

Tugging a delicate lace handkerchief from inside the sleeve of her dress, she dabbed her watering eyes. "Earlier, you mentioned that Teddy gave birth to a little girl?"

My head bobbed stiffly. "Yes, she did."

"Was she permitted to hold her at least?"

"Only briefly. Teddy described her as beautiful; perfect in every way. Ten fingers, ten toes..." The glass in my hand trembled as it touched my lips. "That piece of information she dreaded telling me the most," I conveyed quietly.

"Why?"

"Because she feared the trouble it would create."

Her brow furrowed as confusion crossed her face. "Who made her believe something so absurd? It just doesn't make any sense."

I sipped on my drink and growled. "Therese did."

"Naturally." Mother's eyes rolled dramatically, making me chuckle.

"For years she resisted sharing with me simply because Therese made her believe I'd turn away from her if I knew."

"Why would you? You've loved Teddy since you were children..." Her disbelieving tone switched to disgust. "That dastardly woman certainly has a lot to answer for, traumatising her daughter in such a detestable manner," she spluttered, shaking her head. "Now, I understand your hesitation when I suggested calling her parents.

I'm assuming Teddy's roommates aren't aware of this dreadful situation?"

"They all are. Poppy unwittingly became aware during their time at school together and has remained a loyal friend since, regardless. Scarlett and Dom, on the other hand, were informed only recently."

"It's good to know the girls' look out for each other," she murmured, setting the unusually full glass on the lamp table beside her. Mother sighed languorously, glancing down at her watch. "I must get going, unfortunately. Otherwise, your father shall be wondering where I've disappeared to, and honestly, I don't think I could cope with one of his inquisitions right now." Pushing to her feet, she retrieved her bag from the kitchen, her gaze sympathetic as she slung the skinny strap over her shoulder. "Are you going to be okay, Ari?"

"Yeah, I'll be fine, thank you, Mother." I tiredly pushed to my feet and embraced her warmly. "Thank you for listening or not judging."

"Why would I? Teddy didn't ask for any of this to happen to her." My mother stepped back, her thumb tenderly brushing the lipstick from my cheek. "I'll do whatever I can to support her through this challenging time, both of you."

I gazed lovingly at the one person who had raised me to become the gentleman I was today. "Thanks, Mum. I love you."

Red stained lips curled into a heartfelt smile. "I love you too, son."

Having waved my mother goodbye, I raced upstairs to pack a bag, ensuring I also packed Teddy's belongings in the process. I waltzed into the ensuite with the intention of grabbing our toiletries, only to halt in the doorway. My breath shuddered as my tired gaze raked over the blood-spattered shower and slowly drifted towards the piles of crimson-soaked towels strewn over the floor. Rosa could burn them for all I cared; they'd only ever serve as a painful reminder otherwise.

Fresh tears surfaced, and a lump formed in my throat; distraught screams echoed, and the desperation that surged trying to break down the doors was something I never wanted to feel again.

On the outside, Teddy portrayed a highly confident young woman, but after her disclosure, I realised she was just a scared and broken little girl fighting to break free of her past, and the demons haunting her. Her attempted suicide was undeniably a cry for help; I genuinely hoped I was strong enough to drag her from the dark and into the light, securing us the future I promised in the beginning. Quickly, I grabbed the toiletries and marched back into the bedroom. Whatever was needed was shoved into several bags, and if it meant emptying my wardrobe, then so be it. Teddy's recovery time would be lengthy, and I wasn't about to waste time driving back and forth if I ran out of clothes. Slinging the bags over my shoulders and wheeling a suitcase behind me, I hurriedly made my way downstairs to the garage and roared out of there wishing to never return.

I felt dreadful. The mere few hours of afforded slumber were far from peaceful. Haunted by nightmares of Teddy, my sleep was insufficient and restless. Loving, tender dreams turned heartwrenching in the blink of an eye, jolting me out of my sleep, leaving my mood foul and my temper short.

As I stepped through the doors on the ground floor housing the Inpatient Mental Health unit, my tired gaze scanned the area, looking for the nurses' station. I tentatively approached the young blonde nurse seated behind the protective glass, multitasking as she shovelled down a breakfast of Vegemite and avocado toast in between sips of black coffee.

"Excuse me."

Barely taking a second to glance up from the paperwork on the desk in front of her, she asked, "May I help you?"

"Would it be possible to visit with a patient who was admitted up here last night?"

Her gentle but weary gaze blinked. "Who's the patient?"

"Theodora McGovern." I anxiously observed her eyes scanning the screen in front of her as fast fingers glided over the keyboard.

"And you are?" she quizzed, shifting her scrutinising gaze back to me.

"Ari Jaeger."

"Are you her husband?"

Peeved by the interrogation, I responded tersely, "No, I'm not. I'm Ms McGovern's boyfriend; I accompanied her when she was admitted here last night."

She scratched at her eye and sighed, rolling her chair away from the desk. "I need to speak to the doctor first. Just take a seat while I find him for you," she instructed concisely, pointing towards the small waiting room opposite. I stiffly spun on my heel and inwardly groaned as I stared at the replicated plastic chairs propped against another stark white wall. Horrid chairs or not, I relented, simply because I was too tired to argue.

After what seemed like an eternity, the nurse eventually returned with a middle-aged doctor in tow, his imposing height towering over me as I stood to greet him.

Portraying false confidence, I held out a hand. "Ari Jaeger."

A razor-sharp smile formed below a steely blue gaze. "Doctor Charles Montgomery," he articulated, shaking my hand with quite the firm grip. "Please, come to my office where we can discuss my patient in private." He signalled towards the bright blue door situated directly behind the nurses' station.

Eager, I followed him. His spacious office was warm and womblike, nothing clinical like I initially expected. In one corner sat an identical pair of beige linen club lounges, separated by an antique coffee table. With the inspiration for the muted wall colour drawn from the scattered floral cushions, the entire space indeed offered solace to patients visiting with the good doctor.

"Please have a seat." Eyeing me sceptically, Doctor Montgomery gestured to the beige circular chair adjacent to his rectangular oak desk. His burly physique positioned in an office chair opposite mine, he got down to the nitty-gritty. "Now, with Theodora's case, unfortunately, I can't disclose much in the way of her diagnosis as you aren't her next of kin. What I can tell you is that the sedative we administered last night gave her a well-rested sleep, but she's still not up to receiving visitors just yet."

Scrubbing at my forehead, I let out an exasperated sigh. "It's Teddy."

The doctor's bushy brows knitted above an equally irritated gaze. "Excuse me?"

"She despises the use of her full name, Theodora," I remarked tetchily, wondering if the previous doctor had even heard me.

"I apologise, and I'll make a notation in her folder."

I scoffed derisively, obviously not. "Look, Doctor Montgomery, I fail to see why I can't see my girlfriend? I only want, no – I need to ensure she's all right. I also need to reassure Teddy, that despite what occurred, I'm not going anywhere." My jaw tightened. "We may not be married, Doctor, but I'm the next best thing to her bloody useless parents. Most of this conundrum is their fault as it is!" I hissed, my agitation apparent. "Has Teddy specifically refused visitors or was it your decision based entirely on your professional opinion, Doctor?"

Gauging by Doctor Montgomery's cool-headed demeanour, I speculated he'd heard many a tirade. "I made the decision based on her current state of mind, and for now, she needs rest – not aggravation," he expressed indifferently. "And until I've performed the proper psychiatric assessment, I won't be allowing anyone to visit with Teddy, including family."

My brows shot up questioningly, more so as he proceeded to slide a notepad across the desk, followed by the pen from the inside pocket of his plaid coat. He clicked it, ready to write.

"Now, what I do need from you is some background information as Teddy wasn't very forthcoming during our earlier session."

"You," I growled, pointing a finger, and pushing the chair backwards, "can go fuck yourself!" Seething, I stalked from his office, slamming the door behind me. That sanctimonious fucker, who did he think he was? In all honesty though, my current mood hadn't helped the situation either. I ruffled my hair with both hands; Christ, I needed a stiff drink.

My phone started buzzing. I fished it from inside my jeans pocket and answered, foregoing the usual niceties. "Scarlett; you have impeccable timing."

"Oh, how so?"

"The good doctor's refusing any visitors – including family!"

"Including you, I take it?"

"Not only was I denied access to Teddy, but Doctor Montgomery also refused to grant any information regarding her wellbeing, simply because I'm not her next of kin!"

"That old nutshell doesn't let up, does it? Gimme about an hour, and I'll be there." She paused, exhaling a sigh. "I know we weren't looking to involve my parents," she hesitantly began, "but it's time we called dad at least. He does care about us kids, believe it or not."

"If we must," I grumbled, petulantly. "I'll call Evan myself if that's the case. See you soon." Hanging up, I reluctantly called Teddy's father.

∞

Evan

HANGING UP THE PHONE, my hands shook as I silently cursed at the spiralling shame. Shame for the anguish Therese had inflicted upon our eldest daughter; a pain so easily prevented that I had a hand in. Instead of taking a stand with my wife, I stuck my head in the sand, hoping our problems would disappear if I left my head there long enough. Except they continued to grow like noxious weeds, escalating to a tangled mess.

I hadn't earned the right to act wounded, and it was too late for regrets. Nor was it the time to dwell. I reefed my jacket off the coat rack and snatched up my car keys; my needs weren't of any consequence, my daughter's were, and she needed me more.

23

AS I MARCHED ACROSS the busy carpark, I spotted my youngest daughter rapidly pacing at the hospital's entrance and yelled out, capturing her attention, "Scarlett!"

She rushed towards me, her outstretched arms flinging around my neck as she buried her sobbing face against my chest. Initially, she caught me off guard, but rather than pushing my heartbroken daughter away, I instinctively folded my arms around her, welcoming a notion that was alien to any of us.

"Shh, I'm here now."

Having clearly remembered her mother's words about displaying our emotions publicly, she rapidly stepped away and ran both hands over her cheeks, swiping away her tears as she apologised. Therese and her life lessons had ruined our children, particularly our daughters. Abel always seemed to be the exception to the rule, much to my chagrin.

"Thanks," she mumbled, gratefully taking the proffered hanky from my hand. "How are you? You know, with everything that's happening?"

"I'm as good as I can be considering the circumstances. Nevertheless, it's not about me; it's about your sister. Ari didn't give much away over the phone, in fact, he was quite evasive," I muttered, glancing sideways at my daughter. Judging by her grim expression, she knew more than Ari was prepared to give. "I don't suppose you could fill in the blanks as to why your sister has landed in the hospital?"

She eyed me pensively. "Maybe we should think about sitting down first."

I stiffly nodded and guided her towards a bench seat situated beneath the large shade trees within the lush grounds where we both slowly sat.

Scarlett contemplatively chewed on the inside of her lip, indicating her nervousness. "Last night, while Teddy was at Ari's house...she cut her wrists open with his razor."

"What?" I stared in disbelief. "Why would she do this to herself?"

"All I know is that it had something to do with her rape," Scarlett revealed. "Something must have happened to trigger such a brutal reaction. What it was, I have no idea."

My heart raced. Oh no! No, no, no. I anxiously scrubbed my face. "You know about the rape?" Unable to look my daughter in the eye, my watery gaze remained firmly planted on the grass beneath my feet. Coward.

"Clearly, I do," she blurted angrily. "I had no idea until Teddy recently opened up to me. Also, why was the truth about her sudden disappearance from our lives for several months hidden from both Abel and I?"

She undoubtedly deserved an honest explanation. I sighed loudly and turned at the waist to face her. "Your mother thought it best that you and your brother remained in the dark. She'd stated that dealing with Teddy was stressful enough without dealing with you two as well. It would have caused unnecessary upset to your lives." Disgusted by my wife's egregious actions, my head shook. "I allowed your mother to coerce me; if I hadn't, Teddy might have had a better chance at a normal life. I can't undo my past mistakes, but I can help her now. I owe her that much at least."

Scarlett's crossed arms and narrowed eyes expressed her scepticism. I had to convince her.

"I want to help Teddy recover."

"That means complete disclosure, so no more secrets and no more lies. They clearly haven't helped the situation. Teddy deserves a chance at happiness – without the baggage accompanying her." A worrying silence drifted over her. "Ari also knows about the baby and the lengths mum took to cover that up."

My eyes widened and my head jerked. "Wait, a baby? What, baby?"

"Um, I assumed you knew about that, too....and judging by the look on your face – I'd say no...." Evidently. That piece of information she never shared. "That explains your version of events, then," she added flatly. Her wary gaze followed as I began pacing furiously back and forth across the grass.

"That lying bitch! She told me she'd sent Teddy to a boarding school in Ballarat hoping it would sort her out! I can't believe Therese would do this! How could she damage Teddy more than she already had?"

Scarlett's mouth dropped open and closed just as quickly.

"What was the baby's sex?" I duly asked, swallowing tightly.

"A little girl," she replied gloomily. "Mother prohibited Teddy from giving her a name; there wasn't any point, apparently."

My lips tightened; what that bitch said went, no arguments. "Ari's aware of all this?"

"You sound surprised." I nodded in response. "He has fought for her regardless of the countless times she's tried to push him away."

The thought of Ari and my daughter as a couple had a genuine smile forming for the first time in weeks. "He truly does love her, doesn't he?"

"He has for a long time, and even you know that," she cooed emphatically.

"I do, surprisingly," I simpered, offering a hand to help Scarlett stand. I hadn't ever hidden my fondness for Ari from anyone, including Therese. "Okay, let's go and find Ari." As I proudly wrapped an arm around her shoulders, I sincerely believed Therese had it wrong for years. Hugging my daughter in public felt terrific.

Neither of us had to look overly far. We found Ari close to the nurses' station, the entire length of his body stretched out across several hard, plastic chairs. He wasn't exactly a small man, so how was he even comfortable?

"Ari, we're here," I murmured, gently shaking his broad shoulder. Ari's dark brow creased as he peeled his eyes open and stared up at us with a bleary, bloodshot gaze. He stiffly sat up, wincing as he swung his feet to the floor. "Sorry about falling asleep while waiting for you," he apologised, gingerly rubbing life back into his right shoulder.

"Don't be ridiculous, Ari, you must be running on the smell of an oily rag," I expressed, taking the seat beside him. I studied his weary face closely. He looked haggard and drawn; the dark circles indicative of his exhaustion, concerning me.

"Indeed, I am. Sleep was the least of my worries though," Ari admitted, running both hands through his dishevelled hair. "Have you spoken with Doctor Montgomery yet?"

I gave a brief shake of my head. "No, not yet. Although, the lovely nurse at the desk informed me that he's visiting with Teddy now, and it might be some time before he's available. Do you want to head upstairs to the cafeteria and grab a cup of coffee while we wait? You look like you could do with some."

Ari's apprehensive gaze darted in the direction of Teddy's room. "What if the doctor comes back?"

"I've left my number instructing them to call me when he's finished," I reassured, patting him on the shoulder. "We can't do much right now, and I need a caffeine fix, with a dash of whiskey." Reluctantly, he agreed and rose from the chair, miserably following us to the elevators.

∞

Audrina

PACING ALONG THE FRONT of the French doors in our kitchen, I intuitively grew aware of Jaxson's irritated gaze occasionally glancing over the top of his morning paper. Not surprising considering I'd disturbed his sleep with my tossing and turning, agonising over the disturbing secret our son had willingly shared with me.

The entire conversation had shaken me to the core, and it was taking every ounce of strength not to drive over to the McGovern's and rip them a new one over Teddy. Not to mention the numerous laws they'd broken.

Without shifting his focus from the political article holding his attention in Sunday's paper, Jaxson's loving voice interrupted my musings. "Honey, please sit down before you wear a hole in the floor."

I twisted at the waist and absently stared, meeting the brilliantly blue and adoring gaze that had first captured my attention. Seemed like a lifetime ago now.

His brow furrowed. "What's bothering you? You've been on edge since the wee hours of this morning."

"I'm sorry darling, I'm merely anxious about Teddy is all," I muttered, sliding into the upholstered chair beside him.

Jaxson smiled curiously, patting my hand affectionately. "Why? Did you not tell me it was just sunstroke from yesterday?"

"I did." What was the saying, 'Better the devil you know?' Until Teddy revealed all, I prudently kept my husband in the dark. I deliberately busied myself by pouring another cup of English breakfast tea. "Teddy was dreadfully sick and didn't look well at all. I sincerely hope she's feeling substantially better today."

He sighed. "I'm sure Teddy shall be fine, and Ari shall ensure she's well cared for."

"I'll call him later just to be sure."

"If it stops you wearing out our floors, then, by all means, go ahead," he dryly replied before resuming his reading.

∞

Evan

ARI STARED VACANTLY, stirring the spoon around in his coffee whilst the other ran rampant through his hair, making it truly dishevelled.

"Your coffee's well and truly stirred, Ari," Scarlett murmured, waving a hand in front of his face.

His head jerked as he snapped out of his daze. "Huh? Oh sorry, my mind was elsewhere."

"I noticed. Drink your coffee before it goes cold," Scarlett scolded, making me smile. Bossy girl.

He snorted and picked up the cup, taking a few sips before setting it back on its saucer. "Thank you for being here, both of you. I appreciate it more than you realise. Hopefully, Teddy shall feel the same way," he quietly expressed, his saddened gaze staring at his fidgeting fingers as he consistently spun the gold signet ring he wore around his pinkie.

I regarded him intently. "I need and want to be here. Teddy's my daughter and right now, showing solidarity's important. God knows she needs it." I sighed shakily, placing my cup on the table. "I want to apologise, too...for not supporting Teddy enough, or for not pulling Therese up sooner." Not unlike Scarlett, he searched my face as he attempted to gauge my sincerity.

"It's not me you need to apologise to, Evan, it's Teddy. I, however, agree with you about not putting a stop to Therese and her repugnant behaviour. Teddy won't just take you at face value either. She'll need to see you making a requited effort for it to mean anything before you gain any sort of trust back."

I nodded sagely over the tense but warranted advice. Ari was right; there was so much untold damage to repair, and a Band-Aid solution wasn't the answer. "I'm certainly going to try," I murmured, picking up my buzzing phone.

"The doctor?" Ari mouthed as I answered.

"Evan McGovern." I nodded. "Yes, we are. We'll be right down."

I hung up, meeting his eager gaze. "He's waiting for us in his office."

"About bloody time!" Ari swiftly pushed the chair back, scraping the feet on the tiled floors. His head swivelled impatiently at us as Scarlett and I slowly rose. "Well, what are we waiting for; let's go!" For someone who claimed extreme tiredness, he had quite the sprint. Scarlett and I barely kept up as he ran towards the bank of elevators.

His finger savagely stabbed the button embedded in the wall. He scowled. "Why is the damned lift taking so long? If not for my tiredness, taking the stairs would've certainly been a lot bloody faster!"

"Getting frustrated with the elevator certainly won't make it go any faster," Scarlett teased, her smile fading when dark eyes glared at her.

When the car finally reached the ground floor, Ari stabbed the button for the required level with matched aggression. He was first out before the doors wholly opened, leaving us behind once again. Eventually, we caught up just in time to hear the doctor's booming voice after Ari's knuckles impatiently rapped on his door.

"Come in!" As Ari pushed the door wide open, Doctor Montgomery bellowed, "Mr Jaeger, I told you earlier, I'm unable to disclose any information to you."

"I know, but you can speak with him," he haughtily retorted, entering the room and smugly twisting to point at me.

"You are?" the doctor quizzed curtly, his steely blue gaze cutting to me.

"Evan McGovern, Teddy's father," I sternly replied, holding out a hand to the stout physician.

The doctor's suspicious gaze narrowed over the firm handshake. "Doctor Montgomery, and you must be Teddy's younger sister, Scarlett, is it?"

She shyly nodded, shaking his hand.

"Please take a seat." He motioned towards the beige sofa against the wall and grabbed the iPad from his desk, taking one of the identical seats opposite us.

"Now, since speaking with Mr Jaeger this morning, I've conducted a full mental health assessment on Theodora, sorry, Teddy. Her behaviours are pointing to PTSD or post-traumatic stress disorder with NSSI."

I had to stifle a smirk; obviously, Ari had corrected him over my daughter's hateful relationship with her name. "Layman's terms please, Doc," I requested. "Medical terms are too confusing."

"Sorry. Non-suicidal self-injury, meaning Teddy was self-harming without the intention of committing suicide. I know that may sound strange, but she had reached a point where the pain of the past had accumulated; facing it was no longer an option. However, in saying that, we did have a small breakthrough, and all I can say at this time, it was encouraging, meaning she's open to help. Admissions are never easy."

His interest piqued, Ari sat forward, firing stern questions only the doctor could answer. That wasn't completely true either. "Did she happen to mention why at any stage during this session? Was there any indication as to what or to whom the trigger was?"

Doctor Montgomery fidgeted in his seat uneasily. "I can't disclose any more than I already have. I must protect patient confidentiality, and Teddy only permitted me to tell you that much. I'm sorry, but surely you understand my position?"

A volatile Ari slammed his fist down on the arm of the chair. "How in the devil are we supposed to help if we're kept in the dark?"

I always knew he had a hot temper, but nothing like I'd just witnessed. I held up a hand, hoping to calm him down. "Whoa, Ari, take it easy. Getting angry won't help anyone, and Teddy may tell us why in her own time what triggered her, I'm sure of it. We have to be patient, okay?"

He irately conceded, slumping in the chair, "Fine!"

His thunderous expression only exacerbated the guilt I carried; I knew who the perpetrating bastard was but sought the pleasure of killing him for myself.

Doctor Montgomery leaned forward, steepling his thick fingers in his lap. "Ari, if it's any consolation, Teddy informed me you're aware of the panic attacks and the anxiety, yes?"

A surly Ari stiffly nodded at him. "Teddy apprised me about them not too long ago."

I marvelled along with the doctor. Talking was the first step forward.

"That's wonderful, as it shows immense trust on Teddy's part." He gave Ari a broad smile before referring to the notes in his lap. "She disclosed that you've also witnessed them firsthand as they're happening frequently, along with recurring nightmares, both causing intense mental and emotional exhaustion. We also discussed her mother's unethical approach to the entire ordeal." The doctor pursed his lips disapprovingly. "Therese certainly made herself the victim in all of this, didn't she? Blaming your daughter for these actions was the catalyst for why we're here."

Overwhelming guilt surged. I hung my head in shame as tears dripped into my lap. "Yes, she has," I revealed. "The night of our so-called family dinner, I walked out on my wife. Her feelings regarding our daughter she made abundantly clear then."

The doctor prepared to take notes, his head tilted questioningly. "How so?"

As I divulged every vile word, I nervously glanced sideways. Anger radiated off Ari in waves. "One assertion made was about the relationship our daughter now has with Ari; she needs to quit fantasising..." I swallowed the lump in my throat as Ari's face twisted and his fists clenched. "...as he's too much of a man for a girl like her."

Ari pushed out of the chair and stormed towards the door, reefing it open. It slammed shut behind him.

Doctor Montgomery's empathetic gaze returned to my stunned face. "Give him time to cool off. No doubt he needs it after listening to your wife's unconscionable tirade about the woman he loves."

No shit, Sherlock.

I scoffed. "It's upsetting for all of us, Doc. Which brings me to my next point: I want Ari Jaeger's name entered into that paperwork as Teddy's next of kin," I specified, pointing to the iPad in his lap, my first step on the road to finding redemption.

"As you wish." Doctor Montgomery nodded and immediately began typing. "I'm informing you I'm releasing Teddy today also."

My brows furrowed. "May I ask as to why you aren't keeping Teddy for a longer period?"

"No need. In your daughter's case, I felt a compulsory order wasn't necessary. I assessed her, she answered candidly and honestly by admitting she needed help with her issues. Therefore, as long as she continues her therapy and medications, I saw no issue with releasing her into Ari's care."

"Why Ari specifically?"

Briefly, Doctor Montgomery paused his typing and stared at me with his steely blue gaze. "He appears to be the only person in your daughter's life who provides the stability she needs." His honesty was like a blow to the chest. However, I found myself agreeing with him.

I nodded wisely. "Yeah, I suppose it would be."

"I apologise if I've offended you, but due to mitigating circumstances, I believed it was the best course of action."

A shuddering sigh escaped as I waved a dismissive hand. "No damage done here, Doc, I assure you." I offered a token smile. "What else do we need to know?"

Astutely aware that our conversation was over, Doctor Montgomery's perceptive gaze dipped back to his notes. "I'm prescribing a mild anti-depressant. Teddy needs to take them once daily, preferably at night as they also contain a mild sedative. Other than that, the side effects should be minimal. However, should any problems arise, please don't hesitate to call me."

I watched the doctor speedily type up the prescription, with the printer on the modular shelf unit behind his desk subsequently spitting it out.

"They are slow-release and could take up to four weeks to work effectively," he added, "but over time, Teddy should start to see life a lot clearer. I've prudently set up weekly appointments to ensure close monitoring of her progress also."

"Thank you, Doctor. Hopefully, now, we can look up from here." I blew out a cleansing breath before cautiously approaching my next question. "What about her wrists? Were they bad?"

"Luckily, no. She didn't sever any major arteries as she cut across and not up," Doctor Montgomery explained typing on his iPad. The printer fired up again, printing what I assumed was another script. "There may be some light scarring, but if she applies Vitamin E oil to the wounds, they'll heal and possibly fade. The ED doctor had administered a strong dose of antibiotics already, just as a preventative measure against infection. Nevertheless, I strongly urge she completes the course of antibiotics to be sure. Please keep an eye on her, and if there are any profound changes, please call me," he stressed once more, handing over the prescriptions with an appointment card.

I shook his hand appreciatively. "Thank you again." I assisted a numb Scarlett out of the chair and held onto her swaying figure by the waist. "Come on Scarlett, time to take your sister home."

Wide-eyed, she nodded and clung to me as held back emotions finally spilled over.

24

Ari

"DOCTOR MONTGOMERY," I called out as the doors to the lift glided open. If he was to remain Teddy's doctor, I had to remain in his good graces, which meant swallowing my pride. "I sincerely apologise for my outburst in your office earlier. It was terribly bad mannered of me."

He stared impassively until we reached his office. I observed a wry smile slowly growing, softening the doctor's hard exterior. "I had you worried there for a minute, didn't I?" He closed the door and laughed, watching my entire body sag in relief. "The entire situation has been hugely stressful on you, and these revelations were a lot to take in," he reassured, placing an oversized hand on my shoulder. "Just take it one day at a time, okay?"

I stiffly nodded. "There's an issue regarding Teddy that I need answers to, and regrettably, it's rather personal."

"If it isn't breaking patient confidentiality, then fire away." Again, he eyed me suspiciously and rocked on the balls of his king-size feet, his beefy arms hugging several files to his broad chest.

My father never intimidated me anywhere near as much as he did, and it was making me shift anxiously on my feet. "It's about sex, and before you jump to conclusions just hear me out," I clearly stated before continuing, "Although Teddy was a victim of rape, why does she have such a high sex drive? I highly expected sex not to be a big part of her everyday life. The mere idea, I thought, ought to have left her perturbed, wouldn't it?"

Running a hand through my hair, I explained further, "There were a few instances where she's acted desperate as if she was trying to be rid of something or for reassurance; I'm just not sure which."

Doctor Montgomery raised one bushy eyebrow pondering the question. "It might be one of two reasons; one, she trusts you implicitly, and is aware that you aren't setting out to deliberately harm her. And two, it could be her way of dealing with the trauma of her past, which we class as hypersexuality, an increased libido." My brows furrowed, making him smile.

"Some people become what we as a profession call a sexual anorexic; it's a pathological loss of their sexual appetite for any romantic, and or sexual interaction. They develop such a fear of intimacy, it causes anxiety. Teddy's the opposite. She craves the intimacy, craves the nurturing that she lacked from birth, right through to adulthood. From what I understand it was her nanny, Alice, who acted as that replacement, but still, it's not quite the same as a mother's love, is it?"

"No, it's not," I agreed quietly.

He continued, "As you're aware, bonding with your mother generally begins from the moment of conception, and subsequently afterwards, starting through the birth process. The lack thereof in Teddy's case has had quite a profound impact on her. How her mother handled her attack, coupled with the constant eroding of her confidence, it merely added to those insecurities. Every person and every case, Ari, are different, and sometimes, there's no set way of dealing with it. We simply have to work through the kinks, and slowly iron them out according to the patient's individual needs."

Feeling a little more at ease, I shook his hand and smiled sincerely for the first time in the last two days. "Thank you, Doc. This information helped more than you know."

"Anytime, Ari, and I hope this has enlightened you somewhat to Teddy's behaviours. As I said, take one day at a time. There may be days where she may regress, but I am highly confident with everyone's support, Teddy should make a full recovery. Just try to be patient with her. Take her home, which I am sure she is quite ready to do. Good luck."

"Thank you for everything, Doc." I turned the handle on the door when he caught my attention once more.

"Oh, Ari, one more thing, when you do eventually resume sexual activity, please be sure to use condoms."

I stared quizzically.

"The antibiotics counteract the effects of the pill," he explained, "and in my personal opinion, Teddy's not ready for a child; not at this stage in her life anyway."

I stiffly nodded in agreeance; she most definitely was not ready, not until she was well enough at least. "Of course."

With a few words of encouragement, the gloom had lifted, making life seem less bleak and so much clearer. So much so, as I eagerly made my way towards Teddy's room, the perpetual ache to hold her in my arms had grown as had the reassurance that everything from hereon in was going to be okay. It was now a simple matter of convincing Teddy of the same.

∞

Evan

HAVING REACHED TEDDY'S ROOM, I hesitated in the doorway as my optimism over our reconciliation plunged. Open arms, open heart, and forgiveness only ever happened in the movies, never in real life. If I genuinely sought redemption along with rebuilding the relationship we once had, it would take time as well as a requited effort on my part; I just hoped I wasn't kidding myself.

Scarlett gripped my arm affectionately. "Everything will be fine, Dad, you'll see." I loved that kid's sanguinity. Moving in with her best friend had seemingly rubbed off on her.

I blew out an unsteady breath and slowly turned the door handle, entering what I trusted was the start of new beginnings.

"Hey, Teddy Bear, it's dad," I cooed across the tiny room to where she sat curled up on the bed, her arms tightly hugging her knees, as her saddened gaze stared out the window. The distressing sight broke my heart.

As she slowly turned to face me, the long thick waves of her copper hair tumbled around her shoulders. A frown marred her brow above hazel eyes, tinged with sadness. "Daddy?"

Hope blossomed hearing her sweet voice respond, taking me back to a time when she was a small child. Her excitable little face always the first to greet me after a long day at the office.

My throat tightened. "Yes, it's me, sweetheart." Cautiously, I sat at the foot of the bed and reached out, attempting to grasp her hand. Straightaway, she screwed up her nose and recoiled against the wall, rejecting me. Despondent, I immediately dropped my hand beside me. "How...are you feeling?"

"How do you think I'm feeling?" she muttered, tucking a loose tendril behind her ear, giving me a glimpse of the bandaged wrist as the edge of her sleeve slipped. She rapidly tugged the sleeve back down, covering her wrist from my sympathetic gaze.

"Hey, don't feel embarrassed. I'm not here to judge you. I want to help you, Teddy."

"You want to help me?" she snarled, her eyes darkening. Years of repressed anger had finally bubbled to the surface. "Where were you when I needed you before? When I really needed you, huh? By ignoring everything that happened to me, you're as bad as mother. You let her bully you into submission, and like a god-damned coward, you went along with whatever she decided. Why didn't you stand up to her, *Dad*?" she seethed, swiping angry tears from her cheeks. "Tell me why you abandoned me?"

Her sobs were more than I could bear. "I'm sorry, Teddy, I..." I stabbed at my chest. "I let you down because I was too damned selfish. She told me if I didn't go along with her, she would..."

"Would what?" she pushed impatiently.

Ashamed, my shoulders slumped. Having to actually admit my faults out loud was harder than I ever imagined. "Your mother threatened to expose my affair, the affair I was having with the wife of one of my partners at the firm." An affair I started, and presently remained in.

Wide-eyed and stunned, Scarlett moved further into the room. The revolted expression on her face spoke volumes. "If you were that unhappy, then why not just leave mum?"

My eyes flooded with shedding tears. "She threatened me with full custody, and I refused to walk away and leave you both behind. With the way she was – and still is – I couldn't risk her inflicting any more damage."

"More damage?" an indignant Teddy shrieked. "What more could she inflict upon me that she hadn't already?" she raged lunging, her fists pounding at my chest as hot tears rapidly flowed down her stained cheeks. "You – selfish – prick! How could you? You never gave a flying fuck about me! Only yourself!" Her words were brutal, but if the cold hard truth was what I had to hear to wake me up, then so be it. "I thought you loved me, Daddy! I thought...you...loved me," she sobbed.

"Teddy, stop!" Ari shouted upon entering the room. He tried rushing to my aid, but as much as it killed me, I held up a hand, halting him in his tracks.

"No Ari, she's angry with me. She needs this."

Ari glanced at Scarlett, his face conveying concern over Teddy's troubling behaviour. Resigned neither could do a thing to help, the two of them quietly left the room, leaving me to wear the brunt of her anguish. Deservedly so.

Eventually, Teddy's battle-weary body slumped, and the pounding at my chest stopped. She mournfully hid behind her hands and wept, her reams of tears running seamlessly between her long fingers. Lifting my arms to haul my heartbroken daughter into my lap took every ounce of energy I had. I winced, expressly as she sagged against me.

"Oh, my sweet, sweet daughter, I can't ever apologise enough to you. I'm so sorry that I let you down. You're my little girl, and my actions or lack thereof by not standing up to your mother is something I'll always regret. Can you ever forgive me?"

"That absolution you speak of – you need to earn it before I can even think of forgiving you," she reasoned tearfully. "And for the record, actions speak louder than words."

"I understand completely, and I'll do my absolute best to earn that back." I sighed heavily. "I promise never to let you down again."

∞

Ari

AN ANXIOUS POPPY AND Dominique pounced on Teddy the minute we strolled in the door. Not that she wasn't pleased to see her friends; their fussing was simply too overwhelming. In the end, I had to whisk her away into the bedroom for a shower and much-needed rest.

"Stay with me, please?" she pleaded, gripping my hand tightly.

My brows shot up, shocked by her request. "Are you sure?"

She confidently nodded. "I need your help to change these anyway." Teddy twisted her wrists upright, showing me the soiled bandages.

"All right." Pleased she'd requested my help, I smiled and led the way to the ensuite bathroom.

Purposely, I joined her in the shower and lovingly tended to her every whim, washing her voluminous hair, and gliding a loofah over her body, taking care to avoid her injured wrists.

"They don't look too bad," I noted afterwards as we perched on the beds edge wrapped only in our towels. Laying Teddy's wrists in my lap, I applied fresh ointment to the dry wounds. I flicked my gaze up at her. "I'm not going to fall apart if that's what you're waiting for," I assured her.

Except, she was the first to dissolve, floods of tears falling down her cheeks as her head manically shook. "It was so unfair of me to put you through this. I should never...." A hysterical Teddy wasn't the best scenario. I had to calm her down, anything to prevent her from harming herself again. That would kill me.

"Hey, come here." I gently tugged her into my lap. Her hands clawed, clinging to my shoulders. "Please don't worry about me and stop blaming yourself for this!" Aware I sounded harsh, I winced and softened my tone. "You were crying out for help and believed cutting yourself was the only way, but no longer do you have to feel alone; we're all here for you." I tenderly pressed my lips to her forehead and breathed in her sweet scent. "Let's finish these bandages," I proposed, lovingly wiping away her tears with the pads of my thumbs, "and get you dressed so we can get you into bed for more rest, okay?"

Having ensured Teddy was fully settled before leaving the bedroom, I quietly strolled into the kitchen with the expectation of finding more than one person hanging about. That wasn't to be the case at all. The house was unusually quiet. Well almost.

Someone huffed loudly, drawing my attention to the family room. The sight of my sister's dismal figure stretched out across the sofa had my eyes rolling dispassionately. She was brooding, the magazine in front of her wearing the brunt of her mood as she savagely flicked each page. Perfect. Just what I needed right now – a sulky sibling when my plate was full enough already with Teddy.

What I needed was a drink, and for a change, it was Pinot Noir, not my usual stiff bourbon. For the conversation ahead, it required a clearer head.

Dominique angrily tossed the magazine onto the coffee table and idly rose from the sofa, her bare feet shuffling over the timber boards as she made her way into the kitchen. "Bit early for alcohol, isn't it?" she grumbled, sliding onto a barstool at the island.

"It's five o'clock somewhere in the world," I quipped, opening the bottle. "Besides, the last two days activities warrants a decent drink. Want a glass?"

Resting an elbow on the cool, marble countertop, she lazily sighed. "Yeah, why not." Leaning into her palm, she twirled the ends of her long, raven hair around her forefinger.

I raised a brow and poured us each a glass, sliding one into her hand. "What's on your mind, Dom?" When it came to my baby sister, I was a sucker.

"Nothing's on my mind. Why would you ask that?" Dom voiced, sipping, and swirling the smooth but slightly acidic wine around inside her mouth.

"Don't be evasive, Dominique. You were twirling your hair around your finger." I lifted the glass to my lips, taking a tentative sip. I smirked at her. "You always have when you've wanted something. So, what do you want?"

"I hate that you're so observant," she muttered. "Surprisingly, I don't want anything for a change; I just want to know if Teddy's going to be okay?"

"Oh, then why didn't you just ask me?"

"I wasn't sure how to ask or even what to ask."

I shrugged my shoulders, unsure of what to tell her. "The truth – I haven't the faintest. All I can tell you is that – Teddy shall need an unlimited amount of support, understanding and most importantly, love for her to make it through this harrowing time."

My glazed expression stared at the glass balanced between my fingers. The wine swirling inside was a swift reminder of how quickly my relationship with Teddy had spiralled out of control. If there was any hope of finding that beaming light at the end of the tunnel, I prayed it came before the vortex of the storm had a chance to suck us up.

"Bro, are you, all right?"

Was I really? On the outside, I appeared to be a man, the man and Teddy's rock, but the truth was, on the inside I was crumbling.

I snapped out of my musings and raised a weary smile. "Yeah, sorry, sis, I guess there's just a lot on my mind right now. Anyway, I'm heading outside to have a little chat with Evan. Are you going to be all right with everything?"

"Yeah, I will be. What about you, and don't bullshit me!" She wagged a stern finger at me.

A well-needed laugh rumbled in my chest as I rounded the island and hugged my straight-up sister. "This isn't about me; it's about Teddy. But thanks for asking, sis, I love you."

"I love you, too," she murmured, slyly swiping the wine bottle out from under me. "Now go and relax, but you'll need another bottle because I'm taking this one!" With an evil giggle, she took off in the direction of the stairs. I chuckled.

"Oh, you are your mother's daughter."

Once I'd retrieved another bottle, I made my way outside, joining Evan by the pool, who was already suitably comfortable on a cane lounge. His legs stretched out in front of him, he puffed away on a cigar, the smoke billowing around him in the gentle and cooling breeze.

"May I have one of those?" I politely enquired, pointing to the open box on the table beside the bottle of bourbon, and by the looks of the label, he'd helped himself to my bottle.

"Sure, help yourself. I wasn't even aware you smoked?" His eyes raised in surprise as I grasped one between my fingers and slid it under my nose, sniffing the aromatic tobacco.

"Teddy would prefer if I didn't; she's not a huge fan of the smell."

"A good cigar is the perfect companion for bourbon."

"I agree." I nodded, snipping the end with the cutter, and dragging on the cigar as I held the lighter to it. "Right now, with all that's happening, I thought settling for something less intoxicating wouldn't hurt." I blew out a puff of smoke and raised my wine glass in front of me. "Cheers."

As I took a long sip, Evan drew on his cigar and eyed me inquisitively. "What's on your mind, Ari? You clearly haven't stepped outside for the fresh air, have you?"

My smile faded. "How astute of you, Evan, and yes, there is a matter that needs addressing. One in particular."

"Well, fire away."

"Our session with Doctor Montgomery today was rather interesting, wouldn't you say? You were calm throughout; in fact, I thought you were *too* calm." Puffing on the cigar, I glanced sideways and gauged his body language as his jaw ticked and his body shifted uneasily in the chair, indicative of my intuition. He indeed knew something. "I'm deducing you knew precisely what the doctor was talking about regarding Teddy's attacker, didn't you? Tell me I am wrong?" My impatience with his reticence was growing. "I don't appreciate your silence, Evan."

"The night Teddy was attacked," Evan began, drawing another long puff and exhaling sharply before continuing, "Therese decided to conveniently wait until our last guest had left before revealing the nature of the events that had occurred in our home that evening. Even then, I had to pressure her into revealing the culpable bastard. Naturally, I wanted to report it to the police..."

"You didn't, though, did you?" His jaw ticked, and I deduced he was silently admitting his guilt. I pressed him further. "Therese manipulated you into tabling your rage, and your feelings on the matter, didn't she?"

Blanching at my darkened face, he looked away.

"What did she hold over you?" His reluctance to answer fuelled my harboured rage. Then I did the unthinkable; I lashed out, punching Evan square in the face. The chair he sat in toppled over from the force. "Answer me dammit!"

"I suppose I should've seen that coming," Evan motioned, laying on the ground whilst rubbing his jaw. Blood poured from both his bottom and top lips.

"Foresights a wonderful thing," I roared. "Isn't it? You'd think a man as smart as you would use his noggin for such an occasion!" He glowered as I helped him off the ground. It was apparent that my words matched the sting of my punch. "Hit a nerve did I, Evan?"

"You could say that." Gingerly sitting back down, he winced. "I know, I should have done more; I carry that regret every damn day. Seeing my daughter reduced to this hurts me in ways you can't imagine." He seriously wanted me to hit him again.

"Don't even go there, Evan," I fumed, the dark undercurrent of my tone a subdued warning.

"I honestly thought as the years passed, she would heal and move on with her life," he argued, applying pressure to his lips with his T-shirt. "It never crossed my mind she would still be suffering this much." My jaw dropped in astonishment.

"Well, how obtuse of you," I uttered dryly, picking up the chair and flopping back into it.

"I honestly thought she was moving on with her life, particularly when she announced you two had finally come together. Call that ignorance on my part and bribery from my wife."

"Bribing you about what?"

His Adam's apple bounced in his throat, swallowing his pride I suspected. "She... she was threatening to take absolutely everything from me, including the girls' by exposing my affair with my business partner's wife," he confessed, shakily trying to relight his cigar.

"That's a shitty motive, considering she didn't want the girls' in the first place," I mocked callously, taking the lighter from his quaking hand and relighting the cigar for him.

"You have no idea how manipulating she can be. They're the only reason I stayed. I honestly didn't give a shit about the affair coming out. She knew my girls' were my weakness, and I would hate to think how Therese would have treated them if I hadn't stayed."

"Be that as it may, you still could have intervened and found a way to help Teddy. Counselling through school, anything. At least it may not have gotten this far or worse."

"You're right. I could have…"

"Evan! Ari!" A panicked Dominique frantically called out to us from the edge of the house. I swivelled in my seat. "You both need to come quickly!"

We leapt from our chairs and swiftly ran inside following my sister, the both of us horrified by the piercing screams that resonated through the house.

"Teddy must be having a nightmare," she breathlessly explained, "and we weren't able to get close enough to calm her down."

I bolted to the bedroom.

"Get off me! You're hurting me! Stop! Please!" She was screaming and thrashing about the bed, trying to fight off what appeared to be an imaginary person.

Evan was about to approach the bed, when I held up a hand, stopping him in his tracks. "Unless you want a repeat of this morning's beating, I suggest you don't."

He scoffed. "How do we wake Teddy up then?"

"We don't. I'm hoping the reassurance in my words, and the sound of my voice shall calm her down. Well, that's the plan, and if that fails, I'll call Doctor Montgomery. Poppy, can you find Teddy's iPhone and plug it in please?" I requested without shifting my gaze from Teddy whilst ignoring Poppy's distress.

Evan's brow creased. "What does that do?"

"Music is a calming tool, one of many if you knew her, which you don't," I murmured in an unfeeling manner as I cautiously approached the bed.

He sucked in a harsh breath.

I peered up and stared darkly, daring Evan to challenge me. For a mere second, he thought about it and instead, chose to backdown, watching wordlessly from the sidelines. His worried gaze constantly darting as Poppy hurriedly slipped back into the room, pairing the iPhone with the Bluetooth speaker. The room swiftly filled with the ambient sounds of Attila Fias' classic movie themes.

"Okay," he capitulated. "Whatever works, I guess."

"Teddy, it's me, Ari. No one's hurting you here." With the gentle sound of my voice, the thrashing slowly began to subside. "We're at home, at your house. You're safe here. No one shall ever hurt you again, I promise." As gently as possible, I sat down beside her on the bed, the mattress dipping slightly. I reached over, stroking her forehead with the tips of my fingers. I continuously reiterated my words, keeping my voice a dull whisper. Each word and each touch slowly worked their magic, reducing her movements to nothing more than a sporadic twitching of an arm or a leg.

I briefly glanced over at a doleful Evan. The realisation of my words had clearly set in. With any luck, envy and guilt had risen to the top of that list. I knew his daughter better than he did, and that pained him. His slumped demeanour clearly expressed his feelings as he slipped from the room along with everyone else. Self-pity wasn't an emotion that interested me. Not where he nor Therese were concerned anyway.

I wiped the sweat from Teddy's face, and neck with the tepid face washer Poppy had thoughtfully grabbed for me, using it to cool her overheated body. Much to my relief, both the erratic breathing and the fluttering of her eyelids had slowed to something more evenly paced.

I had a feeling I wasn't far off joining her, my eyelids were drooping, and my head kept dropping. I was exhausted, so why was I fighting the need for sleep? I took one look at the beautiful woman asleep in front of me and tiredly sighed. You are why, I reasoned with myself, citing a perpetual obligation to stay awake just in case you needed me.

A yawn escaped as I scruffed my untidy hair. Something else Teddy teased me about, telling me I spent longer in front of the mirror than she did. That, I doubted. Another yawn. Unable to fight the fatigue any longer, I toed off my shoes, slipping in beside her.

Maybe just an hour or two.

25

STRETCHING AGAINST THE MATTRESS, I peeled my eyes open and glanced out the windows. My sleepy gaze viewed the last rays of light as the sun began to set over the rooftops, shrouding the city in darkness. Curious about the time, I flicked up my wrist and checked my watch. I frowned. So much for an hour or two.

I rolled my head on the pillow, panic surging as I viewed the empty spot beside me. I levered up onto my elbows and called out, "Teddy?"

She replied softly from the doorway of the ensuite bathroom, "I'm right here, Ari." Her sweet voice was music to my ears.

I let out a noticeably, sharp breath.

"I just needed to pee." With her sensuous shape sauntering towards the bed, one of her shapely brows raised intuitively at me.

"Yeah, I know…" Sliding off the bed, I met her halfway and pulled her close. Her long fingers sifted through my mussed hair as her darkened, lifeless orbs framed by blackened circles stared back at me. "I'm fine. Stop stressing, or you'll lose those precious locks on your head. Then what would I have to hold on to when you fuck me?"

Her raw comment had my mouth falling open and quickly closing again. For once, I was rendered speechless. My concerned gaze searching her fatigued face, I collected my thoughts. "Are you okay? You gave us all quite the scare."

"Didn't you hear me the first time? I said I'm fine!" She glared and stepped away from me, her arms defensively folding over her chest.

Shaking my head, I disagreed with her, "You suffered a major breakdown, so how can you act so nonchalant or imply you're fine?"

Teddy's hand waved flippantly around her. "I recovered perfectly well, didn't I?"

"No, you didn't. You're far from it. Don't you see? Given the circumstances, your recovery shall be lengthy, and not just in a day. It could take months, possibly years," I disputed firmly. "But one way or another, we're all going to help you through it."

Perplexed, she stepped backwards until she hit the wall. "What do you mean by 'we', Ari?"

Oh, crap. Dropping my head, I closed my eyes scrambling for the right words. "I meant us...as in Scarlett, Dominique, Poppy, your dad...." I paused and nervously ran a hand through my hair. "....And my mother."

Teddy's eyes widened. "No. No, no, no, no." She pushed past me and crawled back onto the bed, drawing her knees up and under her chin. She hugged them tightly. "Your mother can't help me. She can't know. She'll hate me, Ari," she cried, barely able to breathe from what I assumed was the fear of the unknown.

I climbed onto the bed and knelt in front of her, endeavouring to lay those fears to rest. I made a point not to touch her as I sensed she didn't want to be. "Bollocks! Why would she hate you, or blame you for that matter? If anything, she was confused, but once I explained your past, she understood. Mother's a lawyer remember, so naturally, she has a bad habit of acting terribly pragmatic."

Her head shook disbelievingly. "When I eventually say who attacked me, not one of you will want anything to do with me."

"I could never turn away from you. The rape, and how your mother acted after your disclosure, none of it was your fault," I calmly and softly reassured. "There's something else I also need to tell you."

Teddy gripped her knees tighter and eyed me suspiciously, making my heart thump wildly inside my chest. "What?" she asked, her voice hoarse and barely audible.

My sweat-laced palms rubbed over my thighs. "She knows about the baby...likewise, your dad."

She wailed, hiding behind her hands, "Oh, my god, no!"

Fighting back my tears, I tugged at her hands, tucking them firmly inside mine. "Please don't feel ashamed. Something of this magnitude you won't ever forget, but you can't keep giving your past the power to cripple you either."

A doubtful line etched between Teddy's brows. "How? Tell me how to accomplish the impossible, Ari?"

"By letting others in and facing your past head-on," I countered.

"That's easier said than done." She scoffed. "My mother made me believe it was impossible. She said, *'How could anyone in their right mind believe the rantings of a silly girl like me.'* So why should I believe you?"

I sighed when I categorically wanted to shake her. I refrained. Not one word she spoke was valid; they were all Therese's. That woman was one sharp thorn in our sides. Her lies had impacted Teddy significantly, and if she were in my line of sight right now, I would have happily given her a severe dressing down.

As it stood, she wasn't, so I gave Teddy a question to ponder; I was confident it would have the impact I was after. "Your mother brainwashed you merely to suit herself and her agenda, whatever that may be. Can you name one person in this house who doesn't believe you? Who would it be, Teddy?"

Remaining stoically quiet, I sat back on my haunches, allowing her space and time to contemplate my words. My face brightened as she jumped up, throwing her arms around me, and burying her face in the crook of my neck.

"Oh, Ari, what did I ever do to deserve you?" Teddy sobbed, soaking me with her shedding tears. "I love you infinity, Ari Jaeger."

Bliss washed over me. I enveloped her in my arms, nuzzling my nose inside the thick locks tumbling around her shoulders. "And I love you infinity, my beautiful, Teddy."

"We should go eat something; you must be hungry," I murmured, brushing my fingertips along Teddy's arm. Never before had I felt so gratified.

Ordinarily, an intense discussion such as ours would leave one disgruntled and at a loss, but neither Teddy nor I felt that way. Instead, our optimistic attitude had led us here, back to the bed connecting by other means instead of sex.

"Your bear's hungry, is it?" she teased, tilting her head upwards.

I bent down and kissed the tip of her nose.

"Merciless woman."

She snorted playfully, untangling her limbs, and rolling off the mattress. "You're incorrigible; you know that?"

A smug grin crept across my face. "I know."

She let out a haughty laugh, a genuine Teddy laugh that I recognised. "Dinner, now!"

It was my turn to laugh. Bossy as ever, Miss McGovern had indeed returned.

∞

Teddy

UNDER THE DIM LIGHT of the vintage hanging lamps at the breakfast bar, a lonely figure dolefully sat, holding their head up in one hand and nursing a glass of bourbon in the other. Other than my father, the kitchen was empty. Tentatively, I stood back, observing him from a safe distance whilst inwardly questioning his reasoning to stick around, particularly after I'd beaten the crap out of him. Ari had taken a crack, too, judging by the looks of the fresh bruises on his face.

Ari's head tilted in my father's direction. "Go on," he whispered, giving my shoulder a supportive squeeze. "I'll see to our dinner."

"Okay, thanks," I murmured, reaching up and grasping the hand draped over my shoulder.

"You'll be fine. Trust me on this." He pressed his lips to my temple before making his way over to the oven and bending to grab our plates off the tray inside. The delicious smell of pork meatballs and mozzarella cheese wafted under my nose, making my mouth water and my stomach growl.

Glancing back at Ari who gave me another reassuring nod, I tightened the sash on my dressing gown and blew out my cheeks. "Hi, Dad."

"They look worse than they feel if that's any consolation?"

His confidence barely lessened the guilt swarming my conscious. I scrunched my face, disagreeing with the blasé attitude. "No, not really."

He chuckled. "Anyway, enough about me: how are you feeling baby girl?"

"Better than I deserve really."

Ari scoffed, earning him a defiant eye roll.

"Okay, I'm feeling somewhat better," I corrected, making him smile.

"That's great to hear. You gave us all quite the scare, Ari especially."

"I can't help but feel terrible about my actions and how selfish it was to inflict my pain on everyone else." More tears prickled.

"Hey now, no more crying," he gently chided, circling an arm around my waist, and drawing me closer. "It's going to be okay now."

I nodded sceptically. Accepting my father into my life was a considerable risk, but if I didn't, how could I learn to move forward.

I just hoped he wouldn't let me down. My heart couldn't withstand it.

Kissing my forehead softly, he wiped the flowing tears away with his thumbs. "Life will only get better; you know that, right?"

"I know, and thank you...for being here for me, and for Ari."

"You don't need to thank me, sweetheart. I'm your father; that's what we do for our children. Meant to anyway," he murmured, regret lacing his voice. For the first time in years, I believed him and allowed myself to relax against his hold. "Look, despite the mistakes I've made in the past, I truly want to support you and put everything right, every step of the way. On a lighter note, Ari's an incredible bloke. He's a keeper." He beamed, winking at a smirking Ari. "Without a doubt."

I peered up at my father and smiled coyly. "I know he is."

"Ah, there's my baby girl. You have such a beautiful smile, so let's see more of it, rather than the tears, okay?"

"No more tears," I conceded giggling, wiping my face with the back of my hand.

"Good girl. Now, you go and have your dinner with your young man here, while this old timer heads to bed. See you both in the morning."

"Goodnight, Dad." I basked in the warmth of my father's cuddle, the woodsy scent of his cologne drifting, taking me back to my childhood. Moments I treasured the most, like running and jumping into his arms when he walked through the door after work at the end of each day.

He smiled beatifically, tears misting his hopeful gaze. "Goodnight, Teddy."

I watched my father until he reached the bottom of the stairs before spinning towards a grinning Ari.

"Was I right, or was I right?"

I crinkled my nose and rushed into his open arms, crushing my mouth to his. "I guess so."

Having taken the day off, everyone used the morning to enjoy the big, hearty breakfast with all the trimmings that Ari had cooked. During which, the doorbell unexpectedly rang, pausing the cheery chatter around the dining table.

"I'll get it," Dad offered, wiping the corners of his mouth with the napkin. I watched him push the chair back and saunter from the kitchen until he disappeared down the hallway, my ears straining as the front door opened. "Audrina..."

"Evan! What are you doing here?" she sputtered, obviously baffled by my father's appearance. I almost imagined the stunned expression, too.

"I'm here for Teddy because Ari asked me to be. Please come in," I heard him utter.

Audrina graciously but tightly accepted his explanation. "Thank you."

As I heard the front door close and Audrina's heels scurrying loudly over the timber boards, I raised a dubious brow at Ari.

"Maybe explain mother's flagrant attitude to Evan later," he quietly suggested, leaning closer to me, and out of earshot of everyone else.

"That's a conversation I look forward to," I replied sarcastically just as his mother rushed around the corner, greeting her children and the others with her usual airs and graces.

"Good morning, everyone. And Teddy, darling, how are you feeling?" she asked lastly, bending at the waist to hug me. "You gave us such a fright."

I grimaced. "So everyone keeps telling me."

Audrina took a few steps backward, giving me the once over with a scrutinising gaze. "Dominique phoned to inform me you'd been released from the hospital, so I thought I'd just drop by to check in on you for myself."

Riddled with shame, I blushed. "Um, thank you. I'm feeling a lot better, and until now, it appears I severely underestimated the incredible network of support I have surrounding me."

"Yes, yes, you do. Mine, too; without judgement," Audrina reassured, her astute gaze barely lingering on my bandages as she grasped my hands. "Anything you need, please don't ever hesitate to ask."

Relief engulfed me. "Considering what I've just put Ari through in the last forty-eight hours, this is unexpected...and I can't thank you enough."

Audrina chuckled dismissively. "Ari's a big boy; he can make his own decisions. Besides, this harrowing experience was not your fault," she assured, an annoying sentiment everyone else shared it seemed. "Our entire family shall be right by your side, aiding the road to recovery. Now, no more tears, okay?"

"Everyone keeps telling me that, too." My mouth twitched as I tempted fate and rolled my eyes, provoking a smirk from Audrina. I pictured a pouting Ari and bit on my lip, hiding my laughter. "I'll try, but I won't make any promise's either. But what I do know is that I must face my fears by facing my past..."

"I love your optimism, nonetheless, I implore you, don't allow your past to interfere with paving a future with my son; he loves you dearly."

Sadness clouded over me. "You don't understand, there'll be repercussions, and not just for me...."

Audrina perched on the empty chair beside me and stared, her brows knitting together. "Enlighten me, please, as I don't understand how?"

"When I..." I murmured, turning my head away from Audrina's confused gaze and blinking unbidden tears away.

"When you what, Teddy?"

"You know what, I um...I can't. Not just yet." Shakily, I tucked a lock of stray hair behind my ear. Although, along with speaking his name, the words sat on the tip of my tongue.

Perceptive eyes narrowed. "Okay then," Audrina slowly replied, "I'm sure you'll explain everything to me at some stage. When you're ready, of course."

Her expectations were unrealistically high, so I made a point of pacifying her. "Thank you for understanding." An awkward silence loomed between us. The room had also grown noticeably quiet. I pushed to my feet and craned my head, searching the surrounding spaces for any one of my housemates. "Where'd everybody go?"

"We left to ensure privacy for the conversation ahead." Ari timely stepped inside from the patio and leisurely strolled towards us, circling an arm around my waist. "It made for a less uncomfortable environment that way for all parties involved," he murmured, pressing his lips to my temple.

I leaned into his shoulder. "It was very much appreciated, thank you."

Audrina smiled beatifically at us and pressed a hand to her chest, gushing, "You two are positively perfect for one another."

"Why, thank you, Mother." Ari was highly amused in his usual British manner – dry, compelling me to stifle my bubbling laughter.

"It's true, you are. Now, how about some tea? Ari, darling?"

"I knew the compliment was too good to be true," he muttered just as dryly. "Okay, you ladies go sit whilst I make the tea." Waving us off, he made his way into the kitchen.

"Thank you, darling." Linking her arm through mine, Audrina meandered over to the sofa and settled beside me. Her tiered skirt flouncing as she sat and twisted in her seat. "I don't suppose there are any biscuits to go with that tea, son?" she quizzed, her dark eyes sparkling impishly over the back of the sofa.

"I'm sure there is, your Highness."

∞

Ari

SETTING THE KETTLE ON the gas stovetop, I unintentionally found myself eavesdropping, and chuckling, at the beaming light that was my mother. My eyes rolled repeatedly. Thankfully for me, she was far too entrenched in the conversation to notice.

"Now Teddy, tell me about your job, it sounds absolutely fascinating."

"Haven't I already?" Teddy quizzed.

"Perhaps, but I'm sure there's so much more involved than just simply throwing up a building?"

I smiled broadly. My mother was working an angle, compelling Teddy to focus on everything that mattered to her – her achievements, her love of architecture, and me.

Pausing to lean on the island bench, I took a moment and proudly gazed across the room. With every in-depth detail she gave, an animate joy exuded from Teddy. A pleasure that took me back to our stay at Phillip Island, and oddly enough showing me there was hope after all, making our future together seem clearer, brighter.

The whistle blew alerting me to the fact the water had boiled. My mother noticed it, also.

"How long does it take to make a fresh pot of tea, son?"

I smirked. "As long as it takes the water to boil."

"It's boiled. What's the hold up?"

"Patience is a virtue, Mother," I singsonged, pouring the water into the ceramic teapot and popping the lid in place, leaving the fragrant Earl Grey leaves to stew for a few minutes.

She scoffed derisively. "In a pub, it's not."

"But we're not in a bloody pub!"

"At least I'd be served quicker!"

"Give it a rest, Mother," I mumbled. In the next breath, mother remarked farcically about her supposedly dull job as a lawyer; cue another eye roll.

"Perhaps I ought to have studied architecture as opposed to becoming a lawyer," she mused. "It sounds much more interesting."

"Thank god you had the sense not to, or clients could end up with a house that looked as if a three-year-old had built it from

Lego," I drawled, setting the tray down on the coffee table in front of them.

"Oh, don't be so cynical, Ari. I'll have you know that I'm superb at drawing."

I chuckled mirthlessly. "Stick figures don't count as drawings, Mother."

Teddy listened to us avidly whilst pouring the tea, her amusement growing as the back-and-forth banter worsened. Clutching her stomach, she laughed and rolled against the soft cushions behind her. "Oh, wow, this is so funny; normally, it's Ari and I teasing one another."

"Well, when you can laugh at one another and not get upset by it, it makes for an amazing relationship. I tease Jaxson all the time, and he still loves me." Patting my leg, mother winked at me. Gross mother. "And if you can manage that even after thirty years, well, you are set for the rest of your lives."

I buried my head in a cushion, groaning, "Why me?"

By the time, my mother eventually, and I say that lightly, left, Teddy appeared somewhat better, if only slightly. The morning's laughter was precisely what the doctor had ordered.

"Your mother's hysterical," she randomly voiced, snuggling into my chest as we stretched out along the chaise.

"Yeah, she is funny, ha-ha funny!"

"Hey, that's not nice!" She playfully smacked my chest. "Your mother's a wonderful lady. If only mine was more like yours," she bitterly expressed.

I stroked her arm softly. "I know, but she's not. The upside to my mother is, she thinks the sun shines out of your arse," I murmured, sliding a hand along the gentle curve of her spine, and squeezing her delectable bottom gently.

"By the feel of this..." Her hooded gaze peered up at me beneath fanned lashes as her long fingers explored the bulge over the top of my shorts. "...I would say she's not the only one."

Careful not to grab her wrists, I linked our fingers and raised her hand to my mouth, kissing each digit tenderly. "I love you, however, we ought to lighten up on the sex, if only for a little while."

A glaring Teddy pushed away from my chest. "Why? Do I disgust you now?" Fury laced her question.

"No, you don't," I stressed, thrusting a hand through my hair. "It's important you give yourself a decent amount of recovery time, and before you get upset, I spoke with Doctor Montgomery at length about your sex drive yesterday – only out of concern," I added emphatically, the desolation on Teddy's face causing inordinate distress.

"Concerned about what?" she uttered, shuffling farther down the sofa, and huddling in the opposite corner away from me.

"...About you using sex as a coping mechanism. I'd much prefer we expressed our love through lovemaking, and not because you feel insecure."

"I didn't realise that's what I was doing." Rather than lashing out at my honesty, her anger dwindled, and instead, she grew ultrasensitive. "I thought when we had sex, we were making love." She swiped away the falling tears with the back of her hand.

Not wanting to argue, I sighed and shuffled along the cushions, hauling her across my lap. "We do make love, but there were seldom moments where you were visibly upset, and you almost seemed..." I waved a hand. "...desperate."

Lacing our fingers together, Teddy rolled towards me, snuggling into my chest. "Maybe I am."

"No, you're not desperate per se," I assured, resting my chin against the crown of her head, precariously seeking the right words to say. "I think you're simply wanting to feel loved in the right way and have for some time now. Perhaps those emotions inordinately overwhelm you, confusing you with how you want to convey your feelings."

Teddy remained quiet, too quiet. Maybe I'd upset her after all. I craned my neck, peering down at her.

"Teddy? I haven't upset you, have I?"

"No, I was just thinking about what you said," she murmured, gently swinging around to straddle my thighs and bending her slender legs either side of my torso.

"And?" I cautiously queried.

"And what you're saying makes perfect sense..."

"And?"

"And I'll be sure to speak more in-depth with my therapist about it."

"Good. Now, what do you say to a little canoodling?" I purred, pushing her thick tresses to one side. My lips pressed to her neck, trailing feather light kisses over soft, fragrant skin.

"Will this canoodling include a little foreplay? You know, with just our mouths and hands?" Her husky voice breathed against my ear.

"Oh, I think we can manage that at the very least." Gripping her nape with my hand, I tugged Teddy to me. Our passionate kiss intensified as our desire rose. I lifted her beneath the buttocks, Teddy clinging to my neck as I carried her to the bedroom, fumbling for the handle with my outstretched hand. My foot kicked out swiftly closing the door behind us.

So much for just foreplay.

26

TO HAVE SAID I was immensely grateful with my new assistant Thomas would've been an understatement. His competence in micromanaging the last few days had surpassed all my expectations while I took an indefinite leave of absence from work. It also meant missing the grand opening of JPD in Sydney, compelling me to send Asher in lieu much to the delight of my COO, Jason Kline. What they got up to didn't bear thinking about; anything was possible.

Thomas diverted calls, emailed the necessary contracts for me to sign and had everything else couriered to me. Otherwise, he managed sublimely, surpassing Lila by a longshot. That man was well overdue for a decent bonus.

Apart from the few meetings that required my presence, I managed the day-to-day business from the comfort of Teddy's study. Nor had I left my company completely unsupervised either, I was far too much of a control freak in that regard.

Keeping eyes on the contract in front of me, I reached out for the coffee mug on the desk beside me, bringing it to my lips only to scowl at the taste of the now cold beverage. It was a sign I needed a break. I was also stiff from staying seated for so long and had to stretch before I could even think about standing — another sign I needed a break. Pushing the chair back, I picked up the coffee mug and wandered towards the kitchen, rubbing my bleary eyes in my travels. "Coffee, Evan?" I offered, holding up the cup.

"You look like you need more sleep, not more coffee," Evan remarked dryly, his blue eyes peering over the rims of his glasses and watching me like a hawk. "How much sleep have you had, Ari?"

"Enough," I grumbled.

"Not enough by the looks of it. Those dark bags under your eyes are telling another story. You're exhausted, and in obvious need of more sleep."

Lifting a brow in defiance, I jerked my head towards the piles of notes spread across the dining table. "Speak for yourself, and besides, I need the coffee to keep me awake so I can still run a company and keep an eye on Teddy."

"You're not Superman, and others have willingly put their hands up to help too, you know?"

"I'm aware of that little fact, but I promised Teddy I'd irrefutably remain by her side! Enough people have let her down as it is!" I asserted through clenched teeth as my hand thumped down, swiping the coffee jar off the bench. Glass shattered around my bare feet. "Fuck!"

"Don't move. I'll fetch the broom." Evan calmly rushed past, heading towards the laundry. "Did you cut yourself?"

"No, luckily." I checked my hands and feet to be sure as I carefully extracted myself whilst he swept the mess into a pile before collecting it up with the dustpan.

"You need to take a break from work and get some sleep." About to protest, Evan held up a hand stopping me. "Ari, you're exhausted from burning the candle at both ends. Now, go lie down before you and the floor become intimately acquainted!" he sternly barked, paying no mind to my grumblings nor the rolling eyes. I stormed off to the bedroom; between he and my mother, they were like two peas in a pod – damned bossy!

Quietly stepping into the darkened bedroom and stripping off my clothes, I sank into the mattress and the pillows. Evan was right; I needed the rest. Even my mother had the audacity to agree with him when she called in earlier. As usual I brushed off her concerns, likewise, everyone else's of late.

The fatigue was unlike any other I'd ever experienced. My head and body ached, and my drooping eyes burned. A hangover didn't hurt anywhere near as much. Like a lullaby with an infant, the soft music playing in the room lulled me into a deep slumber, affording me the best sleep in days.

Since Teddy discharged from the hospital, each day from thereon in had proved differently. Habitually, she slept her days away, only to awaken from terrifying nightmares. Aside from one dream, they ordinarily comprised of her repeatedly reliving the rape. Yet it was the one where I walked away from her, uttering the words, *'She was no good for me!'* that terrified her the most. I stupidly attempted to wake Teddy, merely to end up with a blackened cheek for my trouble. A mortified Teddy grew most upset, and no amount of reassurance on my part could have prevented the flood of tears or the self-recrimination that consequently followed.

Her moods fluctuated, giving anyone who tried to console her whiplash. But Doctor Montgomery, with his infinite wisdom, assured us it was merely a side effect of the anti-depressant, and she just needed time to adjust. How much time did one need?

One positive was Teddy's therapy, her attendance anyway, the sessions not so much. With each largely impregnated by self-pity and negativity, I struggled to cope or failed to understand her reasoning behind these loathsome feelings.

That initially bolstered hope was slowly beginning to fade.

Honestly, the balancing act to manage Teddy had proportionally grown. To the extent, I feared my grip on reality could vanish without warning. Not that I ever expressed that to Teddy. She looked to me to remain strong and to pull her up whenever she felt she was falling. Nevertheless, it caused speculation: would she be there to catch me when and if I fall?

During these sessions, I learned to listen and keep quiet, allowing Teddy to purge her fears and thoughts. This was presently one of these moments.

Teddy was in tears as she expressed her feelings of guilt for supposedly burdening everyone, especially me. Despite my reassurances and unwavering support, she refused to shake the feeling. She wiped away a few tears before saying, "We've only made love once since... and that was because I craved an emotional connection."

I gripped the arm of my chair, ready to object, but Doctor Montgomery gestured for me to stay silent. I respected his wishes and leaned back in my chair, posturing self-confidence. It was surreal hearing someone talk about me as if I weren't present, but my stern expression spoke volumes.

"How has it made you feel not having sex as often as you've normally had in the past?"

"I feel rejected, even though I know I shouldn't."

Doctor Montgomery's head inclined slightly, his gaze thoughtfully staring. "Why do you feel rejected?"

"Because Ari hasn't wanted to...and I thought it was because I've turned him off, you know, because of what I did to myself."

That was a load of bollocks right there, and they were words often repeated during many of the conversations we'd had recently. With the occasional swear word slipped in.

"That sounds a little harsh, don't you think?" Umm, yeah, it was.

Teddy ardently argued, disagreeing with him, "No, it's the truth, Doc."

My head shook heatedly as a riotous snort erupted, prompting a deathly glare from both Teddy and the doctor.

Leaning back in his chair, Doctor Montgomery crossed his legs and placed his iPad on the table next to him. "From what I have gathered, Ari cares deeply for you, and I've never seen anyone so torn up or devoted. He's highly concerned about your wellbeing;

without a doubt, the questions he asked about your high sex drive prove just that."

"Oh." Teddy blushed. "I do remember having that discussion with Ari."

"Well, I don't need to explain it to you then, do I?" Doctor Montgomery chuckled. "So, explain what it says about Ari's feelings towards you."

Fidgeting with the shredded tissue in her hand, Teddy clearly struggled with the fact he was right. If only I possessed the same capabilities as he did when getting through to her.

He pushed for an answer. "Teddy, what do you think it means?"

"That...he loves me. Ari also told me he doesn't want me using sex as a coping mechanism any longer." Damn straight, I love you.

"He's right. You need to find a much healthier way to deal with your past rather than through sex, emotionally specifically. I can advise you on coping when it becomes too much for you." Pausing, the doctor picked up the iPad again and continued to make notes whilst they talked, "How did you feel after sex if you initiated it, more so because of an emotional upset?"

"I felt dirty within myself, even though Ari's never been anything less than respectful or patient and loving. But in the back of my mind, I feel like I'm constantly fighting to rid myself of what happened to me. Then I feel guilty – like I'm lying to him. But then, Ari has this way of making me feel whole again," she sniffled. "I'm not making any sense, am I?"

"You're making perfect sense. You trust Ari implicitly with your body, and giving yourself to him proves that. What happened to you was quite traumatic. You had a rough introduction to sex by a man who exerted his power over you with no thought to your feelings before or afterwards. Those memories of your rape won't ever fade completely. However, over time, we can prune them away and nourish your happier thoughts, growing them into beautiful new memories of just you and Ari." He redirected his gaze from the iPad to me, a brow raised questioningly. "Ari, do you agree with me?"

About bloody time! Clearing my throat, I nodded stiffly, replying hoarsely, "Yes, infinitely!"

"That makes a lot of sense to me now," Teddy agreed. Hallelujah! she agreed with something, finally!

"Good, and to assist you with your sleep, I'm switching your current medication to a stronger dose, which ought to improve your sleeping habits."

"Great." Teddy frowned as he rose from the chair and strolled over to the printer, folding the prescription before handing it to her. She begrudgingly accepted it.

"A restful sleep means a clearer head and less anxiety," Doctor Montgomery rationally advised. "Nevertheless, you need to remember, anti-depressants are only ever a short-term solution. Alongside your regular therapy sessions, both should indeed help you with these nightmares. Facing your demons is important, Teddy. I'm also suggesting couples therapy for you and Ari to use as a tool to continue building on your relationship."

Aghast, my head jerked. What was the point of these sessions, then? Perhaps I was merely nothing more than a spectator along for the ride. I was dreadfully confused.

Teddy shrugged languidly. "Do you think there's any chance of me ever having a normal life again?" she questioned, her voice tinged with sadness. "Ari deserves someone better, someone who can give him a chance at a normal life."

Doctor Montgomery stared disapprovingly. "Have you not been paying attention to anything I've said?" he asked sternly. "Most partners would have packed their bags and left by now, but Ari is different. He's resilient and loves you unconditionally. That's why we're here, to help you unpack your feelings of inadequacies."

Teddy's brows furrowed. "But will I ever be normal again?" she repeated, her voice barely above a whisper.

"There is no clear definition of what is considered normal. In fact, if there was, I would be out of a job." He chuckled, holding her hands as she stood up. "To answer your question, yes, your life should start improving. However, this can only happen if you continue attending our sessions and taking your medication regularly in the meantime." He looked down at her, his gaze reassuring. "Let Ari in by enlightening him as to who your attacker was. It's part of the solution, thus a part of your healing."

Teddy's eyes widened, her face blanching at the mere thought. "His reaction, I fear more than my attacker."

Doctor Montgomery dropped his hands, blowing out a disheartened sigh before walking back to his desk. He sat down and began stroking his greying beard thoughtfully. "Once you've made him aware, I'm sure Ari will understand your hesitation," he said in response to Teddy's scepticism. "Look at my suggestion in a positive light; it means that you'll finally have closure and a chance at the 'normal' life you spoke so fondly of just now," he added, his eyes twinkling. Teddy smiled at his words. "Take a chance, and he might surprise you."

"I'll try," Teddy replied, taking another tissue from the box in front of her and wiping her eyes.

Doctor Montgomery smiled in satisfaction. "Good."

Teddy silently and hesitantly nodded. I presumed she was grateful for the doctor's advice, but obviously remained on the fence regardless.

I nodded in agreement, but my lips remained sealed. Expressing my gratitude to the kind doctor, I clasped his hand firmly.

He responded with a reassuring smile and a comforting pat on my back, which lifted my spirits. "Stay positive, Ari. You've done extraordinarily well thus far."

"If you say so," I sceptically grunted.

As Teddy and I departed the room, I ensured I followed Teddy's unexplained request by maintaining a suitable distance. I tried to make sense of it as we walked, but it proved somewhat challenging. I sincerely hoped that one of these days, Teddy might shed some light on the matter.

As soon as we arrived home, Teddy's exhaustion was palpable. She immediately headed to the bedroom for a nap, leaving me to my own devices. I, on the other hand, still bore the effects of the disastrous session we had just attended. Despite her invitation to join her, I declined, feeling too wound up to rest. My refusal only seemed to exacerbate her already gloomy mood, compelling her to ask me why I refused.

"I just can't relax after that farce of a session," I replied, my frustration evident in my tone. Unfortunately, my terse response only served to make things worse, and she slammed the bedroom door in my face, leaving me alone with my thoughts.

I sank into the chair beside my mother at the dining table, feeling the weight of her disapproval.

"I'm not sure your lack of filter is helping the situation, son," she sternly rebuked. My face flushed with embarrassment, and I attempted to conceal my shame by lowering my head into my hands.

The shame of my actions was almost too much to bear.

"I know," I grumbled, my voice barely audible.

Softening her tone, my mother's hand rubbed over my forearm. "How are you holding up, Ari? You could park a car in those bags under your eyes." That alone was indeed self-explanatory.

I pushed to my feet and shuffled into the kitchen, busying myself by making a fresh pot of tea. "I'm okay; it's truly nothing more than tiredness."

Despite my attempt to brush off her probing, my mother raised a brow and eyed me speculatively. "Are you sure that's all it is?"

A sharpened breath escaped as my entire body sagged. "No, not really."

"Talk to me."

I swivelled, facing her, flexing my hands restlessly as I gripped the square-formed edge of the bench behind me. "It's these damned nightmares. They're the same every bloody night, with her fighting this bastard off!" I fumed, my anger intensifying. "I just wish I knew who *he* was so that I could rip his damned head off!"

"Teddy still hasn't told you who it was?" she quizzed cautiously.

"No," I growled, my frustration boiling over. "It would be helpful if she confided in me so I can support her more than I currently am." I spun around, my arms tense with my hands gripping the countertop so tightly my knuckles turned white. Defeated, my forehead banged against the overhead cupboard as I let out a gruff sigh. "The weight of everything is so damned suffocating; I just wish for this madness to stop."

"Given what Teddy's been through, it has been rather traumatic for her. She fears that you might turn away from her. Give her time, son," she reasoned, prudently trying to calm me. "I'm certain Teddy's acutely aware of everything you're doing for her. She's terribly worried about you and told me as much."

"I would never turn away from Teddy; I love her too much. And she needn't worry about me; I'll be fine," I whispered as my mother rose from her chair and ambled towards me. She wrapped her arms around my waist in a warm embrace, resting her cheek between my shoulder blades.

"Teddy feels rather insecure, requiring a high amount of reassurance from you. Please be patient with her." I turned around, relaxing into my mother's embrace.

"I'm doing my best," I replied softly. Grateful for her understanding, I raised a small, affectionate smile. "Thanks, Mum."

She smiled up at me and caressed my stubbly cheek. "That's all right, but please, son, have a damned shave."

I chuckled, feeling a sense of comfort and familiarity wash over me.

As the sun began to set in the late afternoon, my mother and I decided to take advantage of the beautiful weather and spend the time outdoors. We made our way to the pool area, carrying our cups of tea with us. The sun's warm glow lingered in the sky, casting a gentle orange hue over the yard. The pool itself was a deep, shimmering blue, reflecting the light in a way that made it seem almost magical.

As we settled into our seats, I couldn't help but notice the symphony of natural sounds around us: the soft hum of a lawnmower in the distance, the cacophony of birds chirping in the rustling leaves of the trees, and the graceful trickle of the pools waterfall. My mother and I quietly chatted whilst sipping our tea, enjoying the moment's tranquillity.

Suddenly, our peaceful moment was interrupted by a piercing scream.

Oh, fuck! Teddy!

Another scream echoed from inside the house. I rushed from my chair and inside, with my mother rapidly following me. Concern etched her face as I tried to console a distraught Teddy, who, despite my best efforts, resisted my attempts to comfort her. Nothing seemed to be working, leaving me at a complete loss.

My mother immediately took charge and politely asked me to step aside, taking my place on the bed. I helplessly watched on, listening to her speak to Teddy softly and calmingly, holding her close to her breast whilst gently rocking her. Noticeably calmer, my mother accomplished what I had failed to do.

Fury finally boiled over. I aimed for the outside and the fence, a feral, animalistic growl erupting with each ferocious hit, splitting the skin on my knuckles wide open.

"Ari! Stop, son. You'll hurt yourself," Evan barked, snatching up my hand and sharing his apparent displeasure with me, "...Which you've already done." His head shook, and his mouth thinned. "We'll need to get something on these open wounds."

Brooding, I preceded Evan inside, sliding onto a stool at the island bench as he grabbed an ice pack from inside the freezer, wrapping it in a fresh tea towel before passing it to me.

"The first aid kit is in the cupboard above the fridge." I sheepishly applied the icepack and pointed to the overhead cupboards. "I'm sorry I lost it."

Evan opened the first aid kit and started searching for the leukostrips. "Aw, c'mon now, Ari, we all fully understand the toll and impact that Teddy's issues have had on you," he acknowledged, "as you've sacrificed having any life for my daughter. You're doing more than anyone has ever done for her, including me." He removed the icepack and cleaned up my wounds, urging me not to give up. "But you gotta stop thinking you're bloody Superman!" he added.

I snorted loudly. "I know I'm not Superman, Evan; I'm not wearing my red jocks today!"

Evan glanced up and scowled, applying strips of leukotape to my knuckles.

"Sorry, bad joke," I rapidly uttered. "Seeing Teddy this bloody helpless…it just churns me up inside. Every time she has one of these nightmares – it's a rotten reminder of how much I despise the bastard for raping her and what Therese did or didn't do." My lip curled in disgust for even giving Teddy's despicable mother a thought.

"I know; she hasn't helped the situation – and frankly, neither have I, purely out of weakness. The road to any recovery is long, but please remember, there is light at the end of the tunnel," Evan sagely advised, gently patting my shoulder. "I admire your dedication, but please, Ari, for the love of God, ask for more help! There is no shame in asking for it."

"Okay…I promise."

"Oh, Ari, what have you done to yourself?" my mother scolded, rushing up beside me and eyeing my bruised and bloodied knuckles.

"I had a run-in with the fence, no big deal," I replied dismissively, hoping to avoid my mother's irritated glare as I shamefully hung my head.

"This isn't the time to joke, Ari," she sternly admonished. "Are you deliberately trying to upset Teddy?" I silently shook my head.

"Well, I won't tolerate this irrational behaviour of yours any longer. If you continue to act like this, there will be consequences."

I was tempted to ask her how, as I was innately aware I was too old, not to mention too big to be put over her knee for a spanking, but as she glared, daring me to challenge her, I thought better of it.

Instead, I recalled a memory from my teenage years when I intervened in a fight between my brother and the school bully.

My brother Bryson often had a knack for finding trouble, primarily due to his smart mouth. However, one day, he witnessed the school bully harassing a diminutive, younger child, compelling Bryson to intervene. I followed suit. However, Principal Craig learned about our unruly behaviour and suspended us both for a week, greatly displeasing our mother. She was even more outraged when she discovered the bully's mere punishment of yard duty. Seething, she took it upon herself to read the school's policy regarding bullying, which only augmented her anger, and proceeded to give Principal Craig a rather stern dressing down. He certainly learned his lesson and never ignored bullying to the same extent again.

"What were you thinking about?" Mother's frosty tone snapped me out of my musings.

"Nothing, Mother, nothing at all."

27

Teddy

I AWOKE WITH A START and sat up in a rush, sending my thick curls tumbling. A few stray strands stuck to my sweaty face. That, along with the cloudy haze plaguing me, I blamed the lack of sleep, thanks to the attributing nightmares. Typically horrific, like the one just now and the one before that, each dream remaining the same with only one point of difference: I'd lost Ari.

A foreseeable omen, perhaps?

Exhausted, I scrubbed my face and flicked back the sweat drenched sheets, swinging my feet to the floor. In reality, I wished to stay in bed and pull the covers over my head, never to face the world again. An idea Ari would undoubtedly prohibit me from doing – unless I persuaded him to join me. I began to smile at the thought of us never leaving my bed, but he'd most definitely object to the idea under current circumstances.

Disgruntled, I trundled off to the bathroom for a much-needed shower.

I turned on the tap and stood beneath the warm, cascading water, washing away the remnants of my nightmarish sleep. As I lathered my hair with shampoo, I closed my eyes, savouring the sensation of my fingertips and nails massaging my scalp. My tension melted away, replaced by a momentary sense of calm and serenity...

As if on cue, Ari's voice interrupted my peaceful reverie. "Hello there, gorgeous."

I screeched, rapidly covering my breasts with my soap-lathered hands. "Oh, my god, Ari! A little warning would've been nice!"

Ari laughed, ogling my soapy body with gleaming dark eyes. "Why are you covering yourself? It's not as though I haven't seen it all before."

"It's not funny!" I countered, haphazardly running my fingers through my hair as I attempted to rinse out the shampoo. "Besides, it's impolite sneaking up on a lady like that." I paused my rinsing and frowned as he began looking behind the bathroom door and through the cabinets. "What are you looking for?"

His entire face alight with humour, he opened the glass door to the shower stall. "A lady, but there isn't one currently present."

I glared. "Aha, no lady, huh?" I disengaged the handset off the shower rail and began rinsing my soapy skin down, drawing his hungry gaze towards my neck and breasts. "Well, then...." I murmured, choosing the optimum moment to aim the shooting water directly at his head and chest. "You're no gentleman, Ari Jaeger!" I laughed gleefully as his mouth gaped in astonishment.

Soaked through and chuckling, Ari wiped the water from his eyes with his fingers. "I can't believe you just did that."

I raised a challenging brow. "Well, don't sass me then."

"You looked so peaceful, and so sexy. You're impossible to resist," he salaciously purred, his eyes darkening deliciously. My thighs clenched together.

"Well, why don't you join me if that's the case?"

Ari's throat bobbed tightly. "Only if you are sure?"

"I'm sure," I whispered.

"All right, if that's what you want." As Ari peeled the wet T-shirt over his head, my tongue instinctively swept over my bottom lip, and my hungry gaze roamed over the taut muscles of his chest and abs. God, I wanted him. No, needed; I was desperate for his touch to wash away the demons haunting my dreams so much of late.

He tugged his shorts down, stepping out of them and into my arms.

Then I spotted his wounded knuckles and roughly grabbed his hand. "Oh, my god, Ari! What happened to your hand? What did you do?"

Ari shrugged dismissively. "I had a little run-in with the fence, no big deal."

"No big deal? Ari, why? Was this because of me?" Devastated, I clutched my stomach. The thought of him damaging himself sickened me. I hadn't wanted this for him, thus being one of the many reasons I'd suppressed my feelings for so long.

Moreover, why I'd avoided a relationship with him.

That's why my lifestyle was important to me, as it had been the only answer; no emotional ties.

"Yes, it was," he admitted in a barely audible whisper. "I'm frustrated. Teddy, please, I'm begging you, I must know. Who's the bastard that raped you? It's not right that you keep having these bloody nightmares." I looked down at his hands, both clenching into tight fists. "I feel... I feel..."

"Powerless?" I glanced up at him, my throat tightening at the pain etching his face.

Ari frowned and stiffly nodded. "Yes, that's precisely how I felt today; how I feel constantly."

I reached up, caressing the rough stubble along his strong jawline with my palm. "I can't, not yet."

"Why not? Don't you trust me enough?" he fired, visibly upsetting me further.

I dropped my hand and took a step back. "I do trust you! How can you ask that of me? You're aware that saying his name aloud still frightens me."

"Why does it frighten you still, Teddy? You've already told me that we both know him."

Sighing loudly, I slumped onto the bench seat, my back sagging against the cold tiles—a line etched between my brows, recalling

Doctor Montgomery's words in our earlier session. "I'm scared of what you might do. I don't want to lose you either, whether it's you going to jail or you walking away from me."

Ari squatted before me and brushed a stray strand of wet hair off my face. "I promise, once I do know who this prick is, neither will happen, as I can't lose you either," he staunchly conceded, the expression in his eyes as soft as the rasp in his voice. "I love you far too much."

I looked away, my eyes anxiously darting. "I need a bit more time – please. That's all I ask."

Flopping beside me, Ari slumped against the tiles, letting out a frustrated sigh as he closed his eyes. They flicked open again, and his intense gaze stared. "You'll have to tell me sooner rather than later." Adamance laced his voice. "As it's not healthy keeping this inside, and those nightmares you keep having have proven that."

"I know it's not. I'm trying, Ari, I truly am."

"I know you are," he reassured, cradling my head against his chest. "I just want you well."

"I know you do," Teddy sniffled. "I want to be well also."

"Do you know why your mother named you and your siblings using the first four letters of the alphabet in no particular order?" I quizzed as Ari, and I lay naked with our limbs tangled on the bed.

He tilted his head and frowned. "I'm not sure. Maybe she couldn't decide on a name and randomly chose those letters. You could try asking her to find out."

"Your name, Ari," I began, propping my chin on the back of my hand while toying with his chest hair with the other, "originates from Greece. In Hebrew, it means 'lion.' Additionally, it signifies superiority and excellence in thinking. Ari is also a short form of Aristotle, a Greek philosopher who lived back in 338 BC. Furthermore, there was the great Greek shipping tycoon Aristotle Onassis."

"Well, someone's been doing their research." He chuckled, peering down at me. "Is that what they taught you at the School of Architecture?"

I smacked his chest and replied, "RMIT, actually, and don't mock me. But yes, we learnt about provenance and the importance it plays with a home that holds historic value. As in, researching the age of a house and the origin of its name or if the name is missing and needs replacing. It's rather interesting, and similar to a house, parents bestow their children a particular name for a reason."

"Did someone inspire your name, or was it chosen randomly?"

"I believe my mother named me Theodora because it's the female version of Theodore. She wanted another son and frequently reminded me of this fact as a way to make me feel inferior and a pariah. Despite this, my father affectionately referred to me as Teddy Bear, which always annoyed my mother."

Ari chuckled. "I'm sure it did, and you most definitely weren't or nor are you a pariah. You were an adorable child, just like a teddy bear. What happened?"

"I'm still adorable," I protested, jutting my bottom lip.

He laughed and rolled us across the mattress, our lips grazing. Dark eyes tenderly gazed down at me. "No, you're not just adorable; you're gorgeous and adorable."

I ran my fingers through his hair, scrunching my nose at him. "You're just biased."

"Very much so."

A growl erupted, making us both laugh. "I think I'm hungry, so we had better go feed the bear!"

"Ha, yeah, I am a tad hungry," Ari replied, hopping out of bed and slipping on a pair of boxers. "Let's see if your roommates have left us anything," he added before heading towards the kitchen.

I swiftly followed, my mouth watering at the thought of the delicious lemon and basil risoni my roommates had prepared earlier. Ari discovered two plates thoughtfully set aside for us inside the warming drawer. He placed them on the table while I grabbed a bottle of wine from the bar fridge in the butler's pantry.

"Are you allowed wine on your medication?" he questioned, observing from his chair as I poured two glasses on the counter.

"I can have a little, so one glass shouldn't hurt. Besides, it's low-level alcohol, and I'm having it with food."

"Okay, I'm just double-checking and ensuring you won't have any adverse reactions from mixing them."

"I appreciate your concern, but I consulted with the pharmacist," I explained, placing one of the glasses in front of him and taking a seat on his left.

"And the pharmacist knows best," he remarked, clutching the glass stem and swirling the crisp Sauvignon around before taking a sip. "Did you take on board all the good doctor said today?"

I raised the fork to my mouth. "I did. Why, do you think I didn't?" I asked, observing as he stiffened and took another sip before answering me with a noticeable shake of his head.

"I'm sorry, but no. Before you get upset with me, let me explain the reasoning behind my answer, okay?"

I quietly nodded in response.

"Your feedback to Doctor Montgomery was rather negative, and I thought...possibly after a few sessions coupled with the medication, your feelings would convey somewhat differently, as in a little more positively. But not just about yourself, but our relationship also." He twirled the knife and fork nervously, seeming to choose his words carefully, a habit he had recently acquired.

I chewed on my food and words, respectively. "Perhaps over time, with more treatment and once we find a resolution to my issues," I clarified, shrugging nonchalantly, "my symptoms will subside over time."

"Let's hope so." His face glimmered with hope as he slid a gentle hand over mine. "I'd like you to move forward with your life and, hopefully, our future."

"I want that too, more than you know."

We finished our meals in relative silence, and afterwards, Ari shooed me back to bed, leaving him to clear the table and stack the dishwasher, turning it on and the lights off.

Bs I lay in bed waiting for Ari, I began to reflect on our dinner conversation. Ari had indirectly inferred that I wasn't allowing the therapy to work, and the poor bugger had to continually walk on eggshells for fear of upsetting me when he shouldn't have to.

He was right; I wasn't allowing the therapy to work, and his frustration was apparent to everyone except me.

How long before he fell apart entirely due to my selfishness? The lashing out and the state of his knuckles were evidence of that. All that pain, as well as his suffering, was because of me. How could I act so blind?

The chance to smooth things over with Ari wasn't taking place as quickly as I thought. As soon as he entered the bedroom, he went straight to the bathroom, brushed his teeth, and on the way through, picked up his laptop, bringing it to bed.

Occasionally, I looked away from the novel lying in my lap to an oblivious Ari as he busily responded to urgent emails. With each minute that passed, my concentration waned. I began shifting my legs restlessly beneath the covers and fluffing the European pillow behind me unnecessarily.

"You're twitchy. What's bothering you?" he queried, not looking up from the screen or slowing down his tapping fingers.

"I'm just uncomfortable, and the pillow slipped."

Ari turned his head and stared disbelievingly. "Bollocks, you've been huffing and puffing since I came to bed. So, tell me the truth, Teddy, what's going on inside that pretty head of yours?" He closed the laptop and reclined against the pillows, crossing his arms over his bare chest. "Well, I'm waiting," he murmured, raising a well-defined brow, making my heart race.

With trepidation, I closed the book and placed it on the bedside table, my face flaming as I turned to face his scrutinising gaze. "I feel terrible because I've been blind to your feelings. My pain has become yours, and you punching the fence is proof of that." I peered down at the bed, and at his knuckles. "It was the epiphany I needed to wake me up. I haven't been fair to you by not telling you who it was that raped me. You were also right earlier about what you said to me," I paused for a beat, "that I'm not letting my therapy work for me."

Ari sighed and moved the computer from his lap to the floor before hauling me into his arms. "They weren't the exact words I used, but being you, you read between the lines." He lovingly tapped the tip of my nose. "Since our argument at Phillip Island and your recent hospitalisation, I've strived to tread carefully with everything: my actions, my words — all to ensure the utmost sensitivity to your needs. Admittedly, it's been challenging to deal with at the best of times, like today, when you had your nightmare. My mother succeeded where I couldn't, and coupled with today's session, well, that was upsetting."

As I listened to Ari pour his heart and soul out, my guilt grew infinitely overwhelming. "I am so, so sorry, Ari." Tears splashed down my cheeks. "I never meant for you to get hurt in any shape or form — I am so damned selfish," I wailed as shuddering sobs erupted. "...I'll tell your family everything."

"I didn't deliberately set out to inflict damage on myself to pressure you into revealing the bastard," Ari objected soberly, cradling me against his chest, the pads of his fingers gently stroking my dampened cheek.

"I know you didn't." I tilted my head back and looked up at him. "But I need to. Say you'll support me as you need this as much as I do; I know you do."

His nod was resolute. "As long as you're sure, then yes, I'll support you."

I cupped his cheek in my palm. "Thank you."

"Just tell me when, and I'll set it up." He caught my chin and leaned down, slanting his mouth over mine and kissing me tenderly.

I slid my fingers through the thick mass of hair on his head, igniting a fervency between us. But as the kiss deepened, Ari withdrew unexpectedly. His head shook, placing his hand on my chest.

"We need to stop."

Perplexed, I stared at him. "Why?"

Breathless, his dark orbs regarded me intently. "I simply refuse to push the issue with you, and granted we made love that one night, you are still healing. You know I love you, and I am not going anywhere. I'm just worried... worried I'll do something that may trigger a memory and make you regress." He threw his hands up when I clambered off his lap and back onto the bed. "Teddy, say something, please."

I flared in exasperation. "I appreciate your concern and what you are trying to do...but I'm improving every day. Truly, I am. Your love means the world to me, as does your touch. That love and that touch are making me feel whole again. I know that in here...." I reclosed the gap I had opened between us and grasped his hand, laying it over the calm and steady beat of my heart. "Doctor Montgomery's right; I trust you implicitly. I need you to make love to me, Ari, please?"

Ari responded to my pleas by lunging and painfully grabbing fistfuls of my hair, tugging as he drew me closer, our lips crashing together in a heated kiss. His hands swept over me, tearing the clothes from my body, his fingers kneading and plumping every inch. With his unequivocal hunger unleashed, Ari proved he was as equally starved for me as I was for him.

Whilst his mouth worked over my breasts, sucking and rolling my stiffened nipples with one hand, the other slid between the soft flesh of my sex, pumping me. Induced sensations furled as his thumb circled my aching clitoris: desire, lust, a deep-seated love, and pleasure.

I gripped his biceps, digging my nails into the flesh as my legs stiffened and my inner muscles fluttered. I threw my head back and silently cried out, overcome by the climax ripping through my entire body.

Ari pushed me back, his mouth grazing over my heated skin as he worked his way down my torso and disappeared between my thighs, his tongue skilfully lapping at my drenched sex.

My head thrashed against the blankets. "Ari... I can't....."

Miraculously, I did, my body arching off the bed as another climax rippled. I'd barely recovered when Ari silently crawled over me, our bodies crashing against the mattress as we rolled in unison. I reached between us, grasping his length with my hand as I straddled his thighs and eased over his engorged cock. As Ari hissed pleasurably, a delighted smile grew, expressly as I adeptly undulated, taking in his measurable size. Likewise, as his fingertips dug into my flesh at my hips, holding me in place.

But as I slowly lifted and slid back down, Ari's grip eased, allowing my hips to move freely, with each thrust creating a breathtaking fullness. We absorbed each other's pleasure, our mouths slackened and panting as our desire heightened. He reared upwards, skimming his hands softly over my face, over my body, caressing and cherishing every part of me. My head fell back as Ari's lips swept over my dampened skin. His skin radiated an undeniable heat, and each warm, harsh breath fluttered. Everything about his touch was patently light and exquisite.

Overwhelming emotions suddenly surged, and I began pawing at his skin, desperate to be closer.

Sensing the rise in my ardour, Ari's hands framed my face, his reassuring expression soft and so full of love I thought my heart would burst. "It's okay; I'm here, loving you, making love to you."

I let out a cleansing shudder, and wordlessly, my rocking hips slowed, relaxing against his tender hold. And without breaking our intimate connection, he slowly rolled us back over. His head dipping, he took my parted mouth as he sank exquisitely deeper inside of me. Each thrust a slow, drawn-out rhythm.

I arched into him, my hands slipping over his slickened back as my legs wrapped around his waist, digging my heels into his firm, rounded behind.

That's where we remained throughout the night, each touch intimate, with each kiss slow, tender, and meaningful.

28

HAVING SPENT THREE LONG and trying weeks with me, Ari decided it was time to return to the office full-time. My father did the same but went a step further and moved back to his inner-city apartment. The house was profoundly quiet with neither of them here, leaving me bored and listless.

Once upon a time, I cherished my solitude and calm surroundings. However, recent events dramatically changed my perspective — the time spent with my father also played a significant part.

Life had fortuitously given us a second chance to reconnect as the loving father and daughter we once were. Our conversations were endless, and we shared our deepest emotions, helping us to heal old wounds. Additionally, Ari's presence was a constant source of joy, not to mention captivating, permitting us the pleasure of connecting in more ways than one.

That's not to say their ever-present attention hadn't come without its own set of complications. Admittedly, at times, I had reacted negatively and resorted to calling them glorified babysitters, which was unjustified. They were solely concerned for my well-being.

As I nursed my second cup of coffee for the morning, I yearned to return to the job I loved. That's when my aimless wandering led me to the doorway of my study, my bored expression falling over my architect's desk before drifting upwards to the framed artwork hanging on the wall above it.

My first ever design. The sharp, innovative plan scored me my dream job, with Spencer Hughes singing my praises during the interview. To my surprise, he offered me the coveted position that day based on my talent and knowledge. I had worked hard to reach this point and was determined not to squander all my efforts.

As I made my way back to the kitchen, my determination grew. Dumping my cup into the dishwasher, I picked up my phone and swiftly punched out a message for Ari and my father, indicating we needed to talk. Soon. I hit send, causing butterflies. The worry churning inside me was ridiculous. They both knew how much my job meant to me, but then again, after my breakdown, they might disagree with my request, telling me they didn't think I was ready.

I sighed and leaned against the dishwasher behind me, tapping my phone in my hands; how would they know? They weren't me. I just had to remain positive and hoped I wasn't kidding myself.

∞

Audrina

AS I IDLED AT THE KERB, I noticed Teddy engrossed in her iPhone, seemingly oblivious to my presence. I took a moment to observe her closely, noticing a marked difference in her demeanour compared to the last few weeks. Her face was aglow, and her eyes sparkled with an infectious newfound energy. It was a remarkable transformation that brought immense pleasure to my heart.

Her attire added to her radiance. It was simple yet elegant: blue faded jeans paired with a floral short-sleeved blouse in coral and two-tone flats. With one long leg crossed over the other, a foot bounced buoyantly, complementing the smile adorning her beautiful face. I speculated she was swapping texts with Ari, as nobody else seemed to make her smile as he could.

Ari had always remained a reliable presence, calling me throughout the day to discuss complex issues and share his thoughts and concerns. However, lately, our conversations mostly revolved around a more troubling topic: Teddy. Ari was deeply worried about what would happen to her if he wasn't there to protect her. The thought weighed heavily, augmenting his growing anxiety. Thus, increasing my concern regarding his mental health due to the immense toll of Teddy's suffering. Despite my continued efforts to check in on him and ensure he was okay, Ari always insisted that he was fine, leaving me to doubt his assurances.

My son had unrequited fears and rightfully so. Granted Teddy had promised him some time ago, yet she still hadn't revealed whom her attacker was. I advised him to remain patient, which was all well and good in theory, but the reality was, Ari's patience was wearing thin on the subject.

During one of our more recent conversations, he'd suggested I take Teddy shopping, stating boredom was part of her issue. My astute and beloved son knew my weakness, making it impossible for me to refuse such a request. Then, when had I ever?

I honked the horn, gaining her attention. She looked up from her phone and smiled enchantingly. No wonder my son was so enamoured; Teddy was simply gorgeous. She swiftly pushed to her feet and spun at the waist, picking up a small leather tote in a beautiful shade of blue. Slinging it over her shoulder, she bounced towards my white BMW SUV.

Grinning, she opened the door. "Good morning, Audrina," Teddy cheerfully greeted, hoisting her lithe body onto the taupe leather seat using the handle and the sidestep to assist her.

"Good morning to you, too, Teddy." I smiled brightly. "You look lovely today. That coral colour suits you; you should wear it more often."

"Thank you. Believe it or not, I changed my outfit at least half a dozen times." She giggled, stretching the seatbelt across her slender frame, and buckling herself in.

"Well, I'm glad you chose that one; it's cute and feminine."

Smiling, she changed the subject. "So, where are we shopping today?"

"I was thinking Chadstone; we can dine there too, if you like? It's enormous and quite possibly may take us the entire day to get through. How unfortunate for us," I mocked.

"Lucky I wore sensible shoes then. Ari, the naughty boy, also gifted me a credit card with my name on it." Teddy recounted her attempts to argue with my beloved son, but he dismissed her in his typically generous fashion. He insisted on treating her, and to avoid conflict, she reluctantly accepted the card.

"In that case, he can buy me lunch." I chuckled, pulling into the traffic.

I kept the radio level to a minimum, the two of us chatting easily along the way. During which Teddy openly admitted she was indeed bored and ready to return to work. She also requested that I remained mum on the subject until she spoke with Ari and her father. Their reaction to her decision was making her feel anxious. I laid her misgivings to rest.

"I think your fears are unfounded, Teddy. Both Ari and Evan shall be undoubtedly pleased, as am I," I voiced, slowing down for the traffic lights. "We're all striving for the same outcome, and that's your happiness." That alone made her smile.

"Your support throughout this terrible ordeal has meant so much. I can't thank you enough."

"We're a family, Teddy, that's what we do. Although, it would make everyone's lives a little easier if Jaxson knew — and if you shared every aspect with Ari, too."

Guilt washed over her face. "I'm still struggling with revealing that part." As was Ari, but for once, I remained silent; she was visibly upset as it was. Sensing my discontented demeanour, she mollified me. "I'm sorry, Audrina...it's just every time I think I've moved forward enough to tell you all..."

I reached across the centre console and patted her forearm. "I understand..."

"But?"

"Finding the courage to speak up sooner rather than later is vital, Teddy," I stopped myself before I foolishly spoke my mind and ruined our outing. Rather quickly, I changed the subject. "Anyway, let's put this discussion to bed for another day. Besides, we're here to shop," I heartily pointed out as I navigated my way down the ramp into the subterranean garage below the shopping centre: my heart and mind racing as I swiftly found a space and parked.

Gathering my bag from the back seat, I climbed from the car and closed the door, leaning my back against it as I collected my thoughts. The tension caused by Teddy's reluctance had struck quite the nerve, allowing my personal feelings to show when I promised Ari I'd remain silent on the matter—a virtually impossible task when a distraught son called you daily asking for advice.

"Audrina, are you okay?" Teddy called out rounding the boot.

"Just fixing my hair in the window, I'm a little windblown," I fibbed, tucking the loose lock that had slipped from my updo behind my ear. Teddy sceptically stared as I raised a smile and strolled towards her. "Let's shop until we drop, shall we?"

Chadstone Shopping Centre was a three-level complex, plenty enough to whet a shopaholic's cavernous appetite. The enormous complex catered to anyone's needs or preferences. Food options weren't in short supply either, whether you wanted to sit down and enjoy a meal or grab a quick bite. The place was bustling as customers drifted from store to store.

Likewise, as we paused long enough to try on various styles of clothes and shoes from the upmarket stores on the higher levels. Our arms filled up fast with numerous purchases. Mine, naturally more than Teddy's, as she found several pieces she fancied, giving herself an entire new wardrobe for the summer.

We lunched at Calia, a lively Japanese restaurant on the first floor. The interior had a modern feel with timber and stainless-steel finishes, creating a warm and inviting atmosphere. We found an empty seat amongst the square tables near the expansive windows, flopping into comfortable curved leather chairs. We dropped our bags at our tired feet and placed our orders with the server who'd shadowed us.

I smiled politely and thanked them as a bottle of chilled water and two tumblers were set on the table before us. "I never realised shopping was this exhausting." I groaned, pouring a glass and sipping delicately. "Are you enjoying yourself, Teddy?"

"I am. Thank you for asking me to come. The walls and I had grown well acquainted these past few weeks." Her mouth twisted ruefully. "For the first time in a long time, I feel more like my old self."

"You certainly look livelier, that's for sure. Scientific research suggests that shopping releases certain endorphins, which might explain why you feel better," I reasoned between sips of water.

"You may want to keep that bit of information to yourself," Teddy remarked, giggling. "Jaxson might confiscate your credit cards if that's the case!"

"Oh, that would simply not do!" I expressed, mortified. "I'd never allow it anyway. He, however, fails to understand the joy it brings me."

Teddy chuckled. "Like father, like son in that department, I'd say."

I raised my eyebrows and replied, "Oh, that we can definitely agree on."

"Most definitely."

During our chat, Teddy opened up about her blossoming relationship with my beloved son. Our conversation flowed effortlessly. Having known Teddy since she was an infant, I adored her; however, I wrestled with my feelings, terrified that someday she might break his heart. Recent events had merely strengthened those doubts. To my surprise, though, Teddy showed me a ring she'd specifically purchased for Ari. A detailed explanation behind her choice followed: her love for my son was evident, laying my unfounded fears to rest.

"I sincerely hope Ari likes it," she doubted, slipping the tiny box back into its signature gift bag.

I offered her a token smile for the thoughtful gesture. "It's such a benevolent gift, Teddy, and knowing my son as I do, Ari shall love it simply because it came from you."

∞

Ari

"HONEY, I'M HOME!" I playfully yelled, striding through the door. A jubilant Teddy ran and jumped into my waiting arms, her long legs wrapping around my waist. Her fingers weaved through my hair, lovingly tugging as she welcomed me with a wet, passionate kiss.

"Not that I'm complaining, but what was that for?" I breathed, coming up for air.

"No particular reason. Why? Do I need one?" Teddy murmured, her lips and tongue brushing against mine in a tantalising dance. If my cock wasn't rock-hard before, it was now and strained painfully against the zipper of my navy-blue trousers.

Her hips flexed, achingly aware of the bulging predicament inside my pants.

"No, definitely not," I simpered, carrying her into the family room and settling into the deep cushions of the modular sofa. "I think I could handle a greeting like this every day." She smiled coquettishly, melting my heart. "How was your shopping expedition with my mother?"

"It was great. Really great, actually."

"Did you max out your new credit card?"

"No, but I think your mother may have. Hers, not yours," she clarified, giggling at the bemused expression on my face.

"Now, why does that not surprise me?"

"I did buy a few items with yours just to keep you happy, but I also used mine..."

"Well, what did you buy? I am intrigued!" A boyish grin formed as an excited Teddy clambered off my lap and disappeared into the bedroom.

An enchanting smile crossed Teddy's lips upon her return, and as my eyes travelled over the bags hanging off her fingers and boxes she precariously carried in her arms, my eyes widened.

"Wow, did you leave anything behind on the shelves for others?"

She giggled. "Yes, I did, but these," she puffed, setting everything down on the coffee table, "are my way of saying thank you for taking such great care of me lately."

"I don't need gifts to know your appreciation. You smiling as you are now, is more than enough for me," I whispered, shakily grasping Teddy's chin and languidly kissing her plump lips.

Her forehead leaned against mine. "Oh, Ari."

Having opened and admired each gift, I tugged Teddy into my lap and sealed my mouth over hers, showing gratitude with a sedate, passionate kiss. "Thank you for your gifts. I loved every single one of them, the shirts especially."

"Your mum helped me pick them out as she has impeccable taste in clothes." She gazed lovingly, brushing my cheek tenderly with the soft pads of her fingers over my stubbled jaw. "I have one more present to give you, and when I saw this, it reminded me of us," she expressed, stretching across the sofa to retrieve a gift bag she'd stowed away behind one of the oversized cushions. Her head cocked pensively. "I just hope you like it."

"I'm sure I will, whatever it is – because it's from you," I quietly assured as our fingers grazed, sending my heart aflutter.

"Your mum said the same thing to me."

"That's because she's right and knows me as well as you do. But don't tell her I said that," I murmured, raising a brow. "Or I shall never live it down."

"Your secret is safe with me," Teddy playfully whispered, pressing her clasped hands to her lips as she intently observed me opening the bag.

My gaze twinkled. "Good to hear." Straightaway, as I opened the small box, I understood the nervousness and significance behind such a thoughtful gift. The engraved infinity pattern around the tungsten band was the ultimate declaration of love. I lifted the ring from its velvet bed and slid it over my ring finger on my right hand. "This.." I gestured. "...shan't ever leave my finger."

Teddy excitedly clapped. "I'm so glad you like it."

"Like it? I love it." I rewarded her with yet another passionate kiss. "It means the world to me, thank you."

"Does it fit, okay? The saleswoman said if it's the wrong size, they can order another one," Teddy asked as we stretched along the length of the chaise afterwards and snuggled. At the same time, Bach's cello suite played gently in the background, putting me in quite a tranquil mood.

"No need, it fits perfectly." I pressed my lips to the crown of her head. "You look gorgeous today, and I like your top; it suits you."

Teddy smiled serenely. "Your mother said the same thing. She told me I should wear these colours more often."

I snorted. "My mother's full of opinions today. But she's right, you should. You appear a lot better today, too. I deduce it was all that shopping."

"Shopping was partly the reason." Teddy began picking at an imaginary spot on her jeans, a new habit she seemed to have developed of late, primarily when she was unsure of herself.

My head tilted. "What is it, Teddy? You obviously want to ask me something?"

As I watched her nervously blow out her cheeks, I couldn't help but smile at how well I knew her. "I want to return to work; I'm more than ready to."

Her request took me by surprise, but I remained impassive. "Okay, if you are sure, then, by all means, go back," I stated supportively. However, I sensed her disquietude.

"I know there'll be conditions attached."

I gave her a small smile. "All I ask is that you don't overdo it or get yourself stressed, nothing more."

She lifted her head and gazed at me, cupping my cheek with her palm. "Thank you for understanding. Your support means the world to me, particularly over the past few weeks. I know it's been rather taxing on you." The warmth from her hand radiated over my skin, as did the cadence in her voice.

Leaning my head on Teddy's, my fingers lightly strummed her arm. "I love you and wouldn't be anywhere else."

Teddy's requested meeting with her father was a somewhat bittersweet experience for her. On the one hand, she achieved the outcome she sought, but on the other hand, Evan's constant questioning and doubts caused her more angst than she bargained for.

"What if you end up overworked? Or your clients start pressuring you with their expectations? How will you manage it? Manage them?"

Teddy tried to remain calm and composed, but in the end, his relentless attitude proved too much to handle.

"Dad, please, trust that I am making the right decision *for myself*!" she pleaded, her voice quivering as she swiped the rolling tears from her cheeks. "I've weighed up the risks, and I'm prepared to face any challenges that come my way, including overworking and demanding clients. Going back to work is what I need, and I need your support! Please!"

He looked to me for backup. "Ari, what's your take on this?"

"I support her one hundred percent on the provisory she doesn't overdo it."

He stared incredulously. "Just like that?"

I nodded curtly. "It's good enough for me. Besides, I believe Teddy's astutely aware of her limitations, even if you aren't."

Evan's frazzled gaze pleaded with her. "Would you consider taking half days, just to begin with, as a compromise?"

Teddy's head shook defiantly. "No!"

Sighing and running a hand over his thinning hair, Evan gently relented, "Fine, but take extra breaks to prevent fatigue, or call me if it becomes too much. Promise me that much, just to give your old man peace of mind at least?"

A grimacing Teddy hugged her father. "If it keeps you from stressing, then fine, I'll take extra breaks, but no half days!"

Doctor Montgomery shared Evan's concerns regarding Teddy's eagerness to return to work. He agreed only under strict provisions. "You must take your medications regularly to help you adjust. I'm also only a phone call away if you need me. In addition, you must avoid overexertion!"

"I promise. Besides, both Ari and my father will kick my butt if I do," she stated, rolling her eyes at us.

I smirked. "Don't doubt for a second that I won't."

"Good, I'm glad we're on the same page then, Ari." His hardened gaze cut back to Teddy upon emphasising the importance of her fortnightly appointments with him. "This is something I won't compromise on, agreed?" Doctor Montgomery told her rather sternly.

From her chagrined expression, she was less than impressed by the good doctor's scolding, but wisely, she agreed, "Okay, I promise."

As we exited the doctor's office, I trailed a sullen Teddy to the elevator, laughing loudly. "The look on your face..."

"I'm not laughing, Jaeger!" she grumbled, stomping her little foot. "Doctor Montgomery treated me like I was a damned child!" I laughed harder, irritating her further. "Quit your laughing, or I'll tattle on you to your mother."

I immediately stopped and tutted, feigning offence, "Unbelievable. Using my mother against me; that's low, even for you."

She stabbed the button on the wall and shrugged apathetically. "Worked a treat, though, didn't it?" The doors slid open silently, and we stepped inside, a smile flittering over Teddy's lips as I pressed the button. Even as she spun lazily and leaned against the elevator car wall, folding her arms across her chest, her wicked gaze continued to taunt me.

I mirrored her actions; two could play at that game.

By the time we stepped off one elevator and onto another at Bricks and Mortar, Teddy and I were all over each other. Our playful banter continuing as we waltzed through the glass doors, drawing strange looks from Teddy's colleagues as we strolled past them.

Neither Teddy nor I cared, and we simply carried on our merry way towards Spencer's office, laughing.

Spencer's arm excitedly waved the instant we knocked on his open door. "Ari, mate, come right on in!" He rounded the large desk and shook my hand firmly. "And Teddy," he murmured affectionately, toning his exuberant personality down a notch. "It's so good to see you. I take it you are well?"

Teddy nodded tentatively. "As well as I can be, I suppose."

"I've heard you're coming back to us. Tell me it's true, please, as we've all missed you around here."

"I am, only if you'll have me, that is?"

"Of course, we'll have you; you're a tremendous asset to Bricks! Come here!" Overjoyed, he hugged her tightly.

"I'll see you bright and early Monday morning then." She giggled, wrestling out of his stronghold.

"No working Teddy excessively hard, though, she's still recovering," I warned, my amusement fading.

"I completely understand," Spencer readily agreed, his expression sobering. "I understand all too well, as you made yourself pretty clear on the phone the other week when we spoke about Teddy's possible return."

"Um, I'm right here, guys. No need to pretend as if I'm not here," Teddy protested, slipping me a curious glance. As expected, she likely wondered why I hadn't bothered to mention our conversation to her. I'd broach the subject later – once we were suitably out of earshot of everyone else.

Once the visit with Spencer was over, we unanimously decided to head to Vue de Monde in the Rialto Tower for a spot of lunch. With any luck, a nice glass of red would break the brewing tension between us.

Teddy's irritation over my lack of communication had spilt over, and into the restaurant. Marching ahead of me, she refused to oblige my gentlemanly manners and indignantly thumped onto the padded chair.

"I'm perfectly capable of seating myself *without your help*!"

"Fine, if that's what you prefer, who am I to interfere," I tightly retorted, sliding into the chair opposite. I leaned back and crossed my legs, resting my clasped hands in my lap.

"You, interfere? That's beneath you, surely?" she scoffed, glowering at me across the table whilst snatching up the menu. "Acting damned high-handed is another annoying habit of yours. Particularly when it comes down to making decisions regarding my life!" she snapped.

"I thought giving Spencer the heads up on your behalf would ease your transition. I made a call I believed was right at the time; obviously, it wasn't."

"No, really!" I ignored the sarcasm. "You called my boss on my behalf... I felt humiliated, Ari! You embarrassed me by revealing a part of my life I considered private," she whisper-hissed, tears welling.

A tense silence encompassed us as a waiter stopped by our table to take our orders. I swiftly ordered two glasses of Pinot Noir. "Is the choice of wine acceptable enough for you, Teddy?"

"It's fine!"

I waved the uncomfortable waiter away and swivelled in my seat, glaring darkly across the table at my petulant girlfriend. "We're in public; control yourself!"

She snorted derisively. "You sound just like my mother."

My lips thinned. "Charming. Not the comparison I was expecting, but anyway, moving on. I merely gave Spencer a brief run down, informing him you had been unpleasantly unwell and requested that he ease you into the daily swing. I didn't want you bombarded by clients or paperwork on the first day. Call it due diligence." My stern expression softened. "If you must know, he didn't ask for any details relating to your absence, and I most certainly didn't divulge anything private either. I wouldn't do that to you. Even you must realise this?"

"Yet, you told your mother."

"What's the issue with that?" I argued, defensively. "She's my mother and a lawyer, so naturally, I trust her implicitly."

Sharply inhaling, she gazed warily before speaking again, "Granted, she's been very supportive..."

"But?"

"I got the distinct impression that her support was waning," she tentatively murmured, her disheartened gaze firmly focused on the napkin in her fidgeting hands.

"How so?"

"During our recent shopping trip, she raised a certain issue that needs addressing."

I blew out a disheartened sigh, appreciating my mother's frustration significantly over Teddy's reluctance to reveal the bastard's name. "I know you'll tell me soon. She's just concerned, is all." I eyed her speculatively. "Is that the main reason you're upset with me? Over my mother?" She stiffly nodded. "I'll speak with her and politely request she back off, okay? But for now, can we move past this argument and have lunch? I'm about to fade here."

Teddy let out a small laugh. "I told you, there's never a chance of that happening."

29

Teddy

THE PROSPECT OF RETURNING to work had my anxiety mounting. Indicative of my worry was my indecisiveness over choosing an outfit for the day. Why was I worried? It wasn't as if I was starting a new job. Get your act together, Teddy; you wanted this, remember? I closed my eyes and sharply inhaled before shakily exhaling. An exercise Doctor Montgomery had advised me to try and repeat several times until I felt that the angst had finally alleviated itself. Which it had, thankfully. Maybe the good doctor's advice wasn't so bad after all.

I eventually decided on a wrap dress in coral. I tugged it off the hanger precisely as Ari's warm hands slid around my waist.

Breathing in his divine scent, I wilted against him. "Hi there."

"Are you all right, Teddy? You've been in here for quite some time now, and I was beginning to get worried," he stated, planting a lingering kiss on my bare shoulder.

"Yeah, I'm fine," I murmured, rolling my head against his shoulder and peering up at him. "The nerves are just kicking in, no biggy."

His incredulous stare watched me as I began to dress. "Are you certain you're ready to dive back into work then if that's the case? Spencer would completely understand if you changed your mind," he surmised, slipping his hands into the pockets of his black slacks.

"I have to go back; I'm going stir-crazy as it is." With Ari watching avidly, I tied the sash around my waist and flopped onto the cushioned seat at my dresser in the corner of the robe. His reflection stared back at me as I picked up a makeup brush. "I'll be fine, Ari, I promise."

"Okay, if you're sure," he murmured, bending down to plant a soft kiss on the crown of my head. "You look beautiful today, by the way."

My lips rose in an appreciative smile. "Thank you."

"You're welcome," he spoke quietly, his irresolute gaze resting squarely on me as he paused in the doorway. "Have a wonderful day; I love you." With a gentle tap of his fingers on the doorjamb, he strolled from the bedroom, closing the door behind him.

I sagged in the chair, my hands shakily flanking my face as I stared at my forlorn reflection in the mirror. Ari's uneasiness was disconcerting. Yet, at the same time, I understood. One concern he had raised away from my father was the possibility of a setback. A fear he had every right to bring up; he loved me and wanted what was best for me, even if it meant going against everything he felt to support me.

My first tentative step from the lift hadn't meant my trepidation had waned. I inwardly chastised myself; this was getting beyond ridiculous. Ari had suspected colleagues would naturally be curious and intrinsically knew I'd cope better without the probing questions by purchasing a new rose gold watch and bracelet with wide bands to cover the scars on my wrists. Gotta love a man that cared as much as he did.

I inhaled sharply, yanking the etched glass door open, and strolled directly towards Spencer's office. I raised my hand and knocked.

He looked up from the desk and beamed. "Teddy, g'day!" Spencer pushed to his feet and rounded the desk, hugging me tightly.

If it weren't for the mere fact they were friends, Ari would've had a coronary and told my over-affectionate boss to back off, with less subtlety, of course.

Spencer peered down at me, blinding me with his trademark smile. "So glad you're back. We have missed you around here."

"So you keep saying." Laughing humourlessly, I pushed away from him. "I thought I'd pop in and say hi. So now I've done my civic duty, I'll get on with my work."

"Um, on that…" Spencer awkwardly scratched the back of his head and slowly perched on the edge of his bespoke redgum desk. "Mrs Travers proved to be characteristically difficult during your absence. Emily can explain the situation to you."

I huffed and rolled my eyes. Great. The thought of the delightful Mrs Travers had soured my good mood already. "So much for my first day back running smoothly."

"Good luck." Spencer grimaced ominously.

"Yeah, thanks." Giving him a swift view of my back, I stormed down the bright hallway and into my cubicle, throwing my backside into the chair with a thud.

"Hey, girlfriend, it's great to have you back," Emily chirped. "But you don't look happy to be back? Did Spencer tell you about Mrs Tra...vers...," she trailed off.

I raised a brow, displaying my displeasure. "Mrs Travers? Yeah, he did."

Emily slapped a hand to her forehead and slumped in her chair. "Oh."

"Yeah, oh, in a big way," I scoffed, pinching the bridge of my nose. "So, tell me, what did Mrs Imma-pain-in-the-arse want now?"

Running around to my side of the desk, Emily nervously pulled up the house plans on the computer and pointed. "She wanted the ensuite turned into larger his *and* hers, which meant making changes here…"

"Why does she…? You know what?" I viciously growled, throwing my hands in the air. "We will not kowtow to this; it's too late. We finalised the paperwork weeks ago! She does realise this, doesn't she? Actually, do not answer that because I already know the fucking answer!" I gesticulated, fuming.

"She wants the walk-in-robe made bigger, too," Emily squeaked, scurrying back to her desk. "Like Carrie Bradshaw big."

"Oh, my god! Really?" I bellowed, gaining the attention of a passing staff member, and quickly lowered my voice to a dull whisper, "Does she not realise how much rearranging it would take? And don't get me started on the structural side of the build or the bullshit I'll have to go through with town planning at the council – again! Does this woman live just to make my life difficult? I, excuse me, we put so much work into that design," I wailed, thumping my head onto the desk. "And those bloody plans were changed so many fucking times, all to just please that damned woman!"

Noticing Emily's sudden silence, I stopped ranting and jerked my head off the desk. My brows knitted as her gaze conspicuously darted towards the edge of the cubicle. Someone was listening.

"What? What's wrong?"

Biting down on her bottom lip, she discreetly pointed towards the edge of the cubicle frame.

Oh no. I closed my eyes and sighed. Spencer. Slowly, I swung the chair around to face my reproachful boss.

With long legs crossed at the ankles and muscular arms folded over a broad chest, Spencer's towering frame leaned in the narrow doorway. A perfectly sculpted brow suddenly raised sharply above glaringly deep brown eyes, halting the smile I attempted to give in its tracks. Yeah, he was mad.

"At the risk of getting my head ripped off, may I make a suggestion?" he asked, his grim expression sobering.

"Anything to ease my mind over this bullshit would be fantastic right about now," I remarked dryly, only to rush out an apology when he glared. "Sorry."

"Right." He clapped his hands together and rolled a stool over, perching on the seat. "How about we set up a meeting with both

Mr and Mrs Travers? I'll also attend, more as a referee in case tempers are lost." He pointedly glanced at me. "And hopefully, with Mr Travers' help, we can sway Mrs Travers to proceed with the signed off plans?"

I snorted. "That might work, as I'm fairly certain Mr Travers wants to get building sometime this century."

Spencer glared at me again. At the rate I was going, if I didn't fix my sassy attitude before the end of the day, he'd fire me for sure. "That attitude, Teddy, won't help. So please, for my sake, pretend to be nice at this meeting?"

"It'll be a stretch, but since you asked so nicely, I'll try."

He snorted and rose to his feet. "Good. So, on that sour note, I'll call Mr Travers immediately so that we can move forward with this fiasco. Now, both of you," he growled irately, "get back to work."

Damned bossy boss. Frustrated, I poked my tongue out at him.

"I saw that!"

Resigned to the situation being totally out of my control, I turned back to my desk and began hauling out other projects that required my attention.

Emily let out a sarcastic chuckle. "Elise has really gotten under your skin, hasn't she?"

"When hasn't she?" I growled. "From the first instance, she's irked me, and coupled with her demands and haughty attitude, I just want to punch her in the face!"

"Thank goodness Spencer's attending the meeting then."

Speak of the devil; he swanned into our cubicle a few hours later, announcing the dreaded meeting. "The meeting with the Travers is set for nine tomorrow morning, so be ready."

"No worries," we moaned in unison before turning our attention to organising ourselves for the following day's onslaught. A tiresome and necessary evil I quite happily could've done without on my first day back.

Tilting my chair back and stretching, I checked the time on my watch; it was barely two in the afternoon. Could the day have gotten any slower?

I missed Ari terribly, adding to my melancholy. I hated that I'd grown so dependent on him. He seldomly complained though, if at all come to think of it.

My future at Bricks and Mortar was something else I had spent time re-evaluating and discussing at length with Doctor Montgomery. Apparently, in situations like mine, reassessing my future was perfectly normal. There was that word again. The doc was right: what was normal, and why was it even listed in the dictionary?

Sighing despondently, I rolled my chair forward and eyed the paperwork spread across my desk. I had to press on and quit overthinking every facet of my life, another piece of wise advice from the good doctor or Charlie he now permitted me to call him. No doubt, the grumpy old bugger would expect a complete rundown of my first week at the next appointment. So, I made a point of pressing on until it was time to head home.

Never had I been so relieved to see the end of a working day. Itching for a glass of wine, I toed my nude heels off my aching feet in the kitchen alongside my dumped bags before briskly retrieving a bottle of Chardonnay Pinot from the bar fridge.

As I began pouring a glass at the island, Ari's thoughts regarding the implications of mixing alcohol with medication popped into my head. My lips quirked as I lifted the glass to my lips, sipping and savouring the crisp tang of the wine. The taste was so enjoyable that I almost forgot about the work that came home with me. I peered down at the floor and lamented. After several week's hiatus, I was seriously behind and had to catch up, no bones about it. Shit happened, I suppose.

Clutching the bottle around the neck, taking it and my bags into the study, I settled in for the long haul ahead.

Having strolled through the building at 101 Collins, I bypassed my usual stop, a café that served the best lattes in Melbourne, to head directly upstairs. With the Travers meeting set for nine, I had an unusual urge to be early and organised. I blamed Elise and her demands. Both had trodden on my last nerve.

As I entered the office through the glass doors, Spencer's assistant, Andy Denver's early presence at the front desk surprised me. "Hey, Andy, what's dragged you in here with the crows?"

Andy Denver quickly became a welcome addition to Bricks after Spencer's last assistant moved interstate with her husband. With a sparkling personality, she fitted perfectly and got along with everybody.

"Spencer needed a refreshed contract drawn up just in case the meeting with the Travers went south," she replied through a derisive chuckle, pushing to her feet and peering over the top of the desk at my black fitted, sleeveless dress with its scooped boat neckline and A-line leather insert. Her glossy, pink-painted lips gaped. "Wow, look at you all dressed like a mafia boss." She whistled, spotting the sky-high black patent leather heels on my feet. "Slayer heels too there, girlfriend; talk about dressed to kill!"

"That's the plan." I laughed.

"Lemme guess – Mrs Travers?"

"The one and only."

Dropping back into her chair, she groaned along with me. "Good luck with that then, Teddy!"

"Thanks, I'm gonna need it!" I grumbled, swivelling on the spikes of my stilettos and waving back at her.

Rushing down the hallway, I ran into my cubicle, dumping my black tote on my desk before collecting the two previously prepared folders. Taking them with me to the conference room, I strategically aligned them with the head of the reclaimed industrial-style table. Then I set about filling a steel water jug, placing it along with five highball glasses in the middle. I thought about preparing snacks and swiftly changed my mind, wanting to avoid dragging out what would be a painful meeting.

Exhausted, I flopped into one of the Eames replica mesh chairs and relaxed against the backrest with my forearm lazily falling across drooping eyelids. A shuddering breath escaped just as the glass door swung open, and the sound of footsteps clicked across the timber boards.

"Teddy, are you okay?"

My arm immediately dropped to the armrest as Ari's raspy voice pleasantly rang through my ears. "Ari, what are you doing here?"

He glided towards me, his evened pace as tangibly smooth and alluring as the man beneath the expensively tailored navy-blue suit. His tousled hair only added to the attractive view. "You left earlier than expected, so not only did I miss you this morning, but I also missed you last night, too."

Feeling guilty, I smiled tightly.

"You skipped breakfast, too, didn't you?" He grinned, prudently placing a cardboard tray containing two takeaway coffee cups and a brown paper bag in front of me on the table. I blushed profusely. He was onto me. "That's what I thought."

"Thank you." I rolled my chair forward and peeked inside the bag, removing the tasty morsel. The smell was enticing and made my stomach rumble loudly. Eagerly ripping the wrapper open, I took a large bite of the crispy baguette. The combined flavours of gooey egg, salty bacon, and a spicy barbeque sauce prompted satisfied moans. "Oh yeah, this is the ultimate breakfast."

Ari slid into the seat beside me and watched with wry amusement as I began devouring my meal, having to wipe my chin with the serviette. He chuckled. "You had sauce and egg dripping down your chin."

"Oh, whoops, I'm such a grot." I giggled, taking another bite before setting the roll down and wiping my face again with a fresh serviette. "I'm sorry I wasn't awake when you came home last night, but after yesterday I was knackered."

"I'll survive." His hooded gaze swept over my body. "I'll consider it payback for the countless times I've inflicted many a late night upon you. I hope you're not overdoing it already?"

"No, I'm not. I promise," I affirmed, grabbing one of the cups from their tray. I sipped gingerly on my vanilla latte before settling back in the chair and nursing it in my hand. "It's just this client, Elise Travers. She's bloody challenging, and that's putting it mildly. She hasn't been shy about sharing her dissatisfaction either. Which isn't the issue; I'd rather a client happy with the final product *before* we start building."

"I feel the same way; mistakes only add to everybody's costs," he prudently replied, "which nobody wants."

"Exactly. Most of our designs ended in the scrap heap, meaning we had to draw an entirely new draft. And because of these issues, we've bypassed their move-in date by a longshot..." I let out a despairing sigh. "We'd signed off on the final design weeks ago, but while I was away, she changed her mind – yet again. It's pissing me off to no end."

"She's clueless and dim-witted, so don't let her get to you," Ari criticised, waving a dismissive hand at me. "Besides, from what I've heard along the high society grapevine..."

My brows shot up. "By that, you mean Dominique."

A sharp-witted smile crossed his lips, making my head shake in amusement. "Naturally. Anyway, back to my explanation. Patrick only married Elise to spite his ex-wife and overindulges her every whim purely to keep her off his back." The air around us abruptly shifted, causing thought-provoking butterflies to dance around inside my stomach. "I'll tell you what, though," he murmured, rolling his chair closer.

My mouth dried in anticipation. "What?"

"You are... much... much... hotter."

"You certainly have a way with words, Mr Jaeger, and it usually leads to ripping off my panties."

Ari sniggered. "The office incident ring any bells?" The heat swiftly rose in my cheeks. "See, my point exactly. You're rather adept at seducing me, too, particularly in that dress you are wearing, and let's not get started on those heels," he purred in a silken rasp, his sultry gaze molten with lust.

I held up a hand, knowing full well his intentions. "No! Absolutely not! First and foremost, this is my place of work, and secondly, Spencer would fire me on the spot and send me out the door naked." I giggled inwardly, thinking about my mother and the coronary it would give her.

Ari's eyebrows shot up. "But it's okay for you to harass me at my place of work?"

"That's different. You own your company. Who would've fired you if they had caught us?" I retorted, batting my thickly lashed eyes. "You weren't complaining one little bit afterwards, were you?"

I barely had enough time to set my coffee down before Ari lunged, dragging me off the chair and into his lap. I moaned as I felt his firm erection pressing against the back of my thigh.

"I tried complaining, but the moment you lifted that dress..." He gave an appreciative shake of the head. "...I was a goner." He claimed my mouth fervently, his hands roaming and skimming along my body until he found the hem, pushing it to the tops of my thighs. With my lace-topped stockings exposed to his roving gaze, a favourably low growl ruptured.

I framed his face, yielding to the inevitable as I hungrily kissed him back. That familiar ache I craved began to stir, and I swiftly dropped my hands to his waist, tugging at his belt buckle.

A throat suddenly cleared, startling us both.

I looked up. "Oh shit, Spencer." My face flushed, and I promptly abandoned Ari's lap, tugging my dress decently past my thighs as I stood. It was difficult to tell who was embarrassed more: Ari, Spencer, or me.

Ari abashedly waved from the chair and attempted to cross his legs, innocently trying to hide the bulge in his trousers. "Spencer, good to see you, mate."

"Um, great to see you too, Ari," he uncomfortably muttered. "I'll catch you...I mean – I'll see you another time." Discomposed, Spencer quickly retreated to his office, leaving us alone.

"Well, on that embarrassing note, I must be leaving as well, as I'm sure a stack of messages awaits me." Ari awkwardly rose from the chair and smacked his lips to mine, a deep growl reverberating in his chest. "And I...shall see you at home – tonight!"

"That you will." I smiled sweetly and walked with him to the door, waving as Ari viciously stabbed the button for the lift. I laughed at his growing impatience; the sight was just too comical for words.

He scowled and swatted a hand through the air, indicating a spanking was coming my way. A delicious thought that made my nipples harden and my breasts ache: what an enticing vision to have before an all-important albeit dreaded meeting.

The doors slid closed, leaving Ari alone with his predicament and me with mine.

I smirked and returned to my desk; I might make it through the day without killing someone after all.

"Are you planning on assassinating Mrs Travers with your stare?" Emily needled as my hostile stare remained fixated on the door. "Cause if looks could kill..."

"Please, don't tempt me," I remarked irritably, drumming my French-manicured fingernails on the table. "This entire meeting is a joke." Hearing Spencer's booming voice greeting the Travers in the main foyer, I pushed to my feet. "Here we go."

"Ladies," Elise sneered, entering the conference room with the usual flair of dramatics and over-sprayed perfume. Bitch, please. For an unexpected change, her silicone-filled breasts were contained and covered by a long-sleeved cream silk blouse tucked into a lengthier, slim-fitting jade green pencil skirt. Although, the tightly knotted chignon keeping her strawberry blonde hair off her face appeared to be tugging her surgically enhanced nose further in the air.

I forced a smile. "Mrs Travers, thank you for taking the time to meet with us," I murmured civilly, folding my arms across my chest. "However, I believe, and I'm sure you'll agree with me, by promptly putting this unreasonable issue to bed," I confidently articulated, swiftly sliding into a chair far away from the stomach-churning cloud of Elise's perfume, "we can all continue on our merry little way."

"If you say so, *Ms McGovern!*" she snootily disputed, sliding onto a chair beside her equally rigid husband, Patrick.

A tall, slightly built man with short, greying spiked hair and an arctic stare unequivocally trained on me; I greeted him just as coolly and smirked.

Yeah, so not in the mood for dominating men today.

Spencer wasn't either, it seemed, and thudded into the chair beside me, impatiently clapping his hands to gain our attention. "Right; down to business." His eyes zeroed in on Patrick first. "Mr Travers, we have called for this meeting due to the changes your wife, Mrs Travers -" He motioned in her direction. "has requested once again, and as you're aware, these plans were previously finalised through the council. Ms McGovern and Ms Smith -" He gestured towards us. "have spent numerous hours working on new drafts each time to meet your wife's demands." Demanding ways more like it.

Pointing a long, bony finger directly at me, Elise spoke up in an annoying whine, "She maintained whatever I asked for was virtually impossible."

My fingernails dug into the leather armrest. Fighting the urge to reach across the table and punch Elise's lights out was growing increasingly challenging by the second with each lying word that spilled from her botoxed lips. Surprisingly, I used my words instead and vehemently denied the accusation, "That's a blatant lie, and you know it."

"Elise, please, I'll handle this," Patrick sternly voiced without lifting his arrogant gaze off me. "It's apparent to me, Mr Hughes, that Ms McGovern has denied my wife her dream home by refusing her every whim," he argued, the muscle in his square-set jaw twitching as he pinned me with his cold stare. It was starting to grow old already.

Remaining calm and composed, I sat up straighter and squared my shoulders. I produced an A-three-sized black folder, indignantly setting it before me. My tone matched. "Now, Mr Travers, your wife, Mrs Travers, has given you such a delusive representation of myself and Ms Smith. Repeatedly, we adjusted the plans accordingly to suit your wife's needs and desires, to the point our pencils were whittled down to nothing more than toothpicks. They're all here – in this very folder if you don't believe us; *each and every one of them.*"

"I don't doubt my wife, so that won't be necessary!" Patrick sharply replied. "If you're incapable of doing the job we're paying you to do, then perhaps you should reconsider your position as an architect!"

"Mr Travers..." Spencer warned, his agitated voice scarily low as he jumped to my defence.

"It's all right, Spencer; I'm perfectly capable of handling myself," I remarked emphatically, ignoring the vicious stab to the gut. "I insist you do look, Mr Travers, particularly if it settles this pointless argument once and for all."

"If Patrick doesn't want to, then quit forcing him," Elise piped up through clenched teeth. I frowned as her face contorted into something I hadn't ever seen before.

"No, Mrs Travers, I insist your husband reviews these simply because of the inaccurate accusations I'm facing." My brow arched, daring Elise to continue challenging me. "And it's something I take offence to, particularly when my reputation is at stake."

"Mr Travers, I implore you, please! Just check for yourself!" Spencer chided, his dark eyes flashing in anger. "And as for saying

Ms McGovern isn't a great architect...that's completely uncalled for. So, now, I insist that you do, or you can procure your business elsewhere!"

Taken aback by Spencer's tirade, Patrick swallowed his over bulging ego and flicked his hand, gesturing for me to slide the folder over. As he studiously studied each page, Elise's artificially tanned skin suddenly paled: I wonder why?

"Mr Travers, I'll have you know that my colleague and I tried every which way to appease your wife, but to our detriment, the designs never satisfied her. Every time." I was determined to vindicate myself but as Patrick's calm demeanour morphed from smug to downright angry, it seemed as though it was no longer warranted. I observed as his face amusingly matched the lipstick's colour smeared over his wife's botoxed lips. Harlot Red, I assumed, well, if the shoe fitted. The thought made me smile.

"I think I've seen enough!" Slamming the folder shut, he twisted in his seat, turning his glowering gaze on his wife. "There'll be *no further* changes, and the *last* design will be the *final* design! Do we understand each other, Elise?"

"Yes, Patrick," she squeaked, shrinking into the seat from the hostile glare.

Red-faced, he turned back to Spencer. "May I see the paperwork I previously signed, Mr Hughes?"

"Of course." Spencer's face-splitting smile beamed, passing the signed paperwork and itemised bill across the table.

"Now, which was the last we signed off on?"

"Design number twenty. I will warn you, though; if you want any further adjustments to the plans, they will cost you, including a ten percents bonus each for Ms McGovern and Ms Smith, for the inconvenience. The original time frame for the build would also extend by at least, say, another three months, possibly six?" Spencer pointedly explained.

Patrick swiftly rose from the chair, buttoning up his grey pinstriped jacket. "I think my wife has taken up enough of your valuable time already, and I apologise to you all, above all you, Ms McGovern, for the false accusations. It seems apparent I misjudged you and Ms Smith. Both of you have shown dedication throughout this entirely frustrating process," he sheepishly admitted, reefing his wife from the chair by her elbow. "Come, Elise, we are having a serious discussion about your behaviour after we leave here."

I smiled, acutely aware that a stern chat would be the least of Elise's worries where Patrick was concerned.

"Patrick, I can't run in these heels," she whined, protesting loudly as her husband dragged her towards the bank of lifts.

"Now that we've dealt with this little fiasco, I'm heading back to my office, closing the door and having a stiff drink. Alone. You, ladies, may have the rest of the day off. Go home, open a bottle of wine, and drink its entire contents. And before you argue, I'm insisting that you do; it's a one-time offer."

"Oh, we hear you, Spencer. We don't need telling twice," Emily chirped, assisting me with the packing up.

"You won't hear any complaints from me, either. I am gone, like five minutes ago." I laughed, strolling out of the office.

30

AFTER THE VICTORY AT WORK, I was in the mood to celebrate and stopped by the local market, picking up ingredients for dinner. Not forgetting about dessert either, I visited my favourite bakery, The French-Quarter Patisserie, and purchased one of their decadent chocolate cakes with all the trimmings. So worth it.

I dropped the shopping onto the island bench before venturing into my bedroom. I swapped my black dress for a floral maxi dress with spaghetti straps and my heels for bare feet. Ari would undoubtedly be thoroughly disappointed. Oh well. Now, where was that wine? I'd hate to disappoint Spencer, too.

Enticing aromas of garlic, white wine, and vanilla-scented candles permeated the house. White linens, crystal wine glasses and silver cutlery lined the table's centre with a fresh posy of fragrant roses, aligning them between my grandmother's crystal candelabras. The final piece was the music crooning through the ceiling's speakers, setting the mood for the evening's dinner party.

"Honey, I'm home," Ari singsonged.

I giggled upon hearing what had become Ari's signature greeting whenever he entered the house. I also knew the familiar sound of his Italian leather shoes clicking over the timber boards in evenly measured steps.

"Something smells enticing," he murmured, sniffing the air as he entered the kitchen, loosening his tri-coloured tie. He slid it off and shoved it inside his jacket pocket.

I playfully scrunched up my nose. "I'm assuming you meant the food?"

"Of course." He abruptly seized me around the waist and hauled me towards him, laying a hard, passionate kiss on my eagerly waiting mouth.

Twisting my fingers through his dishevelled hair, Ari deepened our kiss and shuffled us backwards until my lower back hit the island bench.

"Baby has most definitely been bad; you've had wine," he breathlessly crooned as his grazing kiss tasted the fruity wine coating my lips. The searing touch flickered my desire, leaving me wet and needy.

"Yeah, you caught me. But how's the taste?"

"Sweet, but not as deliciously sweet as you."

"Ooh, right answer, my love."

"As always," he smugly replied, jerking his chin towards the stove. "Dinner smells divine. What's on the menu tonight?"

"Besides me?" I breathed huskily, nibbling on his earlobe. His splayed hands slid over the curve of my behind and cupped each cheek, lifting me off my feet. His lips pressed to mine in another decadent kiss.

"Oh, don't fret, love, you're my dessert." Ari slid me to the floor and nodded at the stove. "But I need dinner first."

"For that sustenance you speak of?" His lips quirked knowingly. "It's chicken cacciatore with risotto as a side dish."

"Garlic bread?" he cheekily quizzed, pinching a slice of cucumber from the fresh salad and swiftly popping it into his mouth.

I shook my head and smiled. "Hungry, love?"

Salaciously grinning, Ari's jet-black eyebrows rose above a sparkling gaze. "Ravenous."

"Get out of the salad!" I growled, swatting his hand away from the bowl as he pinched a chunk of Roma tomato.

"But I'm hungry."

"Well, you'll just have to wait a little while longer. The girls' should be home any minute. Now, go! And get changed!"

He growled. "Bossy, impossible woman."

Hearty laughter erupted, turning my gaze towards the gorgeous man beside me. Ari's head was thrown back as a single finger wiped his watering eyes after Dominique regaled everyone about an incident at work, leaving both Ari and the girls' in stitches.

He looked up at me and laced our fingers together as his beautiful chocolate brown eyes locked with mine, percolating an unseen desire between us. His masculine scent drifted around the table, leaving me aroused, inebriated and bold. So bold, I glided a hand along his muscular thigh and slid inside the leg of his shorts, grasping his growing erection and fisting his cock beneath the table.

Leaning into my ear, he gruffly whispered, "I think we should take this to the bedroom before the girls' end up with that show they once spoke of."

Barely excusing ourselves, we pushed to our feet and exited the room, leaving the girls' chattering. At the same time, Ari impatiently led me to the bedroom, his mouth attacking me feverishly the moment we slammed the door shut. Pushed against the back of the door, he forcefully tore my maxi dress from my body, breaking the thin straps in the process. My underwear was the next to go as shredded lace floated to the floor.

Ari swallowed hard and stepped back, admiring me with such a scorching gaze that my insides quivered in anticipation. "Pleasure yourself for me."

A shiver excitedly curled around my spine. How could I refuse the aphrodisiac and the Dominant that was Ari Jaeger?

Too transfixed on the hands massaging my rounded breasts and my rolling fingers as they teased my stiffened nipples, his calves hit the edge of the bed. His jaw gaped as my other hand methodically and sensuously drifted down my midriff and over my aching cleft.

I slid my fingers between the soft flesh of the slick folds, rubbing and circling my swollen nub. A display that drove Ari wild as he held his rock-hard cock in one hand, fisting while gently squeezing his tightened sac with the other. His stroking intensified, provoking a raspy groan.

Streams of pleasure shuddered through my body as my fingers pumped faster and my palm furiously rolled over my clit. I was close.

"Don't come yet!" Ari ordered, his voice straining as he fought to stave off his orgasm. "Come here! Now!"

I rapidly closed the small gap between us and sank over him. His hardened length twitching inside me as I slid my fingers into his mouth, giving him a taste of my arousal. He eagerly sucked, twirling his tongue around each digit, lapping up a flavour he enjoyed thoroughly.

Ari emitted a low growl and cradled me firmly against his chest, his mouth seeking out mine. Kissing me long and slow as his fingers trailed along my spine, over the soft curve of my behind, ending between my parted cheeks. The pressure I felt inside my flowering rosebud was euphoric, provoking a lowly groan on both parts.

Everything inside of me tightened as the head of his cock moved against my vaginal wall as his finger plunged inside my anus. With his mouth on my breasts, I was in sensation overload. My climax exploded, making my body shudder pleasurably.

Ari was far from finished. Suddenly, he tugged his finger out and dug into my hips, lifting and rolling us over. My skin dampened as Ari sprawled me against the mattress. He wasn't any better. Beads of sweat had formed across his brow and dripped as he hovered transiently before hooking his arms around my thighs and slamming balls deep inside me.

He hissed as I dug my fingernails into his shoulders, dragging deeply along the slick flesh of his shoulder blades. The pain from the gouging nails triggered an orgasm like no other. His back arched, and his hips flexed, spurting hard and fast inside of me, leaving us both a hot, sticky mess.

Collapsing against the shallow valley between my breasts, he blew out a quaking breath. "I didn't hurt you, did I?"

I laughed softly. "Oh, the irony, I should be asking you the same question."

"I had better go and inspect my wounds then," Ari groaned, heaving his weary body off me and stumbling towards the bathroom.

I staggered after him, watching with wry amusement as he stood askew in front of the mirror, twisting and turning, trying to view the scratches embedded in his back.

"You don't do anything by halves, do you?"

"Oops, sorry." I stared reproachfully at his bleeding wounds. "I guess I got a little too enthusiastic," I muttered, snaking my arms around his waist.

"Enthusiastic? You wounded me," he mocked, pouting. "I'm scarred for life."

"Just think of them as your love wounds."

"Look at the blood; they're more like war wounds."

"I didn't realise I'd dug that hard, whoops." A frown marred my brow from repressed memories, which, in turn, had Ari frowning.

He tipped my chin and gazed vividly. "What's wrong?"

"Nothing's wrong," I vaguely replied, stepping into the shower. The last thing I wanted to do was ruin our beautiful evening by reliving that night. "Come shower with me, and I will wash your war wounds for you, please?"

"Okay, but be gentle. I don't need any more injuries," Ari pouted, joining me under the rushing water. Like always, he sensed my uneasiness and drew me closer, enveloping me in the safest place I knew: his arms.

With Christmas fast approaching, I was trying my absolute best to focus on what to buy everyone. But despite writing several lists, the enthusiasm just wasn't there. Worse still, it had barely passed mid-October.

Work also kept me busy, as did my demanding clients. As my father had predicted, they expected me to pull a rabbit out of a hat simply because they wanted their plans finalised before individual councils closed for the December holidays. In the end, it became too much, not just for me but for Ari also. So, between him and Spencer, they orchestrated an email informing my clients that meeting their demands wasn't possible and they'd have to wait like everybody else. That alone gave me the relief I sought before I cracked under the immense pressure.

Since my return to work, Ari's unwavering support had proved to be a godsend. Ensuring I remained focused, he kept up a punishing daily workout routine, in and out of bed. One that also kept me tired, helping me sleep better than I ever had of late. Another positive aspect was waking up in Ari's arms each morning, bringing a joy I never thought possible.

Yawning quietly, I glanced at the divine figure stretched out beside me. The snoring, on the other hand, was not so much. Laying across his stomach with his strong arms securely wrapped around a pillow, why was Ari sleeping in on such a glorious day? Or how with the room bathed in splendid sunlight. Likewise, with the gentle breeze blowing in off Port Phillip Bay through the open door. Both warranted conditions for a morning run. I just had to wake Ari.

"Come on, sleepyhead; it's time to get up! It's a gorgeous day outside, perfect for our morning run." I ripped the sheet away, landing a harsh smack on one of the most perfectly rounded and naked behinds I'd ever seen. "Come on, lazy bones, move that bootylicious arse."

"I'm already up," he grumbled into his pillow before rolling over and giving me an eyeful of his morning wood in all its glory. I stifled a groan and bit down on my bottom lip. It was so tempting to wrap my lips around that delectable cock, and for once in my life, I resisted the temptation.

"Oh, that I can most definitely see," I simpered, throwing my feet to the floor and standing. "You know what I mean. But be careful; we don't want you snapping it off."

Ari snickered and rolled off the bed anyway. He seized me from behind, poking his erection into my lower back. "You'd be stuffed without it."

I grinned and propped my naked back against his bare chest. "Yeah, that's the only reason I am with you – is for your massive cock."

"Among other reasons," he purred, nibbling my neck and palming my breasts.

"Hmm, your balls."

"Why my balls, do I dare ask?"

"Because you know I own them. They're guaranteed to end up in my handbag at some stage."

"That explains why your bag's so heavy then..."

"Narcissist," I moaned, giving into Ari's groping. We landed back on the bed, our morning run along with my control wholly and solely forgotten.

Stepping through the doors at Bricks and Mortar, I checked my watch and grinned. Regardless of Ari's two toe-curling orgasms, I'd made it on time. Barely actually. With new clients arriving very shortly, which thrilled me as it meant fresh new challenges and ideas, I couldn't afford to be late. But sometimes, one had to make an exception to the rule if the need called for it.

With a bounce in my step, I breezed into the cubicle and slid into the seat behind my desk.

"Well, someone got laid last night," Emily deduced through a chuckle. "Oh, hang on, that would be you every night!"

Focused on the iPhone in my hand, I blushed, biting down on the inside of my cheek, making it glaringly obvious. "So what? I have the best sex in the world with the sexiest man on the planet. Good for me. You have great sex every night, too, so you keep telling me."

Amidst responding to Ari's risqué text, I teased Emily, "By the way, does your dildo need new batteries, or are they energisers that just keep going and going and going?" I giggled, ducking as a pencil came flying past my head.

"Change of subject, Miss Smutty, we have new clients arriving shortly, remember? Therefore, we need to collaborate by getting a few ideas written down and gathering up some of our designs to show them before they arrive. What do you say?" Emily asked, pulling out her notepad.

"Sounds good to me. Although, it would've made our job a whole lot easier if Spencer had given us some clues as to our new client's taste," I hummed, firing up the computer. "Do you even know who the new clientele is yet, Ems?"

"Not a clue." Her response appeared rather vague, concerning me. "I'm in the same boat as you. Spencer only left a note on my desk, happily informing us we had new VIP clients coming in today; no details, though. Possibly a last-minute appointment, I'd say. Maybe they're ultra-rich, or they're famous; who knows? When I finally got a chance to speak with Spencer earlier, he said they'd asked for you specifically. Maybe Mr Travers recommended you to them?" she suggested coolly, flicking her thick, wavy mahogany hair over her shoulder.

"Quite possibly. But regardless of the secrecy, we need to be thorough and organised just in case."

I just hoped it wasn't another Mrs Travers. My nerves couldn't cope with another nightmare client. She was bad enough.

Gathering up the folders with our ideas and designs into my arms, I hurriedly walked towards the conference room, dumping everything on the table.

"Dammit, I've left one behind, so I'll just go and quickly grab it," Emily hollered nonchalantly, running from the room.

"Yeah, okay." My back to her, I waved a dismissive hand and continued laying out our designs, setting them up on the boards in the back corner of the room.

"Hello, Teddy...."

I stilled as the fear paralysed me to the spot; no, it can't be! His voice was just as cold and calculating as I remembered, as was the all-too-familiar smell of his cologne. A wave of nausea unexpectedly hit me like a brick wall as the sickening scent wafted under my nose. I slowly turned and stared directly into the face of my past, his darkened, soulless eyes leering closely at me. *"Emmett."*

31

FEAR HAD MY FEET rooted to the spot, and I couldn't shift even if I tried. The sight of a man who made my blood run cold stood inches away from me. His hands casually slipped into his pockets.

That's where they needed to stay.

I gulped. "What are you doing here, Emmett?"

"Now, that's no way to greet your new client, is it, Teddy?" He shot me a darkened glance and stepped closer, unnecessarily invading my personal space. His cigarette-laced breath was suffocating. "I've missed you...and your...sensuous...*pussy*," Emmett disgustingly articulated in a chilling voice, gliding a finger down my cheek.

I flinched, making the smug bastard smile. "I despise you. You're nothing more than a sick paedophile who ruined my life," I whisper hissed, taking an involuntary step back. To my horror, he roughly grabbed my face, violently slamming the back of my head against the wall. Tears I had bravely fought slipped.

"You listen to me, you little slut, and you listen good; you are mine and always will be. Break up with lover boy, or I may have to inflict the same amount of pain, if not more, on that good-looking sister of yours," he threatened, nuzzling my throat. He inhaled deeply. "Hmm, you still smell so damned delicious." Then, in a sickening move, his tongue darted out, licking my face.

I had to fight the urge to throw up as my stomach roiled.

My bottom lip trembled as I hoarsely stuttered out my veiled attempt to scare him off. "Leave my sister alone or...I... I'll kill you myself."

"And how would you do that, Teddy? Enlighten me, please?" Too psychotic to care, Emmett remained undeterred, his expression indifferent as he tightened his grip on my face, painfully digging his fingertips into my cheeks. "I have often wondered how your pussy feels and tastes these days. It's probably still as exquisite as the day I fucked it, taking away your most precious possession: your virginity." He smirked and shoved a hand beneath my blue wrap dress, brushing the insides of my thighs as his fingers worked their way into my panties, bringing my worst fear to life.

All the air left my lungs as I desperately clawed at his hands, begging, "No, Emmett, please don't do this."

"Hmm, very nice. Bare; just the way I like it."

"You always did prefer your women prepubescent!" I bravely bit back.

Snarling, he plunged his fingers further; I winced as pain lanced through me. "Watch your fucking mouth, whore!"

Frantically, I clawed at his arm and punched at his chest. "Get. Off. Me!"

Again, he remained unmoved and confidently inched closer. "Why? I could take you right here, right now, if I wanted."

My eyes widened at the sheer horror. "No, I won't let you. When Ari finds out, he'll kill you." I had to fight; I couldn't allow him to rape me. Not again.

"Ari won't ever find out, and if he does, what do you think he'll say about you? I'm family, so naturally, he'll believe me. Particularly when I tell him you seduced me, and I simply yielded to a teenage girl's infatuation," he arrogantly jeered.

"You're insane!" A cruel smile grew, and my fearful gaze darted to the opened door, wishing Emily would hurry back.

"No one's here to save you, sweetheart, just like last time." That's where he was wrong. Just as those terrifying words tumbled from his delirious mouth, Bree's excitable voice echoed throughout the corridor, putting a dent in his well-laid plans.

Emmett glanced over at the door and scowled. Slowly releasing his hold on me, he swiftly placed a finger upon his thinning lips, not before mouthing a warning for me to remain quiet.

I sensibly nodded as I attempted to straighten my dress and wipe away my tears, an impossible feat when your hands were visibly shaking.

Bree came rushing in and ran at me, embracing me with her warmth. "Oh, Teddy, look at how beautiful you are. Audrina was right – Ari has you glowing in all the right places," she gushed, twisting at the waist and looking at Emmett over her slender shoulder. "Don't you agree, Emmett?"

"I had no idea he was capable of such a momentous task."

I flicked a deathly glare across the room, one that rapidly morphed into a smile as Bree turned back to face me. "Now, what brings you both here?"

"I need you to redesign my house, silly," Bree chirped, grinning, her baby-blue eyes lighting up. "Now, your co-worker Emily here just showed me quite a few designs; most were yours, of course! Every one of them were simply divine! Honestly, I could've sat for hours exploring your entire catalogue, and only at my insistence did Emily and I finally make our appearance. I felt it was rude of me to keep you, or my husband for that matter, waiting any longer."

"Great." I grimaced, inwardly wishing neither hadn't stalled after Emmett's distressing violation. "Let me show you a few more of mine and Emily's collaborations then," I suggested, deliberately steering her and myself away from Emmett's unnerving stare.

Curious about how they found me, I asked, "May I ask who recommended Bricks and Mortar to you, Bree?"

Emmett annoyingly interjected, "As a matter of fact, it was Jaxson. He informed us that you're the best architect around. And by the quality of your work, I'd say he's right."

I gulped. Oh, God, I wished Jaxson hadn't. "He's just biased. Perhaps I could suggest someone else for this job. Someone with much more experience, at least?" I was barely holding it together as it was, and the thought of interacting with a man I despised for months on end had my skin crawling.

"Now, why would we want anyone else? You're the best, and besides, *it's what I want. I only want you*," Emmett horrifically demanded, making me understand the alternate meaning behind his words all too clearly. I shivered in disgust, likewise at the malice he subjected his lovely wife to. "My wife, too, would be devastated if you refused us. Isn't that right, love?"

She lowered her eyes and speedily answered her dictating husband, "Yes, yes, of course, I would."

Observing their interaction, I frowned and slipped Bree a surreptitious glance; he was indifferent; she was frightened. Her shaking hands and the fear in her eyes told me so—a fear she promptly masked through a tight smile.

Bile rose as realisation dawned: he was abusing her. I gradually turned my head and glared at Emmett reproachfully. The smug bastard's eyebrows rose perceptively.

"Teddy, are you with me?" Bree's chirpy voice jerked me back to the task at hand.

I shifted my blinking gaze back to her and then turned it back to Emmett's, his predatory glare watching our every move like a hawk. I held my own. "For a second there, I thought I was about to throw up; something had suddenly made me feel ill." The smugness dropped, and his gaze tore away from mine. Well, that was a first if I ever saw one.

Bree's brows knitted together, and then continued addressing her ideas as if nothing had happened. "I love these two," she articulated, grabbing the drawings off their boards and setting them down on the table. As Bree pointed to the design aspects she liked, I jotted them down, consciously aware that Emmett was within proximity. Too close.

I caught him in my peripheral vision, thankfully giving me a chance to move away from his annoyingly unwelcome, incessant touching.

As if he'd read my mind, he grabbed the back of the dress and held me steadfast, leaving me unable to shift to the other side of Bree where I wanted to be – away from him.

His touching was unrelenting, to the extent, he gripped me in a bear hug as they were leaving, expressing he was thrilled to have acquired my talent. I felt the opposite. He lingered a little too long for my liking, and pushing him off me proved to be quite challenging.

"I wasn't, and I'm still not done with you," he chillingly warned quietly in my ear before pressing his lips to my cheek. The pit of my stomach dropped; he meant every menacing word.

I rushed to step back, my heel catching in the crack between the timber boards, causing me to stumble slightly.

Thinking quickly on my feet, I politely excused myself under the pretence I had a meeting with my boss regarding another project. I rapidly spun on my heel, my steps quickening upon feeling the sting of Emmett's suspicious gaze as it bore holes into my back.

He had every right to doubt me; I'd lied. Spencer had left hours before to confer with another client on the other side of the city and wouldn't be back until later, if at all. I needed an escape, and his office was conveniently empty. It also had a lock on the door.

I knocked and waited a few seconds, plastering a smile on my face as I reached for the door handle and opened the door. My voice trembled as I said, "Hello," to Spencer, nearly giving me away. As I leisurely stepped over the threshold and closed the door, the tears I'd miraculously held in for the last hour trickled over, blowing into full-blown sobs as I hit the floor.

For years, whether at family functions or any other party my mother forced me to attend, I successfully managed to avoid Emmett at all costs. According to her, keeping up appearances was far more important than my suffering. Then, the reality of coming face-to-face with that despicable man for the first time in years had left me insufferably rattled, to the point that my mood sent everyone ducking for cover.

Without offering any explanation to Emily, and only when I felt it was safe enough to leave, I took off from work, checking every facet of the building, including the darkened corners of the garage, as I ran to my car. I spent the entire drive along the busy streets as I sped towards Ari's Beaumaris home, tugging at my blue wrap dress, desperately trying to rip it from my shaking body. I ended up screaming in frustration when the seams refused to budge. That's when I resorted to cutting the wretched thing off before throwing its tattered mess in the kitchen bin. My lace panties copped the same treatment.

My wild shrieking unwittingly alerted Rosa. Mortified by my nakedness and unsure where to look, she scuttled back to the kitchen where she remained as I sat at the piano in only my bra, playing whatever dark piece came to mind.

Then Ari came home, his buoyant mood retreating the instant I shrank away from him. I couldn't even bring myself to look at him, and the one time I did, I immediately looked away. The resemblance to that piece of shit was disturbingly similar, something else I had overlooked for years – until now.

Ari was at a loss. Whenever he tried sparking a conversation, I snapped, yelling at him to leave me be. Bedtime was even more awkward. I showered alone and dressed in the ensuite as dealing with his forlorn gaze was more than I could bear. Then, adding insult to injury, I slept in one of the spare bedrooms, again not wanting to be touched. In all fairness, I should've just gone home, but believing Ari's was where I needed to be to feel safe, I stupidly drove straight here. What a colossal mistake on my part.

Even now, I warred with my head amidst trying on several outfits in Ari's walk-in. I procrastinated, with each one feeling unworthy in my eyes, until I finally settled on a white halter neck dress and a pair of white wedged sandals. Throwing the entire outfit on, I stormed stony-faced past a quietly observing Ari on the way to the bathroom. "Are you all right this morning, Teddy?"

My reply was short and curt, "I'm fine!" I snatched up the hairbrush and roughly ran it through my tresses before pulling my thick mane off my face, hoping to make it resemble a messy bun. Not quite. It looked like shit, but it had to do.

"Okay then," he reacted quietly and raised his hands in defence. "Are you sure? Because you seem..."

I marched behind him into the bedroom. "I seem what, Ari?"

His wary gaze eyed the swinging brush in my hand. "Out of sorts – and angry."

"I slept like shit, if you must know."

"Are you due for your period? Because normally..." Ari had to duck as the brush flew past his head. His lips thinned into a disapproving line. "I was about to say your sleep is usually erratic when you are due. Sorry for even talking this morning." He hastily marched from the bedroom, slamming the door behind him.

I slumped onto the bed and winced inwardly, disgusted with my treatment of him, the one man I'd solely come to depend on for support. It was unfair of me to take my frustrations out on him. He deserved better than a tossed hairbrush at his head for something as simple as showing concern.

I needed to apologise.

Rushing from the bedroom, I bolted down the stairs, hoping to catch Ari before he left for the office, if he hadn't already. Thankfully, he hadn't. Sitting at the glass dining table, he ate the eggs benedict Rosa, his housekeeper, had cooked for him.

Tentatively, I approached. "Can we talk, please?"

"Should I duck for cover again?" he muttered.

"No." I cautiously slid into the seat beside him, my fingers flexing restlessly in my lap.

He stared reproachfully. "What's put your knickers in a twist?" Ari was irritated and justly so. "Well, I'm waiting for an explanation."

Finding the words to explain was harder than I thought. "I had a new client yesterday... one that was unexpected."

A frown marred his brow. "Who?"

"I can't tell you."

"Why can't you?"

I stammered, "I...I just can't."

Ari's cutlery dropped loudly onto the plate. "We're back to this again, are we? Your refusal to disclose? Only recently did you promise me no more hiding!"

Tears pricked my eyes. "I'm trying, Ari, I truly am."

"No, you're not! I thought we were finally moving forward! How many times do we have to keep circling this subject before it makes me fucking dizzy?" His strong jaw was rigid and ticking as if a grenade was about to go off, and I was the trigger. "Was it – him? At least tell me that much."

Tension radiated between us. Apart from Phillip Island, I'd never seen him so angry with me. I couldn't answer him, which was ridiculous, considering I was the one who wanted to talk. Instead, I mournfully looked away, upsetting him further.

His fist slammed against the glass tabletop, making me jump. "For crying out loud, Teddy, tell me!" he roared before shoving his chair back and rising from the table.

Heat crept into my cheeks as the tears flowed.

"I can't take...."

"Yes!" I yelled through my sobs. "Yes, it was him! Are you happy now?"

Wide-eyed and stunned, Ari quietly slumped back onto the seat while I wept, nursing my head in my hands. "I'm sorry, Teddy, but I need more. Who is he?"

I jerked my head up and shook my head violently. "No, I can't."

He glowered and pushed back to his feet. "Well, I don't know if I can help you anymore."

I gaped in disbelief, watching as he stalked out of the kitchen and into the garage. The BMW's throaty engine revved, and the tyres squealed, followed by nothing but silence. He was gone. I dissolved into floods of tears and collapsed to my knees; I had broken us for good.

32

Ari

THE WORD REGARDING MY LESS THAN sunny disposition had spread like wildfire to every corner of my building. Consequently, the staff made a point of steering clear when they saw me coming, except for one foolish individual: James Newman, my head architectural engineer. Of all days, he chose this one to hand in his resignation, adding to my aggravation.

Once I stopped ranting, I calmed down enough to hear the man out. Not actually leaving until mid-March the following year, he'd acted considerate enough to allow me a sufficient amount of time to find a replacement — one who was up to my exacting standards.

I chuckled. The man knew me well, as did all my staff. A tough nut to crack, that much was right. To be given a lucrative position in my company, they had to impress me by showing what they had to offer above other applicants. Generally, most people in my employ stayed until retirement, if that's what they chose, and only rarely was anyone fired, usually with good reason.

Asher Bradford, my lawyer and best friend, on the other hand, was one of the select few who dared to challenge me, and get away with it.

"What's eating you today, bossman? You're so gloomy today and acting like you've swallowed an entire lemon tree."

"You want to be fired?" I uttered dryly, rolling up my sleeves as I strolled across the room to look out the windows at the city below.

He defied me by having the courage to guffaw at my words. "You wouldn't dare. You need me, plus you love me too much," Asher confidently retorted.

"Try me," I growled, glaring menacingly. I pressed my forearms to the glass and peered downwards at the ant-sized traffic bustling below. Cars and people rushed by, most headed in the same direction as Bricks and Mortar, making me wonder how Teddy was feeling.

"Wow, you do have your knickers in a twist today," he noticed, perching on the arm of the sofa and crossing his arms over his chest. He studiously gazed. "Seriously, Ari, what's eating you? Is it Teddy?"

I shoved my hands through my hair and huffed, "Yeah. We argued before I left for work, and it didn't bode well with either of us."

"All couples argue from time to time." Asher cocked his head thoughtfully. "Or does it have something to do with her past?"

A flare of exasperation escaped my lips. "That it does. The fact Teddy keeps holding back on details, one in particular, is frustrating the absolute fuck out of me!"

"What are you going to do?"

I gave a desolate shrug. "I don't know at this stage."

"Do you still love her?"

"Teddy's the love of my life, and that won't ever change."

"Do you want a little advice as your friend, not your lawyer?"

"Do I get a choice?" I gloomily enquired.

He grinned. "No."

I ran another hand through my hair and snorted. "This advice had better be bloody free."

His jaw grew rigid, conveying I might not like his advice regardless. "Have you thought about giving an ultimatum or even considered having a break from Teddy?"

I looked at him as if he was mad.

"That's what I thought. Maybe you should. But before you go climbing on that high horse, listen." He leaned forward, setting his elbows on his knees, clasping his hands between the wide spread of his long legs as he sighed. "Since becoming involved with Teddy, you haven't been yourself, more so since she ended up in the hospital. You're falling apart. Something's gotta give, man – before you do."

Asher meant well, and I trusted his opinion significantly. His advice and words had merit to them also. He certainly gave me something to deliberate, that's for sure.

We had been best friends since high school, with our parents following, becoming fast, close and personal friends. Even as we branched off in different directions after high school, we still consciously tried to hang out whenever the opportunity arose.

Asher was the complete opposite of me in every way and not just in looks. Where I was dark, broad-chested, and muscular, Asher was blonde, tall, and chiselled, his eyes a startling azure blue – although quite the draw card for the ladies, it was usually to his detriment, too.

Where I wanted to settle down with one woman, Asher was happy to date every woman within the state borders of Victoria, sometimes venturing further north, or west, when he grew bored. What we shared most was mutual respect, and not just for each other, but all that we represented. Predominantly, our connection extended to our families as well as the business.

Throughout our school years, we were both highly competitive in every sport. Our games generally resulted in a visit to the emergency department with our mothers' by our sides, scolding both of us for our delinquent behaviour. Honestly, nothing had changed, nor had our mothers'. Asher and I could recite their speech flawlessly – before they'd even begun our dressing down, infuriating them further.

Asher also knew the depth of my love for Teddy, often sharing his concerns, whether they were warranted or not. He guarded my secrets with his life, and for that, I was grateful.

Just when I thought my day couldn't have gotten any worse, it did. A distressed Spencer phoned to inform me he'd ordered Teddy home in a flurry of tears, and when I queried as to why his answer hadn't shocked me at all.

She'd behaved similarly insufferable at work, too, snapping at anyone who crossed her path or even looked at her the wrong way. His staff had complained, unable to tolerate the fluctuating mood any further. Spencer subsequently hauled her into his office and reprimanded her. Then he thoughtfully suggested she head home for some much-needed sleep, setting her off again.

Whereas others would have fired her on the spot, Spencer's impartial attitude sent his staff home for some reflection and quiet time. Teddy ought to thank her lucky stars that she had such an understanding boss.

Snatching up my belongings, I slammed the door to my office wide open, startling even my ordinarily cool-as-a-cucumber PA Thomas.

He regarded me carefully. "Mr Jaeger, is everything all right?"

"No, everything has gone to pot. I'm leaving for the remainder of the day as I have a rather contentious issue requiring my immediate attention. Please ..."

"Reschedule your meetings? Consider it done." He gave me a token smile and waved me off. "Go do what you need, and I'll take care of business here."

I gave a satisfied nod. As per usual, my ever-faithful assistant took everything in his stride. "Thank you, Thomas. See you tomorrow."

"Teddy!" I barged through the bedroom door and found her huddled in the corner of her wardrobe, sobbing her heart out. I took one look at her distressed state and knelt on the floor beside her, hauling a reluctant Teddy into my lap. "Hey, what's going on? Does this have something to do with yesterday?"

"Y...yes," she stammered in a whisper, prompting my jaw to clench.

"Why was he there, and how did he know you worked at Bricks and Mortar, Teddy?"

Her lower lip trembled as she struggled to find her voice. "Your...your dad told him."

"Why would...?" The reason suddenly dawned on me, making my spine stiffen. "It was someone within my family who raped you, wasn't it? And the sole reason you've been so disinclined to tell me."

Her head stiffly nodded against my chest, confirming those suspicions. "Who, Teddy? Who was it?"

"I... I can't!" She shook her head furiously. "I can't. He threatened to come after Scarlett. Ari, you have to go! You shouldn't be here!" Crying with trepidation, she scrambled off my lap and heaved. Unable to shift my bulky weight, the panic set in further. "You have to go! We can't be together; he threatened to hurt my sister!"

I dug my heels in. "I told you before, I am not going anywhere, nor am I leaving you in this panicked state! Expressly after what happened the last time you were this upset!" Rising from the floor, I grabbed a flailing Teddy and tugged her into my arms. "I am not leaving you, ever," I softly reiterated as I fought to hang on in more ways than one.

Laying on the bed beside Teddy, I watched her closely as she jumped and fidgeted in her sleep. The fight with her had grown arduous, leaving me agitated and utterly exhausted. Lying alongside Teddy also allowed me the time to speculate who the culprit might be. Whoever he was, the thought of the unknown made my lips curl in repugnance.

Mentally, I began to rattle off a list of possible suspects, crossing off those who were either too young or weren't even born around the time of the attack. Only a mere few sprang to mind, one more in particular than the others. But, until Teddy revealed who *he* was, my hands were tied, frustratingly so.

Careful not to disturb Teddy, I slipped off the bed and into the hallway, tugging my phone from my pocket in the process. As I dialled, I just prayed my mother was available. Thankfully, she answered straight away. "Hey, Mum."

"Ari, what's wrong? You sound awful."

I sagged my back against the wall and sighed heavily. "I know it's out of the way, but is there any chance you can swing past Teddy's, please?"

"Nothing's out of the way for you; you know that." Her benevolence raised a small smile, at least. "Is everything all right?"

"No, it's not," I wearily acknowledged, rubbing my aching temples. The tension had tightened into a vice-like grip on my head. "Teddy's had another breakdown, and not only that, she revealed something else to me about her rape."

"Oh?"

"Yeah, oh. I would rather discuss it in person than over the phone."

"Okay, but I need to finish this deposition first. I should go so I can. Love you."

"Thanks, Mum, I love you, too." I attempted to stand upright, only to sway. "Whoa." Unsteady, I reached out for the wall with my hand, giving myself a minute to regain my equilibrium before letting go. From there, I aimed for the kitchen, figuring alcohol was as good a cure as any painkillers.

Having filled the glass with bourbon, the magnitude of the situation finally hit me; I was on the brink of losing it. Alcohol wasn't the answer, but I threw the warm amber liquid down anyway. I poured another before lowering my throbbing head against the cool, marble benchtop, closing my eyes, even if it was just for a minute. Other than the soft humming of the air conditioner on the roof, it was relatively peaceful.

That silence was short-lived as Teddy's piercing screams rang through the house, triggering an automated response as my head jolted and my arms flailed, sending my tumbler crashing to the floor. I bolted for the bedroom, my bulky frame practically barging through the bedroom door to find a distraught Teddy curled up against the headboard, wide-eyed and wailing.

"He was here, in my room!"

"Did you have a nightmare?"

Her head shook vehemently. "No! He was here! I know he was. You need to check the house!" Her lower lip quivered as I stared disbelievingly. "You don't believe me, do you?"

If I said no, it would only crush her severely broken spirit further. "It's not that I don't believe you, Teddy…" I exhaled sharply. "Are you sure you saw him here?"

"He was here, Ari!" she screeched with the high pitch resounding through my aching head.

"Okay," I softly agreed, holding up one hand in defeat as I clutched at my skull with the other, anything to alleviate her fears. "I'll go check."

"Thank you," she uttered tearfully.

After checking every square inch of the house, I returned to the bedroom. "There's nobody here," I reassured, sliding onto the mattress beside her and reclining against the soft pillows. "It must have been just a nightmare," I murmured, fighting to keep my weighted eyelids open. "Come here, please? I don't want to argue; I just need to hold you."

Teddy cautiously eyed my outstretched arm and slowly curled her rigid body along the length of mine.

I rolled into the soft curves and strummed the pads of my fingers up and down her arm. A smooth and relaxing motion that eventually encouraged her to shuffle closer.

I briefly gave up the fight and allowed my eyes to close, blowing out a contented sigh as I relished the closeness. But upon hearing the front door open and slam shut, I grumbled, "That must be mum. She said she would be here soon." Reluctantly, I forced my burning eyelids open and, likewise, lifted my head off the pillow with

Teddy's red-rimmed eyes gazing inquisitively at me as I set my feet on the floor.

"Why is your mum coming over?"

"I asked her to." Yawning, I ruffled my hair and twisted at the waist. "I wanted to talk to her and possibly seek some advice."

"Oh. I see," Teddy muttered reproachfully.

My lips set into a hard line as I pushed to my feet. "You have your shrink; I have my mother," I tersely responded, marginally turning my throbbing head. "You're not the only one who's entitled to vent!" I stalked from the room, flexing my arms. Christ! I needed a workout desperately.

I yelled out, "Mother?" No answer. Well, that was strange. My brows creased. Oh no. I bristled and clutched at my hair; she was telling the truth! The fucker had indeed been in the house. "Fuck!" A feral growl erupted, alerting Teddy that something was indeed wrong.

"Ari? He was here, wasn't he?" The pain and terror on her face shredded me further. I was such a bastard.

"Stay in the room, and don't come out until I say so! And lock the bloody door!" I firmly ordered, gripping the front door handle.

I sprinted out the front door, scouring the front garden and the neighbourhood for any sign of our crafty intruder. Annoyance flared. I stormed back inside, speedily checking every door and window, locking and bolting any that weren't.

"It wasn't your mother at all. It was him?"

Hearing Teddy's frightened voice, my head whipped around. "I told you to stay in the room!" Her face dropped. "... I'm sorry."

Her eyes swam, becoming pools of hurt and grief. "You're sorry? Is that all you've got to say?"

I raised my chin to the ceiling and sighed. "What else am I supposed to say? Yes, I was wrong for not initially listening to you, but you've had similar nightmares before, so what was I meant to think?"

Rather than argue, she crumbled to the floor, howling loudly in despair.

I dropped alongside her and promptly cradled her against me. "Shh, you're safe now as I secured the house, ensuring I locked every bloody door and window. I even set the alarm so the sly bastard couldn't get back in even if he tried, and if he does – I shall beat him to within an inch of his life."

She nodded stiffly into my chest, clinging to me as she cried harder than ever.

Teddy's fingers clung to my striped linen shirt. Hysterical sobs had turned into shudders, ultimately leaving her far too drained to fight the exhaustion any longer. The deep sleep I thought she was in was fleeting, with her waking and screaming every few minutes, terrified by yet more nightmares.

In tears and at the end of my tether, I desperately called Doctor Montgomery, scheduling an emergency appointment as soon as possible. But Murphy's Law dictated that too. The good doctor was away on a fucking holiday right when we needed him the most. Talk about inconvenient.

Short of making Teddy divulge who he was, what more was I to do? I loved Teddy, but I was just as exhausted as she was. If something didn't give soon –

Just about to doze off myself, I heard a light tapping on the front door, disturbing me. Perfect timing, mother. I sighed despondently and carefully extracted Teddy's clingy grip from my shirt, ensuring I had firmly tucked the pale blue blanket around her shaking figure before slipping off the bed. Without me beside her to comfort her, I quietly prayed that she remained asleep. Sighing heavily, I opened the door and padded from the room, closing it gently behind me.

Pressing in the code for the alarm, I unbolted the front door and stepped aside as I opened it. Motioning for my mother to enter, I held a finger to my lips. "Teddy's asleep, finally. So, we need to be quiet."

Her eyebrows shot up, observing me as I bolted the door shut and reset the alarm once more. Nonetheless, she wordlessly leaned a hand on the wall and removed her heels, carrying them through to the kitchen. She paused at the island bench and looked down at the floor, quizzing me, "What happened here?"

I scrubbed at my face. "I completely forgot about this wretched mess."

Mum thoughtfully grabbed the dustpan from a cupboard inside the butler's pantry and began interrogating me as she scraped the glass fragments off the timber boards. "Why is the house locked up like Fort Knox, Ari?"

"That would be because … the bastard that raped Teddy broke in and scared the fuck out of her while she was sleeping," I seethed, taking the dustpan from her hand, noisily disposing its contents into the bin under the sink. For once, she overlooked my swearing.

Gasping incredulously, she straightened. "No? Really? The audacity of that man."

"Yeah. Teddy tried to tell me…"

"And you refused to believe her, didn't you? Tell me that wasn't so, Ari?" she quietly probed, eyeing me reproachfully as a hand flew to her throat. Her disappointment in me reflected my own.

"No. I tried to say it was just another nightmare. I even went as far as searching the entire house – meticulously. Not long afterwards, we heard the front door open and close…."

"And you thought it was me?"

"I did."

"He was still here, with you both in the house?" she enquired, sliding onto a barstool. I stiffly nodded. "Oh, my god, no wonder Teddy was beside herself. What did you do?"

"I chased after him, but it was too late; he had gone," I fumed viciously, throwing the dishcloth into the bin. "Do you want a drink? For the conversation ahead, I suggest you have one." Under the assumption she'd say yes, I moved about the kitchen, grabbing a bottle of her favourite Shiraz from the pantry and two glasses from the overhead cupboard. No wasn't part of my mother's vocabulary, not when it came to alcohol anyway.

"Sure, why not? If I'm going to have to listen to bad news, I cope better when I'm drunk," she joked, removing her pale pink jacket and slinging it over the back of the stool beside her.

A small smile danced on my lips as I sat the glass in her outstretched hand. "If that's your coping mechanism, I'm surprised you aren't drunk all day, every day at work, then?"

"True, I ought to be, but I have a feeling the bar association may not let me keep my job if I was," she simpered, taking a sip. "Now, what is it you need to tell me?"

"The person who raped Teddy is someone directly linked to our family." Surprisingly, my voice remained eerily calm, unlike my mother's. Hers raised an octave higher than it needed to be. Her glass also paused mid-air as she took a moment to register what I'd just said.

"What do you mean, directly linked?"

Pouring a glass for myself, I propped my hip against the bench and lifted the glass to my lips, downing a generous mouthful. "Meaning it was someone within our family."

Mother's glass suddenly came into contact with the marble; miraculously, it stayed in one piece. "Wh... who was it?" She fought back the tears, her chest rising and falling with each rapid breath. "I need to know, Ari?"

I shrugged. "I'm clueless. Still. Teddy won't tell me for the reason that this prick threatened Scarlett."

"When he was here?"

"Noooo, not here..." I held my mother's confused gaze. "He was Teddy's new client yesterday."

"Oh, good grief." She scowled. "You had better refill my wine then," she suggested, holding the empty glass out for me.

"It also made me better understand the strange behaviour I walked in on, too."

Mother wore the same quizzical expression I had only the day before.

"I arrived home to discover Teddy seated at the piano wearing nothing more than her bra. Her mood was – well, let's just say it was as dark as the pieces she played. I couldn't say or do anything right. She refused to let me touch her, so much so she slept in one of the spare rooms."

"Oh, dear."

I scoffed. "You're telling me. Then I discovered Teddy's dress along with her panties in the bin, both of them shredded into tiny little pieces, only after Rosa brought it to my attention."

"What the hell did he, whoever he is, do to Teddy?"

"I don't know – yet. But I endeavour to find that out and why this mongrel was even at Bricks and Mortar."

"Wait," she paused, holding up a hand, "not the wine; I need more of that. How would this dastardly man have known to go there?"

"According to Teddy, Dad told him." I waved a hand dismissively and headed over to the sofa, taking a second bottle of wine with me and thumping my bare feet down on the edge of the coffee table; I smirked. "You could always ask dad who he was."

"I could," she hesitantly agreed, following me. "But then Jaxson may start asking questions. The lawyer in him won't be able to help himself," she swiftly advised, bursting my bubble. She elegantly sat askew beside me, perching her chin atop her furled hand. "No, Teddy has to be the one to tell us. The last thing she needs is you flying off the handle and landing yourself in jail for assault, young man."

I grabbed the second bottle of wine and topped up both glasses, scoffing, "Nah, it'd be for murder."

"That's not even funny, Ari Jaeger," she admonished, smacking my arm. "Not even your father or Garrett could have you acquitted for that, as good as they are."

"True. Let's get drunk, Mother," I proposed, clinking her glass.

"I already am."

33

Teddy

LOUD AND EXCESSIVELY HIGH-SPIRITED laughter boomed throughout the house, disturbing a nightmarish sleep. A noise that forced me out of bed and into the bathroom, where I stood in front of the mirror and stared at my hideous reflection. The raw sight of my bloodshot eyes and pale skin disgusted me; ugh, I needed a shower and promptly undressed.

Jumping beneath the water, I used the time to reflect on the past two days and the toll my reluctance was taking on Ari. He wasn't himself anymore; gradually, my past was stripping away the man he once was. Audrina's comments might have annoyed me, but in retrospect, she was right; I had to face my demons once and for all. Otherwise, I might end up losing Ari for good. They were words left unspoken, but her expression had spoken volumes. He was her son; she was just a mother bear simply protecting her cub.

Once I had dried off and completed my usual ritual with the moisturiser, I slipped into a baby pink strapless sundress with a short, flouncy skirt, hoping some colour might pep me up some more. I also dragged out the hairdryer and blow-dried my freshly washed hair, leaving the soft waves to flow around my shoulders and down my back.

Feeling somewhat respectable, I strolled from the bedroom and into the kitchen. But as I took one look at the rubbish scattered across my countertops, my jaw hit the floor. No longer were they spotless. Numerous rows of wine bottles littered the island, as did the empty chip packets and whatever else they got their hands on. I huffed and began clearing the mess, reefing, and slamming the bin drawer closed several times. More screams and laughter erupted from the family room, temporarily diverting my attention to the drunks responsible for the mess playing Pictionary. Surprisingly, Ari heard me banging about over the blaring music.

"Ted...dy! You. Are. Up!" He hiccupped as he approached, weaving his swaying body around the furniture.

"And you are extremely drunk," I chided, looking up at him. "How much have you had to drink?"

Squinting eyes struggled to stay open as he pinched his fingers together and slurred, "Only dis much...."

"I bet you haven't eaten anything either," I impatiently quizzed.

Ari's delightful lips lifted. "Nooo..." I reached out to steady him as he wobbled. "Ta...you...are...da...best!"

I hummed reproachfully. "I'll order a few pizzas. At least they'll help soak up the alcohol."

"Okay. I lurve you, Teddy."

I smiled tightly and grabbed my iPhone from the charger. "I know. Now go and sit down before you fall over."

"'Kay." Giving me a drunken smile and a sloppy kiss on the cheek, Ari attempted to manoeuvre his way back to the family room; he failed miserably and toppled headfirst over the arm of a chair. Swearing loudly, his, along with everyone else's riotous laughter, swiftly followed.

Ari blinked one eye open and promptly closed it again. "Who turned on the lights?" he grumbled, his head diving beneath his pillow.

"Feeling a little under the weather, are we, Ari?" I muttered dryly, strolling from the bathroom.

"Don't talk so loud."

Out of my peripheral vision, I noticed the slight lifting of a pillow as one bleary chocolate orb intrepidly followed me, moving about the room.

"I'm not. But you need to get out of bed." I added to his hangover misery by ripping the sheet off. I flicked his bare backside with the wet towel, making him flinch and yelp out in pain. "What the fuck, Teddy!"

A wolfish grin formed as his head poked out from beneath the pillow. "We need to talk," I firmly told him, leaning across the mattress.

"Can I shower first and have several large cups of coffee before we have this...talk?" he distastefully probed; his voice hoarse due to his antics the night before.

I gagged, screwing up my nose. "Yes, you can, but please brush your teeth thoroughly. Your breath smells like a winery; by that, I mean the bottom of the barrel."

"Fine, I'm going," he growled, chucking the pillow across the room. He pushed to his feet, nearly tripping over the sheet tangled around his ankles as he tried to walk.

I giggled. Ari exhibited his displeasure by smacking my lacy-clad behind as he strolled past. "Ow!"

"Paybacks are a bitch!"

A freshly showered Ari stepped into the walk-in robe, his lips harshly smacking mine. "Is that better?"

I deeply breathed in his enticing scent of mint, citrus, and roses. "Much. But you know what would make it even better?" I purred, skating my splayed hands over his naked torso and past his waist to cup his balls. "Some clothes."

Gratified by my touch, he groaned. "Now I smell nicer; how about some tender lovemaking?"

"No, we don't have time." I guffawed and walked away.

"Oh, that's pretty cold, lady; you can't just leave a man standing here with this..." He moaned, pointing at the steely erection poking the air. "Not even just a little one?"

"You and I both know we don't do quickies. Now get some damn clothes on!" I ordered firmly before leaving him grumbling under his breath.

"So damned bossy!"

"I'm dressed!" Ari stated matter-of-factly, strolling into the kitchen, his arms gesturing to the tan chinos and the denim blue shirt rolled up to his elbows, displaying muscular, veiny forearms.

I raised my brows over the top of the mug I had nursed between my hands. "So, you are," I murmured, blowing on the piping hot Earl Grey tea.

"Can I have coffee now...please?" he asked politely, wrapping an arm around my waist, his lips gently brushing against my cheek. "You smell amazing."

Emmett's words were still raw, and instinctively, I flinched. "Thank you, and so do you. Now, you need to sit so we can have this talk." I shot him an apologetic smile as his chocolate gaze slid over me.

"That sounds both ambiguous and ominous." He sighed and rounded the bench, sliding onto a barstool. He flanked his aching head in his hands.

Exhaling shakily, I turned to the bench behind me and sat my cup down as I set about making Ari that much-needed cup of coffee. "I spent quite a bit of time reflecting and thinking last night about my rape, ...and how I behaved yesterday..." I cleared my throat, "... The last few days, if I'm to be honest." Tentatively, I slid the freshly made cup across the countertop before continuing, "I've arranged for us to meet up with your parents today for brunch at their house."

"Is this the ominous part you needed to prepare me for?" he simpered, grasping his cup by the handle and slowly sipping the extra-strong brew.

I rolled my eyes irritably. "No, it's not. I want to disclose everything."

He gaped, staring. "That means..."

"I know what it means, Ari!" His face fell; I swiftly apologised, "I'm sorry, I didn't mean to snap."

"I know," he whispered, searching my troubled gaze for any sign of uncertainty. But there was none found. Without question, I had to reveal all. Dealing with the fallout could come later. "And I'm fully aware that relinquishing this information won't be easy."

"Thank you for understanding. It's just — I want to get the ball rolling on sending this bastard to jail, and your dad is the only lawyer I trust to set this right."

He nodded sagely. "All right. Now we've discussed the why; let's discuss how on earth you organised a brunch with my mother when she was extremely drunk last night?"

My mouth quirked. "I didn't. I spoke with Jaxson when he came to drag her out of here. He said he would arrange the day around me after I explained that I had a crucial legal matter that required both his and Audrina's presence."

"And Dad agreed without asking why?" Ari quizzed, raising a brow in surprise when I replied with a yes. "Well, let's get this show on the road then, shall we?" Sliding off the stool, he held out a hand and pulled me into his arms, reassuring me with his words and a soft, tender kiss. He tasted of peppermint toothpaste and coffee. "Granted, none of this will be easy; you know that, right?"

"I know." I let out a shuddering breath and reached around him, grasping my black clutch off the bench. "Let's go before I change my mind — and by the way, I'm driving. You'll still be over the limit." Grinning, I snatched up the keys to his beloved BMW and hurried out the door. My black patent leather five-inch heels clicked as Ari trailed after me, his bottom lip petulantly dragging behind him on the timber boards.

"You're so brutal today."

Having to speak Emmett's name aloud to someone other than my therapist had my stomach in knots. I doubted I'd make it to Ari's parents, let alone the outskirts of Toorak, without needing to throw up in the gutter.

The dread I felt Ari sensed. He clutched my free hand, laying it in his lap. The soft pad of his thumb stroked across my knuckles, soothing me somewhat. "Stop fretting."

I scoffed, "Easy for you to say. You aren't the one with your head on a chopping block."

He snorted derisively. "A tad dramatic, don't you think?"

"No, it's not," I claimed, slipping my hand from his hold and wrapping it tightly around the steering wheel. My fingers flexed restlessly over the supple leather. "Albeit I instigated the brunch, the foreboding I currently feel, well, that's inevitable. I'm still worried about your mother's reaction once I say his name and if she'll ever speak to me again." I swallowed the bile that had risen in my throat before continuing my self-recrimination, "And your dad, as sweet as he is, what if he doesn't believe me?"

He gave an exasperated growl. "The lawyer in dad won't be able to help himself, and he can spot a liar a mile away. Trust me; it's a gift. And as far as my mother goes, she adores you. Perhaps if you'd given me the heads up first and told me this fucker's name, I could've helped prepare both you and them, hopefully staving off any fallout." A darkened gaze darted sideways, briefly glancing my way before sliding a pair of tinted sunglasses over his eyes. His sullen expression spoke volumes; it seemed my not revealing Emmett sooner remained quite the contentious issue.

Well, wasn't brunch going to be a barrel of fun?

Upon our arrival, a rather hungover and unusually quiet Audrina greeted us in the open doorway. "Teddy, darling, how are you?"

I giggled. "Better than you by the looks of things."

Bleary and bloodshot eyes rolled in amusement. "You at least look radiant, and I simply love that black and white chevron dress.

And look at those legs; they must stop somewhere, surely?" I laughed. Beneath her horrendous hangover, Audrina's chatty personality still shined. But while complimenting me, she remained oblivious to the anxiety hiding behind my façade, as well as the radiating tension between Ari and me.

"Thank you. How is your head after last night?"

"Oh, don't ask," she croaked. "But I had a marvellous time if that's any consolation for my suffering."

I scrunched up my nose. "Possibly not."

"Dad, it's great to see you," Ari greeted, pushing his sunglasses through his thick hair and wincing at the glaring light drowning the entryway.

"It's good to see you too, son." Shaking the proffered hand, Jaxson smirked at his son's less than jovial salutation. For me, he beamed and enveloped me in a firm and warm embrace. "And the delightful, Teddy, it's great to see you again. I must say, though, my wife was right, making a pleasant change; you do look radiant."

Her hands flying to her hips, Audrina shared her outrage. "Hey! I'll have you know I am always right, Mister!"

"Of course, you are my darling," he simpered, pressing a loving kiss to her forehead.

Ari cracked a smile and snorted. "Nice save, Dad."

"I always know how to placate your mother, son," Jaxson murmured, jiggling his eyebrows. "The tricky part is knowing what to placate her with."

Ari screwed up his face. "Dad, TMI."

"Now let's go through to the kitchen and have this brunch. I'm famished, and if I don't eat soon, I may begin to fade away into a shadow," Jaxson boomed, ushering everyone out of the elegant entryway and through the formal living room.

"I hardly think so, Jaxson. I believe you're over-exaggerating there a little." Audrina chuckled, taking his hand.

"Sounds like Ari," I muttered, following right behind them.

Having strolled into the stylishly modern kitchen, the four of us took our respective seats at the sizeable rectangular oak table. I picked up the linen serviette and unfolded it, laying it over my lap before helping myself to fruit salad, Greek vanilla yoghurt, and a glass of pineapple juice.

"Aren't you having more than that?" Ari demurred, whispering in my ear.

"No," I argued, "my stomach's in knots, and I'm worried if I eat more than this, I'll surely throw it up."

As Jaxson piled the plate up in his hand with bacon, eggs, hash browns, tomatoes and mushrooms, his perceptively bright gaze eyed us over the table. "What are you two whispering about over there?"

"Nothing, Dad." Ari smiled, giving nothing away.

Breakfast was a strangely quiet affair, with only Jaxson and Ari exchanging words over the government's latest policies. Both agreed only to disagree as they typically argued their difference of opinions. Politics wasn't my forte as, generally, it bored the hell out of me.

Audrina, too, appeared disinterested in the conversation, which was unlike her. Commonly, she became incredibly involved in their discussions. I suspected she was too hungover and instead remained quiet, poking at the eggs on the plate in front of her. She looked just how I felt: sick to the stomach.

Quiet fell over the table. I figured now was as good a time as any to reveal the real reason behind this impromptu brunch.

I set my spoon down on the plate and anxiously peered up at them. "Jaxson, Audrina, there's something I need to tell you both about me," I shakily began, "but what I'm about to reveal could change everything." Reaching for Ari's hand, I inhaled sharply and laid down the gauntlet, ensuring I left nothing out.

I attained the end without throwing up, at least. Ari squeezed my hand, which I initially believed he was gesturing a job well done. I thought wrong as he frowned and raised his hand, silently questioning why I hadn't mentioned my attacker yet.

"I was getting there," I mouthed.

His lips thinned, pressing into a disapproving line. I shared my displeasure over the testy attitude and snatched my hand away. I glared before returning my attention to his parents.

Jaxson directed his perplexed glance at his wife. "I gather by your less than shocked demeanour; you knew about this already?"

Audrina slid a shaking hand over his and nodded bleakly. "I'm sorry, honey, I am, but it wasn't my secret to tell. You do understand, don't you, Jaxson?"

"Yes, of course I do." Jaxson gently smiled. "At least that explains your odd behaviour and absences of late. What I don't understand is why you felt you couldn't inform me sooner?" he addressed softly, glancing at each of us.

"Because I was far too ashamed to tell you." Humiliation burned my cheeks. "It was hard enough telling Ari, and then when I found out Audrina knew...," my voice trailed off. "Deep down, and thanks to my mother's constant disparagement, I worried that you would think me less of a person, deeming me unworthy for your son."

"No, Teddy. I would never think that of you." Jaxson's lips pressed together in a reprimanding line. "We love you like a daughter and would never turn on you for something that was entirely someone else's doing." He switched seats, moving beside me and grasped my hands, regarding me intently with sympathetic blue eyes. "You poor, poor girl, having to live through this harrowing ordeal alone is just dreadful. Well, no more. We shall find this bastard and send him to jail."

"You won't have to look far," I professed, my head hanging shamefully.

Confused, Jaxson blinked. "What do you mean we won't have to look far?"

I opened my mouth, but the fear of speaking his name had left me mute.

"It's all right, Teddy. You no longer need to feel afraid." Jaxson lifted my chin, and through tear-filled eyes, there was a certainty. A certainty that I wouldn't have to face my demons alone any longer, giving me the strength to say his name out aloud finally.

"It was your brother, Audrina. It was Emmett," I blurted before bursting into tears.

AUTHOR'S NOTE

Teddy and Ari will be back in Book 2: Clouded Judgement.

The fallout begins….

www.ingramcontent.com/pod-product-compliance
Lightning Source LLC
Chambersburg PA
CBHW022348020726
47500CB00002B/179